# MOUNTAIN GRUMP

MOUNTAIN MEN BOOK THREE

S.J. TILLY

Mountain Grump

Cover: Lori Jackson Design

Model Image: Wander Aguiar Photography

Editors: Jeanine Harrell, Indie Edits with Jeanine

& Beth Lawton, VB Edits

*This book is dedicated to all the state parks. May you continue to thrive for all the future generations of ducks.*
*And for the park rangers. May the North Star always guide you.*

Visitor
Center

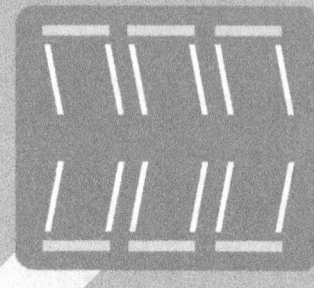

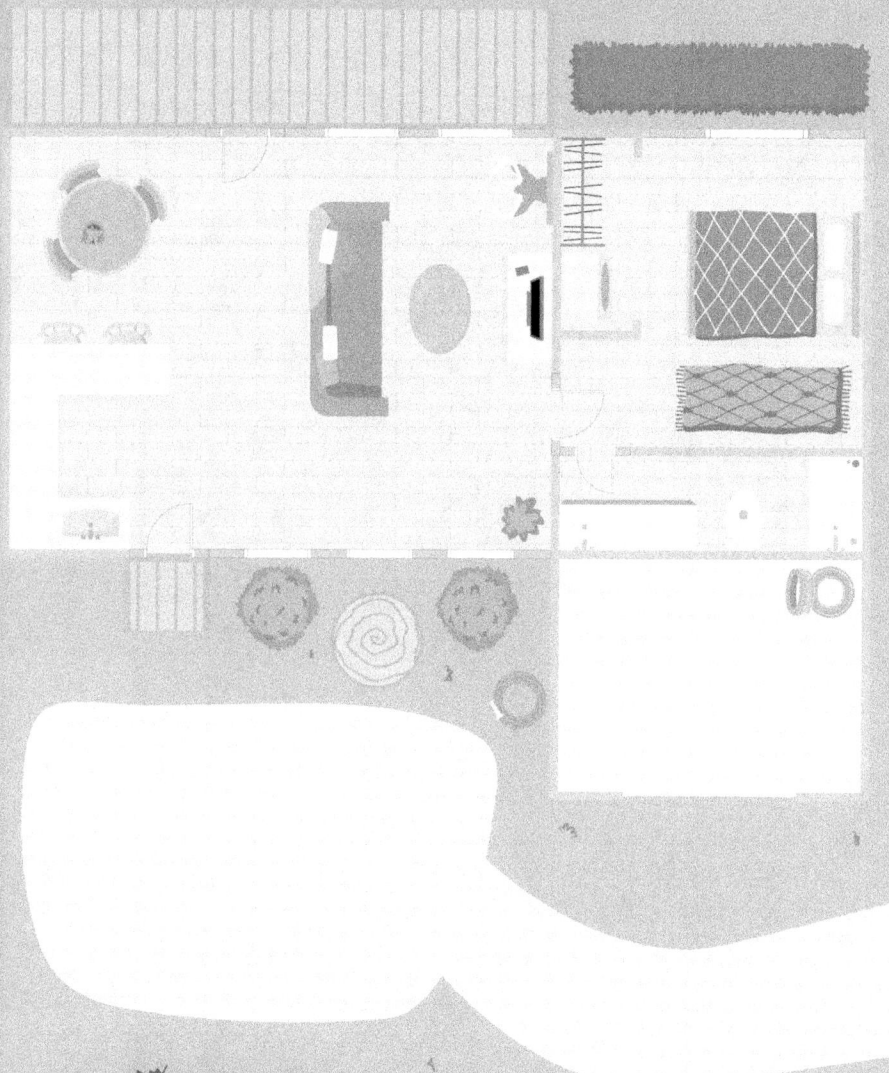

# Tilda's House

# CHAPTER 1

# ETHAN GRANT, PARK RANGER

MOSS FLATTENS BENEATH MY BOOT, AND I PAUSE.

*Is that... humming?*

I tip my head to the side, holding my breath.

*That's humming.*

I start walking again.

Lonely Peak State Park is practically my home. I spend more time here than at my house, and I know every square foot of it.

So I know that out here, at the border of the park, there shouldn't be anyone.

At least not someone who can produce a high, girly hum.

The pine and aspen trees are thick in this part of the forest, filtering the afternoon June sun and forcing me to duck under another low branch as I follow the sound.

Jack, the old man who owns the place on the other side of the park border, should've been back weeks ago. He always disappears for the colder months, claiming he's gotten too old for winters in the Colorado Rockies. But he still spends more time here than not in the summer. Which, for Jack, starts in May. So he should've been here already.

But he's not.

I know he's not because I've been checking.

The humming stops.

I stop.

Silence stretches.

The humming starts again, quieter, farther away. And I continue my stride.

A moment later, the old barbed wire fence that separates state park property from Jack's comes into view.

I stop again.

The fence is just as shitty as it was the last time I saw it. The wooden posts have seen better days. The center strand of wire is sagging. But the top wire...

I take a step. Then another.

*Is that a fucking ribbon?*

I take two more steps, reach out, and touch the purple ribbon wrapped around the top strand of barbed wire.

*What the fuck?*

I look to my right.

The ribbon extends down the wire a dozen feet, ending in a bow around a fence post.

I look to my left, toward the humming.

The ribbon continues, bows tied around each post, disappearing from sight, into the trees.

*This* is park property. The fence, the land. No way did Jack put this up.

It's the girliest vandalism I've ever seen. And harmless or not, it doesn't belong.

I grip the ribbon and tug.

The surprisingly sturdy fabric snags on a barb.

I pull the switchblade out of my pocket and slice through the ribbon.

I tug on the cut piece.

It snags again.

I grit my teeth and slowly walk along the fence, unwinding the ribbon from the barbed wire.

*What sort of person would spend the time required to do this?*

It snags again. I cut it again.

Jack wouldn't do this. And I've never known him to bring a woman out here. So whoever is here is trespassing. And defacing public property.

I continue down the fence line.

Unwind. Snag. Cut. Repeat.

My irritation grows with every step, and all the while, the humming persists.

I don't recognize the song, but it sounds off-key.

On the other side of the fence, but still out of sight, is Jack's gravel driveway. It's only about thirty feet away, but the forest extends past the fence, and where the tree line finally ends, the ground slopes downhill, toward Jack's house, so none of it is visible from here.

Which again begs the question, who would *decorate* a fence you can only see when you're standing next to it?

I take another step.

Unwind another foot of fucking ribbon.

Cut it.

Carry on.

The humming continues.

Jack's driveway is over a quarter mile long, and it makes a ninety-degree turn halfway down, so if you're coming from the road, you can't see the house until you're practically on top of it. But Jack has a multitude of no trespassing signs that start at the mailbox. So even if somebody turned down the driveway by mistake, it's obvious this is private property.

I slice another length of ribbon, flip my blade closed, and slide my knife into my pocket.

The rest of this purple bullshit can wait. I need to know who's here.

Careful not to catch my clothes, I duck between the top two strands of wire, officially leaving park land.

My brain focuses on the humming.

*Did someone break into Jack's place?*

*Am I gonna have to kick out squatters?*

A few strides later, I'm out of the trees, and Jack's driveway comes into view.

It rained this morning. Not enough to wash away the tire tracks that I'd swear weren't here last time. But enough to leave little murky puddles in the uneven surface.

I take another step and lift my gaze.

Jack's front door is open.

The garage door is open.

His truck is parked half in, half out of the garage.

But it's not Jack I see in front of the house.

Standing with their back to me is a stranger. And they're hanging...

I narrow my eyes.

*Is that a string of fucking crystals?*

No, it's definitely *not Jack* hanging crystals from a tree branch.

It's a woman.

A woman with long lilac hair curling past her bare shoulders.

A woman in a pink dress so short that when she reaches up as high as she can to hang another string of crystals, I can see her underwear.

Bright white, full-coverage cotton panties.

*They shouldn't be sexy.*

They're *not* sexy.

But the plump ass they're plastered to...

The soft, curvy body that's wearing them...

The expanse of smooth bare legs below them...

I swallow.

Then I feel like a total creeper.

Dragging my eyes away from the stranger's ass, I sweep my gaze over the property.

It doesn't look like the front door was broken in.

There are no signs of anyone else. No vehicles except Jack's old pickup.

4

But there is... *stuff*. Like the cardboard moving boxes visible through the open door.

*What the fuck is going on?*

If Jack sold the place, I'd know about it.

If he sold this place, *everyone* would know about it. Lonely isn't a large town. And even though we aren't all buddies around here, news travels fast. And a house going up for sale is considered news.

Looking at the front of the house, left to right, you see the window over the kitchen sink. The front door with two low concrete steps leading up to it. A trio of windows that look into the living room, with a pair of bushes under the first and third windows—the middle one died a few years back. Next is the single bedroom with the single bathroom, but the view of that is blocked by the garage, which is attached to the front of the house. Making the structure an L shape.

The driveway comes up from behind the garage and continues all the way to the front door. There aren't really lawns at elevation this high. The growing season is short, and grass grows in clumps. But scattered around on either side of the driveway are a handful of trees.

And each and every one of them has strings of crystals hanging from their branches.

I shake my head.

The humming stops, and my attention moves back to the woman.

She bends down, grabbing something out of the box at her feet. Simultaneously flashing her panty-covered ass at me again.

My body reacts on its own.

My stomach clenching. My chest heating.

And it pisses me off.

This nonsense ends now.

"Who are you?" My voice comes out too loud in the quiet.

The woman lets out a scream, obviously startled by my appearance.

She spins to face me and something shiny flings from her hand.

I'm too far away to do anything, so I just watch as her foot—covered in a little yellow shoe—catches on a rock.

Her pretty hair flies around her face, obscuring my first glimpse of her features. And she loses her balance.

The shiny thing lands in a muddy puddle with a splash.

And I continue to stand, helpless, as the woman in the pink party dress falls onto the rough gravel.

# CHAPTER 2

## TILDA WRIGHT, MOUNTAIN FAIRY

THE PAIN RADIATING FROM MY KNEES AND HANDS IS muted by the thudding of my heart.

*Someone is here.*

*In the middle of nowhere.*

*At the top of a freaking mountain.*

Fear shoots through my veins as I scramble to my feet.

A boot crunches over the ground, and I shove my hair out of my face as a man steps onto the driveway.

From the direction of the woods.

*If he's here to do me harm...*

He takes a step forward.

I step back.

"Stop." His gruff voice cracks through the air between us.

I hold my hands palms out. "Y-you stop." My voice shakes, revealing my nerves.

He halts and holds his hands out in a similar gesture. "I didn't mean to scare you." His tone is gentler than it was before but still not quite friendly.

His hands are huge, and his forearms are covered in tattoos.

His tan button-down short-sleeved shirt is tight across his muscular chest.

His dark trimmed beard frames his not-smiling mouth.

And his eyes...

I blink.

He's wearing a baseball hat that puts his eyes in shadows, but they look like they're two different colors. One green, one brown. And they're full of suspicion.

*Did he really just come from the woods?*

*Is he a forest man?*

I lower my eyes from his intense ones, and that's when I see it.

The gun at his hip.

I stumble back. "Don't shoot me."

He drops his hands to his sides. Closer to his gun.

A shriek creeps out of my throat, and I glance around, looking for a weapon.

"Shoot? Lady, I'm not—"

I spot my box of suncatchers on the ground and run toward it.

Crouching down, I reach inside.

My knees sting with the movement, and I have one second to glance at the trickle of blood running down my right shin before I stand back up, brandishing my scissors. "B-back up." I hold my arm out straight, trying to get the points of metal as close to him as possible. "Which one of them sent you?"

"Sent me?" The man furrows his brows. "What the fuck are you talking about? Who are you? Where's Jack?"

That makes me pause.

That name.

My great-uncle.

I swallow.

Then I swallow again.

"Jack's dead." I can't say it any louder than a whisper.

The man jerks back. He doesn't move his feet. Doesn't step away. But his weight shifts. Like the ground swayed beneath him.

His serious expression doesn't change. "When?"

"Two weeks." I wet my lips, my mouth feeling dry from the rush of adrenaline. "My cousin didn't send you?"

He shakes his head slowly, looking at me like he can't understand what I'm saying. "No one sent me. I'm not here to shoot you." He lifts his hands away from his sides, like he's reminding me he didn't pull the gun from its holster.

Like he's inviting me to look him over.

So I look at the forest man.

The size of him.

The air of intensity.

The dark, wavy hair sticking out around the edges of his hat.

And if I wasn't scared for my life, I might appreciate how absolutely attractive he is.

*Might.*

He's big and built and wearing boots with dark green pants.

He's in a uniform.

But he's not a cop.

He's...

My gaze moves back to his hands.

The one near his holstered gun is empty, and the other one is holding...

I gasp and use my scissors to point to his hand. "Is that my ribbon?"

He looks down at the pieces of wadded-up fabric in his grip, then back to me. "This is paraphernalia. Where's Matty?"

*Para...*

It takes my brain a second to comprehend his words. But when they do...

My heart squeezes painfully in my chest. "*Matty?*"

"Yeah. Jack told me if something ever happened to him, his grandkid Matty would take over the place. So." The grouchy man takes a step toward me. "I'll ask you again. Who are you? And where is Matty?"

My shoulder muscles give out, and I drop my arm to my side, lowering my weapon. "I'm Matty."

# Chapter 3

## Ethan

I blink at the beautiful girl.

No.

It can't be.

But then I think about all the times Jack talked about him. *Her.*

Matty. Grandkid.

Did he ever say *he*?

My jaw clenches.

That sneaky bastard knew exactly what he was doing.

He must've known all along that he'd ask me, like he did, to keep an eye on his grandkid when they take over the property.

He knew I'd say *yes* more easily if I thought Matty was a guy.

Knew I'd argue about it if he told me the person inheriting his cabin was a gorgeous little sexpot in a frilly dress and pretty white panties.

He knew I'd keep my fucking distance if he told me Matty was a damn girl.

*And what a girl she is.*

Standing here, just a few strides away, I can see all of her.

The pink on her cheeks.

The golden brown of her eyes.

And the twig stuck in her hair, next to her ear, making her look like some sort of alluring, curvy mountain fairy.

*The cleavage.*

Her heaving cleavage in her little strappy dress that belongs on a bedroom floor, not doing yard work.

Then I take in the mud smeared on her skirt.

The bright red streak of blood running down from her scraped-up knee.

And fuck. I feel bad for frightening her.

"Matty, I'm—"

"Tilda." She speaks over me, then lifts a shoulder. "Or, well, Matilda. Technically. Uncle Jack was the only one who called me Matty."

"Tilda." I say it slowly. Feeling the letters on my tongue. "I'm sorry for startling you." I dip my chin toward her knee. "Are you okay?"

She nods, but her lips are pressed together, so I don't believe her. Then she visibly swallows when she glances back down at my gun. "Um, who are you?"

"I'm Ethan." I use my empty hand and point to the badge on my shirt. "Park ranger."

She looks toward the fence, then back to me. "You work in that park?"

"Lonely Peak State Park, yes."

She bites her lip, glancing back down at the ribbon in my grip. "Can I see some ID?"

I lift a brow. "Do you know what a park ranger ID is supposed to look like?"

Tilda shakes her head, her purple curls swaying with the motion.

"Then how will you know it's not a fake?"

She bites her lip. And I feel like an asshole.

But I'm not here to be her friend.

I'm not here to be her anything.

I simply told Jack I'd keep an eye on his grandkid. And

pointing out the flaw in her plan might be rude, but if she's going to live out here—way the fuck out here, all alone—she needs to be smart about her choices.

Which reminds me that she didn't hear me approaching. I wasn't even trying to be quiet.

"There are bears out here. And mountain lions. And coyotes and foxes and moose." Maybe it makes me more of an asshole to point it out so bluntly, but so be it. She needs to be careful.

"I know. Uncle Jack told me about the wildlife. I was humming so animals would know I was here." She drops her gaze back to the torn ribbon in my hand. "Why'd you do that?"

I give the shreds a shake. "You can't tie shit to the park fence. Even if it's just some silly ribbon."

Her eyes snap up to mine.

And fuck, she's pretty.

Even with the scraped-up knee and dirty skirt, she looks ready for a tea party in the forest.

A dirty tea party. One where she sits on my lap and I bury my face in her tits.

I clear my throat. "You need to take the rest of it down."

"Seriously? It's not hurting anyone."

"Seriously." I cross my arms. "Be happy I'm not giving you a ticket."

Her mouth pops open. "A ticket? For some ribbon?"

"Doesn't matter if it's ribbon or razor wire, it's illegal to vandalize public property." I pull an arm free and gesture to a strand of beads hanging from the tree next to Tilda. "It should be a crime to do this too."

"To hang suncatchers?" She sounds truly surprised at my attitude. "I think they're pretty."

"Nature is pretty enough on its own." I roll my eyes when I spot another tree with another strand of *suncatchers*.

"Yeah, but it doesn't take away from the natural beauty. It enhances it," Tilda argues.

I shake my head and huff. "You're ridiculous."

And... she flinches.

It's the smallest movement.

The tiniest reaction.

But I see it.

And I hate it.

I open my mouth, wanting to tell her that I meant to say *that's* ridiculous. Explain that my words came out wrong. *Worse.*

But she speaks before I can, her voice back to a whisper. "My family didn't send you?"

She asked about her family earlier. When she saw my gun.

And... *What the fuck?*

"I don't know your family. Just Jack. And he's only mentioned you."

She nods, slowly.

Her expression stays the same. Neutral.

But her eyes start to shine.

"Tilda..."

Her mouth tips up into a fake-as-fuck smile. "I'll take the ribbon off the fence." She blinks, and I feel something tighten inside me as I watch a pair of tears roll down her cheeks. "Was there anything else?"

She looks like a doll. Her features frozen in a mask of pleasantness. But the tears...

They make my chest hurt.

And I don't reply.

I can't.

# CHAPTER 4

## TILDA

RIDICULOUS. FOOLISH. STUPID.

*A silly girl with silly ideas.*

The thick, heavy weight of disappointment fills my bones.

My family has always called me those things. Called me names. Made me feel *less than*.

Fat. Dumb. Frivolous.

But to hear it from a stranger.

A man who doesn't even know me.

*You're ridiculous.*

Another tear breaks free, and I curse it in my mind.

*Never show weakness.*

*Never show pain.*

My knee throbs.

My heart hurts.

*Never let them see your loneliness.*

I glance around at my suncatchers. The pieces of tinted glass snag the sunlight and throw it back across the branches as a rainbow.

I thought doing this would make me feel better.

But... not today.

Not anymore.

I drop my scissors into the box on the ground.

Thinking I could defend myself against a man with a gun with a pair of craft scissors... *that's* ridiculous.

Stupid.

Silly.

I take a step back, focusing on the man's chin, not meeting his eyes. "Have a good day, Park Ranger Ethan."

He takes a step toward me.

And my eyes move back to the gun on his hip.

He stops.

And before he can say more, before he can insult me further, I turn and walk to the front door of the house.

*My house.*

I hurry up the front steps.

*My front steps.*

I grip the door handle, not reacting when the metal connects with the scrapes on my palm, and I step inside, shutting the door behind me.

# CHAPTER 5

## ETHAN

SILENCE SETTLES AROUND ME AS I WAIT.

But the front door doesn't open.

Tilda doesn't appear in a window.

And I have no reason to follow her footsteps. No reason to knock on her door.

But those fucking tears.

I don't get it.

*Was it the cut-up ribbon?*

*Was it talking about Jack?*

And why do I feel sick to my stomach?

I tip my head back and look up at the sky.

*Jack, what the fuck were you thinking, leaving your mountain house to a girl like Tilda?*

I lower my gaze and shift it to Jack's old-ass pickup truck and try to picture pretty Tilda driving it.

I try to picture her climbing into it.

Tilda's not *shockingly short*. But she's below average height, whereas Jack was tall and lanky. Meaning he had no use for running boards, so he never installed them.

Tilda's going to need a fucking step stool to get into the driver's seat. If she doesn't, and she wears a dress like the one she's wearing now, the whole damn town is gonna know what her panties look like.

*I don't like that thought.*

A breeze blows through the trees, and a few of the suncatchers swing in the wind.

I stand by the fact that this shit is unnecessary.

But... maybe... it's not as horrible as I first thought it was.

Sighing, I step forward, then crouch down and stick my hand into the murky puddle.

My fingers find what they're searching for, and I pull the strand of beads out of the muck.

I drape them over the edge of the box holding even more suncatchers and glare down at Tilda's discarded scissors.

The tool she brandished as a weapon.

*Don't shoot me.*

*Which one of them sent you?*

*My cousin didn't send you?*

Standing, I stare at the front door.

*Is her family trying to kill her?*

I look around the property.

It's remote. Hard to find if you don't have the address. But there's no security. No gate. And if someone who wasn't supposed to be here found her...

It's remote. Hard to find.

Unease crawls up my arms, but I shake it off.

Jack would've told me if his family was homicidal.

She must just be overreacting.

The edges of my mouth pull down.

*Would a woman who smiles through her tears ask questions she didn't mean?*

Feeling like a total piece of shit, I turn away from Jack's house and toward the fence.

I don't slow my stride as I climb the small hill.

And I don't slow as I enter the forest.

When I reach the fence, I brace the hand not full of ribbon on top of the post and hop over the barbed wire.

I make it two steps past the fence line before I stop and turn around.

The cut end of the ribbon hangs limply, already frayed. The once cheery decoration is now torn and sad.

I inhale the scent of pine.

Then I take two steps.

# CHAPTER 6

## TILDA

I LEAVE MY SHOES BY THE FRONT DOOR AND WALK through the house.

*My house.*

The entryway is just a rug.

The kitchen is on my left, with its U-shaped countertop and the sink below the window that looks out over the front yard.

Two stools are tucked under the far side of the counter, looking into the kitchen. And behind that is the dining area, which consists of a small square dining table and three nonmatching chairs.

The living room is on the right. I have my boxes of stuff lined up along the back of the couch and more against the wall under the front windows.

The couch is made of brown fabric that feels like velvet and is printed in a faded foliage design. There's a low coffee table before it, all facing the wall that separates the bedroom—*my bedroom*—from the main living area. And against that wall is a six-drawer dresser with an ancient TV and a DVD player sitting atop it.

But the pièce de résistance of the home is the deer head mounted in the far corner of the living room.

The unseeing eyes watching you as you watch TV.

I don't hate it as much as I did this morning.

I mean, I still hate it, but it does draw the eye toward the back of the house.

To the wall of windows.

*My windows.*

*My windows.* In *my house.* Because Uncle Jack is dead.

I press my teeth into my bottom lip as I pass behind the couch.

*I'm not going to cry.*

It's a *ridiculous* thing to tell myself since tears are already sliding down my cheeks.

It's only another second before I reach the solid wood back door, which matches the front door.

Sniffing against my emotions, I pull it open.

The screen door beyond doesn't have a screen in it, so I just step through the empty frame barefoot, onto the back deck.

The best part of the house.

*My house.*

Using the back of my hand to wipe at my cheeks, I lower myself onto what I imagine was Uncle Jack's favorite chair.

It's sturdy. The same as the one on the other side of the door. Same breathtaking view.

But this chair is slightly more worn.

Slightly more comfortable.

Slightly more loved.

I sniff again. "What a day."

I want to shut my eyes. Want to close them and pretend the last two weeks haven't happened. But the sight before me...

I inhale.

Trees surround me, but they don't reach the deck. There's maybe a fifty-foot radius of shrubs and patches of grass around the house. But past that... it's forest. Thick, lush forest.

Nothing like the Vegas landscape I came from.

Nothing like the city.

But that's not even the best of it.

The forest is just the start.

Because straight ahead, the ground dips.

The trees lower, following the slope of the land down.

And what it reveals... is mountains.

Actual snowcapped mountains.

It's June. It's already hot back home.

*What used to be my home.*

But here... Here it feels magical.

I blink away what I hope will be the last tears of the day and focus my eyes on the distant peaks. They're miles away. Miles and miles. But it feels like they're mine.

Like they belong to me, as much as this land does now.

And... it's the prettiest thing I've ever seen.

"I get it now, Uncle Jack," I whisper into the vastness beyond. "I get why you kept this place a secret."

# CHAPTER 7

## ETHAN

A RAVEN SCREAMS AT ME FROM OVERHEAD.

"I know," I sigh as I tell her.

She screams again, then floats over the treetops, out of view.

I watch the spot where she disappeared, betting she'd like some ribbon too.

My hands are shoved into my pockets, clutching the ruined fabric. And the urge to toss the pieces into the sky, offering them up as an apology, is strong.

Strong enough that I clench my jaw and stomp my boots harder than necessary as I continue through the woods.

*Tilda was breaking the law.*

*It is my job to uphold the law.*

Somewhere in my mind, nineteen-year-old Ethan is swinging his leg, trying to kick me in the ass, muttering something about *pretty girls* and *acting like a total fucking loser.*

I narrow my eyes—at nothing—picturing my young, naive self.

*You don't know shit,* I tell my younger self. *Just you fucking wait.*

My phone vibrates in my cargo pocket, and I finally release my grip on the ribbon bits to pull it free.

Heaving out a breath, I answer. "Sister."

"Brother. Whatcha up to?"

I look at the forest surrounding me.

I'm far from any of the hiking paths. Far from where I parked my truck on the service road.

Far from any reasonable answer.

I'm here because I was curious. Wanted to see if Jack was finally back.

*Jack.*

Something wraps around my throat.

I don't know that we were friends exactly. But to be honest, I don't know that I'd call anyone my *friend*.

I've lived in this state my whole life. Never lived *in town*, but Lonely has always been the closest town. The school I went to. But everyone I knew from before, when I was young... we don't stay in touch. Not since looking after my sister became my life. And not now that my work has become my life.

"You alright?" Sandra asks, bringing me back to our conversation.

"I'm good." I lie. "Bad service." Not a lie, but not relevant. "We still on for dinner tonight?" I'm not really in the mood, but canceling would just lead to more questions.

"Yep. Usual place?"

"If you don't mind driving." Our usual place is closer to me than it is to her.

"Nope, I don't mind."

I duck under another branch and come out onto the service road, putting my truck in sight. "Just call to confirm dinner, or do you need something?"

I'm being short, but Sandra ignores my attitude. "That's all, Bro-than. I'll text when I'm on my way."

Hanging up, I unlock my truck, and I push all thoughts of the mountain fairy named Tilda out of my mind.

# CHAPTER 8

## TILDA

MY STOMACH GRUMBLES, AND I SIGH.

Time to make some food.

I shift forward in the chair, planting my bare feet on the deck, readying myself to stand, and my knee protests.

When I fell, I landed on both of them. But my right knee clearly took the brunt of my weight. The sun felt good on my legs, but now that I'm looking at the mud and blood on my skin, I feel itchy.

My next sigh turns into a groan as I stand.

I'm glad my body tends to run hot, because the weather here is certainly cooler than I was expecting, and I'm dressed for a desert summer.

But the mild temperature is appreciated since I didn't break a sweat hanging my suncatchers. Hauling my boxes into the house was a different story. But it was a good distraction from... everything.

Reaching through the empty screen-door frame, I push open the inside door and step through.

One of these times, I'm sure I'll trip on the lip of the screen door, but right now, stepping through it is a tiny touch of fun that I desperately need.

*Stop it.*

*Stop feeling sorry for yourself.*

Standing in the space between the living room and kitchen, I hold my arms straight out from my sides, close my eyes, and take a deep breath.

*I'm fine.*

*I'm better than fine.*

*I have a house.*

*I have property.*

*A truck.*

I have a home that's *mine*. That no one can take from me.

*I'm fine.*

I take another breath and slowly lower my arms.

*But Uncle Jack is gone.*

I squeeze my eyes shut tighter. And I breathe.

Two weeks ago today, a man knocked on my apartment door. When I answered, he handed me an envelope without a word, then turned around and left.

The envelope had my name handwritten on the front, in neat block letters.

I shut the door. I opened the letter. I read it. And then I sat on the floor. Right there. In the entryway to my tiny studio apartment. I sat on the floor, and I cried.

And I read it again.

*Uncle Jack is dead.*

The letter explained it all. But...

I lift my arms and breathe again.

He had a terminal illness.

But he never told me.

Never told anyone.

*Breathe.*

He knew it was over. Said he wanted to control his own destiny. So...

*Breathe, Tilda. Just breathe.*

He chose death with dignity. Physician-assisted dying.

He did it his way.

I drop my arms and open my eyes.

Uncle Jack, *Great-Uncle Jack*, brother of my mother's mother, arranged his death.

And he arranged my life.

The house is in my name.

The land is in my name.

The check for twenty thousand dollars was in my name.

And the plane ticket... the driver...

He had it all planned.

Two weeks ago, I got the letter. The one in Uncle Jack's handwriting, telling me that he loved me. That I was his hope and his joy. That he was sorry we didn't spend more time together. That he was sorry he didn't visit more often. That he was sorry he couldn't tell me his plan.

The letter that had a single house key taped to the paper.

Two weeks ago, I put my notice in at my apartment.

I put my notice in at my jobs.

I started the process of selling my furniture.

I deposited the check, purchased moving boxes, and packed my belongings.

Two weeks ago...

A traitorous tear rolls down my cheek.

This morning, I answered the door again. And the same man who delivered the letter was once more standing on the other side of the threshold.

But this time, he spoke.

He asked if I was ready.

And then he helped me carry my boxes and my one suitcase down to his waiting van. Before driving me to the airport and helping me carry my boxes all over again.

I didn't know you could check cardboard boxes as luggage. But you can.

Uncle Jack knew that. He prepaid for it.

And when I landed in Denver this morning, there was another driver waiting. Another van. All paid for.

Two hours later, the new stranger slowed to a stop in front of this very house.

*My house.*

The stranger waited beside the van while I unlocked the front door with my key.

And he waited while I had a breakdown. Right here, where I'm standing now.

Two minutes later, I found the garage door opener sitting on the kitchen counter, on top of a box of microwave popcorn, the brand I used to love as a kid. Which led to another breakdown.

Then, with red-rimmed eyes, I went back outside, and the nice stranger helped me put all my boxes in the garage, next to Uncle Jack's old pickup truck.

It didn't feel right having someone else in the house. Not yet.

It felt right to do that work by myself.

Of course, at the time, I didn't realize that even though the garage is *attached* to the house, it's not *connected*. So I had to haul them all across the gravel-patch yard area through the front door.

I open my eyes and look at all the boxes.

I'll unpack tomorrow.

Taking another slow breath, I cut through the living room to the door next to the dresser with the TV, into the one and only bedroom.

*My bedroom.*

The bedroom part is on the left. And navy-blue curtains are pulled open, showing off a pair of windows that have the same amazing view as the back deck.

There's a bed, with royal blue bedding folded inside a clear plastic storage cube sitting on top of the mattress. It has a plain wooden headboard pushed against the far wall, opposite the door, and a pair of matching nightstands.

Across from the foot of the bed, sharing a wall with the TV in the living room, is a closet, with room to hang my dresses beside the stacked washer and dryer.

And to my right is the sole bathroom.

There's just the one, but that's all I need.

I step into it and think the same thing I did the first time I came in here.

*My bathroom is spacious.*

It has a long vanity with a single sink and lots of counter space. Plain white cabinets below match the floor-to-ceiling cabinets to the right of the vanity. On the other side of the sink is a toilet. And then the shower.

It's plain. But it's bigger than the one I had in my apartment.

The house is bigger than anything I've ever had to myself.

My fingers fumble as I attempt to pull down the zipper on the side of my dress.

I pause and stare at myself in the large mirror.

"You're fine." My hair is a mess. My eyes are sore. My throat aches. "You are going to be fine."

With purpose, I reach for my side zipper again and pull it down.

I exhale with accomplishment, then slide the straps down my shoulders and let the mud-stained material fall to the ground.

My bra and underwear go next. And as I drop the white material to the floor, I bite my lip.

When I fell... did that man see...

I shake my head.

It doesn't matter.

Who cares if the grumpy ranger jerk saw my underwear.

Or my butt.

Or my thighs that aren't toned.

I turn away from the mirror.

The plain white shower curtain is loud as I draw it back, revealing a clean porcelain tub with a standard shower head jutting out high up on the wall.

*Uncle Jack was tall.*

I swallow.

He may not have lived here full time. And I may not have been here before. But I can see him in the details.

This was Uncle Jack's home.

Was.

Because now it's mine.

Reaching down, I turn on the water, and I cross my fingers, hoping the hot water situation works.

I've only ever lived in apartments. I've never had to deal with water heaters before. I don't know the first thing about them.

I've never even owned a car.

Standing next to the tub, waiting for the water to warm, I shake my head. "What were you thinking?"

I shake my head again, remembering the out-of-body feeling when I deposited the twenty-thousand-dollar check Uncle Jack gave me.

I knew he wasn't hurting, but I didn't think he had that sort of money sitting around.

Or maybe it was his retirement? That he didn't get a chance to use.

Tears build along my lashes. Again. And I groan.

It's too quiet.

That's the problem.

And it's going to remain a problem because there's no internet here. Barely any cell service.

Maybe I could get internet? But I don't really know how to go about that either. I'm so far away from *everything*. I doubt the company I used in Vegas can just come plug a router into the wall. And, well, twenty thousand is more money than I've ever had in my life. But it's not enough to live off, so I need to make it last.

*I'll start to worry about my job situation tomorrow.*

The house is paid off. I don't have rent or a mortgage. So minimum wage might be enough. I have to figure out how the utilities work, but I know how to grocery shop on a budget. And electricity, garbage, and water can't be that much.

Or am I on a well?

Unsure what my water source is, I look back down at the water pouring out of the faucet into the tub.

Not wanting to waste it, I bend and stick my hand under the flow.

*Hot!*

A real smile pulls across my mouth, and I pull the little doodad on the faucet to redirect the water to the shower head. There's a pause. A stutter. Then steaming water shoots out with a hiss.

Excitement fills me as I step under the stream and pull the shower curtain closed behind me.

Then I remember that I haven't unpacked my toiletries.

I don't even know which box they're in.

My shoulders slump. "Crap."

I'm tempted to just stand here, let the water do its work, but I have blood on me. And dirt containing who knows what caked onto my cuts.

Dripping wet, I step out of the shower onto the white bath mat.

Crossing my fingers, I take hurried but careful steps across the bathroom to the tall cabinets and pull open one of the doors.

A massive bottle of shampoo and a six-pack of bars of green soap—minus two—stare back at me.

"Yes!" I snag a bar of soap and start to turn back to the shower, but then I see the empty towel bar on the wall.

I open the other cabinet door and spot a stack of white towels. After grabbing one, I drape it over the towel bar, then step back under the spray of water.

Fifteen minutes later, I reemerge from the shower. My hair is twisted back in a damp braid, not washed, but the rest of me—forehead to toes—is scrubbed to a squeaky level of clean.

Standing, I let water drip off me for a minute before pulling the curtain back and reaching for the towel.

As I dry myself, I can't help but notice that the towels smell nice. Like laundry. And I wonder what his process was like when he packed everything up at the end of the summer. Clearly, he did all the laundry, putting towels away, packing up the bedding. But even then, I haven't noticed much dust.

I think about the box of popcorn on the counter. And how it seems like he left it there for me.

*Did he have this plan even last fall? When he closed up the house, did he know then that I would be the one coming back here, not him?*

His letter mentioned that he didn't live here full-time but that he hoped I would. Saying I was young and tough enough to deal with the winters and to stock up the cupboards in case I got snowed in for a few days.

The notion of being stranded freaked me out when I read it. But being here now... I could see myself spending a few days curled up on the couch, enjoying the snow from the warmth of the indoors.

When I go to wrap the towel around my body, I sigh. "Uncle Jack, I love you. But what the heck?" The top corners of the towel barely meet, and the bottom half... does not. "Did you steal this from a hotel?"

I let go with one hand, and I look for a tag.

It's some brand I don't know. Which, when I think about it, makes sense. I doubt hotels embroider their names on their millions of towels.

Seriously, though, I'm pretty sure this is stolen property.

Vowing to find all my bath items before I shower again, I step out of the tub and hang the towel back on the bar.

Then I move from the white-themed bathroom to the blue-themed bedroom. And I'm grateful that the wood floors from the main living area carry into the bedroom because blue carpet would be too much.

I glance through the open door that leads into the living room and note all the brown.

Brown couch. Brown rugs. Brown natural wood cabinetry.

Brown dead deer head, which is out of sight from this angle but never out of mind.

Blue, white, and brown. The three themes of the three rooms. *My rooms.* Because this is my flipping house.

Uncle Jack was always nicely dressed, but not exactly what I would call fashionable. More comfortable. And I'm not sure if his need for neatness is of a diagnosable nature, but the careful way everything is put in place feels very much like him.

But since neatness is not one of my traits, I'll be breaking up these color themes as soon as I get more of my stuff unpacked.

I need to be smart about my money, but I'll be making a wish list of things to buy when I get a job. Like a large throw blanket or some sort of cover for that hideous couch.

Crossing the room, I go to the short dresser under the window and open the second drawer down.

I grab one of my pajama shirts, a light pink one with gray stitching, and pull it over my head. It's baggy and stops at my upper thigh.

Then I open the top drawer and take out a pair of my hip-hugger undies.

Earlier, after the driver left—after I walked through the house, touching every piece of furniture; after I stood on the back deck, mouth open, staring at the view; after crying, for the hundredth time—I found the keys for *my truck* hanging on the fridge from a magnetic hook. Which prompted me to open the fridge.

Completely empty.

Not even a condiment inside.

Same with the freezer.

I opened the cupboards.

Dishes in perfect, neat stacks but boasting a variety of mismatched vintage patterns.

A stack of glass Tupperware containers.

A cabinet full of mugs from different vacation destinations.

The tall door beside the fridge revealed the pantry cupboard with cans of soup, boxes of flavored rice, two jars of spaghetti sauce, and two boxes of noodles that are not spaghetti shaped. Plus, a blue tacklebox full of condiment packets, sorted by type and then by restaurant.

Uncle Jack was a strange mix of eccentric meets backwoods with a dose of military sparseness.

Knowing I'd end up hungry, like I am now, I grabbed the truck keys. Went to the garage. Climbed in the truck. Started the engine. Pulled the truck halfway out of the garage. Realized I was going to have to make a four-point turn to get aimed back down the driveway correctly. Had a slight panic attack. Put the truck in park, right where I was. Turned the engine off and walked back inside.

So instead of buying groceries, I unpacked my clothes. Most of them.

Pulling my underwear up my legs, I'm glad I did. Forgetting about my toiletries was an annoying oversight, but it was nice to get my clothes out of drawers rather than digging through my suitcase.

I was planning to unpack the rest of my stuff right then and there, but the next box I opened happened to be my suncatchers and ribbon.

*My ribbon.*

I can't believe that hot ranger showed up out of nowhere.

Can't believe he knew about Uncle Jack calling me Matty.

Can't believe he destroyed my ribbon like that.

In the plainest sense of the term, sure, I *vandalized* the fence. But *come on*. Like, how grumpy do you have to be to get mad over some ribbon?

*And* I can't believe he's making me take down the rest. He already ruined it. The least he could do is complete the removal process himself.

Exiting the bedroom, I cross to the front door and make sure the dead bolt is locked.

Tomorrow I'll deal with the ribbon. And with unpacking. And driving into town for groceries.

Tonight...

I cross the kitchen to the pantry cupboard and grab a can of chicken and dumpling soup.

Tonight, I'm having popcorn and soup for dinner.

The sun glows orange as it sets, sending its colors through the wall of windows at the back of the house, making it feel like I really am the only person in the world out here.

I rip the plastic off the popcorn bag, then put it in the microwave and swing the door shut.

The first pop goes off, sounding like a tiny gunshot.

I grimace.

I can't believe I asked *Ethan* if he was going to shoot me.

I don't really think my family will kill me for this place.

I purse my lips.

Probably not.

But when they find out about it. That I got it. That I moved. That it came with money...

It's not going to be pretty.

# CHAPTER 9

## ETHAN

THE DOOR SWINGS SHUT BEHIND ME, AND THE SCENT OF burgers and whiskey surrounds me.

Sandra just texted saying she'll be here in five. Meaning I'll see her in ten.

Jessie, the bartender, waves at me.

I cross the small dining room of the inn and stop across the bar top from her. "Evening."

"Hey, Ethan. Whatcha getting?"

"Two waters, two ginger ales, and two of the veggie dinners."

Jessie grins. "Meeting your sister, I take it?"

I nod.

"I'll get your order in, then bring the drinks over."

"Appreciate it." I tap my knuckles on the bar, then find a table along the wall.

My water is half gone and my soda glass is covered in condensation when Sandra pushes through the door and drops into the chair across from me.

She came straight from the hair salon she works at, but it's an artsy place that has no uniform. So her outfit—a crop top under red denim overalls—isn't a surprise.

Her pixie-cut hair is dyed black, like the last time I saw her.

But the piercing through her brow now has a purple diamond thing on one end.

"Hey, Brother." Sandra grins at me.

I dip my chin. "Sister."

I FORK THE LAST OF MY FRIED BRUSSELS SPROUTS INTO my mouth, my eyes moving back to Sandra's damn eyebrow jewelry.

"Are you even listening to me?"

I drop my gaze to meet Sandra's. "No. Where would I buy ribbon?"

My sister lowers the portion of the mushroom Philly cheesesteak hoagie she was lifting to her mouth. "Ribbon? Like for wrapping presents?"

Her face is scrunched up as she looks at me like I asked her to help me build a bomb.

But no matter how right I was, I still feel like an asshole for ruining Tilda's ribbon. I could've taken the time to untie it, rather than ruin it.

I set my fork down.

*Matty.*

I still can't believe Jack was so sneaky. Talking about his grandkid for fucking years without actually telling me anything.

My shoulders sag.

*I can't believe Jack's dead.*

Which makes me feel like an even bigger asshole. Because Tilda, Matty, Matilda, just lost a family member.

Even though I'd never met her—and by all recollection, she's never been to Jack's cabin before—she must've been close with him.

I think about my gun locked in the glove box of my truck.

Jack never said anything about anyone else in his family. Never gave any hints about them being violent. But...

*Don't shoot me.*

*Which one of them sent you?*

I need to talk to Tilda.

"Are you dying?"

I blink at my sister. "Not any more than usual."

She rolls her eyes. "Wow."

"What?"

"Don't *what* me. I'm *what-ing* you."

I lift a brow.

She wags a finger at me. "Nope, don't give me that look. You're the one asking about ribbon."

"And that means death?"

"Not inherently. But..." She picks her sandwich back up and gestures at me with it. "Explain yourself."

"I just need ribbon." I regret ever bringing this up. But I'm in it now.

"Like to wrap a present with?" Sandra asks with her mouth full.

I shove my empty plate a few inches forward and cross my arms. "Yeah, I guess. But not that papery shit. Cotton stuff."

"Cotton. Stuff."

Gritting my teeth, I uncross my arms and shove my hand into my pocket. Then I withdraw a six-inch piece of ribbon.

I threw the rest of it away at the Visitor Center, but this bit fell on the ground, rather than into the trash can. And when I picked it up... I put it back in my pocket.

Sandra shoves the last chunk of sandwich into her mouth, then reaches for the ribbon.

I pull my arm back. "Your hands are dirty."

She widens her eyes while making a show of cleaning her fingers with a napkin.

When she holds her clean hand out, I reluctantly drop the length of fabric into her palm.

"This from a case or something?"

I furrow my brows. "A case?"

Sandra nods, holding the ribbon by one end, examining the color. *The color that matches my little Mountain Fairy's hair.* "Yeah, a case. Like, what's the mystery? Is this about a missing hiker? An empty campsite? Did you find it near a puddle of blood?"

I stare at the psychopath across from me. "No." Images of blood trickling down Tilda's knee flash into my mind.

And then more...

Finding the house empty.

Finding blood on the floor.

Finding a scrap of ribbon stuck to a branch.

Tilda disappearing...

"No." I say it louder.

Sandra just shrugs and holds the ribbon back out for me. "Okay. So, what then?"

"I just need to get more. Just like this." There's no way I'm telling her about Tilda. No way I'm admitting that I'm buying ribbon for a girl. She'll never let it go.

"A craft store would have it. There's a place not far from my work that should have something. I can send you the name."

I nod as I shove the ribbon back into my pocket. "I'd appreciate that."

Sandra picks her phone up off the table and taps at the screen a few times. "There." She sets her phone back down and narrows her eyes at me. "You sure you're okay?"

I wrap my fingers around my water glass. "Jack's dead."

My sister's face falls. She never met him, but she's heard me talk about him. "What? How?"

I open my mouth and pause. "I don't actually know."

"Did you...?"

I shake my head. "He didn't die at the house. I just heard about it today." From his grandkid. Who I agreed to keep an eye on. Who I thought was a boy. But who's actually a girl, straight from my fantasies, and instead of helping her, I made her fall, then cry.

*Not off to a great start.*

"I'm sorry."

I lift a shoulder, not sure what to say.

Jack was someone I saw on occasion.

We didn't go out to dinner.

Didn't talk on the phone.

But for the better part of two decades, since I first started working at the park, I've spent my summers stopping by his place. Talking shit. Listening to his stories. Having the occasional cup of coffee on his deck.

I exhale. And the weight of his loss settles across my thighs, pressing me into the chair.

I don't really have friends.

But I think he might've been one of them.

And now he's gone.

# Chapter 10

## Tilda

MUSIC IS PLAYING.

I blink my eyes open, and it takes me a second to remember where I am.

I'm sprawled on the ugly brown couch, with an empty bowl of popcorn and an empty bowl of soup on the low coffee table in front of me.

I groan as I sit upright.

While my soup was heating, I ventured through the living room and decided to open the top drawer of the dresser that the TV is sitting on. And then I grinned. Because it was full of DVDs. Spines up, titles on display, the entire drawer was filled with them. So was the next drawer and the next... Every drawer. Completely stuffed.

Turning on the TV, I knew there was no cable. Not even the usual over-air channels or whatever they're called. And without internet, I couldn't stream anything. So finding a bunch of DVDs... better than finding gold.

At first glance, they seemed to be in random order. But then I noticed that each drawer had a genre. And within that, each drawer was alphabetized.

Disney. Documentaries. Action Movies. Rom-coms. TV sitcoms. And the bottom drawer... all WWE wrestling videos.

I snorted a laugh when I found those.

Since internet is probably out of my budget, and because I'm not picky about my entertainment, I opted to start with the top drawer, first on the left. Which is how I fell asleep to *A Bug's Life*.

It's summer, but man, it's not hot up here at night at... whatever elevation this is. And since I was too lazy to get up for a blanket, my legs are cold.

I roll out my neck, then get to my feet and circle the coffee table. I'll deal with the dishes tomorrow.

Rubbing my eyes, I make my way to the bathroom and pat myself on the back for putting my toothbrush in my purse and not in some random box I have yet to open. I keep my eyes mostly closed while I brush my teeth, wanting to go right back to sleep, but as I sit on the toilet, I notice the same thing I've noticed all day.

The silence.

Not just quiet. *Silence.*

Bone deep. No sounds at all. Proof you're completely alone, type of silence.

My nerves tingle and my heart rate picks up.

If only there was a local sexy ranger who wasn't a total turd and could keep me company.

Hands washed, I turn off the bathroom light, then go back into the living room.

I know it's locked.

I'm positive.

But I still move to the front door and make sure.

Then I make sure all the windows are latched.

Then I double-check that the door to the back deck is also locked, even though there are no stairs down to the ground from the deck. It's not so high off the ground that someone couldn't climb it.

When I'm positive every opening to the outside is secure, I turn off the living room lights.

But when I stop in front of the TV, I don't turn it off. Instead, I hit Play on the DVD player.

The movie starts again as I walk into *my bedroom*.

Maybe someday I'll get used to the soundless nights out here on the top of a mountain.

But not today.

Not my first night.

# CHAPTER 11

## TILDA

"Yes!" I pump my fist in the air, then grimace when I see how close I came to smashing my knuckles against the counter.

Tempering my enthusiasm, I crouch lower and pull the vase out from under the kitchen sink.

Pretty wildflowers are growing in front of *my house*, and I want to bring some inside to cheer the place up.

It's great that this place is bigger than anything I've ever had before, but it needs a little help in the personality department.

Standing, I glance over at the dead deer staring at me from the corner of the living room.

*Air Bud* is playing on the TV, too quietly to cover my sigh.

*I need to find a way to spruce that freaking deer up too.*

I fill the vase half full of water, then set it next to the sink and dry my hands on my skirt.

I chose my pale blue sundress today.

It's a little plain. Knee-length. And made from jersey cotton, so it hugs the contours of my body more than my more structured dresses do. But I like the white bow woven into the low neckline and the fact that it has a built-in padded bra. The boob situation is nearing indecent, but I'm not in the mood to care. If I have to

43

remove my ribbon and go get groceries today, then I'm going to be comfortable. And this dress does that.

I pick the vase back up and slip my feet into my leather sandals, then open the front door.

Bright morning sun greets me, and I smile against the warmth.

Before I start, I tuck the vase against my body, careful not to spill the water, and reach under my skirt.

From the pocket sewn into the thigh of the thin shorts I have on under my dress, I pull out my phone.

After unlocking it, I open my music and hit Play on the one album I have downloaded.

The soundtrack to *Moulin Rouge!*

I was flipping through apps on my phone this morning while lying in bed, trying to see if I had anything that could entertain me without internet, when I stumbled across my music library.

Back home—back in Vegas—I streamed music when I wanted it. Never saw the point of buying songs.

Now I see.

But thankfully *past me* bought this soundtrack on impulse years ago. Which I'd forgotten about until I came across it.

Music playing, I slide my phone back into my pocket, my skirt falling back to my knees.

Humming yesterday was annoying. I'm not a good hummer. Or singer. But I know I have to make noise while I'm outside.

Or at least I'm pretty sure about that.

I don't really have a way to check that fact until I go into town later, but I swear I remember Uncle Jack telling me something about making noise so you don't accidentally surprise a bear with your presence.

Better safe than sorry, I let the tune distract my thoughts as I step off the front step and head toward the box I left outside yesterday.

As I bend down, reaching for the scissors I threw in here, I notice the strand of beads draped over the edge of the box.

Every bit of it is covered in a thin layer of dirt, and it takes me a moment to remember that this must be the strand I dropped yesterday.

*Did the grouchy park ranger pick them up?*

Leaving the strand where it is, I grab the scissors and head for the first patch of flowers.

# CHAPTER 12

## ETHAN

I TURN OFF THE ENGINE.

There's no need for me to be on this side of the park.

Not this far out.

There's no need for me to go check the perimeter fence.

Not after checking it yesterday.

There's certainly no need for me to see if Tilda is home.

There's no need at all.

But... I climb out of my truck and stride into the woods.

# CHAPTER 13

## TILDA

I ROLL MY LIPS TOGETHER.

The ribbon is gone.

There's nothing on the fence.

I turn left, then right, double-checking that I'm not in the wrong spot. But this is where I tied the ribbon that Ranger Grumpy Pants complained about. And I'm ninety-nine percent positive he told me to remove the rest of it. Which would mean that he left some of the ribbon on the fence. But...

Nothing.

It's all gone.

Holding the metal part, I tap the plastic handle of the scissors against my skirt, matching the beat of the song playing from my hip.

Part of me wonders if I'm losing it.

Maybe there never was a sexy park ranger with tattoos and two different colored eyes...

I spin in a slow circle.

*I'm in Colorado.*

*Uncle Jack is gone.*

*I woke up in his old house because I live here now.*

*I put ribbon on this fence yesterday, but it's gone today.*

Facing the bare fence again, I inhale deeply.

I didn't imagine Ethan.

And I'm not imagining the burst of color a few yards ahead of me, on the other side of the fence.

I don't remember seeing these flowers yesterday.

And... they're purple.

I left my vase back on the front step, and it's already full of flowers. But the purple ones are so pretty. And there was still another vase under the sink. So... I want these.

I just need to figure out how to get over there.

And I need to ignore the sign that I read farther down the fence yesterday. The one saying *No Entry to State Park from Private Property.*

Honestly, the sign feels a little insulting. Because who—other than the occupant of *my land*—would even see this sign?

And really, what's the difference between where I'm standing right now and fifteen feet in... that direction? *East?* Who knows. But really. These are man-made lines. And those flowers are pretty.

I examine the fence, judging my options.

I don't bother entertaining the idea of hopping over the fence. Not in a million years could I do that.

Not even if I was being chased by Bigfoot.

I narrow my eyes at the darker spots in the forest.

*Bigfoot isn't real... Right?*

The song in my shorts changes to something slower, more mysterious, and a shiver skitters down my arms.

*Nope. Not thinking about Bigfoot.*

I grab the wire where it's not barbed, next to where it's attached to the post, and give it a shake.

The big staple-looking thing holding the wire in place isn't loose, but it also doesn't feel strong enough to hold my weight.

Not that I'd be able to climb over the fence with any sort of agility.

I'm going to have to duck between the middle and top strands of barbed wire.

But they aren't that far apart. And I'm not a wisp of a girl. I'm substantial.

And I don't feel like getting tetanus today.

Pursing my lips, I look along the fence line.

Two posts down, the center strand of barbed wire sags a little more than the others.

Stopping before the sad-looking section of fence, I wonder again if this is worth it.

It's just a few more flowers.

And I'll probably tear my skirt.

But... the petals are a deep shade of purple.

And there are so many of them.

And they'll make my new house that much cheerier.

Determined, I put the scissors between my teeth and bite down, like they're a rose and I'm doing the tango.

With my right hand, I find a spot between barbs and try to push the top strand up, creating as much room as possible. With my left hand, I bunch up my skirt, holding it so the material is tight around my upper thighs, then I duck through the fence.

My hair catches on the top wire.

My skirt catches on a barb below me.

I lose my balance and have to slam my foot down on a patch of slippery moss.

I let out a shriek as my foot slides forward six inches.

The scissors drop from my mouth onto the ground.

And when I let go of my skirt while trying to catch myself, my dress catches on the barbed wire. Again.

All to the soundtrack of *Moulin Rouge!*

# CHAPTER 14

## ETHAN

I PINCH THE BRIDGE OF MY NOSE.
This girl cannot be real.

# CHAPTER 15

## TILDA

SCISSORS BACK IN HAND, I TAKE A CALMING BREATH.

Climbing through the fence wasn't my most graceful moment, but all is well. Nothing seems torn, just disheveled.

The song playing from my hip reaches a crescendo as I take the couple of steps to the first cluster of flowers.

I bend, aligning my scissors with the base of the stem.

The singer holds a high note.

And a voice sounds from beside me.

"Don't cut that."

I scream.

My arm jerks.

The scissors shut.

And I tip forward.

# CHAPTER 16

## ETHAN

I CLENCH MY STOMACH MUSCLES AND GRIT MY TEETH, urging my blood to stay where it is.

But Tilda is on her hands and knees before me.

Ass in the air.

And my thoughts are backstroking through the gutter.

Because I want to kneel behind her.

I want to kneel behind her, flip her skirt up onto her back, and...

She pushes herself up so her hands are no longer on the forest floor. And she twists her torso to glare at me.

Her purple hair is a curly mess.

Her cheeks are hot with emotion.

Her hands have dirt on them.

And she looks exactly like the troublesome mountain fairy she is.

She points a finger at me. "You, sir, are a bastard."

She's not smiling at me this time.

Not masking her feelings.

And I like it so much I have to work to keep my expression even.

"Well?" She drops her hand.

"Well, what?" I step closer, leaving only a few feet between us.

"Well, aren't you going to argue?"

I lift a brow. "I've been called worse."

She huffs. "I believe that."

The urge to smile grows, but I keep my lips flat. "Plus, you're not wrong."

Tilda puts her hands on her hips, drawing my attention down her delicious body. "What, that you're a jerk, or that you were born out of wedlock?"

This time my smirk wins. *Wedlock? Who says that?* "Both, actually. Though, considering my parents aren't alive to defend themselves, I'll just admit I'm a jerk."

Her shoulders slump, and her fists fall from her sides. "Oh... I'm sorry."

Probably shouldn't have casually mentioned the orphan detail. But it's been twenty years, and I didn't really consider how fucked up that might sound.

The pretty girl presses her lips together.

Better for Tilda to be mad at me than pity me, so... "You need to pay better attention to your surroundings."

Her mouth drops open. "Excuse me?"

I gesture around. "I've been here since you decided to *illegally* cross through the fence, and you didn't notice me at all."

She glances back at the fence, and I know we're both remembering how that went.

My smirk grows.

# CHAPTER 17

## TILDA

"WELL, I'M SORRY." I SHIFT, PLANTING MY RIGHT FOOT on the ground, then I press my hand against my raised knee and push up to standing. "I was told I'm supposed to make noise while in the forest."

"You are." He lifts that annoying brow again. "But you can still listen. Or use your eyeballs."

Previous sympathy gone, I mumble under my breath as I bend down and pick up the flower I cut and my scissors. "*You* could use *your* eyeballs."

"Okay." He points at the flower in my hand. "*That's* illegal."

I look down. "Flowers?"

"Picking flowers in a state park. They're protected."

"But I didn't pick it. I cut it."

His eyebrow stays up.

"It'll grow back," I argue, raising my voice over the music.

He sighs. "The law doesn't care *how* you retrieve them. Just that you *don't*."

Irritation flares in my chest as he pulls a small pad of paper out of his pocket. "What's that?" I use the flower to point at his hand. "Are you giving me a ticket?"

He nods.

I stomp my foot, careful not to trample any flowers. "Seriously?"

He pulls a pen from his chest pocket and starts to write. "Same last name as Jack?"

"No," I grit out.

He looks up at me.

I don't want to tell him. But I don't know if I can get arrested by a park ranger. And I don't really feel like finding out the hard way. "It's Wright. With a *W*. Like the airplane brothers."

He takes a step closer. "Can you turn that music off?"

"No," I say stubbornly.

He tilts his head, brow furrowing. "Where is it coming from anyway?"

I feel my cheeks darken. "None of your business."

His gaze lowers to my waist, and my frustration at everything grows.

Him. Life. The fact that I fell *again* because of *him*.

I want to leave the music on just to be obstinate. But it is pretty loud. And I'm no longer in the mood for this playlist. "Can you turn around?"

"No." He repeats my earlier answer back to me.

I'd leave the music playing, just to bother him, but it's making me feel... *ridiculous*.

"Please?" I ask between my teeth.

"No," he says again, hovering his pen over the pad as he keeps watching me.

I press my lips together and angle my body so the side with the pocket is away from him. Then I shift the scissors into the hand with the flower, reach up under my skirt, and pull my phone free from my pocket.

I turn off the music, then slide my phone back into my pocket.

"Happy?" I face him.

"Ecstatic," he deadpans. Then he goes back to writing.

*Writing* a mother-flipping ticket for picking a flower.

Anger building, I crouch down and cut another flower. Then another.

I can't believe this man snuck up on me again.

I don't know how big this state park is, but it seems super unlikely that he would happen across this same little piece of land two days in a row.

*At least I didn't imagine him.*

*Not that the reality of him is any better. Even if he is hotter than I remember.*

I cut another flower and glance up at him, hoping to sneak a peek at his rugged good looks.

But of course, he's staring right at me.

"What are you doing?" Ethan sounds exasperated.

*Well, that makes two of us, buddy.*

I cut another flower. "If you're giving me a ticket, I might as well earn it." I cut another one.

"Tilda Wright." He basically sighs my name. And I hate how good it sounds.

*It's been way too long since I've gotten laid.*

"Ethan Grump." I take two steps away from him, then crouch down and cut three more at once.

"You need to stop."

"Why?" I hold his gaze as I cut another one.

He shakes his head, and I notice that he's not wearing a hat this time. Yesterday he had a baseball hat shading his face and covering his hair, but today... he's on display.

*Shame we don't admire stick-in-the-mud jerks.*

"Because, Bad Girl," he says slowly, annoyingly, "if you cut too many, the fine will go up."

*Bad girl?*

Heat rolls around in my belly. But I refuse to acknowledge it.

I look down at the cluster of flowers in my hand, trying to count them. "What's the number?"

He huffs, like I'm the one being unreasonable. "I'm not telling you that."

"Guess I'll take my chances, then."

I take a few more steps toward a pretty blue flower I hadn't noticed before.

"Miss Wright," Ethan snaps, and I freeze. "Do *not* cut that flower."

I look down at the unique bloom. "Is it poisonous?"

"No, but that is the Colorado State Flower, and if you cut that in front of me, you will be in even bigger trouble."

I am so sick of this man scolding me.

So freaking sick of it.

"Fine." I step away from the flower and glare at the man staring at me.

Judging me.

The man who called me ridiculous.

He lifts his chin. "What?"

"I didn't say anything."

"No, but you want to." He goads me. "Holding back doesn't seem like your style, Starlight."

I narrow my eyes at him.

I don't know what starlight means, but I'm sure it's some sort of insult. "Just write the ticket."

He sighs, then rips the top sheet off the pad and holds it out to me.

I stare at it.

The urge to use my scissors and cut it into a dozen pieces flares bright.

He gives the paper a little shake. "You gonna take it?"

"You gonna admit your butthole looks like an asshole?"

My eyes widen as they snap up to meet his.

I didn't mean to say that.

Not out loud.

Ethan's mouth opens.

And I prepare myself for anger.

But then... he laughs.

A full-body, *so loud it scares the birds out of the trees* kind of laugh.

And *whyyy* does that make him even hotter?

He closes his fingers around the ticket, crinkling the paper in his large grip.

"Just go," he laughs, shaking his head.

I look from his smiling mouth to the crumpled ticket in his hand, then back up to his eyes.

He uses the back of his hand to wipe at his eyes.

*Is this man crying?*

He points back toward my property. "Before I change my mind."

I'm torn between wanting to laugh with him and wanting to shove that ticket into his open mouth.

But... if he's letting me go.

I turn my back on him and pick my way back to the fence, avoiding stepping on flowers and branches.

When I reach the property line, I want to wait. Want to stand here and wait until he's disappeared back into the woods so he won't watch me struggle again.

Because I'm sure I'm going to make an even bigger mess of this than I did coming through it the first time.

But I also don't have money to burn on wildflower tickets, so I'm taking this getaway opportunity. Even if it makes me look *ridiculous*.

I toss my scissors to the ground on the other side of the fence and bunch up my skirt in my free hand.

But I can't toss the flowers. I don't want to damage them. And I can't hold up the top wire with my hand full.

A hand reaches past me, gripping the top wire and lifting it.

I don't turn to face him.

He's close.

So close.

Closer than he's ever been.

If I turned, our faces would be inches away.

If I turned, I might brush his chest with my shoulder.

Ethan lifts a big, booted foot, and he presses it down on the middle strand of barbed wire, creating a bigger opening than I could ever do on my own.

Taking the kindness, I duck through the fence, my dress not catching at all.

With my back to him, I let go of my skirt.

"Did you remove the rest of the ribbon?" I ask quietly.

But I know he hears me.

"Put some ointment on your knees, Starlight."

# CHAPTER 18

## TILDA

I TWIST THE VASE ON THE DINING TABLE.

I twist it again.

"He's not even that hot."

I turn away from the collection of flowers.

"He's not," I tell Deerdra. Because it feels slightly more sane to talk to a dead deer over dying flowers. "Honestly, he's not my type."

Deerdra stares back, sensing my lie from across the room.

I throw my hands up. "Fine, he's everybody's type."

Then I try to picture him at some snooty brunch with royalty, a princess at his side. And... yep, he'd look smokin' in a suit and tie too.

And if the tie was a little bit loose. Circling his neck, with room for me to wrap my hand around the silk and drag him closer.

He could call me Bad Girl again...

"Nope." I shake my head.

I'm not going to fantasize about the man who cut up my ribbon.

*The same man who removed the rest of the ribbon after telling me to do it.*

60

After grabbing the keys for the truck—*my truck*—I snag my silver clutch off the top of one of the boxes and open the front door.

Something quacks. Loudly. And I shriek.

Taking a quick step back into the house, I swing the door shut and slap a palm to my chest.

My heart is thudding so hard you'd think Bigfoot shouted at me.

*I really have to work on my startle response.*

Taking two steps to the side, I lean over the row of boxes I still have to unpack and look out the window into the front yard.

Movement draws my attention, and I spot a duck waddling across the gravel driveway, away from the house and toward the forbidden state park property.

His little brown tail wiggles back and forth with each step.

"Wait," I whisper, placing my fingers against the glass.

Rushing, I move back to the front door and pull it open.

"Hi!"

*It's been one night, and I've already lost what's left of my sanity.*

Then the duck lets out one of his air horn quacks again.

And I grin.

I grin all the way to Uncle Jack's truck.

*My truck.*

"Can't believe you left me with a truck." I roll my eyes as I climb into it.

*Climb* in the literal sense of the word.

This old beast of a truck isn't one of those cute ones you see in Christmas ads with a tree strapped down in the back. No, this is the one you'd see parked in front of a house in a horror movie. Where the cast is stranded in the forest and they come across a house with a light on...

*Nope. Not going there.*

Seated, I pull the driver's door shut and buckle my seat belt.

I drop my purse on the bench seat next to me, then remember I need the key that I put in there.

Because this truck is *that old*.

I stick the key in the ignition and turn it, and just like yesterday—when I took the truck on a five-foot test drive—the engine turns over smoothly.

Like so many other things, I wonder how far out Uncle Jack planned his departure from this world.

*How did he leave last fall without his truck?*

After shifting into drive, I turn the wheel and work my way out of the narrow garage.

# CHAPTER 19

## ETHAN

LEAVING MY WORK TRUCK IN FRONT OF MY CLOSED garage door, I turn off the engine. But I stay where I am.

My thoughts are on Tilda.

*Still* on Tilda.

And even though I have absolutely no reason to go back to her house, I want to.

It's only a few miles from here as the crow flies. Except the park is between us.

I drum my fingers against the steering wheel, wondering if there's a reasonable excuse I could use for driving over there right now.

I could smooth out the crumpled ticket that's still in my pocket and give it to her.

The corner of my mouth twitches as I think about her trying to insult me.

*Admit your butthole looks like an asshole.*

I shake my head as the smile takes over my features.

*Who even says that?*

*What does that even mean?*

Shoving my door open, I finally exit my truck.

And as I walk to my front door, I wonder what Tilda will have for dinner tonight.

# Chapter 20

## Tilda

No one looks at me funny.

No one whispers behind their hands while watching me.

No one pays me any special attention as I push my cart through the aisles of the grocery store.

I don't know why I was so stressed. I just figured, in a small town, everyone would know everyone, and I would stand out as an outsider.

But no.

I'm not even the only person here with hair dyed a color from the rainbow. I saw a guy in the produce section with a blue mohawk.

My shoulders relax, and I slow to a stop as I enter the bakery section.

My cart is barely half full. Partially from feeling overwhelmed, partially from not knowing what to get.

Back in Nevada, I mostly ate takeout and frozen burritos. Takeout isn't really a daily option anymore. I may not have anything better to do than drive the thirty-seven minutes to town, but I also can't be blowing my money on excessive gas use. And considering that pickup is as old as I am—*or older, I have no idea*

—I doubt she's getting good gas mileage. So... I need to shop wisely.

I look at the apples and blueberries in my cart. The ramen. The boxes of mac and cheese. The case of ginger ale. The loaf of bread I'll keep in the freezer. The peanut butter and blueberry jam.

Heat builds in my cheeks.

I'm turning thirty soon, and I'll be the first to admit that I am not a good cook.

Maybe I could be. One day. And I'd like to learn how to bake bread...

But I need to research recipes before I just start grabbing stuff.

I lean forward, about to push my cart toward the cookie display, when a tiny girl bolts in front of me.

My spine curls as I hunch forward, absorbing my momentum before the wheels can move.

"Sorry," someone with a deep voice says from beside me, surprising me even more than the child did.

Thankfully the air is already stuck in my lungs, so I don't scream the way I probably would have otherwise.

*Small mercies.*

The extremely handsome man dips his chin at me as he strides past.

My blush deepens, but blessedly, he doesn't notice as he chases after his child. "Ursa, quit running."

*They really must breed them differently in the mountains.*

Exhaling, I look both ways, then continue on to the cookies.

Ten minutes later, I've doubled the contents of my cart. Mostly with frozen foods that I can hopefully get home before they thaw, and with more bakery items than any one person needs.

But it's not my fault this small-town grocery store has a top-notch bakery section. And I think I can freeze most of the muffins and stuff if I wrap them tightly in the cling wrap I also put in my cart.

Before I exit the freezer row, I try to recall my mental grocery list.

Butter. Ground coffee. Creamer. Coffee filters. Frozen veggies, to offset the frozen pizzas. Hot sauce. Ranch, to offset the veggies. Crackers. Dish soap, because I forgot to pay attention to whether there was any. Laundry soap, because same reason. Garbage bags, with a mental note to figure out how to set up my garbage pickup—which I've never had to do before.

Deciding I've remembered as much as possible, I push out of the aisle and steer toward the checkout.

Only two of the registers have lights on, indicating they're open. And there's one person in each line. Which is stressful because there's no obvious choice.

*What if I pick wrong, and the other one clears out right away? Do I back up and switch lanes? Or do I stay put?*

My pulse thuds, and I pull in a breath through my nose.

*Get it together, Tilda.*

*It's a grocery store, not an exam.*

An older woman with a cart overflowing with bags of charcoal wheels her way into one of the lines, and I exhale with relief. *Choice made.*

Acting as though I wasn't on the verge of a total breakdown, I maneuver into the other lane.

There's a couple ahead of me, talking to the cashier like they know her, and I make sure to smile when they all look my way.

Reminding myself that this is all normal, and to stay calm, I unload my items onto the conveyor belt as the other three people chat casually.

I have about a third of the things still in my cart when the couple leaves, and the cashier turns her attention to me. "How you doin'?"

"Good, thank you," I lie convincingly. "Yourself?"

"Oh, can't complain." She smiles. "You have your bags?"

My mouth is starting to form a matching smile, but then I replay her question. "Bags?"

"Yeah, hon." At my blank expression, she nods toward all the food I've placed on the belt. "Grocery bags."

That ache of panic starts in my chest again.

"I don't have any." It comes out as a whisper.

And just like that, I feel so dumb.

So out of place.

So far from home. Even if it was a home I didn't like.

And damn it all, I think I might cry again.

But the woman never stops smiling. "That's alright. I forget mine all the time too. We'll do paper ones."

I inhale, then I do what I've done my whole life.

I match her smile.

I push the feelings of anxiety and unworthiness down into my belly, and I pull the sides of my mouth up. And I let my round cheeks round even more. And I pretend.

I embrace the pageantry.

And when I turn my back to the cashier, I brush my fingers under my eyes. Then I take the rest of my groceries out of my cart and act like everything is fine.

# Chapter 21

## Tilda

Setting my mug of coffee down on the arm of the chair, I pull the zipper of my hoodie all the way up to my throat, then I sit.

It's not early morning. Because why get up early when it's not necessary? But the sun is still rising, and the air has a distinct nip.

Settling into the chair, I imagine Uncle Jack sitting right here, drinking his coffee just like this.

I take a sip, the steam warming my nose.

Then I spill coffee down the front of my hoodie because the world's loudest duck lets out the world's loudest quack from somewhere below the deck.

I hold my mug out with one hand and use the other to brush the liquid off my sweatshirt.

"Crap on a cracker."

The duck lets out a quieter quack, and I snicker.

"Okay, fine. On a quacker."

He lets out a double quack.

I stand and walk to the railing, looking over the edge in time to see the same duck butt from before waddle around the side of the house.

Since I need to wash my hands anyway, I turn around and

69

head for the back door, hoping I can catch Quackers in the front yard.

Reaching through the screenless screen door, I use the side of my hand to depress the door handle and push the door open.

I set my mug on the counter and grab a hand towel from next to the sink, then rush the few steps to the front door and yank it open.

The soft thwaps of flat feet on damp earth pull my attention to the edge of the driveway, where the duck is once again making a break for the park.

I only ever crossed the boundary that once, and I didn't get more than a few yards past the fence, but there must be a lake nearby. Or some form of water. Ducks like that, right?

I'm tempted to chase after him. But I don't. Because that would be crossing a line.

Of insanity... Animal cruelty... It's a toss-up.

Back inside, I wash my hands and use the towel to dry off the side and bottom of my mug, then I take my coffee to the front window and stand there in my dirty hoodie, looking out over the front yard.

I hung up the rest of my suncatchers yesterday, put the box away, and parked the truck in the one-car garage—took three tries to back it in, but I eventually got there.

Now with the light shining down on my suncatchers, everything sparkles. And a rare sense of pride fills me.

Quackers seems to like it too, since he keeps visiting.

Except he's not staying.

I hold the mug with both hands and lift it to my lips.

I really need to go back into town so I can use the internet and find out what ducks like to eat. Maybe there's a type of food I could buy to keep him around.

I can't say for certain, but I feel like I read somewhere that you aren't supposed to give ducks bread. Even though every TV show ever always shows ducks swimming around in a pond and people tossing bread at them.

I purse my lips.

Maybe I could set up a bird bath?

Do ducks like bird baths?

They're birds so...

I take another sip.

I did my best to pay attention to the town, aptly named Lonely, as I drove through it. And if I'm recalling correctly, I believe there's a hardware store across the street from the nicer gas station. They should have something.

WITH THE IGNITION OFF, I UNBUCKLE AND PUSH MY driver's door open.

It slams shut, and I jerk my arms back, narrowly avoiding my hand getting smashed.

I huff and pull the strap of my cross-body bag over my head.

*Let's try this again.*

I twist on the bench seat and use both hands to shove the door open, keeping one hand braced against the handle this time so the wind doesn't smash it shut on me again.

My red skirt whips around my ankles, the maxi length saving me from flashing my goods to the whole town.

Okay, *whole town* is probably an exaggeration since there are a few other vehicles in the parking lot but no people. But the main road is right beside me, and, like I remembered, there's a gas station directly across the two-lane highway.

Halfway to the front door of Lonely Hardware, I wonder if I should've brought the paper bags from my grocery trip with me. But they're back home under my kitchen sink, so it's not like I can get them now.

While I was paying for my groceries last night, I noticed the reusable bags for sale at the register. I was too busy holding my composure together to buy any, and I didn't want to give away the fact that I have none, but I bet they have some here.

Mind made up, I push the stress away from my shoulders and walk into the hardware store.

Duck food and shopping bags. I can do this.

# Chapter 22

## Ethan

I lean against my truck as my gas tank fills.

I've been working to clear a downed tree off one of the service roads all morning, and I'm streaked with dirt and sweat. I should stop home for a shower and a change of clothes, but I need to get a load of gravel spread across a trailhead before the day is over, so there's no point in cleaning up yet.

My shoulders ache, and I roll out my neck.

*I'm getting too old for this shit.*

Pushing the bill of my baseball hat up, I use the back of my other hand to wipe sweat off my forehead.

The pump clicks, and I remove the nozzle from my gas tank and secure the cap.

When I turn toward my driver's door, my attention is drawn across the street to the hardware store parking lot.

My brows lower as I narrow my eyes.

*Is that Jack's pickup?*

It's empty.

I move my gaze to the store's front door.

I wonder...

As if summoned with magic, my lilac-haired Mountain Fairy emerges through the sliding glass doors.

There's a bag hooked over her elbow, flapping in the wind. And in her arms, she's carrying... something.

I can't tell what it is, but the way she's slightly leaned back tells me it's heavy.

I feel my fingers flex.

*If she hurts herself...*

I take in the rest of her. And I swallow.

Her body is wrapped in red fabric.

The top of her dress is hidden behind the large bag of whatever she's carrying, but her pale arms are bare.

The skirt dances around her feet, and I instantly worry she'll trip over it, since, unlike the other dresses I've seen her in, this one goes to the ground.

But Tilda doesn't trip.

She disappears around the passenger side of her truck, out of my view.

I can see the far door open. Then close. And I expect her to circle around to her driver's door, but instead she walks back the way she came. Back into the store.

Curious what she's up to but knowing it's none of my business, I get into my truck.

I turn on the engine, and I put the shifter into drive, but I don't take my foot off the brake.

I wait.

And I watch.

It only takes half a minute before the doors open again.

And I shake my head.

Because Tilda has reemerged, only instead of a heavy bag, this time she's carrying a bright blue kiddie pool.

It's practically as tall as she is. And it's going to act like a fucking sail in this wind.

On cue, the hard plastic pool catches a gust, and the bottom flies up and away from Tilda.

I take my foot off the brake.

Tilda staggers.

This will be my third time meeting Miss Tilda Wright, and I don't want it to be my third time watching her fall.

Especially on pavement.

I drive to the exit.

Keeping an eye across the road as I wait for the sparse traffic to pass, I watch Tilda turn, putting her back to me, as she tries to blade her way through the wind.

The pool flies free of her grip.

I step on the gas.

Tilda rushes after the pool, her long hair whipping around her head.

I have to take my eyes off her as I make the turn into the parking lot.

When I look back, she's got a hold of the pool again and has almost reached her truck.

I leave an empty parking spot between our trucks, but she doesn't seem to notice me pulling up beside her.

Shoving my shifter into park, I push open my door at the same time she presses the pool to the side of her truck, trapping it between the vehicle and her body.

I slam my door shut, and the noise finally catches her attention.

Tilda turns her head to look over her shoulder, but the wind today is relentless, and it blows her hair over her face, obstructing her view.

She tries to reach up to brush it away, but the pool starts to shift, so she puts her hand back down.

I cross the few feet between us and stop beside her. "Need help?"

Tilda tries to toss her hair out of the way, but it doesn't work. "Ethan?"

There's a tone to her voice that I can't quite nail down. *Relieved? Hopeful?*

"Yeah, Starlight." Moving slowly, I reach up and slide my thumb along her jaw, catching a handful of her wild hair. Her eyes snap to mine as I tug her hair, just a little, while I hold it back.

Her light brown eyes stare up at me.

*She's so fucking pretty.*

My fingers tighten in her hair, and her lips part.

*Christ.*

*Focus, fucker.*

I tip my head toward the pool in her hands. "Fancy a swim?"

She rolls those pretty eyes. "Yeah. I love rolling around in eight inches of water."

I press my lips together, stopping myself from saying something I shouldn't, and clear my throat. "What's it for, then?"

She huffs. "None of your business."

I was expecting her to say she was going to turn it into a garden. Or some sort of fairy pond. But her evasiveness...

I arch my neck to look through the back window, trying to see what else she bought.

"What are you doing?" She shifts, trying to block my view. Which is cute, since she's a solid foot shorter than my six foot three.

"What was in the bag?"

"What bag?"

I lower my gaze back to hers. "The bag you carried out before you went back in for this damn pool."

Not many people can stare me down. My heterochromia usually throws them off, and they end up looking back and forth between my eyes, trying to confirm that my irises are, in fact, different colors.

It's never bothered me. But Tilda... I like that she doesn't do that.

I like that she looks at me like she's seen me a hundred times before.

Like she's used to me.

She narrows her eyes. "Are you following me?"

It's so hard not to smile around this girl.

And that's not something I'm used to.

I'm not a smiley type of guy.

"Well?" She lifts her brows.

This time, I don't fight the urge, and I let the edges of my mouth pull up.

She's acting put out over my presence, but she's also not telling me to let go of her hair.

"I was getting gas. I'm not stalking you." I flex my fingers, and I appreciate how soft the strands of her hair feel against my rough palm. "Tell me what the pool is for, and I'll help you strap it down."

I peek into the bed of the truck, confirming there are no ratchet straps visible. They could be in the back seat, but I doubt it.

"If you call me ridiculous again—"

I shake my head. "I won't." Remembering the look on her face when I did, I stroke my thumb across the smooth skin behind her ear. "I never should've called you that. I'm sorry."

She stares up at me. Looking... stunned.

Like no one has ever apologized to her before.

And I hate that look on her face almost as much as I hated her tears.

My shifted grip sends strands of hair flying again.

I release my hold of her hair, then use both hands to pull all her hair back. It takes a couple tries, but once I have a hold of it, I grip it with one hand at the back of her head like a ponytail.

I pull my baseball hat off and pass her hair through the hole in the back, then tug the bill down to secure it onto her head.

Too late, I realize it's probably damp from sweat, but Tilda doesn't recoil.

She doesn't pull away.

But she's not looking me in the eye anymore.

No, she's looking at my mouth.

I slide my tongue over my bottom lip, wetting it. And I swear she sucks in a breath.

*Fuck.*

My body reacts without my permission. My stomach muscles tighten, like they always do around her. My balls throb. My cock...

I drop my hands from the hat. "Keep your back to the wind, and it'll stay on."

She nods.

"Do you have any straps inside the truck?"

She shakes her head.

"Can you hold this for another minute while I get mine?"

She nods.

The edge of my mouth pulls up. Again.

I step back, then cross the empty parking spot. Unlike Tilda's two-door, bench-seat, thirty-year-old pickup, I have a four-door model that's just a few years old.

I open the rear door and grab the set of ratchet straps I keep on the floor.

Turning back, I catch Tilda's eyes on me before she turns her head forward.

*Look all you want, Fairy Girl.*

Moving to the back of Tilda's truck, I lower the tailgate and climb into the bed.

With the baseball hat on her head, she can't see me as I stand above her. But when I grip the top edge of the pool, she lets go.

When it clears the side of the truck, I lower it into the bed, then stand in the center of the pool, holding it in place.

Jack didn't believe in replacing things that weren't broken, hence this old-ass truck, but the engine is in great condition, and he bolted half a dozen tie-down anchors in the bed. Making it easy to secure things with straps exactly like the ones I'm using.

I crisscross the straps over the kiddie pool and tighten them as much as I dare, without cracking the plastic.

Still crouched down, I turn my head and meet Tilda's eyes.

She's been waiting silently. Watching.

"You know how to loosen these?" I indicate the yellow strap.

She shakes her head.

I show her how.

Then I tighten it and show her again.

"If it sticks, just give it a little jiggle. Okay?"

She nods.

From my place in the bed, I look through the back window, and this time I can see the item lying on the passenger side of the front seat.

I slowly turn my head back toward Tilda. "Duck food?"

She crosses her arms, pushing up her tits.

But I keep my eyes locked on hers as I lift a brow.

She lifts one right back.

And I find myself fighting another fucking smile.

Standing, I step over the straps, then brace my hand on the edge of the truck bed and jump down.

I close the tailgate and round the side of the truck, but when I stop before Tilda, the look of defiance has withered away into something else.

I frown. "What is it?"

She rolls her lips together. "I wasn't planning on getting the pool. I figured I'd get a bird bath or something for the duck to play in."

"Okay..."

She looks down, my hat's bill blocking my view of her face as she slides her hands into hidden pockets at her hips. "I'm not stupid."

Something unpleasant strikes me in the center of the chest. "I know you're not."

She doesn't look up at me. "It's just that I saw the pool and thought it would be perfect. But I didn't think about the wind. And if you hadn't shown up..."

I step forward, putting myself so close she has to tip her head back to avoid the front of the hat hitting my chest. But she only lifts her head enough to avoid collision, not enough to see me.

She pulls her hands out of her pockets, like she might reach for me, but then she lowers them to her sides.

79

"If I hadn't shown up, you would've gone back in to return the pool, and they would've sold you some straps." I reach behind her, gripping the makeshift ponytail, and tug, tipping her head back until our eyes meet. "And I promise that someone in there would've been more than happy to help you."

I almost growl at the thought of another man crawling all over her truck. Holding her hair back. Getting this close.

But then Tilda stops my spiraling thoughts because she reaches her hands up... and this time, she touches me.

Palms against my sides, bracing herself as the wind pushes against us, Tilda finally touches me.

*And goddamn it, I want her hands everywhere.*

But I focus on the conversation. "I know you're not stupid, Starlight," I tell her gently, meaning it. "Just like I know you've never lived alone in the mountains before."

Her fingertips flex, just the smallest bit, but I feel it in my bones. "That obvious?"

I tip my head to the side, letting her see the hint of a smirk. "Little bit."

Her shoulders drop, but not in defeat. More like she's letting go of tension. "I've lived alone, but never in a house. I've never even owned a car."

"You do have a driver's license, though, right?"

Her expression turns back to the annoyed one she gave me yesterday. "I have a license. I know how to drive."

I give her a slow nod, like I maybe don't believe her. *Even though I do.* In the hopes of breaking her even further out of her self-doubt.

"You're a pest." She moves like she's going to press her fingertip into my chest. But I'm still holding her hair. So when she shifts, I do too, and instead of a fingertip, she flattens her palm against my pec.

Her gaze drops to where her hand is.

And then a car horn honks.

# CHAPTER 23

## TILDA

I snatch my hand away from Ethan's chest.

Then I drop my other hand from where I was practically clinging to his side.

His firm, muscled side.

*What is wrong with me?*

This man has my senses twisted in knots.

He's manhandled me. Helped me.

*Apologized.*

No one has ever apologized to me. Not for calling me names.

I inhale, trying to slow my pulse as I take a step back. "Thank you."

Ethan nods once. "Put a couple of big rocks in the pool before you fill it up. Water's heavy, but they'll help weigh it down on these extra windy days."

I watch his dark, wavy hair whip around, and I start to lift my hand, knowing I need to give him his hat back but feeling strangely reluctant to do so.

He shakes his head. "You can give it back when you're done with the straps."

I lower my hand. "Okay."

A vehicle door slams nearby, and I remember the honk that broke us apart.

We both turn to look at the newcomer who parked nose to nose with Ethan's truck.

"Hey there, Ranger." The guy is around my age, give or take, with shaggy hair and a tall, lanky build.

"Fisher." Ethan turns to face the man as he greets him, putting himself between me and the new guy.

I hear a chuckle and lean to the side to look around Ethan's wide shoulders.

The man grins at me.

Ethan steps to the side, blocking my view again.

*What is he doing?*

I lean the other way.

And the man, Fisher, grins at me again.

"I assume you're here to buy bait or some shit." Ethan holds out an arm, gesturing toward the front door of the hardware store. "Don't let us stop you."

A snort escapes me before I can stop it.

*Ethan really is a grump.*

Fisher ignores Ethan's bad manners and holds his hand out, keeping his attention on me as I peek around Ethan's side. "Name's Fisher."

Keeping his arm up, now with a finger pointed toward the hardware store, Ethan uses his other hand to slap Fisher's down.

"Ethan!" I gasp while attempting to hide my amusement at his rudeness.

When I try to step around him, he hooks his arm back around my side. "Tilda, this is Fisher. Fisher, this woman is none of your business."

Fisher presses his tongue to the inside of his cheek, like he, too, is trying not to laugh. "Tilda, nice to meet you." He tips an imaginary hat my way. "I have a *girlfriend*, and we love to double date, so if you and whoever you're seeing"—he cuts a glance at

Ethan—"want to go out sometime, just call Black Mountain Lodge and ask for me."

"Thank—"

"She won't be doing that." Ethan tries to push me farther behind him as he speaks over me.

Fisher just grins before snapping a salute. "Ranger." He drops his hand and does a little bow in my direction. "Miss."

I bite down on my lip as Fisher straightens and strides away from us toward the store.

Ethan slides his hand down my hip as he drops the arm that was hooked around my side and slowly turns around to face me.

I tip my head back so he can see me lift my brows. "What, *pray tell*, was that?"

"Fisher. I already told you."

I snort. "You're rude."

I swear his lips twitch with the start of a smile, but instead, he rolls those fascinating eyes, then nods toward my truck. "Go feed your duck, Matilda."

My feet stay planted for a second, not wanting to go.

The first time I met Ethan, I was embarrassed and mortified.

The second time I met him, I was embarrassed and irritated.

The third time... this time, I started out embarrassed. But then he touched my face and gripped my hair. And he...

Heat rolls in my stomach.

This time, it feels different.

*He* feels different.

Ethan takes a step back. "Now, Starlight."

I take my own step back, widening the distance between us. "Why do you call me that?"

Ethan lets his gaze lower slowly, trailing it down my body, then back up, until he meets my eyes again. "I'll tell you later."

Then, after dousing my dormant hormones with gasoline and lighting them on fire, Ethan turns, climbs into his truck, and drives away.

# CHAPTER 24

## ETHAN

I'M FILTHY.

Clothes twice soaked in sweat and caked in dirt.

I'm not fit to be seen in public.

But as I slow to a stop, exiting the park, I flip on my blinker, and I turn the opposite way from home. Toward the craft store.

# CHAPTER 25

## TILDA

PEELING MY DRESS OFF, I MAKE A FACE OVER THE FACT that I can smell myself.

It took approximately fifteen minutes of struggling to get those stupid ratchet straps to release.

After that, I wrestled the pool out of the truck and into a spot I liked, right below the center living room window in front of the house, between the two bushes. So if Quackers decides to use his new *pond*, I'll be able to watch him.

This was followed by me circling the house, searching for large rocks to weigh down the pool. Which meant carrying the large rocks. Which was then followed by accidentally spraying myself with the hose after I failed to connect it to the spigot properly.

By the time the pool was actually filled, I was tempted to just cut a slit in the duck food bag and drop it on the ground. But I resisted and instead filled an old Halloween candy bowl with duck food and set it a couple feet in front of the pool.

The bag with the remaining forty pounds of food sits just inside my door, ready for refills.

And right next to it, on top of a cardboard box that still needs to be unpacked, are the yellow straps I need to give back to Ethan. And his baseball hat.

After dropping my dress on the floor, I grip the top of my undies and bend forward, shoving them down my thighs.

I've only been here a couple days, but between falling, spilling coffee, and setting up a duck habitat, I have enough dirty clothes to do my first load of laundry.

The stacked washer and dryer set in my bedroom is hardly new, but I've had to use communal apartment laundry my whole life, so machines of my own are literally a luxury.

The appliances are white. The bottom one is the washer, and it opens from the top. And through some feat of engineering, the dryer is mounted above it.

I'm not that short, but I'm glad all the dials are below the front-loading dryer door, because I'd never be able to reach them if they were at the top.

Naked and grinning, I open the washer lid.

Nothing happens. Nothing lights up. There isn't a chime.

But these machines are probably twenty years old, so maybe they don't do anything fancy like that.

I shove my clothes in, pour a capful of laundry detergent, then shut the lid.

I turn the load-size knob to medium, turn the temperature knob to cold, and then turn the washer-cycle knob to casuals.

Then I press start.

And nothing happens.

None of the indicator lights turn on.

There are no sounds coming from the washer.

Nada.

The machines are tucked in the corner of the closet, but I use the flashlight on my phone to look behind them, and yes, they're plugged in.

Or at least it looks like they're plugged in.

I press start again.

Still nothing.

A breeze slides in through the open bedroom window, reminding me I'm naked.

I press the start button three more times.

I turn the knobs to all different settings.

I open and close the lid.

I open and close the dryer.

I try to turn the dryer on.

Not. A. Thing.

Dropping my head back, I glare up at the ceiling.

I'm not really a heaven or hell girl. But I am a *human energy has to go somewhere* girl.

"Uncle Jack." I lift my hands and cover my nipples. "If you're out there somewhere, can you let me know if these are supposed to work?"

A loud quack replies from somewhere outside.

# Chapter 26

## Ethan

Music plays from speakers overhead. Old-school hip-hop that I wouldn't expect in a store like this. But the volume is low, and it's somehow... welcoming.

Welcoming in an overwhelming sort of way.

Overwhelming in a *I've never seen so much color in one place* sort of way.

There are displays of paper in every color and pattern imaginable. Rows of paint. A wall of flowers—that must be fake but looks incredibly real.

Candles. Beads. Unpainted birdhouses.

It's chaos.

It's a mountain fairy's dream.

I take a step farther into Which Crafts.

The store isn't huge. Not a big-box chain store like I was imagining. But it's not tiny. Rows of bookshelves create aisles, displaying items for sale. Origami birds and paper hot-air balloons hang from the ceiling.

And... I inhale. It smells... *nice*. Like cedar and roses.

I don't know if adults buy other adults gift cards, but if they do, and if I ever have cause to buy Tilda a birthday present, it should be to this place.

Taking another step into the store, I wonder if that's what I should do. Let her buy her own replacement ribbon.

But that's not really a gift at all. Even if it meant that she'd be able to pick out her favorite, she'd have to drive all the way here to do it. And a forty-five-minute drive isn't the end of the world, but it's not convenient. And it makes a gift card feel more like a task than a present.

"Welcome," a scratchy voice hails from deeper in the store. "Can I help you find something specific? Or are you browsing?"

The person sounds completely serious. Which is kind of them, since I couldn't look more out of place in my filthy ranger uniform.

I move toward the voice, pressing my arms tight against my side as I maneuver between two displays of delicate stationary. "Yes, I'd like help. Please."

I feel like I'm going to break something just by being here.

"What is it you're looking for?" the person asks from my left as I'm turning right.

Careful not to bump into anything, I shift my attention to the left as I answer. "Ribbon."

Except I don't see anyone.

I glance to my right.

Still no one.

*What the fuck?*

"A specific kind?"

My head snaps back to the left, and my wildlife training is the only reason I don't stumble when I spot a person standing not more than two feet in front of me.

I doubt they're even five feet tall, but I don't believe I missed them. They had to have been somewhere else.

I blink.

Bright green eyes blink back at me while they lift bleached eyebrows that match their shaggy bleached hair.

Standing here amid all the color, they stand apart almost as much as I do. The white hair. A boxy, oversized gray linen shirt and matching loose pants. Unassuming.

I dip my chin in greeting, then answer their question. "Purple."

They grin. "We have that. Any other defining features, or shall I show you the options?"

I shove my hand into my pants pocket and pull out the piece of ribbon I just can't bring myself to throw away.

The shop worker hums, then holds out their palm. "May I?"

I drop it into their hand.

Holding it taut, they lift it up to the light. "We don't have this exact brand, but I have something very similar."

I lift a brow, impressed. I hadn't expected anyone to know the brand of a ribbon just by look, but everyone has a specialty. "Similar is great."

They nod and hand the piece of Tilda's ribbon back to me.

I shove it into my pocket, then press my arms against my sides again as I follow them toward a display along the side wall.

The shop employee hums along with the music as they stop in front of a shelf filled with nothing but purple ribbon.

They tip their head side to side, then reach up and pull down a spool.

It's a little lighter than the one in my pocket. But that means it's a little closer to the shade of Tilda's hair.

They hold it out to me, and taking it, I rub the pad of my thumb along the surface. It looks like cotton, but it feels like silk. And there's a white—almost silver—thread woven along each edge.

If Matilda Wright were a ribbon...

"It's perfect."

The employee grins up at me. "Anything else?"

# CHAPTER 27

## TILDA

I SLAM THE DRYER DOOR SHUT AND PRESS THE START button.

It's been a while since I've been in a public laundromat, not an apartment one, but this place is surprisingly nice.

For some ignorant reason, I was thinking small mountain town meant out of date, but I was wrong. The building is clean, brightly lit, and the machines all have card readers. Which is so much better than having to turn a twenty-dollar bill into quarters.

Today's been productive.

I unpacked a few more boxes, and now I've washed all my dirty clothes, the used towels, and the bedding I brought with me, since I hadn't washed it before packing.

I also used the laundromat's Wi-Fi to download three seasons of my favorite baking show onto my tablet and five That's What I Call Music albums to my phone.

I at least get one bar of service on my cell at the house so I can call 911 if I need to. But that's about it.

Turning toward the big wall of windows along the front of the laundromat, I look through the glass at the twenty-four-hour gym across the street.

While my laundry was in the wash phase, I pulled up the

website for the gym and found that the front door is run by an app on your phone. I also found an option for a free three-day trial.

It uses my phone number, so I'll only be able to do this freebie thing once. But I have fifty-eight minutes left on my dryers, and I'm ready for a walk. The gym is just a handy surprise.

I was planning to just stroll down the street. But I don't know the town well, and even though it seems safe, I don't love the idea of leaving my laundry unattended. But since the treadmills in the gym are lined up facing that building's wall of windows, I'll be able to literally watch my dryer while I walk.

I reach up and tug on the bill of my hat.

I thought it looked cute with my oversized T-shirt and bike shorts. And there's the bonus of it looking like it belongs to a man —*since it does*—meaning that maybe it will make me look like I belong to a man.

In a hot way.

In a *please don't approach me* way.

I take a deep breath, then stride toward the door.

This feels a hundred times more stressful than going to the grocery store that first time.

But I can do hard things.

The door swings open, and I step out onto the sidewalk.

*I'm going to go to the gym.*

# CHAPTER 28

## ETHAN

I CLENCH MY JAW AS I DO ANOTHER BICEP CURL.

*What is with this girl?*

I do another rep.

*Is she ignoring me, or does she really not see me?*

I do another.

*Does she have any idea how tempting she looks?*

I set the weights down.

I'm facing the back wall of the gym, where all the free weights are lined up. But the wall is covered in mirrors. So even with my back to Tilda, I can still watch her.

And I can watch the fucking creeps who are also busy watching my girl.

I pick up a heavier set of weights.

Okay, she might not be *my girl*. But she's more mine than theirs. Solidified by the fact that she's wearing *my* fucking hat.

When I spotted her, it was the first thing I noticed. Because it made her look like *mine*.

I sit on the reclined bench and start doing shoulder presses.

Sweat drips down my forehead. More has my shirt sticking to my back. But I don't slow down.

Neither does my heart rate.

I'm sure I look like the biggest perv of all, the way I'm staring. But I can't help myself.

Tilda is walking. Not running. Not jogging. Just walking.

But her ass is swaying with each step.

Her thick, juicy ass.

Her ass that's wrapped in shorts so formfitting they might as well be painted on.

I squeeze the dumbbells even tighter.

Her top half is draped in a giant shirt, and if it wasn't bunched at the top swell of her ass, it would probably cover her lush cheeks.

But it is bunched up. And the bright blue material of her shorts is basically a beacon for my attention. A neon light for the moth that runs my brain.

I close my eyes and do another three reps. But the image of her is still there, taped to the back of my eyelids.

*I can still see her long lilac braid as it caresses her spine.*

*I can still see her bobbing her head along with the music playing in her headphones.*

*I can still feel her hair between my fingers. Can still feel her hands against my sides.*

I open my eyes.

*I should talk to her.*

Lowering my weights, I set them on the ground in front of me and pull in deep breaths as I stand.

*I can't talk to her.*

I sit back down.

What would I say? It's not like I can tell her what to wear. I learned that didn't work when I was nineteen and in charge of my twelve-year-old sister.

And maybe these damn shorts *are* better than a dress. Because knowing Tilda, she'd find a way to fall and flash her panties to everyone.

I grit my teeth.

The real problem is that I don't want anyone else looking at her. End of story.

I close my eyes again and roll out my shoulders while I focus on slowing my breathing.

I'll just walk over there and see how she's doing. See how the kiddie pool setup went.

*But maybe she's ignoring me and doesn't want me to talk to her.*

Tilda got here just after I did. I'd just started a set of squats, looked over, and spotted her walking through the front door.

I looked right at her. Didn't try to act sneaky about it at all. But she looked right past me.

Or pretended not to see me.

Either way, she didn't acknowledge me. She also didn't stop at the cubbies. Didn't go to the bathroom. Just walked right to the first treadmill, put her headphones on, hung her purse from the handle of the machine, and started walking.

It was an impressive display of confidence, considering I'm positive she's never been in here before.

As my pulse finally returns to normal, I wonder if she somehow didn't notice my truck in the lot when she parked. There were only a handful of other vehicles, so the ranger truck shouldn't be hard to miss. But I've also managed to sneak up on Tilda three times in a row without even trying.

I open my eyes.

*I'm going to talk to her.*

My eyes scan the mirror.

Her treadmill is empty.

I snap my head to the side just in time to see her walk out the door.

Then, two heartbeats later, I watch Clark walk out the same door.

I stand up.

# CHAPTER 29

## TILDA

I FEEL REFRESHED AS I STEP OUT OF THE GYM. AND I decide it was a good idea to come over for a little walk. I'm not sweaty, but I do feel accomplished.

I reach up and touch the bill of my—Ethan's—hat.

When he put it on me yesterday, it was a little sweaty. And that should have grossed me out. Usually, just the idea of someone else's sweat makes me want to gag.

Except when it comes to grumpy park rangers with mismatched eyes and tattoos and muscles for days... I'm apparently unbothered.

Not simply unbothered by his sweaty hat. I liked it.

Shaking my head at myself, I exhale.

The entrance to the gym is on the side of the building, so I turn, planning to head back the way I came, down the little walkway that leads to the sidewalk.

But as I take a step, I feel something brush against my shoulder.

# CHAPTER 30

## ETHAN

I'M OVERREACTING. CLARK, THE MARRIED MECHANIC, just happens to be leaving at the same time as Tilda.

I reach the door before it closes.

He's going to walk to his car and not say a word to her.

But he doesn't turn toward the parking lot.

He reaches for her.

This motherfucker *reaches* for her.

He doesn't call out.

Doesn't introduce himself.

Doesn't let her know he's behind her.

He just *reaches for her.*

*I don't fucking think so, Clark.*

I lunge forward, darting my hand out and catching the back of his shirt a moment before he makes contact with Tilda.

My fingers tighten in the fabric, and I jerk him away.

He stumbles, too surprised to even make a sound, but he keeps his feet as I force him to walk toward the parking lot. Away from Tilda.

# CHAPTER 31

## TILDA

I PULL MY SHOULDER AWAY FROM THE LIGHT TOUCH.

*If there's a bug on me...*

I reach across my body and brush at my sleeve as I try to see what touched me.

Then I pause.

Because striding away from me is Ethan.

He's dressed differently than I've seen before.

He has black gym shorts on, revealing more tattoos on his calves. And his thin white T-shirt clings to the bulging muscles in his back.

I can't see his face.

Can only see the perfect shade of dark brown hair.

But it's him. I know it is.

And he's holding another man by the back of the shirt, manhandling him down the footpath toward the back of the building.

*What the...?*

*Was Ethan in the gym?*

I watch, mouth going dry, as I take in the transparency of his shirt.

Ethan is sweating like he just finished a workout.

He was totally in the gym.

And I didn't see him.

I move my attention to the other guy's back.

I purposely didn't look at any of the people when I got here.

When I approached, I looked through the windows and decided which treadmill I wanted. Then, when I entered, I was able to walk straight to it without making eye contact with anyone.

So I never saw Ethan.

But apparently, he saw me.

I watch, confused, as the two men—one dragging the other—round the back corner of the building and disappear.

*Was that other guy following me?*

# CHAPTER 32

## ETHAN

"WHAT THE FUCK?" CLARK WAITS UNTIL NO ONE CAN see or hear us before he starts to struggle. "Let me go."

I don't let go.

In fact, I give the man a shake.

He's almost as tall as me. Heavier than me. But I'm still stronger.

"*What the fuck*, is that I'm going to end you if you go anywhere near that woman again," I grit through my teeth. "*And* I'm going to download the footage from the security camera, showing you reaching for her." I lengthen my stride and make him walk faster to the truck that I know is his.

"Fuck off, Ethan. I didn't—"

I give him another shake. "I'm going to keep that video. And if you so much as look at another woman, I am sending it to your wife. And to the local news."

I shove him as I let go of his shirt, and he has to catch himself against his door.

Then I turn around and stride away.

"You're not actually gonna show her," he calls after me. "Right?"

"Find a different gym," I snap back.

# CHAPTER 33

## TILDA

THAT WAS... HOT.

I don't even know what that was, but it was hot.

I glance toward the road.

*Should I just go?*

I glance back to the spot where Ethan and the mystery man disappeared.

*Should I see what's happening back there?*

I bite my lip.

I don't know what I should—

Ethan rounds the corner.

Striding toward me.

Eyes locked on mine.

And it's... he's... Gods, he's so intense.

The easily startled animal inside me wants us to back away.

The incredibly horny animal inside me wants us to run toward him.

But I do nothing.

I just stare.

And hold my breath.

# CHAPTER 34

## ETHAN

HER EYES ARE WIDE. AND HER CHEST IS RISING WITH rapid breaths.

But she doesn't back away.

And when I close the distance between us, I do the only thing I can.

# CHAPTER 35

## TILDA

ETHAN'S HAND DARTS UP, AND HE GRIPS THE FRONT OF my baseball hat. *His hat.*

My mouth opens, ready to protest if he tries to take it.

But he doesn't.

He uses his hold to spin the hat around, twisting the front to the back. And without letting go, he tugs the bill down, tilting my face up.

Then, with my lips still parted, Ethan kisses me.

His mouth slams against mine.

He shoves his tongue between my lips.

He grips my hip with his free hand.

And he kisses me like I've never been kissed before.

This man who's been rude.

This man, who appeared from the woods and into my life.

This man, who confuses me with each interaction, kisses me.

And I do the only thing I can.

# CHAPTER 36

## ETHAN

SHE KISSES ME BACK.

Tilda, my Mountain Fairy, arches up into me.

My Starlight presses her lips against mine.

My fucking Firecracker drags her tongue against mine.

This girl, who fell into my life just days ago, kisses me back.

And her hands.

*Fuck me.*

Her hands grab at me.

They claw at me.

They take hold of me.

Her fingers twist in the damp fabric clinging to my side. And as she tugs, pulling me closer, her grip shifts again, and then her hand is against my bare skin.

Her fingertips are against my hips, just above the band of my shorts.

I slide my hand from her side, over the swell of her hip, to the center of her back, my pinkie resting against the top of her ass.

Her shirt is still bunched there.

And I shift my hand.

So it's under her shirt.

Against her skin.
Her incredibly soft, so warm skin.
And I do the only thing I can.

# CHAPTER 37

## TILDA

HE PULLS ME CLOSER.

Impossibly closer.

Our bodies are flush.

My head is tipped all the way back. I'm on the tips of my toes. And my hands have moved to his lower back, under his shirt, just like his hand is on me.

It's reckless.

All of this is reckless.

I don't actually know this man.

But my body recognizes him.

His energy.

His need.

His... desire.

The pressure on my forehead disappears as he releases his hold on my hat.

I feel the loss.

And without meaning to, a sound—something needy—leaves my chest.

The missing hand smacks down against my ass.

I gasp.

He tilts his head, shoving more of his tongue into my mouth.

His hand doesn't lift away. It stays on my ass cheek, squeezing, fingers digging into my soft flesh.

And I do the only thing I can.

# CHAPTER 38

## ETHAN

SHE MOANS.

She fucking moans, and my hardening dick throbs at the sound.

I want more of that.

More of this.

*All of her.*

But we're standing in the middle of town. Outside my gym. In front of a glass door.

And as much as I want to, I can't fuck Jack's great-niece on the sidewalk.

I give her luscious ass one more squeeze, then I pry my mouth away from hers.

My eyes open slowly, and dammit, I should've turned away without looking at her.

Tilda is blinking up at me.

Her lids look heavy.

Her lips are a deeper pink than normal. A little puffy. And the expression on her face says she wants this just as much as I do.

I take a small step back, and her hands drag around my sides with the movement. My hands do the same, moving to her hips.

The summer air that swirls in the space between us feels almost cold. And I want to plaster my body to hers again.

But I don't.

"You need to pay better attention." My words come out gruffer than I intended, but my throat is so clogged with lust it's a miracle I can speak at all.

"Pay attention?" Her eyes drop to my mouth, apparently not bothered by my tone. "To what?"

Tilda's voice is so breathy that I know I'll be replaying it tonight. When I'm alone. In bed.

"Yeah, Firecracker. You need to pay better attention to your surroundings."

"But..."

I shake my head. "Don't argue with me. Not right now." Lifting my hand from her hip, I reach back and grab the bill of *my hat* again. "Go home." I spin the hat back around. "We'll talk later."

Then I do the only thing I can. The only thing that will keep me from throwing her over my shoulder and carrying her to my truck.

I turn and stride back into the gym.

# CHAPTER 39

## TILDA

I WATCH ETHAN DISAPPEAR INTO THE GYM.

*What on earth...?*

Without my permission, my hand reaches up and my finger-tips brush against my lips.

My phone alarm beeps from the little purse that's somehow still hooked over my shoulder, letting me know I have two minutes until my dryers are ready.

# Chapter 40

## Ethan

Keeping my promise to that prick, Clark, I walk straight to the small office at the back of the gym and use my key to unlock the door.

I tap the space bar as I drop into the chair, waking up the computer.

Then I type in my password and open the video feed.

The live view of the door shows that the walkway is empty.

I click on the parking lot feed, confirming that Clark's truck is gone. But I also don't see Tilda or her truck.

Maybe she parked on the side street, not knowing the lot was behind the building.

Clicking back to the front door feed, I rewind it.

Only I don't make it to the spot where Clark reaches for Tilda. Because the sight of us... entwined...

I hit Play.

The camera is in the eaves above the door, so the angle shows my back.

My size blocks most of Tilda from view, but her hands...

I lived it.

I felt it.

But seeing it... seeing the way she was grabbing at me.

I watch as her hands slide around to my back.

I can still feel it. Can still feel her hands on my skin.

Can still fucking taste her.

If I'd remembered to lock the door to my office, I'd be tempted to beat one off right now.

But I didn't lock the door.

And I can bring this video home.

It only takes a few clicks for me to download two videos.

One that shows the seconds before and after Clark tried to touch what's mine. And the second is everything that happened after.

I email them to myself, then shut down the computer and exit the office.

I'm tempted to go straight home so I can watch the second video at my leisure, but I go back to the free weights.

I've done plenty for the day, but the adrenaline boost of having Tilda's tongue in my mouth is making me feel twitchy. And I want to burn off that energy before I drive home.

My gaze automatically moves to the mirror, my eyes searching for that purple braid. But she's not here.

She's gone.

She's...

I narrow my eyes.

*What the hell?*

Turning so I can look directly out the front windows, I watch Tilda walk out of the laundromat across the street.

Her arms are full with two laundry baskets stacked on top of one another.

She stops at the driver's door of her truck, which is parked in plain sight in the laundromat lot.

*Why is she using a laundromat?*

Tilda sets the baskets on the ground, opens her door, lifts the top basket, sets it on the bench seat, then leans into the truck as she pushes the basket across to the passenger side.

All I see is her ass.

Her shirt is still bunched up at her lower back. And even from across the street, those damn blue shorts demand my attention.

*Flame. Moth.*

One foot pops up off the ground as she leans in as far as she can.

I take a step forward.

Her foot lowers, and she pulls herself back.

Then she picks up the second basket of laundry, sticking her butt out.

I think I groan.

This time, Tilda doesn't have to lean in as far, since she's only sliding the basket into the middle seat. And my balls thank her for it.

With her laundry situated, Tilda follows the baskets into the truck and closes the door behind her.

Confused, I stay where I am and watch her drive away.

# CHAPTER 41

## TILDA

I CAN FEEL MYSELF GRIN AS I STEP CLOSER TO THE window.

Quackers, my friendly neighborhood duck, is in her new pool.

Joy overwhelms me.

At her apparent happiness.

At my sense of achievement for doing something right.

At the day that turned out to be pretty freaking good.

I shuffle a few inches closer to the glass, trying to be quiet, since the window is open and I don't want to startle her.

While I was at the laundromat earlier, I used the internet to do a little research on ducks. And I learned that my duck is a girl. *A mallard, I'm pretty sure.* And I confirmed that no, you aren't supposed to give ducks bread.

I also learned that there is a high probability that Miss Quackers will migrate in the winter, flying away to warmer pastures. And there's a good chance her favorite color is either green or blue.

Quackers lets out a loud quack and splashes her wings against the water.

My grin widens.

I wonder if I should take one of the chairs from the back deck and put it out front.

It's not like it's ever more than just me out there, and if I set the chair far enough from the pool, maybe Quackers will still come play while I'm out there.

I glance across the living room at the back deck.

If I try to do it now, I'll definitely scare Quackers off.

I eye the two boxes that I have left to unpack, sitting beside me below the windows.

The yellow strap things are still on top of one of them, and as tempted as I am to sit on the other box, I'm confident I'll crush it.

So I'll stand here.

Shifting my weight, I cross my arms and lean closer to the glass.

Quackers steps up onto one of the big rocks I put in the pool, then hops up onto the ledge.

She lets out another squawk, then hops to the ground.

I start to frown, assuming she's about to leave, but then she waddles over to her food dish.

My frown morphs back into a smile as she chomps away.

*I need a picture of this.*

Spinning away from the window, I rush over to where I left my phone on the coffee table and hurry back. Just in time to see Quackers pop her head up, ruffle her feathers, then take off flying.

"Well, poop." My arms hang at my sides.

*Of course she'd take off right when I got my camera.*

I look back down at the food dish.

She'll be back.

I start to turn back toward the living room when another noise catches my attention.

An engine.

Following Quackers's lead, I let my flight mode activate and I hustle out of view, putting my back against the front door.

The sound of a vehicle gets louder.

I reach back and make sure the dead bolt is locked.

Maybe it's a delivery. Just the UPS guy.

I bite my lip.

Except I haven't ordered anything.

I look at the setting sun through the back windows.

It's a little late for the post office. And they put all my regular mail in the mailbox.

My heart starts to pound.

I need a guard dog.

Or a bear.

Or a...

I lean to the side and look out the window.

A familiar white pickup with green lettering down the side pulls into view.

I flatten myself to the wall again, and this time my heart thuds for a whole new reason.

*Ethan is here.*

I look down at myself.

*Why did I put on my oldest pajama shirt today?*

The engine cuts off as he parks on the gravel in front of *my house.*

If I try to run for my bedroom, he'll see me through the windows.

*I really need to get curtains for the living room.*

I look down at myself again.

I'm in my standard pajamas. A pair of non-thong underwear —today it's bright green boy shorts—and a giant T-shirt that fits like a dress. This one is white, and even though it goes past my butt, it's so worn you can see the green of my undies through it.

*Maybe I can make it to the bedroom and change without him seeing me.*

*Maybe he parked facing away from the house.*

Then I hear a door slam shut, and I know I'm stuck.

I hold my breath, like it's a masked man approaching and not the man I made out with two hours ago.

A few seconds pass, then a fist pounds on the other side of the door.

I knew it was coming.

I know who's there.

But my stupid body still reacts as though it's completely surprised by the noise, and I let out a little shriek.

I slap my hand over my mouth.

"Tilda."

Even through the door, his voice crawls across my skin, making my nipples tighten.

I lower my hand to my throat. "Yes?"

"What are you doing?"

"Um..." I can't think of a single answer. "Nothing. What are you doing?"

"Visiting you."

"Why?"

I swear I can hear him sigh through the door. "I have something for you."

My eyebrows raise. "Really?"

"Really."

"What is it?"

"Tilda?"

"Yeah?"

"Open the door."

I bite my lip.

*Do I really know this man well enough to let him into my house?*

"Please."

*If he's going to ask nicely...*

I run my fingers back through my mostly dry hair, pushing it out of my face, then I turn around and open the door.

# CHAPTER 42

## ETHAN

THE DOOR OPENS, AND I STEP FORWARD.

I open my mouth to ask why Tilda was hiding, because I could tell she was standing against the door, but then she comes into focus, and I can no longer remember my question.

The sun is setting on the other side of the house, and the glow coming through the window outlines the woman before me.

She's...

My eyes lower.

Christ.

She's hardly wearing anything.

I went home. Showered. Thought of her. Resisted touching myself. Put on jeans and a ratty flannel.

And she...

She's wearing nothing but a see-through shirt.

*I'm here to check on her.*

*I'm here to be a decent human. To check on Jack's Matty, like I said I would.*

I flex my jaw.

*I'm not here to fuck her.*

"Why were you using the laundromat?"

She blinks at me. "W-what?"

I clear my throat and use every shred of willpower I can find to keep my eyes on her face and off her tits.

"Why aren't you using the washer and dryer here?" I try to keep the sharpness out of my voice, but I don't quite manage.

Tilda digs her teeth into her lower lip as she crosses her arms over her tits.

I relax my shoulders.

I'm here to help.

"Is there a problem with them?" This time I manage to sound civilized.

She starts to move her arms, like she's going to uncross them, then remembers she's covering herself and keeps them crossed. "They don't work."

I keep my eyes on hers. "Show me."

She hesitates, just for a heartbeat, and I feel like I should step back. Offer to leave. Apologize for coming here in the first place.

But then she turns and walks toward the bedroom.

*Her bedroom.*

My feet follow. And my eyes drop.

The outline of her green underwear is visible through the see-through top she's wearing. And I watch as each step makes her ass jiggle.

My cock notices the movement too.

I press a palm against my thickening length and lift my gaze to the ceiling.

I asked to see her washing machine. She's bringing me to that. Not her bed.

But when I follow her into the bedroom, my eyes go straight to the damn bed.

The bedspread is dark purple. It's smooth, with the top corner folded down, like she just made the bed. Her pillowcases are pink with a delicate floral design, and they also look perfectly smooth.

It's all quite pretty.

Girly.

Very Mountain Fairy.

The sound of the closet door opening drags my attention away from the bed.

I spot the stacked washer and dryer in the corner of the closet, then watch as Tilda pulls a gray hoodie off a hanger before she steps aside.

I keep my focus on the appliances but see her pull the sweatshirt on out of the corner of my eye.

Shame. But for the best.

I test the dials. Press buttons. But it doesn't react.

My hand reaches for the dresses hanging beside the machines, but before I touch them, I look over my shoulder at Tilda.

She's standing just a few feet away, hoodie zipped and her hands in the pockets.

I tip my head toward her clothes. "May I?"

She nods.

I slide the hangers down the bar, bunching her pretty dresses together. Then I lean in and look behind the machines, making sure they're connected correctly.

"Have you been in here before?"

I straighten, then answer Tilda's question. "The house, yes. But not the bedroom."

"Then how did you know these were here?"

I turn to face her. "I remember Jack talking about getting them serviced not too long ago."

"Oh." She glances at the dryer over my shoulder. "Why'd you come inside?"

*What a way to word that.*

I glance at the bed, then clear my throat again. "Jack invited me in for coffee a few times."

Tilda hums.

"Have you checked the breaker?"

Tilda slowly shakes her head.

"I'll do it. Where is it?"

She bites her lip again, and an unpleasant emotion crawls through my chest as I watch her lower her chin to her chest.

"Don't worry about it," I say before she can tell me she doesn't know. "I'll be right back."

Striding out of the room, I glance around the main living space, then step out the front door and cross over to the garage.

There is no side door, but Tilda left the main garage door open after returning home, so I step through and immediately spot the electrical panel on the wall where the garage backs up against the house.

Opening the panel, I think about all the times Jack complained about this garage.

Saying how small it was. How the overhead door should've been put on the back side so it'd be easier to get in and out of. There was another time when he told me that he wanted to convert the garage, expand the house, then build a proper two-car garage on the other side of the driveway.

Dreams that never became reality.

I find the breaker labeled *Laundry* and see that it's in the off position.

The rest of the breakers are on, so I don't know if Jack flipped this one before he left for the winter or if it got tripped, but I push it to the on position.

Done, I close the panel and head back to the house.

Tilda isn't visible when I step inside, and when I close the door behind me, I take a moment to untie my boots, and I leave them next to Tilda's pile of discarded shoes.

This time, as I cross through the living room, I look around.

The TV has the old animated version of *Alice in Wonderland* playing quietly on the screen.

A handful of brightly colored pillows are on the couch, and a trio of candles on a tray sits on the coffee table.

S.J. TILLY

And I didn't fail to notice the duck pool and bowl of food in front of the house.

I start to smile as I think about Tilda giving safe haven to a wild duck, but as soon as I step into the bedroom, my smile vanishes.

# Chapter 43

## Tilda

The lights on the washer and dryer are on.

Ethan fixed it.

By checking the breaker box.

It's so simple.

And I feel so stupid.

Heat flares in my eyes, and I blink.

I hate feeling stupid.

Ethan's steps are quiet as he enters my bedroom, but I can feel him as he stops beside me.

"Thank you," I whisper, but I can't meet his eyes.

"You're welcome." Ethan shifts so he's in front of me, blocking my view of the appliances.

I still don't look up.

I don't want to see pity on his face.

Don't want him to look at me like I'm an idiot.

I just...

I bite my lip harder.

This is my new start.

A place where no one can criticize me. A place to make my own. And I've already messed up so many times.

Warm fingers grip my chin, and Ethan tips my head up.

I blink again, willing my eyes to stay dry, as I finally meet his gaze.

Ethan's brows are furrowed. "What's this look for?"

His concern feels real.

His genuine intentions... real.

*He feels so real to me.*

And every time he sees me...

My hands lift and drop to my sides as defeat takes over.

Ethan leans down, putting our faces inches apart, as he continues to grip my chin. "Firecracker, what's this look for? You didn't do anything wrong."

"I should've known how..." I swallow, my voice going quiet. "I'm not st—"

Ethan pushes my chin up, cutting off my word. "Woman, I know you're not stupid. I've never once thought that. Not ever."

He seems so... mad. *On my behalf?*

So I admit the truth. "I *feel* stupid. And I hate it. It's the worst feeling."

He furrows his brows again. "Because of the breaker box? Tilda, lots of people don't know how those work."

"Yeah, but this is *my house*. I should—"

He presses my chin up again.

"You should learn as you go. How long have you owned this house?"

He loosens his grip so I can reply.

"A couple days," I sigh, knowing the point he's trying to make.

"And did your parents teach you this stuff growing up?" He asks it like he knows the answer.

I think about my dad, who cowered around my mother, hardly a figure in our lives before he up and left when I was nine.

Then I think about my mother, who never did anything herself, always called maintenance when something needed fixing in our apartment, and who always told me to *go to my room* when they came over, so *I'm not in the way*. Meaning I couldn't even watch them fix stuff if I'd wanted to.

But in the decade since moving out, when I lived on my own in my own apartments, I couldn't tell you if I had a breaker box.

And that makes me feel stupid too.

"My dad made me help with everything," Ethan says, like I asked him the question he asked me. "Didn't matter if I wanted to or not. He had me running power tools, chopping wood, holding the ladder, and flipping breakers on and off while he tinkered with shit he probably shouldn't have been tinkering with."

The start of a smile tugs on my lips. "He sounds fun."

Ethan huffs, "He was a pain in the ass."

*Was.*

My bit of a smile drops.

For a moment there, I forgot that Ethan mentioned his parents were gone.

He'd said it so casually, when I'd called him a bastard one of the first times we met, that I almost didn't believe him. And I have to stop myself from wondering which is worse—good parents who die too soon, or bad ones who stay forever.

"My parents didn't teach me any of that stuff." I don't hide the sadness in my tone. "But I should—"

He shakes his head. "Stop beating yourself up."

"But—"

He takes a step into me, and I take a step back. "If you'd fixed it yourself, you wouldn't have gone to the laundromat today. And then you wouldn't've come into my gym." He takes another step forward, and I step back again, bumping against the foot of the bed. "And if you hadn't come into my gym..."

My eyes lower to his mouth. "You wouldn't have kissed me."

The edge of his mouth pulls up, just a little. "Correct."

I watch his lips, and I think about all he's done for me.

How he took down the ribbon that I was supposed to remove.

How he decided not to give me a ticket.

How he helped me with the pool.

How he fixed my washer and dryer.

I lift my gaze back up to his as my hands lift to his sides. "You act like a bad guy, but I don't think that's what you are."

Ethan shifts closer, and I feel his muscles move beneath the soft flannel he's wearing. "No? Then what am I?"

I watch him watching me. "I think you're a good boy."

His lids lower.

His body goes tense against mine.

And then the hand on my chin shifts so he's palming my cheek. "Say that again." He moves even closer, until our bodies are flush. "Call me that again."

"Ethan?" I slide my hands up his stomach, over his pecs, to his shoulders. "Are you my Good Boy?"

# CHAPTER 44

## ETHAN

HEAT SPEARS THROUGH MY BODY.

I've heard the phrase before. Heard it and... felt a certain way.

But hearing Tilda say it, in her sweet voice, it rewires something in my brain.

Dropping my hold of her, I bend my knees, grip her around the waist, then lift her as I topple us onto the bed.

She lands on her back, and I drop on top of her, bracing my elbows on the mattress above her shoulders. And before she can say another filthy word, my lips connect with hers.

Tilda moans into my mouth.

Her knees spread, and I wedge my body between her thighs.

I lower more of my weight onto her.

Tilda presses her heels into the backs of my legs, pulling me closer.

She's so soft beneath me. So warm.

I rotate my arm so my elbow is still on the mattress, but my hand is tangled in her hair.

*This fucking hair.*

Our kiss becomes more frantic.

More hungry.

And then she's gripping *my hair*, tugging on it like I'm tugging on hers.

*Good Boy.*

I roll my hips, grinding my length into her.

We both moan, the sound merging into one where our mouths touch.

And fuck, I don't remember the last time I was this hard.

# CHAPTER 45

## TILDA

MY HIPS TILT AS MY BODY TRIES TO GET PRESSURE *right there.*

Because Ethan's cock is *right freaking there.*

I open my mouth wider, and he plunges his tongue deeper.

I scrape my teeth over it.

Tasting him.

Warning him.

Begging him for more.

I grip his hair tighter as I squeeze his hips with my thighs.

This isn't like me.

Wanton behavior is *not* like me.

But there's just something about this man.

He rocks into me.

Something about him makes me feel so alive.

His weight shifts above me, and my eyes open.

Ethan's eyes slide open at the same time, and he pulls his face back, putting an inch between our lips.

I start to lift my head, wanting his mouth on mine again, but his hold on my hair tightens, pinning me to the mattress.

Then I feel his other hand. On the back of my bare thigh.

Ethan lowers his forehead until it's resting against mine. "Is this what you always wear to bed, Firecracker? Just a thin shirt and some panties?" He slides his palm down, slipping his fingers under the fabric of my underwear until he's gripping my bare ass. "Answer me, Bad Girl."

I shift my feet so they're pressing into his lower back. "It's practically a dress."

Ethan grinds into me, rolling his hips in a firm circle. "Of course it's a fucking dress," he growls.

The thick piece of denim over his zipper is lined up perfectly with his hard dick, and when he rocks against me again, he wedges the fabric of my panties into my crevice, putting pressure exactly where I need it.

I gasp as I release his hair and claw at his shoulders.

His fingers dig into my butt cheek as he tries to widen my legs even more. "That feel good?"

Ethan doesn't give me time to answer before he rocks his hips again, sending me closer to the point of no return.

"Ethan... I..." I cling to him as I lift my hips.

"Fuck," he pants against my mouth. "Are you going to come for me?"

I squeeze my eyes shut.

I shouldn't.

It's only been a moment.

A handful of minutes.

But...

Heat rolls through me.

The fingers in my hair shift so he's cupping the back of my head. "Open your eyes, Matilda."

I do.

His are right there, staring into mine.

One green iris, one brown, and their focus is entirely on me.

His hair is hanging down over his forehead. His cheeks are flushed.

And his intensity...

Ethan grunts as he thrusts his dick against my entrance.

That heat inside me starts to boil.

It's been so long since anyone other than me has given me an orgasm.

It's been so long since I've had anyone put their hands on me.

It's been so long...

And that timer is about to reset to zero.

My breath starts to get choppy. And more than a touch of panic fills my chest as the overwhelming need to release fills me.

My muscles clench, preparing for detonation, trying to stave it off.

Then he slides his hand farther inside my panties, and his fingertips edge toward my core from behind.

"That's it." Ethan rocks into me, holding my gaze. "That's it, Starlight." The tip of his middle finger brushes my entrance. "Let go."

My body listens. And I let go of my control.

My eyes slam shut.

My back arches.

My core convulses.

My pussy gushes with pent-up lust.

And I feel Ethan's fingertips delve deeper. Feel him wedge two of them against my opening. Not pushing inside, but feeling my muscles pulse.

He groans.

He groans, and he pistons his hips.

He ruts over me like a wild animal.

And I keep coming.

My core keeps pulsing.

My hands keep holding on to him.

And then he starts to tremble.

Like he's trying to hold back.

*Like he's about to come.*

My eyes slide open, and I find his closed.

*He is.*

This stunning man.

S.J. TILLY

This masculine creature.

This grumpy ranger is about to come just from humping against me.

My insides flutter anew.

My pussy squeezes so hard I know his fingers have to be soaked.

And I know I need him to fall with me.

I slide my fingers back into his hair and grip the strands roughly.

He groans.

And I smile. "That's my Good Boy."

His eyes snap open.

I press my hips up into his thrust. "Do it, Ethan. Be a Good Boy and come for me."

"Fuck." Ethan drops his face into the crook of my neck.

His hips thrust once. Twice. And then he's rocking against me.

Groaning into my ear.

Coming in his pants.

# CHAPTER 46

## ETHAN

I COLLAPSE ON TOP OF MY LUSTY LITTLE FAIRY.

Wetness coats my cock, making my boxer briefs feel sticky and uncomfortable, but I can't find it in me to be embarrassed.

I probably should be.

I might be tomorrow. Or maybe in a few minutes. But right now...

My lungs fill with the scent of Tilda.

Right now, I feel content.

At home.

Calm.

I'm sure I'm crushing her.

But I can't move yet.

Tilda strokes a hand down my side as she releases her hold of my hair. Then she goes limp beneath me. Her knees fall open, and her arms drop to the mattress.

"Wow," she breathes.

"Fuck," I exhale.

Tilda lets out a sound that might be a laugh, but my weight is probably preventing her lungs from properly filling.

With great effort, I push up onto my elbows and my knees so I'm hovering over her.

She blinks up at me with those almost golden eyes, and I'm at a complete loss for words.

*Do I thank her?*

*Do I apologize for making us both come so quickly?*

*Do I ask if she wants to do it again?*

The loudest duck I've ever heard quacks from somewhere outside the house, pulling my attention over my shoulder.

When I look back down at Tilda, she's biting her lip.

And she's... cute.

So cute and pretty and sexy and...

I just dry humped Jack's great-niece on his bed.

The duck quacks again.

I start to mildly panic about how to proceed before I decide to keep it simple.

I drop my head, press a kiss to Tilda's lips, then push up and away.

Standing at the foot of the bed, I get a fantastic view of the damp spot on Tilda's panties before she presses her knees together.

I lift my gaze to meet hers. "Good night, Bad Girl."

Her mouth starts to pull into a smile, and I have to go.

Have to leave before she offers to let me stay.

Because if I stay, I'm going to fuck her. And Matilda Wright isn't the kind of girl you casually have sex with. She's someone you get serious with.

Striding out of the bedroom, I pause as I pass the cardboard boxes.

I pull something out of my back pocket and trade that item for the ratchet straps.

I glance back at the bedroom door as I step into my boots, then, without lacing them, I exit the house.

Where a female mallard squawks at me.

# CHAPTER 47

## TILDA

I STAY WHERE I AM, FLAT ON MY MATTRESS, AS I LISTEN to the front door open and close. As I listen to Quackers. As I listen to Ethan turn his engine on and drive away.

I can hardly believe that just happened.

I mean, I can. Because the kiss we shared outside the gym was the most passionate kiss of my life.

Well, until the one we shared while Ethan made me come by rubbing his hard dick against me.

"Wow."

Swinging one arm over, I roll onto my side and climb off the bed.

I'm not even mad about Ethan's orgasm 'n' dash. If he'd stayed... well, I probably would've just stripped, pulled all his clothes off, then spread myself back on the bed.

And even though that sounds freaking amazing—and I'm positive I'd enjoy the experience—I don't actually know him that well. And grumpy is one thing, but I need to make sure he's a decent human before I let him put his big dick inside me.

I roll my lips together as I open the drawer with my underwear.

*Doth my vagina deceive me? That dick was* big.

Setting aside a new pair of undies, I reach under my sleep shirt, pull my green ones off, toss them into my now-working washer, then carry my new pair into the bathroom.

Refreshed, I walk on bare feet into the living room, planning to lock the front door, then make popcorn to eat in bed while I watch TV on my tablet.

But before I make it to the door, I stop.

The yellow straps are no longer sitting on top of my box.

Ethan's hat is still there. But the straps are gone. And in their place...

I press my teeth into my lower lip and step forward.

Then, slowly, I reach down and pick up the spool of purple ribbon.

"How?" I whisper.

I run my finger over the surface, around the narrow circle the spool makes.

The ribbon is so soft.

It's not silk. Not linen. But something between.

I hold the ribbon closer to my face, admiring the silver thread woven into the edge.

I bite my lip harder as I look out the window to where Ethan's truck was parked.

*When did he buy this?*

*Where did he buy this?*

*Why did he buy this?*

It's so... thoughtful.

I stare down at the ribbon in my hand.

It's odd because he's the one who destroyed my ribbon in the first place. But I think I understand him now. I think I get that he's a stickler for the rules.

That him ripping that other ribbon off the fence had nothing to do with me.

But this...

I peel up the tiny star sticker holding the end of the ribbon down and stick it to the side of the spool.

This is something he had to go out of his way to find.

I doubt a store in Lonely carries this.

I run the fabric between my fingers.

Ten minutes later, with a bowl of popcorn in hand, I make my way back across the living room.

The TV is playing credits, and even though I'll be in the other room, I decide it's time to put in a new movie.

I snap the *Alice in Wonderland* DVD back into its case, then open the top drawer of the movie dresser.

I slide Alice into place but pause as my fingers touch the next one in line.

I look over at Deerdra, and the new purple bows tied around her antlers, and decide to skip over *Bambi*.

# CHAPTER 48

## TILDA

THE COFFEE IS WARM AND SWEET WHEN IT REACHES MY tongue, and I take my time savoring the moment.

The sun is rising on the front side of the house, and sitting in the shadows on the back deck, I'm glad I traded my pajamas for my pale blue sweatpants and matching hoodie.

I take another sip.

*Last night...*

I breathe in the crisp mountain air.

Last night was *an experience.*

We didn't even get naked, but it was still quite possibly the most sexually intense moment of my life.

I'm twenty-nine. I've been with guys before.

But none of them were like Ethan.

None of them demanded my attention like a gravitational pull.

I think back to that day nearly three weeks ago, when a stranger knocked on my door and changed my life with a letter.

I think about the sadness and the fear and the little bit of excitement I felt.

Sadness over losing Uncle Jack. Over not getting to say goodbye.

Fear over the unknown. Over leaving the only city I've ever known.

I smile at the forest that surrounds me.

Excitement over the possibilities.

Excitement of escaping what had been laid out for me.

The chance to alter my timeline.

But even then, even with the idea of a new future before me, I never counted on Ethan.

Never could've dreamed him up.

I lift my empty hand and bring my fingertips to my lips.

Even if we stop here.

Even if I only ever see him again in passing.

Even if I never touch him again.

I have no regrets.

My smile grows as a sense of pride fills my chest.

*I can't believe he came in his pants.*

*Because of me.*

Taking another sip of coffee, I appreciate the stillness around me.

It's amazing, the difference between here and where I came from.

If I'd had a patio to sit on at my old apartment—which I didn't—I'd be listening to traffic. To horns honking. To sirens. To people talking and laughing and shouting.

I wouldn't be in sweatpants.

I'd be in a skimpy dress, and I'd still be sweating my boobs off.

I'd be drinking an iced coffee, not a hot one.

I close my eyes and listen to the sounds of the mountain.

The leaves shifting in the breeze. The happy, chirping birds.

*I really, truly get it, Uncle Jack.*

I'm still not sure what I'll do for work. But I'm not going to stress about it. I'll get by.

My eyes open, and I tilt my head to the side.

*Is that...?*

I stand and carry my coffee through the empty screen door, into the house.

My bare feet are quiet on the floor as I cross the living room.

*Beauty and the Beast* was playing while I fell asleep, but this morning, I turned the TV off.

I decided to absorb the silence.

But then I opened the windows, and the house filled with birdsong. It's still quiet, but not the overwhelming silence I've been dreading.

And through the open front windows, I hear the unmistakable sound of a vehicle coming up the driveway.

Opening the front door, I step outside, mug in hand, and wait for Ethan.

The noise of tires on gravel gets louder.

My mouth starts to pull up into a smile as my bare toes curl against the cool concrete steps.

But then the vehicle comes into view. And my smile stops.

Because it's not a white pickup truck. It's a black SUV.

I freeze.

*They found me.*

I take a step backward, up the stairs.

*They...*

With the engine still running, the SUV stops, the driver's door opens, and a man I don't recognize steps out.

*Not my family.*

Not my family, but still a stranger in a black suit.

I take another quick step backward so I'm standing at the threshold, able to sidestep and slam the door shut if needed.

Sensing my unease, the man holds up his hands. "Morning."

My gaze zeros in on the white envelope in his grip.

The same type of white envelope that was delivered to my apartment nearly three weeks ago.

He stops when he's still several yards away. "Miss Wright?"

"Who's asking?" I try to keep my voice steady.

He holds the envelope higher. "I have a delivery for you, prearranged for today by a man named Jack."

I bite my lip.

He could be lying.

This could be something else.

But... I don't think that's true.

Slowly, I move back onto the top step and hold my hand out.

The man crosses the distance between us and sets the envelope on my palm.

He dips his chin. "Have a good day."

Then he turns around, gets back into his SUV, and rather than attempt to turn it around in front of the house, he backs down the driveway, disappearing from view.

With my heart working overtime, I stare at the envelope in my hand.

*Jack sent me another letter. And I have no idea how to feel about it.*

But ten minutes later, the winning emotion is undeniable.

Dread.

# Chapter 49

## Ethan

A MAN IN A SUIT STEPS INTO THE VISITOR CENTER.

I keep my expression flat, giving him the same look I give everyone. But what I really want to do is narrow my eyes.

Everyone is welcome at the park, but this corporate bozo is not here for a hiking map. I'd bet my savings on it.

I prefer working in the field, getting my hands dirty, sweating through my shirt. But today I'm stuck in the Visitor Center, dealing with guest questions, selling park passes, and other general bullshit.

The front two-thirds of the Visitor Center is filled with interactive educational displays, taxidermized wildlife, state park merchandise, and a variety of free maps and brochures.

The back third of the building contains the employee office—which is a walled-off room tucked into the back corner. And then a hallway that leads to the rear exit, which opens up to a picnic area.

The door to the office is partway down the hall, and it's controlled with a keypad, so only employees can enter.

It's a typical slightly outdated office with workstations along one wall, storage on another, and a communal fridge in the back.

The front of the office, where I'm standing, has a large cutout in the center of the wall, above a bar-height ticket counter. It makes me look like I'm working a concession stand, complete with a roll-down door overhead that we close and lock at night.

It's annoying if someone needs help on the floor because I have to backtrack to the employee door, walk up the hall, and out to the front. But I guess it's better than just a desk out in the open where people can bother you from all sides. Gives a way for people to pay for their merch or buy their park passes without me having to move.

I continue standing behind the ticket counter and watch Suit make a face when he spots the stuffed skunk on the wall.

*No need to be afraid, Soft Hands. It's dead. It can't spray you.*

He clears his throat and keeps walking.

I narrow my eyes at him, glaring at him from the shadows under the brim of my formal ranger hat—the one we're required to wear while we're working in the Welcome Center.

He stops on the other side of the cutout, the counter between us.

I cross my arms. "Toilets are in a separate building." I lift my chin back toward the front entrance. "Quarter mile down the road."

"Uh... What?" He furrows his brow.

"Sorry," I say in a nonapologetic tone. "You looked like you needed to go."

"No, I..." He shakes his head. "Are you Mr. Grant?"

I have a name tag pinned to my shirt that says Grant, so I don't answer.

He looks down at my name tag, back up at me, then takes an envelope out of his inside jacket pocket.

He holds it out.

I keep my arms crossed.

Suit sighs and sets the envelope on the counter. "A man named Jack paid me to deliver this."

*Jack?*

I have to work to keep my expression steady.

Suit doesn't say more. He just turns and heads back the way he came.

When he disappears from view, I uncross my arms and pick up the envelope.

My name is written on the front in neat block lettering.

I've never seen Jack's handwriting before. Never had cause to. But looking at it now, I know it's his.

I pull out the single sheet of paper and unfold it.

DEAR ETHAN,

# Chapter 50

## Tilda

Dear Matty,

I hope you're enjoying the house. If my timing is correct, you've been here for about a week. Plenty of time to fall in love with the property.

I'm sorry for springing all this on you.

And I'm sorry to do it a second time. But I need one more favor from you. I need you to go back to Vegas.

Tomorrow.

It's just for the day, and I've already arranged everything.

A man will meet you at the Peaks Airport. (See addresses below.) He will fly you to Vegas, drive you to the meeting with my lawyer, drive you back to the plane, and fly you home. You'll be back before you know it.

But I do need you to go.

The rest of our family will also be there to hear the reading of the will. And I know it will be unpleasant, but I also know you can do it.

You can do the hard things, Matty.

*I BELIEVE IN YOU.*

*LOVE FROM THE BEYOND,*

*UNCLE JACK*

I smooth the paper on the kitchen counter and read it again.

Back to Vegas.

Back to my family.

I swallow.

I don't want to go.

I don't want to see them.

I don't want to hear whatever crap they're going to say to me.

I don't want to do it.

Not at all.

*You can do the hard things, Matty.*

I press my teeth into my lip.

If it wasn't a handwritten letter from Uncle Jack, I might ignore it.

Might find a way to justify missing the flight.

But he asked me.

*From the Beyond.*

I roll my eyes and release my lip from my bite.

Even in death, he's dramatic.

And even in death, he knows I'll do it.

# CHAPTER 51

## ETHAN

I SHOVE THE LETTER BACK INTO THE ENVELOPE.

Then I stare across the empty Visitor Center.

*Fucking Jack.*

My phone rings.

Mind racing, I pull it from my pocket and answer.

"Mr. Grant?"

Irritated at all this, I run my tongue along my teeth before answering. "Who is this?"

There's a chuckle. "Jack warned me you weren't very friendly."

I grunt.

"There's a new deposit in your account from Peaks Airport," the man tells me.

"Who is this?" Suspicion rolls in my gut.

Peaks is a private airport about forty minutes from here. Where I keep my plane. Where I sometimes do charter flights.

But it never goes down like this.

"Jack hired you to fly a person to Vegas tomorrow morning. The flight plan has already been registered, and your request for time off has already been granted." The man says it so nonchalantly that it makes me grind my teeth. "When you land, there will be a car waiting for you to use."

"Who. Is. This?" I grit out each word.

He's talking about Tilda. He has to be.

And if he thinks I'm going to just deliver her—

"My name is Richard. And tomorrow I'll be reading Jack's will. Matilda Wright *must* be present. It's of the utmost importance."

I grind my teeth. Again.

"After the reading, you'll drive her back to the airport and fly her home. If all goes smoothly, you'll be back in time for dinner." He hums, like we're in some sort of accordance. "Safe travels, Mr. Grant."

Then he hangs up.

And I lower the phone.

# CHAPTER 52

## TILDA

MY GPS TELLS ME TO TAKE THE NEXT LEFT, AND I FLEX my grip on the steering wheel as I approach the tiniest airport I've ever seen.

Slowing, I turn into the driveway. Then I stop because there's a chain link gate blocking my entry.

An older woman steps out of the little guard shack and approaches my truck.

Keeping my foot on the brake, I roll down my window. "Good morning."

The woman smiles. "Morning. Name?"

She looks down at the tablet in her hands.

"Um, Matilda Wright." I don't know how security works in a place like this, but I figure I should use my official name.

"Gotcha." The woman taps her screen, then lifts her gaze back to me. "Have you been here before?"

I shake my head.

"You're leaving out of hangar five, off to the right." She lifts her arm and points in that direction. "Park in one of the spots behind the building with the five on it. Then enter through the side door. Pilot's already here."

I force a smile. "Okay, thank you so much."

"Have a nice flight." She dips her chin, then walks back to the little guardhouse.

A moment later, the gate slides open.

Filled with stress and trepidation, I take my foot off the brake and roll forward.

*It's just the reading of the will.*

When I got that first letter from Uncle Jack back in Vegas, telling me about the house and the twenty thousand dollars, I was shocked beyond belief. But I've had weeks to accept it. So even though today is going to be unpleasant, at least I won't be taken off guard like the rest of my family.

I turn my truck to the right and coast toward building five.

For the hundredth time since the letter was delivered yesterday, I silently ask Uncle Jack why I have to be there today.

Because yes, I know what's coming, which is good. But what's *not good* is knowing that every single one of my relatives is going to have a total and complete meltdown when they find out Uncle Jack left everything to me.

*Me.* The pariah of the family.

I take a mindful deep breath as I pull into one of the six parking spots behind building five.

There are two vehicles. A black pickup truck and a blue four-door something. One of which must belong to the pilot.

My stress increases as I force myself to exit my truck.

I make sure my keys are in my mini backpack, then I slip my arms through the straps, lock the truck doors, and slam my door shut.

I was stressed about my family when I was at the gate, but now that I'm looking around, I'm scared for an entirely different reason.

*This is an airport for tiny planes.*

Which is why that guard lady said my pilot is here. Because this is going to be a tiny, little plane. And it's going to literally be just me and the pilot.

I wipe my palms down the skirt of my dress.

*Why would Uncle Jack book me a private plane?*

*Why wouldn't he just get me a normal ticket out of a normal airport?*

I don't know much about planes. Hardly anything. But I'm pretty sure flying to Vegas in a windup toy is going to take longer than flying in a commercial jet.

I narrow my eyes at the sky.

*Is that why I had to be here so ungodly early?*

Then I think about how much longer it would take me to get to the Denver airport and to go through security... Maybe the travel time evens out?

Except this has to be way more expensive.

And scarier.

*Don't these small planes crash all the time?*

I wipe my palms down my skirt again.

*I can do hard things.*

I repeat the words to myself as I follow the sidewalk around the corner of the building.

*Would that count as doing a hard thing, though? Dying in a plane crash? Because it's not really me that's doing it. It would be more of a thing that's happening to me.*

When I reach the side door halfway down the side of the building, I wipe my palms down my skirt for the final time. Then I push open the door and step into the brightly lit airplane hangar.

And it's exactly like the movies.

The building is wide with metal walls and a concrete floor, and an orange airplane sits beneath an open overhead door.

Voices come from the other side of the aircraft, but the people they come from don't seem to notice my arrival.

I take a few steps farther into the hangar, but my black combat boots don't make any noise, so I clear my throat.

The voices cut off, then a man in his sixties steps around the back of the plane.

He swings a towel onto his shoulder and grins at me. "Morning, Miss. You the passenger?"

I nod.

*Okay, he looks seasoned.*

*I bet he's flown this route a hundred times.*

*Maybe this won't be so bad.*

"Good." He claps his hands together. "We just wrapped up, so perfect timing. Do you need to use the restroom before the flight?" He shrugs as he asks it, like he knows it's an awkward question. "There's no bathroom on the plane."

I can't stop myself from biting my lip as I look over at the plane.

I hadn't even thought about the bathroom situation. But it doesn't look like you could even stand up in the plane.

I nod. "In that case, yes, please."

"I'll show you—"

"I'll take her." A familiar deep voice cuts through the air.

I turn and see *him* walking over from the front of the plane. "Ethan?"

"Ah, you know each other." The older man keeps grinning.

I glance at him, then back at Ethan. "Are you going to Vegas too?"

He tilts his head but doesn't answer my question, just holds his arm out in invitation. "Come on."

I glance at the other man again, but he's looking at Ethan. "I'll double-check that nothing got added to the schedule, but you should have the runway to yourself for the next hour."

"Good." Ethan nods, then locks eyes with me. "Let's go."

I'm trying to follow the conversation, but my nervous system is working overtime right now.

*I don't want to fly in a tiny plane.*

Ethan settles his hand low on my spine, below my backpack and just above my ass.

Heat soaks through the fabric of my dress, and the pressure finally gets my feet to move.

"So..." I look up at Ethan as we exit the hangar. "This can't just be a coincidence, right? Did Uncle Jack hire you as like my bodyguard or something?"

His fingers flex. "Bodyguard?"

I try not to notice how handsome he looks in his dark red flannel as I nod. "Yeah, are you just supposed to keep an eye on me or something?"

He blinks down at me. "Starlight, I'm not going to Vegas as your bodyguard. I'm flying you there. As your pilot."

# CHAPTER 53

## ETHAN

SHE STARES UP AT ME. HER CURIOUS EYES LOOK INTO mine, like she's trying to decipher my words.

I increase the pressure on her lower back as she starts to slow.

"I'm sorry." Tilda shakes her head. "You're too handsome. What did you say?"

The edge of my mouth twitches. *She's such a goofy girl.* "What do my looks have to do with anything?"

She lifts a hand and gestures toward my face. "It's distracting."

I lift a brow. "*It?*"

Tilda sighs as she drops her hand. "Your handsomeness."

"Truly, I never know what's going to come out of your mouth,"

She stops walking. "Did you really say pilot?"

My gaze drops to her lips, her teeth biting into the plump flesh.

I rotate so we're facing each other.

I slide my palm to her hip and reach up with my other hand. Using my thumb, I free her lip.

*And I want to kiss her so badly.*

Tilda's hands grip the front of my shirt, holding me in place.

I always feel like a beast when I'm near her. And especially this morning.

I'm in my usual clothes. Old jeans. Old flannel. Old boots. And she looks ready for a party.

Her hair is down around her shoulders in curls that I know are as soft as they look.

Her black boots match her black leather backpack.

And I won't lie, the combat boots are hot. But it's the dress.

It's her bright yellow dress that's going to distract me all fucking day.

I don't know what type of material it is. Probably something you could find in that craft store. It looks lightweight, almost lacy. It has cap sleeves and a deep V-neck that shows a delicious amount of cleavage. It's snug over her chest, but the skirt flares out in a series of ruffling layers, creating a ballgown look, even though it ends at her knees. And there's a bow on her side. Making me wonder what happens if I untie it.

I bet it all unravels.

*I hope it all unravels.*

And... I need to remember I'm here for a job. And that job does not include having sex with Tilda in my plane.

I take a step to the side and slide my hand back to her spine. "We need to get going."

Tilda walks with me, staying quiet as we approach the restrooms.

"I'll meet you back here," I tell her just outside the doors.

She nods and walks into the small building ahead of me.

Two minutes later, Tilda walks out and stops before me. "Ethan?"

I dip my chin.

"Are you really flying this plane?"

I dip my chin again.

"But..." She looks up at me with imploring eyes. "But you're a park ranger. I've seen you."

This time the corner of my mouth definitely twitches. "I'm not denying that I'm a ranger. I'm just also a pilot."

"How?"

"Classes. Hours of flying. The usual." I reach out and gently grip her elbow.

"Are you good?" she whispers.

I slide my grip down her forearm. "I'm good." I squeeze her wrist. "Come on and I'll show you."

# CHAPTER 54

## TILDA

I FIDGET WITH THE SEAT BELT CROSSED OVER MY CHEST and stare out the windshield while I try to breathe.

My mini backpack is tucked away in the back seat. And I don't know what's scarier, just the two of us in this tiny plane, or if there were *two more people* in this tiny plane.

I reach down to double-check that I still have my phone wedged under my thigh.

I do.

I'm assuming there won't be any service while we're up in the air. But if I can get myself out of this anxiety phase, I want to take some pictures. Gods willing, I'll never fly in a miniature plane again, so I want to make the most of it. Assuming we don't die.

Ethan taps things on the screen in the center of the dashboard, or whatever it's called, and I wonder if I have time to run back to the bathroom.

I don't really have to go again, but knowing I won't be able to go for the next few hours is stressing me out.

But before I can ask, the propeller starts to whirl.

"Ethan." My voice comes out as a quiet croak. I try again. "Ethan."

He turns to face me, but instead of replying, he hands me a headset.

He puts his own on, adjusting the little microphone piece in front of his mouth, then he does something with the controls, and we start to roll forward.

Focusing on breathing, I pull the clunky headphones over my ears and mimic his actions so the mouthpiece is near my lips.

"What is it, Firecracker?"

I jolt at the sound of Ethan's voice through the headphones.

I glance at him, then look back out through the windshield. "W-why do you call me that?"

It's not what I was going to ask him. But he's already told me he's a pilot. The other dude in the hangar seems to know him as a pilot. And asking Ethan now if he's *super sure* he knows how to fly a plane seems pointless. Because we're moving.

We exit the hangar, and I squint in the morning sunshine.

Ethan shifts and reaches back between our seats.

He leans, and I'm about to offer to help him with whatever he's trying to get, but then he pulls his arm back and holds a glasses case out to me.

I take it and look up to thank him. But I pause.

I don't know how he put them on without me noticing, but Ethan is wearing a pair of dark aviator sunglasses. The lenses are nearly black, and the thin metal frame is silver.

And... wow.

*How do sunglasses make him even hotter?*

I swallow.

"Put them on, Tilda."

Watching his mouth move, I don't jump when he speaks this time.

Carefully, I unsnap the case and pull out a pair of glasses identical to the ones Ethan is wearing.

Clearly these are here for his passengers, not just for me personally, but I silently like that we match.

And I like that he's prepared, because I left my sunglasses in my truck.

I lift them to my face and slide the earpieces under my headphones, settling them on my nose.

When I look back over at Ethan, I swear I catch the hint of a smirk.

"How do they look?" I try to give him a smile, but my insides are too twisted to pull it off.

I can't see his eyes through his lenses, but I watch him tip his head, and I can practically feel his gaze drag down my body.

I lower my hands to my lap and fidget with the glasses case.

This isn't a *super* low-cut dress, but it is low. And the V-neck, along with the way the cut pushes my girls up, means my cleavage is on full display.

Had I known I was going to be climbing into a tiny, little plane, I probably would've worn something else. Perhaps a denim jumpsuit. But I didn't know. And I dressed for confidence.

Remembering why we're flying to Vegas doubles my anxiety.

Fingers grip my chin.

I focus on my reflection in Ethan's glasses.

"It's going to be fine." His words are soft against my ears. "Say it back to me."

I pull in a slow breath through parted lips. "It's going to be fine."

Ethan drags his thumb across my jawline before he lowers his hand.

Then he pulls the glasses case free from my grip and puts it back, somewhere behind my seat.

There's a crackle in my headphones, then a new voice comes through. "Clear for takeoff."

Ethan steers the plane into a turn, and my stomach sinks into my butt when I see the runway stretch out before us.

The engine gets louder.

*Or I think it gets louder.*

Maybe that's my heartbeat.

Maybe this is all a dream.

*Please be a dream.*

We start to roll forward.

Faster.

Faster.

I wrap my fingers around my seat belt, holding it as tight as I can.

A warm hand gently grips my wrist. The one closest to Ethan.

He pulls my hand down, setting it on his thigh. "You want to know why I call you Firecracker?"

Swallowing down my panic, I look from the runway to Ethan's profile. "Because I'm fun?"

He looks at me. "Because you're a threat to the natural order."

My jaw drops.

And Ethan grins.

Actually *grins*.

*This—*

Before I can think of an insult, Ethan pulls the controls back, the nose of the plane lifts, and the ground drops away below us.

# CHAPTER 55

## ETHAN

TILDA'S FINGERNAILS SCRAPE AGAINST MY JEANS AS SHE mumbles something too quiet for me to understand.

I try to focus on flying. But my dick keeps focusing on her fingers.

When I glance over, Tilda has her chin tucked down to her tits, her other hand still clinging to her seat belt with a white-knuckle grip.

I can't see her eyes through the dark sunglasses, but I'm positive she has them squeezed shut.

"Tilda." I speak calmly into the mouthpiece. "Relax and breathe."

She sucks in a noisy breath.

"Relax," I tell her again. "Breathe."

Her exhale comes out in a huff that almost sounds like humor.

I glance over again.

Her face is turned toward me this time.

"Something funny?" I lift a brow.

I notice, but don't comment on the fact that her grip on the seat belt has loosened.

Her breath puffs against the microphone. "It sounds like you're trying to walk me through sex."

I slowly turn my head back to look at her. "Excuse me?"

"Relax." She tries to mimic my deeper voice. "Breathe."

*Firecracker.*

"Tilda?"

"Yeah?"

I face forward. "Keep breathing."

I hear her inhale through my headphones.

Then I hear her squeak as I bank the plane toward the mountains.

# CHAPTER 56

## TILDA

A WARM PALM SETTLES ON TOP OF MY HAND, AND I OPEN my eyes.

Then I gasp.

I knew we'd have to fly over the Rockies to get to Nevada, but... wow.

Just wow.

Ethan gives my hand a gentle squeeze, and I twist my wrist, flipping my hand over so we're palm to palm.

"It's..." I take in the wilderness spreading below us. "Amazing."

His fingers slide between mine as he grips my hand in his. "Another one of your sex lines?"

"You wish." I don't give the comeback the proper attitude because I'm too busy looking out the window.

Silence stretches between us, the hum of the engine filling my head.

We're flying lower than the commercial plane that brought me to Colorado did.

I don't think we're going as fast either.

So the mountains are closer.

More vivid.

More detailed.

It's like a Bob Ross painting come to life.

The gray rocky slopes.

The blanket of evergreen trees.

My eyes scan it all, and I notice that all the trees seem to stop growing at about the same spot on all the mountains.

I'm sure Ethan knows why. Probably something to do with temperature or oxygen or wild chipmunks eating all the nuts. But I'm too busy looking to ask.

It's so—

The plane shakes, and I let out an embarrassing squeak.

Ethan flexes his fingers around mine. "Just turbulence. It's normal around the mountains."

I squeeze his fingers back. "Why's that?"

"Mountain waves." He answers in a calm tone. "Wind coming from the west moves up over the mountains and causes mayhem."

I press my lips together and inhale through my nose, trying to slow my racing pulse. "It's cool that you know that."

Ethan grunts.

"What?" I focus on his response and not the new round of shaking.

"You shouldn't let yourself be so easily impressed."

I turn my head and gape at him. "Excuse me?"

"You heard me."

I move my attention back out the window.

And... he's not wrong.

Years and years of people disappointing me, for one reason or another, have left me expecting the least.

So, yeah. My bar is probably too low.

I sigh. "You're right."

"Usually." Ethan says it so blandly that I have to smile. "But what precisely are you referring to?"

"My standards." I shrug, keeping my eyes on the mountains. "Pretty sure my expectations aren't just low. They're lying on the floor."

It stings a little to admit it, but it's the truth.

Ethan doesn't reply. And when I glance over, I think I see his jaw tick.

Then I realize that might've come off as insulting.

"Oh, um, not you. I don't just mean our... Well... You know." I struggle to find the right words.

I like Ethan as a whole. But now my cheeks are getting hot as I think about the last time I saw him, when he made me come just by grinding on me.

That wasn't below average.

That was an A-plus experience.

"Do you have an ex-boyfriend I need to kill?" Ethan's tone is angry.

"Huh?" I'm back to looking at him. "Why would you...?"

"Your expectations on the floor. Did someone hurt you?"

My face scrunches up. "What? No. It's not—" I try to think of the best way to explain myself. "I wasn't referring to any of my exes. Of which there are few. It's my family that sucks. Not like *hitting me* sucks. They just... suck."

Nerves, ones that have nothing to do with flying, crawl across my skin as I think about the people waiting for me on the other end of this flight.

I try to slide my hand free from Ethan's, but he tightens his grip.

"The first time we met, you asked me if I was going to shoot you. You asked if your cousin sent me."

I grimace. "That may have been an overreaction."

"Most people don't assume a relative is trying to kill them for no reason."

I let the warmth of his hand comfort me against the unpleasant memories. "He's all bark."

"But..." Ethan prompts, knowing there's more.

I shrug. "But... he also told me he was going to kill me the last time I saw him. So when you show up, out of the freaking woods, with a gun, on the day I move in... I may have overreacted."

"What were his exact words?" Ethan ignores the part about him coming out of the forest.

I've never told anyone this story.

Telling my mom or anyone else in my family would be pointless.

I had some friends, but they were all people I knew through work, and I didn't want to involve them in my emotionally abusive trauma.

But with Ethan... "Honestly, I couldn't tell you why I was even at this family event. I hated going to them. It was just... easier to go than deal with the harassment of not going."

It's an uncomfortable truth. And all the more reason to be grateful to Uncle Jack for my new house. My escape.

Ethan's thumb rubs a calming line against my hand. "I get it. But now you never have to choose between the two."

I swallow against his understanding, glad that I'm finally sharing this. "We were at his mom's place, my Aunt Gunnie's. In early April for our grandma's birthday. She's Uncle Jack's sister. Or *was*, I guess. But they didn't get along. I don't think Uncle Jack liked anyone but me. And I don't mean that in a bragging sort of way. He and I... we aren't filled with spite and entitlement like the rest of them. Really, I don't know why they're all so nasty."

A weight shaped like disappointment settles on my chest.

I really don't know why they're all so rotten.

I know every family has its drama. But this group... I don't think they've ever been happy in their lives.

*Have I ever been happy?*

That weight gets heavier, and I finally release my hold of the seat belt to rub at my sternum.

Maybe I haven't been *happy*, but living on my own for the last decade has definitely been better than living with any of them.

And maybe I'm just not happy *yet*. But...

I flex my fingers against Ethan's. I look out the window at the endless beauty below me. I think about my new home and my ribbon and my duck...

I'm going to be happy.

Soon.

"And your cousin?" Ethan's reminder cuts through my optimism.

"My cousin is a toad."

Ethan makes a choking sound that almost makes me smile.

"Ralph, my cousin, apparently heard our moms talking about how Grandma's health wasn't doing well. And when I was stepping out of the bathroom, he cornered me and told me that he'd kill me if I tried to take what was his." I shake my head as I say it. It's true. "I don't know why he would even think Grandma would leave me anything. I mean, maybe she has some savings stashed away. But I'm pretty sure she'd give it to her weirdo cult friends before she'd give it to anyone in the family. She certainly wouldn't give it to me."

"Do they think she has more money than Jack?"

A laugh bubbles out of me. "For sure. None of them have talked to Uncle Jack for probably a decade. Last time I saw him was like four years ago, when he passed through town and took me to lunch. If they ever find out he left me twenty grand, they'll flip out."

I didn't mean to say how much money Uncle Jack left me. But when I glance over, Ethan doesn't look shocked, so maybe he knew Jack had money.

I clear my throat. "Anyway, this thing you're bringing me to is the reading of Uncle Jack's will. And I'm assuming everyone will be there, because they're a bunch of greedy greed bags. I really hope the will doesn't say anything about the check. It's gonna be bad enough when they find out he left me a house. And a truck. And land. I'm also hoping the will doesn't list out the address, but they're greedy, not stupid. So I'm sure they'll find a way to figure it out." My insides sour at the idea that any of them might show up at my new house. "I know Uncle Jack didn't live in

Lonely all year. So maybe today has something to do with that? Or maybe that place was a rental. Whatever it was, I know he wouldn't give it to any of them." I look at Ethan and ask him because I don't have anyone else to ask. "Do you know where he went when he wasn't in the mountains?"

"I don't. He never said."

"Oh."

"Do you know for sure that your family will be there today?"

I shake my head. "Not for sure. But pretty much everyone, except my dad and a few other cousins, lives in Vegas. I lived there my whole life too. Until now."

Ethan makes a humming sound. "If everything is already in your name, do you really have to go?"

It's a fair question. "Legally, I don't know if it matters. But Uncle Jack left me a letter specifically asking me to. And he knows I hate all these people as much as he did, so I'm assuming there's a good reason."

When Ethan doesn't reply, I look over at him.

After a moment he speaks. "You'll point out *Ralph* to me."

The way he says my cousin's name lightens some of the earlier heaviness.

I nod. "Promise. I mean, I hope they don't follow me back to the airport. But if they do, he's the smarmy-looking one a couple years older than me."

"No one is following you back to the plane, Tilda. I'm going with you to the lawyer's office."

"Oh, you don't have to—"

"I was hired to fly you and drive you."

I press my lips together.

*I was hired.*

I want to pull my hand free from Ethan's.

I want to stop touching him. Stop absorbing his comfort.

But I can't do that without calling attention to my hurt feelings.

And they shouldn't be hurt.

*It's stupid for me to feel hurt.*

Ethan is the pilot.

He's flying me right now because he was hired by Uncle Jack.

I know that.

*I knew that.*

But I forgot.

I got caught up, and I forgot.

Ethan isn't here for *me*.

He's here for a job.

A paycheck.

Grateful for my dark sunglasses, I turn my head and look out the window.

# CHAPTER 57

## ETHAN

Silence stretches between us.

Too late, I realize that my words came out wrong.

But I can't backtrack and pretend I wasn't hired for this job. I was. She has to know I was.

If she'd been the one to ask me, I could've turned the payment down and done it for free.

But she didn't. And the money was already deposited into my account through the booking system before I even agreed to it.

"Could I have a water, please?" Tilda's question is quiet. Timid.

"Yeah." My reply comes out scratchy, and I decide we'll share the water.

I loosen my hold on Tilda's hand and reach into the back seat for a water bottle.

She doesn't do it the second I let go.

She waits until my arm is stretched back.

Waits until I can't stop her.

Then she slides her hand off my thigh and into her own lap.

That disgusting, guilty feeling that I'm beginning to associate with treating Tilda poorly slithers through my chest.

She doesn't need water.
She just didn't want to hold my hand anymore.

# CHAPTER 58

## TILDA

THE PLANE SHAKES THROUGH ANOTHER PATCH OF turbulence, and I grip the water with both hands.

*Breathe.*

*Relax.*

I repeat the words in my head over and over.

And I remind myself that I'll find my happy.

Not today.

Today is...

Well, today is going to stand as a good reminder. A life lesson.

*I can count on myself. And no one else.*

I inhale.

Exhale.

Relax.

I squeeze the water bottle tightly, glad it's made of metal so it doesn't crinkle under my hold.

It's not fair to be upset at Ethan. He's done nothing wrong. I just... forgot. For a moment.

The kisses.

The... bed.

It's blurred my vision.

It was fun. But it meant nothing.

I start to bite my lip, then stop myself.

*I'm not nothing.*

*I'm just not for everyone.*

Memories of my mother shouting at me try to wedge their way into my psyche. But I ignore them.

*You're such a little shit. No one is going to put up with this stupid, fanciful behavior. If you ever want a man, you need to grow the hell up.*

Okay, so I don't ignore them as much as I'd like to.

But staring out the window at the bright blue sky beyond, I think about that ribbon. The one Ethan bought for me. The spool he left sitting in my living room without saying a word.

That was fanciful.

Indulgent.

And even if it was just his way of apologizing for destroying the ribbon I put on the fence, it wasn't nothing.

*He's* not nothing.

I take another breath, a calming one to steady my voice. "Thank you for the ribbon. That was really nice of you."

Out of the corner of my eye, I see him glance my way. But I keep my attention forward.

After another heartbeat, his voice rumbles through my headphones. "It was nothing."

I let the side of my mouth pull up into a smile. "It wasn't nothing."

# CHAPTER 59

## TILDA

"WE'RE GOING TO START OUR DESCENT."

I jolt at the sound of Ethan's voice.

We've spent the last couple hours flying over mountainous terrain, not talking. Ethan focused on flying. I focused on getting through the day.

My fingers pluck at my skirt.

"Matilda," he says quietly.

Keeping my stress hidden behind my dark lenses, I finally turn to look at Ethan, wishing there was a longer version of his name like there is for mine, so I can have something else to call him. "What's your middle name?"

"Ford."

I purse my lips. "Family name?"

He nods.

"Car company?"

He shakes his head. "Different family."

"Spaceships?"

His lips twitch as he shakes his head again.

"Mother's maiden name?"

"No, but it came from her side. Every male born has it somewhere in their name. Supposedly."

I hum. "Is Grant your last name? I saw it on your shirt." I hadn't noticed the first time we met. But I saw it the second time.

He nods again. "What's your middle name, Matilda Wright?"

"Iris." Unclenching my fingers from my dress, I reach up and touch one of my purple curls.

"It's a pretty flower." His voice is so soft, his words so gentle.

I purse my lips on an exhale. "Ethan Ford, tell me you'll land us smoothly."

He reaches over the gap between our seats and wraps his fingers around my wrist. "Matilda Iris, I'm going to land us smoothly." He pulls my hand toward him, setting it on his thigh.

Ethan releases my wrist, taking the controls in both hands, but I leave my palm where it is.

And I close my eyes.

I close my eyes to the ground below us.

Close them on the situation before me.

Close them, just for now, while I gather my courage.

And when our tires meet the ground, I take one more breath in the dark.

One last breath before the next part.

# Chapter 60

## Ethan

Worry claws at my throat as we pull onto the parking ramp beside our destination.

Tilda didn't say anything during the landing.

Hardly said anything as we made another bathroom stop, then transferred to the car.

She's been silent the whole ride.

And now, as I park and turn off the engine, I worry that she's shutting down.

I know she doesn't like her family, that she doesn't want to be here. But this reaction is stressing me out.

As I push open the car door, I wonder if I should just turn the engine back on and drive us right back to the airport.

Tilda doesn't need to be here for this.

She already has Jack's house and land. Sitting in a room with her relatives as they find out is unnecessary. And, if I'm reading the family history correctly, more than a bit cruel.

*Why would Jack put her through this?*

With one leg out of the vehicle, I turn my head toward Tilda. "You don't have to do this. We can go."

Still wearing my extra pair of aviators, Tilda gives me a tight smile. "I'm okay." She unbuckles her seat belt. "But as soon as this is done, we go straight back to the plane."

I want to argue. But I dip my chin instead, leaving my sunglasses on the dashboard.

We slam our doors shut at the same time and meet at the back of the car.

Tilda pauses beside me.

The black glasses, with the black boots and leather backpack, mixed with her fluffy yellow dress, make her look even more badass than she did before.

I want to tell her that.

Want to tell her that I haven't stopped thinking about the other night.

How good it felt having her beneath me.

How I need to have her there again.

I want to tell her that I'm becoming enamored.

*Obsessed.*

That I'll help her through anything. That I'll happily punch Ralph in the fucking face if it will just make her smile.

But I don't want to derail her.

Don't want to make this about me.

So I keep my mouth shut.

And I hold my hand out.

She tips her head up, and I watch myself in the reflection of her lenses as she makes her decision.

Tilda blows out a breath. Nods. Then puts her hand in mine.

Satisfaction blooms inside my rib cage as I close my fingers around hers.

Tilda falls into step beside me as we walk together down the ramp to street level.

I keep my grip firm and use my hold on her to turn Tilda to the left.

Before she got to the hangar this morning, I studied the map of this location so I'd know where to go. I didn't tell her that. And she doesn't question me. Just follows. Giving my confidence another boost.

I know I fucked up with how I said things on the plane, but I can still show her that today isn't just about a hired job.

Heat radiates up from the concrete as we make our way down the wide sidewalk.

Summer in Las Vegas is not for the faint of heart.

And not for people dressed like lumberjacks.

I reach up with my free hand and undo the top couple buttons of my flannel.

I'm probably showing more bare chest than is respectable. But, fuck, it's like being in hell out here.

Tilda's fingers flex against mine. "You okay, Ranger?"

"Hot."

She huffs and reaches across with her free hand to the front of my shirt.

My steps falter as she undoes the next button.

A fingertip taps against my chest, and I look down at the tattooed skin she's revealed.

"I'm suddenly better." I try to say it dryly. But it comes out as a rumble.

Tilda hums and drops her hand.

I focus on slowing my heart rate as we cross an intersection.

Then we're here.

I squeeze Tilda's fingers. "This is it."

We slow and turn to face a three story building.

It looks like an old courthouse, complete with a wide stone staircase leading up to the front door, and is the current home to two dozen businesses. One of which belongs to Jack's lawyer.

I wait for Tilda to take the first step, then I walk beside her up the stairs.

"It's on the first level. Turn right when we get inside, then it's on the left."

Tilda nods, and I let go of her hand so I can open the door.

She takes the aviators off and puts them on top of her head, the earpieces disappearing into her hair. Then she walks in ahead of me.

We turn down the hall, the directory on the wall confirming this is the way to Richard and Son. Spaced out between the doors on either side of the hall are plain wooden benches. And our footsteps echo between the high ceilings and the marble floors.

Ahead of us, a door opens, and a woman steps out into the hall.

Tilda tenses, and her hesitation has me lifting my hand on instinct and placing it against the center of her back.

She straightens her shoulders and whispers under her breath, "Here we go."

"There you are." The woman snaps it like an accusation.

"Hello, Mother." Tilda's tone is formal and cold.

And her mother... is average.

Average appearance. Size.

Short brown hair dyed a shade too dark to look natural.

Clothing that is conventionally nice but not memorable.

She's unremarkable.

Nothing like Tilda.

And I've never instantly hated a person more in my life.

"We've been waiting." There isn't a single shred of affection in her tone.

As our steps slow, I lift my hand and make a show of looking at my watch, letting the awful woman see me do it.

*We're ten minutes early.*

She glances at the movement but just as quickly dismisses me.

Before something else can come out of her mouth, another woman steps out of the office.

Followed by a man. An older woman. And then a paired couple.

I must make a noise because Tilda hums an agreement. "There's a lot of them."

Together, we come to a stop before the crowd.

The woman standing next to Tilda's mom makes a clicking sound as she looks Tilda over. "Yellow... With your complexion?"

"Watch your mouth," I growl.

The old bitch gasps as she looks at me. "Excuse me?"

I hold her gaze, letting her see how serious I am.

And I keep my expression flat when she finally notices my eyes and flinches.

Tilda's mom huffs. "Tilly—"

"Don't call me that." Tilda cuts her off, and I almost smile.

"Ma-tilda." The older woman rolls her eyes as she emphasizes the name obnoxiously. "Can we please get started?"

A male voice calls something from inside the law office, and the shitty not-mother woman shouts back, "We're coming."

Tilda gestures toward the office. "After you."

Her family files back through the door, and I dip my head, speaking quietly against her ear. "Do you want me to come in with you?"

She keeps her attention forward, on the enemy, but shakes her head. "Thank you, but no."

"You're sure?"

She nods, then tips her head up to look at me. "I'm sure, Ranger."

Accepting her answer, I straighten and let my hand slide down her spine as she steps away.

When the door closes behind her, I sit on the bench beside the door. And wait.

# CHAPTER 61

## TILDA

THE LAW FIRM IS SMALL, JUST A WAITING ROOM AREA with a woman behind a reception desk and one office.

The door to the office is open, and my cousin Ralph is standing at the threshold, sneering like the rat he is.

I ignore him, making sure our shoulders don't touch as I step into the office.

Everyone else is still standing, whispering to each other, so I circle around them and claim one of the four visitor chairs in the room.

A man about my dad's age sits on the other side of the desk.

He nods at me. "You must be Matty."

"I am. Nice to meet you." I give him a tight smile.

The familiarity of hearing the name my uncle called me helps to settle some of my nerves.

I smooth my skirt over my lap. Being in a room with this much family is a nightmare. But knowing Ethan is waiting in the hall—that he'll fly me out of here as soon as I ask him to—makes this all slightly more tolerable.

Ralph sniffs, like he's fighting a cold, and leans against the wall nearest me.

*Gross.*

Mother takes the chair next to mine, then Ralph's parents—Aunt Gunnie, who doesn't like my yellow dress, and her ever-silent husband—take the remaining chairs. Everyone else stands behind us.

I keep my attention forward.

I just have to sit through a few minutes of the lawyer talking.

Just have to sit through them finding out about the house.

Then I'm out of here.

The lawyer clears his throat. "Thank you all for coming in today. I'm Richard—"

"Where's your son?" Ralph scoffs, like he's catching the lawyer in a sneaky lie.

Richard keeps his expression blank as he turns to address Ralph. "I'm the son. My father was also named Richard."

I bite down on the urge to smile. *Eat it, Ralph.*

The lawyer returns his attention to the rest of the room. "Jack requested that we have a formal reading of his will, and as all required parties are present, I shall begin." He waits a beat, letting his eyes linger on my relatives, then looks down at an envelope on his desk. "This is a letter written by Jack." Richard picks up a golden letter opener and slices the sealed envelope open.

Then he unfolds the paper and begins to read. "Hello, dear family. Thank you for gathering here today, in the event of my death."

I press my lips together because this would be an inappropriate time to laugh. But *really, Uncle Jack?*

Not that the dramatics of a letter should surprise me.

"Though I hate most of you—"

I can't prevent my snort. Because *really, Uncle Jack?* But I lift a hand to my mouth as I half-heartedly turn it into a cough. "Sorry. Continue."

Richard nods. "I feel it is important for you all to be here for this, so there are no misunderstandings. And I assure you, Richard has approved all my requests. There is nothing illegal, nothing that can be done by any of you to undo what I've set in motion. So, please, sit there and take it." The lawyer uses *zero inflection,* and it makes the whole thing that much more absurd. And satisfying. "To my sister and nieces, I leave you nothing."

My mother and aunt gasp.

I suppress another laugh.

"To my brothers, I leave you nothing," the lawyer continues. "To any others who have gathered, if your name is not Matilda Iris Wright, I leave you nothing."

Satisfaction mingles with the nerves in my stomach.

This is the whole point. I knew this was coming. But with every pair of eyes on me, I internally brace myself.

"To my Matty, I leave you my house in the mountains. By now, you should already be residing there and familiar with the property. And I hope you've been drinking your coffee on the deck." I swallow, wishing I could tell them that I do. That I love it. "To my Matty, I also leave you everything on the property. My truck. My belongings. And the check from my savings for twenty thousand dollars, to get you going."

"What is the meaning of this?" Mother hisses at me, as though I'm the one reading the letter.

I keep my eyes forward.

"Twenty fucking thousand?" Ralph pushes off the wall and steps toward the desk. "Are you fucking kidding me?"

The rest of the group erupts with sharp, angry words.

Richard pulls something small from his desk drawer, lifts it to his mouth, then presses the metal whistle between his lips and blows. Loudly.

Everyone shuts up.

I press my fingertips against my lips, physically suppressing my smile.

This is a nightmare but also satisfying.

Richard lowers the whistle and goes back to reading. "I've provided my lawyer with a whistle. Please don't embarrass me in death and make him use it."

I press my fingers harder against my lips.

"Before my final bestowment, I want to tell you all something. You didn't break me. Your snide comments. Your attitudes. Your remarks and put-downs. You never broke me. I didn't stay away because I was afraid of you. I stayed away because I found a better family to surround myself with. And if you weren't such an unpleasant group of assholes, I'd hope for you to make similar connections. But you are, so I won't." The lawyer pauses, turning just the slightest bit so he's facing me directly. "Except you, Matty. You didn't let them break you either. And with time, you'll make your own family. Through friends or children, I care not how, just that you do. And to help you in your venture, my glorious little flower, I have one more thing for you."

My fingers tremble against my lips.

*I will.*

*I will find my own family.*

*I'll make my own happy future.*

*In Colorado.*

I swallow. Wishing I'd spent more time with Uncle Jack in the past years.

The corners of Richard's eyes crinkle. "Matty, I leave to you my investment account."

My eyebrows lift.

*There's more? Beyond the twenty thousand?*

"It's already in your name. And will be dispersed to you, by my accountants, over four years. Each year, on your birthday."

My heart thuds behind my ribs.

Today is Friday. My birthday is next Tuesday.

The room is silent. And from the edge of my vision, I can see everyone leaning forward. Waiting for the detail.

The *how much.*

"There is a catch, my dear. One I will insist on. And before you wonder your precious purple head about it, know that if you don't comply, the money will go to *them.*" Richard looks up from the letter and slowly sweeps his gaze across the room. And I just *know* Uncle Jack wrote something telling Richard to do that. He looks back down to the letter. "Before I tell you *the what*, ask me how much."

The lawyer lifts his eyes to mine.

I lower my fingers to my chin. "How much?"

He holds eye contact. "Two million."

I blink.

I swallow.

I choke on my inhale.

"Dollars?"

The edge of Richard's mouth pulls up into a smirk. And that look... That look tells me he wasn't just Uncle Jack's lawyer. He was his friend. *His family.*

"Dollars." He confirms with a nod. Then he lowers his eyes to the paper again. "Now ask me what you have to do."

I can feel the outrage pouring off my family members.

Can feel the tension ready to burst through the room.

*Two. Million. Dollars.*

*How on earth did Uncle Jack have two million dollars?*

I slide my hand lower, until it's covering my throat. "What do I have to do?"

*Uncle Jack loved me.*

*He's leaving all of this to me.*

*He won't make me do something awful.*

*He just won't.*

Richard's gaze slides over the paper as he reads. "You must be married. By your thirtieth birthday."

My thirtieth birthday.

The one on Tuesday.

"What?" The question comes out quieter than a whisper.

I have five days.

If I can count today. And my birthday. I have five days to find someone to marry me.

I slump in my seat, squishing my little backpack between my body and the chair.

My mother stands.

Ralph steps closer to the desk.

Shouts fill the room.

But instead of listening, I close my eyes and focus on breathing.

*Two million dollars.*

I part my lips and pull in deeper breaths.

Two million, and if I don't get married in the next five days, it goes to these people.

These horrible, selfish, greedy people.

*He knew.*

Uncle Jack *knew.*

If the money were to go anywhere else—charity, *strangers*—I wouldn't stand in the way. I wouldn't force some random person to marry me. I'd let the money go. I'd let it go literally anywhere. Except to these people.

These undeserving, hateful people.

A sound gets trapped in my throat, and I don't know if it's humor or horror.

I shake my head.

*Well played, Uncle Jack.*

The movement dislodges something from my hair, and I open my eyes just in time to catch the sunglasses as they slide off my head.

I gently grip the shiny metal frame.

And I stare at myself in the reflection of the lenses.

*Ethan's* lenses.

I pull in another ragged breath.

Uncle Jack gave me his house.

He befriended the park ranger next door.

He told Ethan about *Matty.*

He knew Ethan would come by. That we'd meet.

Uncle Jack hired Ethan to fly me to this meeting.

Hired him to drive me to *this meeting.*

This meeting, where I'd hear his demand of marriage.

Uncle Jack knew Ethan would be here with me.

Arranged it that way.

The sound crawls out of my chest again.

Uncle Jack knew exactly how this would go down.

He set it up perfectly.

Set *me* up perfectly.

I blink at my reflection.

*Well played, Maestro.*

Except... It only works if Ethan agrees.

*And why would Ethan agree?*

Richard blows his whistle.

Silence falls.

And everyone turns to me.

I sit up straight.

I lift my gaze.

*I think about the way Ethan kisses me.*

*I think about the way he felt on top of me.*

*I think about the way he holds my hand.*

*And I decide to bet it all on Ethan Grant.*

Clearing my throat, I stand. "Marriage won't be an issue. My fiancé is sitting in the hall."

The shouting starts again.

# CHAPTER 62

## ETHAN

I CLENCH MY HANDS INTO FISTS ON TOP OF MY THIGHS.

This bench is uncomfortable, but the uneven boards below my ass aren't enough to distract me from the shouts and the fucking shrill whistle sounds coming from the lawyer's office.

I should've gone in there with Tilda.

Should've insisted.

Because whatever is going down isn't going down smoothly.

Obviously, her nasty family members weren't going to be happy about Tilda inheriting everything. Or almost everything.

But to yell?

I'm a bastard. A grumpy piece of shit most of the time. But I can't imagine a single scenario that would make me shout at a family member.

That whistle sounds again, and I turn my head toward the closed door.

*How loud must that be inside the fucking office?*

Silence follows.

I glance down at my watch.

The plane should be refueled and ready to go by now.

I'll see if Tilda wants to do a quick stop for food on the way back to the airport. Maybe I'll take her to that burrito place I like. We can get them to go. Eat them in the air above the clouds.

It's my favorite meal.

And when we're back home, maybe I can ask to come over.

Maybe we can—

The door to the office swings open and slams into the wall.

My wildlife training once again comes in handy as I don't react to the stampede of Wrights—or whatever their names are—as they pour out into the hall.

And head straight for me.

Slowly, I straighten my spine and loosen my fists.

"Is this him?" One of the horrible women points at me. "I thought this was your driver."

Ignoring her, I keep my attention on the door.

More people file out.

But none of them are my girl.

My jaw clenches.

But then pretty purple hair appears, and I stand.

Her eyes are wide.

Her teeth are digging into her lower lip.

And her fingers are twisted into the top tier of her skirt.

*Matilda is nervous.*

*And I don't like that.*

The need to be near her takes over, and I step forward.

Tilda's mother moves to stand right beside her daughter.

Matilda still looks worried. And stressed. But my Firecracker shoots a glare at her mother before taking a step to the side, so their shoulders are no longer touching.

But then Tilda's mother puts her hands on her hips, flaring her elbows out so she's once again touching her daughter.

Before she can lose it, I reach out and grip Tilda's wrist, causing her to let go of her skirt.

I tug her to me, and Tilda moves so she's standing at my side.

Close enough that our arms touch.

Her mother flits her gaze down to where I'm still holding

Tilda's wrist. Then she narrows her eyes at me. "Are you really here to marry Matilda?"

Under my hold, Tilda's muscles twitch.

But I continue to stare at her mother.

*Am I really here to marry Matilda?*

She's not saying it like some wild guess.

She's saying it like an allegation.

Like Matilda told her that's what I'm here for.

*Am I here to marry Matilda?*

Her skin is warm against mine, and I can feel her pulse thumping under my touch.

I remember the feel of her under me.

I remember the sounds she made against my mouth.

I remember the way she reached for me when she was scared on the plane.

And I remember Jack asking me to keep an eye on his Matty.

Remember his letter.

So, if Tilda is claiming that we're here to get married...

I slide my grip lower, so our hands are palm to palm. "What business is it of yours?"

Tilda reaches across her body and grips our combined hands with her free one. "Mother, I already told you. We're getting married this weekend."

"Where?" The older woman glares at us.

"Again," I say slowly, like she didn't understand the words last time. "What business is it of yours?"

Mother Wright presses a hand to her chest. "If you think I'm going to allow you to marry my daughter—"

"Allow me?" I give my head a slow shake as the side of my mouth pulls up into a smirk. "That's not how this works."

The woman sneers at me. "If you think—"

"I think that for as long as I've known Tilda, I've never met you." She doesn't know the length of time is approximately a week. And she doesn't ask. She just assumes. I drop my smirk. "So

I hardly think your permission or blessing or even *presence* is of importance here."

Mother Wright looks like she wants to claw my eyes out.

I have half a heartbeat to wonder if I've gone too far, but then Tilda makes a little squeaking sound. And I know it's her suppressing a laugh.

Knowing I haven't offended Tilda, and taking it as permission to keep being a dick, my body relaxes.

The other woman, who I believe is Tilda's aunt, crosses her arms. "We're coming as witnesses."

Tilda's purple curls brush my arm as she shakes her head. "No. I don't want any of you there."

One of the older men gasps.

I look down at Tilda. "Are they always this horrible?"

Her eyes are filled with an emotion that looks a lot like appreciation as she meets my gaze. "Always."

I make a sound. "I see why you've never introduced us."

Someone new gasps this time, and I lift a brow.

Tilda presses her lips together.

"We aren't just going to take your word for it, Ma-tilda. So if you're going to insist on marrying this man, then we're going to insist on being your witnesses." Disdain laces each of her mother's words.

Tilda and I continue to look at each other.

"Will they stick around if we wait to get married tomorrow, as planned?" I ask, assuming a Saturday wedding was a part of the lie.

Tilda blows out a breath as she nods. "Afraid so."

Something happened in that room, with that lawyer, that is making it imperative for us to marry.

Or, at least, for Tilda to marry.

And I'm here.

The only option.

Convenient.

I stare into her captivating eyes. And I don't have to take time to think about it. If Tilda has to get married, she's not getting married to anyone else.

This might be an irrational decision, but whatever we do can be undone.

And if it can't...

I flex my fingers around hers.

"It's up to you, Firecracker. We marry tomorrow and have these clowns on our heels for twenty-four hours. Or we can find the closest chapel and get married right now."

"Threat to the natural order?" she whispers up at me.

I dip my chin. "Every damn day."

Her nose flares as she inhales.

I've never been able to read anyone like I can read Tilda.

Her eyes are filling with hesitancy. And I know she wants to talk to me. I can feel her need to explain herself.

But we can't do that here. Not in front of her family.

So, I raise my brows. "Today, then?"

The tip of her pink tongue slides out and wets her lips. "You're sure?"

*Sure I want to call you Wife?*

*Sure I want to drag my thumb across your lip where your tongue just was?*

*Sure I want to be reckless in a way I've never been reckless before?*

*Sure I want to be your Good Boy...*

I lean in closer until our mouths are just inches apart. "I'm sure, Starlight."

Tilda squeezes my hand, and her exhale dances across my lips.

"How do we know this isn't some kinda setup?" A male voice cuts into our moment.

I turn to face the man.

He's in his thirties.

Average like the rest of this group.

I tip my head toward the man. "This him?"

Tilda sighs. "Yeah. That's my cousin Ralph."
I hum. Then I let go of Tilda's hand.

# CHAPTER 63

## TILDA

ETHAN STOPS A FOOT AWAY FROM RALPH.

And I swallow.

Ethan dwarfs him.

His height. His muscles. His aura of intensity.

Ralph has to tip his chin up to maintain eye contact.

And I wish so badly that I could take a photo of this moment without breaking it.

"I had a cousin." Ethan's tone is conversational as he unbuttons one cuff. He shrugs and starts to roll up his sleeve. "Second cousin, technically. Last I heard, he went missing in Eastern Europe. That was a few years back. Might still be alive. If anyone could do it, it'd be him."

Ethan shifts and works on his other sleeve.

Ralph takes a step back. "What does your missing cousin have to do with anything?"

"When I was a kid, my parents left me in his care for a weekend. He took me hunting." Ethan takes a step forward. "I was too small to carry a rifle, so he gave me a knife. And when he shot a deer, he taught me how to clean it. I slaughtered the second one on my own. In under ten minutes." Ethan slides his hands into his pockets. "I cut myself a few times, trying to work that fast. Blood makes things... slippery."

Ralph tries to take another step back, but bumps into his father. "W-what's the point of this story?"

Ethan leans a little closer. "You remind me of that weekend."

Ralph makes a squawking sound.

*Holy. Crap.*

I run my damp palms down my skirt.

*Did I just get turned on by watching Ethan threaten Ralph?*

Ethan turns back to me. "Your mom and one other person can come as witness."

My aunt steps forward. "I'll go."

She says it like it's a sacrifice. And not something she's volunteering to do.

"Fine." Ethan holds his hand out to me.

I wrap my fingers around his. And I let him lead me down the hall, back the way we came, to the main entrance of the building.

My family members clamber behind us, running back into the office, gathering the items they left strewn around.

"Ethan." I keep my voice low as I give his hand a tug. "I can—"

"We'll talk on the plane." His voice is just as low.

I want to tell him about the letter.

Explain myself.

*Ask him why the heck he'd agree to marry a practical stranger, no questions asked.*

But I keep my lips pressed together because I can hear footsteps approaching, and I know there's no time.

Ethan looks over my head, back down the hall. "They really are awful. No wonder Jack only ever talked about you."

Warmth spreads through my chest.

That isn't exactly a compliment, since it'd be hard to be worse than them. But it's still a nice thing to say. And a good reminder that Uncle Jack might've been out of line with this marriage request. But he still loved me.

I almost smile.

Then I remember I'm forcing an innocent man to marry a girl he doesn't really know.

A girl who comes with horrible in-laws.

The almost smile disappears.

Ethan pulls his phone out of his pocket with his free hand. Then he flexes his fingers around mine. "Move your hand to my elbow."

I glance up at him. "Huh?"

He lets go of my hand, then bends his arm. "Hold my elbow. I need both hands."

I shift closer to Ethan. Then I reach up and hook my hand into the crook of his bent elbow.

I lean against his arm and watch him search for a *chapel*, then select walking directions for the closest option.

*Fairytale Chapel.*

Pulling the aviators off the top of my head, I slide them on.

We walked into this building less than thirty minutes ago. And now we're about to walk out so we can get married at the *Fairytale Chapel.*

*Fairytale.*

I blink behind the dark lenses.

Honestly, I didn't think I'd ever get married. No particular reason why. I just haven't really been lucky in the love department. So... I assumed.

But I'm a lover of dresses. And sparkly things And love stories...

So even though I didn't think I'd ever be walking down the aisle, I still imagined it.

What I'd wear.

What flowers I'd have.

The sort of man I'd marry.

I sneak a look at Ethan.

His boots match mine. Only his are functional. Broken in. And... huge.

But everything above that... we're opposites.

He's big and gruff and strong.

I'm short and soft and still working on being assertive.

Ethan slips his phone back into his pocket, having apparently memorized the directions. Then he reaches out and shoves the front door open, holding it so I can walk through ahead of him.

Releasing my hold of him, I do. And then I look back just in time to see him let go of the door after he steps through, not holding it for my approaching family.

I bite my lip to keep from laughing.

It would probably come out hysterical. And I'm afraid if I lose my composure now, I may never regain it.

Ethan glances down at me, then, as is becoming our habit, he holds his hand out, and I take it.

He dips his chin, and as the door reopens behind us, we descend the steps to the sidewalk.

We stay quiet as we retrace our steps and pass the parking ramp.

I have so many things I want to say. To ask. But Ethan is right, we can talk later.

After we get married.

I grip Ethan's hand tighter as stress fills my body.

He's being so cool about all this.

And I know we can just get a divorce. There was nothing in the letter about length of time.

I tighten my hold on Ethan's hand even more when I remember that it did mention a time period.

It said I'd get the money on each birthday, over four years.

*What if I need to be married for four years?*

I can't do that to Ethan.

Can't make him give up four years of his life.

*Maybe I can offer him a cut of the money.*

I roll my lips together.

What amount of money would be appropriate? Ten percent? Fifty?

*Am I supposed to let him date other people?*

My stress turns to nausea.

I'll do just about anything to keep this marriage legal if it means keeping Uncle Jack's money out of the claws of my family. But the idea of watching Ethan date other people while pretending he cares about me... I don't think I could do that.

*Maybe I just need to be married? Maybe the person doesn't matter?*

I could divorce Ethan when he wants to break up and then find someone else to marry before my next birthday.

Ethan's thumb drags against the back of my hand.

I look up at him.

"On the plane."

As always, he can read me too easily.

I blow out a breath, then nod.

Ethan comes to a stop, and I stop beside him. In front of a light blue door under a pink neon sign that reads *Fairytale Chapel*.

"One last question." Ethan keeps his voice low, just for me.

Internally, I brace myself.

Ethan lets go of my hand, then reaches up and carefully removes my sunglasses.

With the dark lenses gone, I'm sure he can see the worry in my eyes.

He turns the glasses around, then puts them on top of my head, how I had them before.

Then he holds my gaze.

It's intense.

*He's* intense.

But the longer I look into his dual-colored eyes, the calmer I feel.

And even though I don't know him well, I trust him.

I can feel his trustworthiness.

He's someone I can count on.

Maybe not to be my *one and only forever and ever.* But I can count on Ethan to do the right thing.

I can count on him to protect me against the feral herd behind us.

"What's the question?"

He wraps his fingers around my wrist, sliding his grip down until our fingers are entwined again. "You okay with drive-thru burritos for our wedding lunch? We can eat them in the air."

His words enter my mind slowly.

But as they register, my lips pull up into a smile. "Honestly? That sounds perfect."

An elaborate plated dinner was my childhood fantasy. But burritos, in a plane, over the mountains, as we flee my family after a hasty Vegas wedding... not a bad second choice.

The blue door opens. And Dolly Parton steps out.

My eyes widen.

"You Matty and Ethan?" Her voice gets less confident as she looks between us.

And as I look at her, I realize I'm a doorknob and she's a Dolly Parton look-alike.

Though with the way today is going, getting married by a superstar would hardly be the biggest surprise.

Then, like Ethan's lunch question, Dolly's sinks in.

*Did she just ask for us by name?*

Ethan and I look at each other, then back at Dolly.

I lift the hand not holding Ethan's and wave. "I'm Matty."

Dolly sighs. "Oh, a straight wedding. Okay."

She couldn't sound more disappointed. And I have to fight not to laugh.

"Wait." Aunt Gunnie steps up right behind us. "I thought their wedding was scheduled for tomorrow."

For once, Aunt Gunnie has something useful to point out. Because yes, the fake wedding I lied about was *scheduled* for tomorrow. At a nonexistent wedding chapel.

"Nope." Dolly pops the *p*. "Today's the day. And right on time."

*Uncle Jack.*

"Jack," Ethan huffs as I think about the same man.

We glance at each other again, and I'm glad he came to the same conclusion.

It would be easy for Ethan to pin this on me. Accuse me of setting it all up. For who-knows-what reason. But people have gotten angry at me over less.

The more Uncle Jack weaves his web, the more I wish I'd known him better.

I can't imagine the emotions someone must go through when they choose to pass the way Uncle Jack did.

I can't imagine approaching my death willingly and not being terrified.

But this...

I look around at the colorful interior of the small chapel as we follow Dolly inside.

This plan... This scheme that Uncle Jack put together...

I bet he was grinning.

*I hope he was with someone he loved.*

I hope they gave him peace.

But I bet Uncle Jack thought about this moment before he closed his eyes for the last time.

I bet he thought of me, on my wedding day, stunned and stressed and still going through with it. Because amassing that sort of money and giving it all to me, that was the biggest *fuck you* he ever could've landed on our family.

Humor and glee and sadness braid themselves around my heart.

But I still walk forward.

"No," Ethan snaps, looking behind us. "The mother and the aunt. The rest of you wait outside."

Glee grows inside my chest, and for this moment, I let it win. Because I can see it.

When Ethan yells at my family, I can see why Uncle Jack liked him so much.

# Chapter 64

## Ethan

The Dolly Parton impersonator shook our hands, gave our phones to her assistant so he could use them to take photos, then handed Tilda a bouquet of fake roses.

They're pretty enough. But you can tell they aren't real.

I glare at the roses. The reddish-orange color isn't bad, but it's not right.

Tilda should have pretty purple flowers for her wedding.

Jack clearly laid this whole trap out for us to spring, and we sprang it, so it seems the least he could do is get the fucking flowers right.

But then I take the whole of Tilda in. The frilly yellow dress. The wavy hair I want wrapped around my fist. The boots and the way her cheeks are blushing pink.

I guess the roses work.

"Do you want a matching boutonniere?"

I drag my eyes up to meet Tilda's and shake my head at her question.

"You sure?" She gives me a soft smile. "The color would match your shirt."

I look down at my red flannel. And realize my buttons are still half undone.

"Shit." I quickly do up the buttons.

Tilda snickers. "You could've left it open."

"No, I could not." I smooth down the material. "I might be wearing an old flannel shirt to our spur-of-the-moment wedding, but I will not have my chest out."

Tilda snorts. "Chest out?"

"What else would you call it?" I roll my shoulders back, feeling claustrophobic in this narrow, low-ceilinged room.

The walls are covered in more fake flowers. Making the space even narrower. The carpet is a light blue that I bet matches the front door. And the pews, that can fit maybe two people each, are neon pink.

It's chaos.

"I'd call it hot."

My gaze snaps back to Tilda.

She's always so free with her compliments, but it still takes me by surprise every time.

I should tell her how pretty she looks.

*Should've already done that.*

But if I say it now, it won't feel sincere.

I shift closer to her. "I'll unbutton it again as soon as we're done."

Tilda lifts the bouquet to cover her smile. Then her brows go up as I watch her sniff the fake flowers. "These smell like roses."

She holds them up for me, and I lean down, inhaling. Then I shrug. "I like the way you smell better."

Satisfaction flows through me at her stunned expression, glad I was able to get my own compliment in.

I reach up and tap her chin. "Close your mouth, Firecracker. It's not the honeymoon yet."

Tilda's mother gasps from somewhere nearby, but I ignore her and wink at my soon-to-be wife.

# CHAPTER 65

## TILDA

HEAT FLARES ACROSS MY SKIN AS I KEEP STARING UP AT Ethan.

*I can't believe he just said that.*

"Alrighty." Dolly steps back into the room. "If everyone is ready."

Standing at the back of the room, we face forward. And "I Will Always Love You" starts to play through the speakers in the ceiling.

The whole situation is borderline insane. Add in Ethan making comments about my mouth and a honeymoon. Then finish it off with a classic song about love... My nervous system doesn't know what to do with itself.

Ethan gently grips my elbow and lifts my arm out to my side, with my hands still clutching the roses before me, and he hooks his arm through mine. Then we start down the short aisle.

I know it's all fake.

I know that even if the license is real, the marriage isn't.

I *know* all that.

But I still feel a slight thrill of excitement over the fact that I'm marrying this man.

This rugged, handsome, stern Good Boy.

And even if it's all for show... There's nothing stopping us from having a little staycation bedroom honeymoon when we get home.

*Maybe it's romance.*

*Maybe it's trauma bonding.*

We stop before Dolly, a flower-covered podium between us.

I glance down, expecting to see a bible on the surface, but it's a Dolly Parton cookbook.

I bite my lip, a grin of absurdity fighting to break through.

The volume lowers, but the song keeps playing.

Dolly smiles at us, her hands extended toward us, palms up. "Did you come with your own vows?"

"No." Ethan's tone is serious. "We prefer a traditional ceremony."

I bite my lip harder as laughter vibrates through my body.

Dolly dips her chin and lowers her arms. "Completely understandable." Then she opens the cookbook.

# CHAPTER 66

## ETHAN

"I DO." TILDA'S VOICE IS STEADY AS SHE PROMISES TO always love me.

And I know it's fake.

Know it's not real.

But having this Mountain Fairy promise to be mine forever...

My chest expands on a deep inhale.

As Dolly lists off my requirements, I focus on the feeling of Tilda beside me.

Focus on the warmth of her arm against mine.

Focus on the way she leans into me.

And it might be a setup. Some elaborate game laid out by a dead man.

But, as I focus on the way I feel, I decide I don't care.

I don't care if it's fake.

I want it.

I want Matilda Iris Wright.

"And do you, Ethan Ford Grant, promise—"

"I do."

It doesn't matter what the rest of that sentence was going to be.

I'll do it.

Dolly makes a sound of appreciation. "Then I command you to be husband and wife, for the rest of this ever after. You may kiss your bride."

I slide my arm free, face Tilda, grip her shoulders, and turn her to me.

My wife's eyes are wide.

A little startled.

I slide one hand up the back of her neck and into her hair.

I curl my fingers into the strands, tugging just a bit, tilting her face up.

Then I kiss my bride.

# CHAPTER 67

## TILDA

HIS LIPS PRESS AGAINST MINE, AND FIREWORKS IGNITE
in my blood.

Ethan's hold on my hair is a delicious pull, and I arch
into him.

His tongue presses into my mouth, and I open.

I take him in.

I let the flowers get crushed between our bodies as we shift
closer.

Ethan spreads his other hand across the bare skin of my upper
back.

And I wish we were going to a hotel instead of an airplane
hangar after this.

I moan around Ethan's tongue.

"That's quite enough," Mother hisses from her pew.

Ethan's lips pull up into a smile against mine.

I smile too. Unable to stop myself.

Ethan pulls back, but instead of straightening, he lowers his
head and presses his open mouth to the top swell of my breast
above the low-cut neckline of my dress.

"Ethan," I gasp and let go of my flowers with one hand, grabbing on to his shirt for balance.

The volume of the song, which is apparently on repeat, increases.

I let my eyes close.

Ethan lifts his mouth from my chest.

His lips softly press against mine.

I open my eyes.

Ethan's exhale is warm against my lips. "Ready to go, Wife?"

*Wife.*

Ethan slides his fingers down the back of my neck as he removes his hand from my hair, sending a shiver down my spine.

My aunt whispers something to my mom, reminding me of our audience.

Playing along, I give the front of his shirt a light tug. "Yes. Now, be a good husband and take me home."

He doesn't smile at my words. He clenches his jaw.

And I'm more than ready to go home. Because no matter how we got here, the attraction between us is real.

Ethan drags his gaze down my body, and I feel it like a rough caress.

*Yeah. The attraction is real.*

# CHAPTER 68

## ETHAN

THE NAVIGATION SCREEN FLICKERS.

I narrow my eyes.

Our flight so far has been uneventful.

Easy sailing.

We ate our al pastor burritos after we got to altitude.

And before Tilda fell asleep in the copilot seat, she told me a few stories about Jack causing havoc at family gatherings when she was a kid.

We talked about what it was like living in Vegas.

We talked about a few things. But not the wedding.

Not the clearly set-up situation we found ourselves in.

I can still feel her lips against mine.

Can still hear her asking me to be a *good husband*.

And goddamn... this girl has my number. Because just thinking about how those words sounded coming out of her mouth has my blood flowing south.

I shift in my seat, not sure why I'm even trying to lie to myself.

My dick has been half hard since it was first suggested that I was going to marry Matilda Wright today.

The screen flickers again.

I focus back on my immediate task of flying us over the Rocky Mountains.

The weather is currently clear. But weather is tricky out here. It can change with little notice.

I look out the left window, then I turn my head to the right, looking past Tilda, out her window.

The skies are clear.

The screen flickers.

The engine stutters.

Then the engine quits.

Stops.

Goes quiet.

And the screen goes black.

*That's not good.*

# Chapter 69

## Tilda

My eyes blink open, and I look at the blue sky stretching before me.

The plane shakes, like we're flying through turbulence, but it stops a moment later.

I yawn.

I didn't mean to fall asleep. But seeing my family always exhausts me. And I didn't sleep well last night since I was stressing about today.

*Today. Who could've seen that coming?*

I shift in my seat, opening my mouth to ask Ethan how much time is left, when I notice something.

The quiet

The lack of rumble.

I stare out the windshield at the propeller.

It's spinning.

*Is it going slower?*

"Ethan?"

He's doing something to something on the complicated dashboard. The dashboard with a blank screen in the middle.

I lift one side of my headphones.

It's too quiet.

"Ethan?" Panic laces my tone.

He sighs and drops his hand from the dials back to the steering wheel thing.

"Ethan?" I whisper it this time.

He looks at me. His dark glasses block me from seeing his full expression. But he doesn't look worried.

*Maybe it's fine? Maybe I just thought it was loud before because I was nervous.*

"We're going to land," Ethan says calmly.

And I look forward, back out the windshield.

But there's nothing.

No airfield.

No city.

Just mountains and an endless forest.

I try to keep my voice even. "Where?"

"Up ahead. There's a strip of clear land beside a stream."

My heartbeat starts to dance. "Why?"

Ethan sighs again. Like he's annoyed. "Because the engine stopped."

*Because. The engine. Stopped.*

I look back out the front. "But... the propeller..."

It's still spinning. I can see it.

"The air is pushing it."

My next breath is choppy.

*The air...*

*It's just spinning.*

*The engine stopped.*

I clutch at my seat belt, gripping the straps over my chest tightly. "We're going to crash?"

"No." His tone is stern, and I focus on his mouth. "We're going to land."

My throat feels so tight it hurts to swallow. "Ethan."

"Starlight. Remember what I told you?"

I shake my head.

"I'm a good pilot. Remember?"

I nod. "I remember."

But remembering doesn't stop my hands from trembling.

"Relax." He holds his hand out. "Breathe." I force my fingers to release the seat belt and put my hand in his. "I'm going to land us smoothly." He sets my hand on his thigh. "Now you say it."

I press my palm down against the warm denim. "You're going to land us smoothly."

I repeat that sentence in my mind. Over and over.

And I try to tell myself to be calm.

I try to keep my breathing even.

But then Ethan pushes the control forward, and the nose of the plane angles down.

Toward the ground.

My pulse feels too loud.

I dig my fingertips into Ethan's thigh and curl my other hand tighter around my seat belt.

I hold my breath.

"Breathe." Ethan's voice speaks directly into my ears.

I inhale.

The ground is getting closer.

The trees are becoming more defined.

I look out the side window.

My heart stutters.

We're below the mountaintops.

There's nowhere to go but down.

"Relax." Ethan sounds just as calm as he did before. "I need you to breathe and relax."

I try.

I drag in a lungful of air.

We're getting lower.

A sound of distress tangles in my chest.

"Repeat what I told you."

I struggle with another breath.

I can see the stretch of grassy land next to the river below.

It's mostly bare. Looks like smooth earth. But it looks too small.

It looks too short.

And too far away.

"Wife. Repeat what I told you." Ethan's voice is louder this time, pulling my attention to his profile.

I look at his jawline.

Look at the way his wavy hair curls around his headphones.

I glance at his tattooed forearms, the muscles shifting as he controls the plane.

I purse my lips, and my inhale doesn't rattle as much this time. "You're going to land us smoothly."

Ethan turns his head toward me. "I'll never let anything happen to you, Starlight."

I bite my lip.

"Tell me."

"You'll never let anything happen to me."

"Never."

Heat stings the corner of my eyes, but Ethan can't see it through my aviators. And I'm glad.

Because I can't distract Ethan.

Not when he's about to... land us smoothly.

*Please, gods, let him land us smoothly.*

I face forward, keeping my hand on his thigh, and I try to relax.

The clouds are above us now.

I try so hard to relax.

The plane vibrates through a patch of rough air.

I try really hard to relax.

But it's not possible.

So I fake it.

I keep my lips parted and my inhales quiet.

I trap my little backpack between my boots on the floor.

And I squeeze the hell out of my seat belt but try to keep the hand on Ethan's thigh steady.

And we go lower.

Ethan stays silent.

The ground gets closer.

The forest spreads out on either side of us.

Mountains surround us.

I can make out rocks jutting from the water below on my side of the plane.

We're going too fast.

It feels like we're going too fast.

But I can't close my eyes.

I didn't look the first time, when we landed in Vegas. I didn't look because I was scared. I didn't watch Ethan land the plane.

But now, as the forest floor rushes up below us, I can't look away.

I can't close my eyes.

My mouth is painfully dry.

My palm aches where the seat belt is digging into it.

The plane tilts to the left. To the right.

My muscles tighten.

The ground is so close.

We tilt left, to the right again.

The ground is filling the windshield.

"Relax, Matilda."

Ethan's voice is strong and steady.

I exhale.

I force my limbs to relax.

The nose of the plane tips up.

My next breath catches.

And then the plane touches down.

Our tires connect with the ground.

We're still going too fast.

*We have to be going too fast.*

Ethan's thigh shifts beneath my hand as he depresses the brakes.

We start to slow.

The ground dips.

We bounce.

I press my lips together and swallow the distress trying to crawl out of my throat.

We slow a little more.

The stretch of clear land narrows ahead of us.

The river turns.

The trees get closer on Ethan's side.

The sound claws at my throat.

"Counts as smooth," Ethan grits out through my headphones. "But this part won't be."

"What—"

Then I see it.

The lone tree.

It's not huge.

But it's not small enough.

We're going to—

The tip of Ethan's wing slams into the trunk.

A sound escapes my chest.

And the collision forces the plane to swing toward the forest.

My eyes finally squeeze shut.

We rock.

And then we... stop.

I force my eyes open.

We're facing the thick tree line. But it's still yards away.

We... landed.

*We hit a tree.*

But we landed.

Warm fingers wrap around my wrist, and I look down.

Ethan has reached across, and he's prying my hand away from the seat belt.

I let him.

And I let him turn my hand over.

He holds my wrist with one hand and uses the other to trace the indents left in my palm.

"Bad Girl. I told you to relax." His voice vibrates through the headphones. "No more hurting yourself. I told you I wouldn't let anything happen to you. Don't make me a liar."

Heat trails across my skin where he touches me.

He lowers my hand to my lap, then reaches across and unclips my seat belt.

Glancing at his chest, I see he's already unbuckled himself.

My heart is still beating wildly behind my ribs, and when I look out his window, I swallow.

The tip of the wing is all smashed up and somehow still stuck to the tree trunk.

A memory of being a kid, roller skating, and holding my friend's hand as she swung me around in a circle flashes in my mind.

Only today, the tree is my friend, and the plane is the roller skates.

"Arms," Ethan softly commands.

I shift and let him help me slide my arms free from the straps.

"Look at me." Ethan reaches up and takes his sunglasses off.

I do the same.

Or I try to.

But my hands are shaking too badly.

*Why can't I stop shaking?*

Ethan makes a shushing sound and takes my glasses off for me.

I know my eyes are shining.

I know a few tears have slipped free.

His brows furrow, and holding both our sunglasses in one hand, he smooths a thumb across the rounded part of my cheek. "Don't be scared, Starlight."

"I-I'm okay." I take a slow breath. "I'm okay." I say it with more conviction this time.

"Yes, you are. And you're going to keep being okay." He pulls his hand away from my face, giving one of my curls a light tug as he lowers his hand. "I have a satellite phone. I'm going to make a call while I pack us a bag. Then we need to go."

I blink at him.

*Need to go?*

Slowly, I turn my head to look out the windshield. At the forest.

At the mountains beyond.

At the *nothing but wilderness*.

My pulse doubles.

*We're stranded.*

I was so concerned with landing. With *not dying*. I didn't think...

My hands start to shake again.

I didn't think about the *where*.

I didn't think about the fact that we just crashed a plane in the middle of the Rocky freaking Mountains.

Fingers grip my chin. And Ethan turns my face back toward his. "Matilda. I won't let anything happen to you."

"We-we were in a plane crash," I whisper.

He shakes his head. "We experienced a controlled emergency landing."

"But..."

"The tree hit *us*. But we're fine. You're fine."

A sliver of humor—or mania—cracks through my wall of panic. "Rude of the tree."

"Incredibly." His eyes trace over my features. "I'm sorry," he whispers.

I look back out his window at the tree that dared to hit our wing. Then I meet his gaze. "You did a very good job crashing the plane."

His tongue presses against the inside of his cheek. "Controlled emergency landing."

I nod. "Right. Controlled emergency crash landing." My sliver of humor slips away. "What do we do now?"

Ethan drags his fingers down the front of my throat before

dropping his hand. "Now, you grab your little backpack while I make a call. Then we start walking."

I swallow. "We can't stay here?"

It's not that I can't walk. It's just that I have no idea how to survive in the Colorado wilderness.

Assuming we're in Colorado. Not that the state matters. I don't know anything about surviving in any wilderness.

"There's a cabin a few miles from here. And if we leave now, we'll get there before dark."

The mention of *dark* has my heart thudding all over again.

I don't want to walk through the woods. But the idea of sitting here, with the windows surrounding us showing nothing but darkness...

"Is it safe?"

"Park ranger, remember?" Ethan lifts a brow as he reminds me of his profession.

*Right.*

I nod. "I guess if there's anyone to crash in the mountains with, it'd be you."

"Not a crash."

# CHAPTER 70

## ETHAN

TILDA IS HUMMING TO HERSELF ON THE OTHER SIDE OF the plane.

I helped her down, then she said she would reorganize the items in her tiny backpack so she could fit the sunglasses and the water bottle in it.

I told her I have a large backpack that can fit everything. But she insisted on helping.

*I'll take the bag from her later.*

There's a compartment in the rear of the plane that has my backpack, a few items of clothing, a handgun, a flare gun, and most importantly, a satellite phone.

I don't know what the fuck happened to my plane, but her radio is of no use anymore.

There's no cell service here, so my phone is also worthless, but before I power it down to save the battery, I pull up a contact I've never used before and type the number into the sat phone.

It rings twice.

"Who the hell is this?"

"Ethan Grant. Is this Stoleman?"

"I'm not great with names."

I roll my eyes. "We met at Peaks Airport, west of Colorado Springs. You told me to call if I needed anything."

The man on the other end of the line makes a humming sound. "Okay, ringing a bell. You the ranger?"

"Yeah."

"And what is it that you need?"

"An extraction."

"From a hot zone?"

He asks the question casually, and I lift a brow.

"From the Rockies. Had to put my plane down when the engine quit."

"Well, shit. Damage?"

I sigh, looking at my poor wing. "Clipped a tree with my wing. Even if I had power and a runway, she's not flying."

"Bummer." It's kind of a dick thing to say, but Stoleman sounds sincere. "What're you transporting?"

*Transporting. Hot zones. I thought this guy seemed a little shady. And I was right.*

"I'm not transporting anything."

"Okay." He says it like he absolutely doesn't believe me.

Tilda's humming changes to singing, just loud enough for me to hear.

"My wife is with me." The words taste good as I say them.

Tilda's off-key note falters.

An unexpected urge to smile tugs at the corner of my mouth.

I can't believe I had to put my plane down

Can't believe my wing got fucked up.

Can't believe that the first time Tilda put her safety in my hands, I failed spectacularly.

And yet... If I'm going to be stranded in the woods, headed to a secluded cabin in the middle of nowhere, there's no one I'd rather be with.

And not just that there's no one else I'd prefer. I'm glad she's with me. Being with Tilda is better than being alone.

I swallow. The urge to smile fades.

I like her.

I like the way I feel when I'm around her.

Tilda starts humming again.

It's still off-key. And it's perfect.

I like her a fucking lot.

"So..." Stoleman sounds legitimately confused. "You're not being shot at. And you got nothing but your lady with you. You just need, what, a ride home?"

"Pretty much."

He huffs out a laugh. "This is gonna be an expensive ride."

I shrug. "Figured as much."

"There a reason you're willing to pay top dollar for a private ride out rather than calling the *proper authorities*?"

It's a fair question. So I answer him. "I believe I'm on national land. And the place I'm heading to definitely is."

"Oh?" Stoleman's interest is piqued. "And where are you heading?"

"To my cabin." I tip my head to the side. "One of them."

"And this cabin you own, it's in a national forest?"

"Yep."

"You *are* a park ranger, right?"

"Yep."

"So you know that's like *super* illegal, yeah?"

I roll my eyes again. "I got the impression that wouldn't bother you."

The man chuckles. "Why, Ranger Grant, whatever gave you that impression?"

Stoleman and I met one night last fall.

It was late. Past dark. And I'd never seen him there before.

He was in the hangar next to mine, and we closed our doors at the same time. Done for the night.

He was dressed in all black, carrying a large duffel, and I introduced myself.

When we shook hands, I noted the smoke smell.

Bonfire. Not cigarette.

I asked if he took the lease out on the hangar beside mine. He told me it belonged to a buddy of his, but he was in town for the weekend and keeping an eye on things.

We exchanged numbers. And went our own ways.

I haven't seen him since.

Not sure his friend even still has a plane there.

"There won't be a strip for landing," I tell him. "It'll have to be a chopper. Not your friend's plane."

Stoleman grunts. "That's back up north. But I know a guy with a helicopter."

"Good."

"Hmm, what time is it?" Something creaks, like Stoleman's shifting in a chair. "Dude's kinda old. And he never does anything the next day. But if you can hold tight until Sunday, I can tell him to pick you up at noon."

"That'll work. Ready for the coordinates?"

Furniture creaks again. "Ready."

I tell Stoleman the memorized coordinates.

"You got food? Or do you need the pilot to bring calories?"

"We'll be fine."

"If you say so." I hear a door open and close. "This a sat phone number?"

"Yeah."

"I'll call tomorrow at noon if there's a change of plans. If you don't hear from me, he'll be there Sunday. Give him the code word Bunny."

I shake my head. "Sure. What's the cost?"

"I'll pay the pilot. Then I'll decide."

"Decide what?"

"If I'd rather have money or a favor from a ranger."

I open my mouth to tell him cash is the only payment he'll get, but the line goes dead.

After powering off the phone, I secure it in the front pouch of the backpack.

I checked everything before we left this morning, but I do another once-over to make sure it's all here.

First aid. Bag of protein bars. Two empty water bottles with attached filters. The flare kit. An emergency blanket.

I attach the holster to my belt and secure my handgun.

Then I lock the doors of the plane.

Tilda is already looking my way when I round the tail. "Everything okay?"

I nod. "Come here. We're going to fill the water bottles."

She glances at the river just yards away. "Handy there's water here."

"It's pretty fresh, but the filters will still be good." I pull the extra bottles out of my backpack as we walk toward the river's edge.

"You've been here?" She shakes her head before she's even done asking. "Never mind. You already said we're going to a cabin nearby."

I crouch on a large flat rock and place the bottle into the stream. "I usually come in from a different direction. And by land. But I've utilized this river before." I hand her the bottle and the cap, and she twists the top on as I fill up the second bottle. "There's a well at the cabin, so we'll be fine. But first rule of being in the wilderness, fill up on water whenever it's available."

Tilda gives me a soft smile. "First rule? Will there be a test at the end of the stranding?"

"Yeah, but don't worry, I grade on a curve." I pull the extra flannel out of my backpack. "Put this on."

Vegas was hot. Here, it's not.

Tilda shrugs her backpack off and takes the flannel.

And while she's putting the shirt on, I grab her tiny bag and shove it into my larger one.

"Ethan," she sighs.

"Button up," I tell her, while I pull the zipper closed on my backpack.

Along with providing warmth, the sleeves will help protect her from the sun and tree branches.

Tilda pulls in a sharp inhale, and I jerk my gaze up to her, wondering if she somehow hurt herself.

But she's not looking at herself.

Or at me.

She's looking across the river.

"Ethan."

I've seen enough people reacting to wildlife, so I keep my movements slow as I turn, still crouched low.

I expect a bear.

There are lots of black bears out here.

But it's not a bear.

"Cat," Tilda whispers, just as I see it.

The mountain lion.

# CHAPTER 71

## TILDA

FEAR AND AMAZEMENT TWIST AROUND MY ORGANS.

It's a mountain lion.

*It's a mountain lion.*

The river isn't that wide. Isn't flowing so fast that something couldn't swim across it. Isn't a good enough barrier between my soft body and those sharp teeth.

"Ethan." I want to reach for him. Want to jump on his back and make him carry me out of this place. But I don't dare move.

*Are you supposed to stay still for mountain lions? Or is that just T. rexes?*

Ethan slowly stands to his full height.

He rolls his shoulders back and spreads his fingers wide as he rotates his wrists so his palms are facing the giant feline.

I don't know why he's doing that. But he's the park ranger. So I do what he does.

"Go on now." Ethan's tone is deep. Commanding.

The mountain lion, standing on the opposite bank, swishes its long tail.

"This side of the river is mine."

My eyes flit away from the cat to the man.

The man who called me his wife to the person on the phone.

The man who is talking to a freaking *mountain lion* like it's a pesky neighborhood dog.

*Gods, he's hot.*

A chirping sound snaps my attention back across the river.

*Did the cat make that sound?*

"That's it. Go on." Ethan lifts his arms another inch.

I do the same, causing the flannel I just put on to fan around me.

The mountain lion chirps again. *Weird.* But then it—*she?*—turns around and strolls away from the water into the trees.

Ethan keeps his arms out but turns his head to look at me.

The edge of his mouth pulls up as he gives me a once-over, taking in my mimicking pose.

"So." I try for my own smile, but I think that was the fourth round of anxiety-induced adrenaline today, and my composure is waning. "That was a big cat."

"An adolescent, I think."

Ethan glances back across the river, then drops his arms.

I look too, and I can't see the cat anymore.

I lower my arms. "Is that a good thing or a bad thing?"

Ethan shrugs. "Hunger is more important than age. They wouldn't have walked away so willingly if they were hungry."

I stare at him.

*Hunger.*

As in, *she wants to eat us.*

"H-how long does it take a mountain lion to get hungry?"

Ethan pulls a face. "Sorry, I didn't mean to scare you."

"I'm not scared." I'd be more convincing if my statement didn't come out shrill.

Ethan moves closer to me, reaching up and pulling my hair free from the collar of the flannel shirt. "They can go days without eating. Sometimes over a week. We'll be fine. I promise you."

"But if it comes back?"

Ethan drops his hand to his hip.

I follow the movement. And notice the gun.

"I don't want to shoot anything out here. But if I have to, I will. Now tell me you trust me."

I resist the urge to glance across the river.

If Ethan says he'll protect me...

I place my hand on his chest. "I trust you."

# CHAPTER 72

## ETHAN

I HOLD HER GAZE. AND I NOD.
   *I trust you.*
   I told her to say it. Gave her the words.
   But still...
   I inhale the weight of it.
   *She trusts me.*
   And I won't ruin that.
   *I can't ruin that.*

# Chapter 73

## Tilda

"He had a whole box of them." I tell Ethan about the Dolly Parton books I found in the cabinet above the fridge. "Pretty sure that... cookbook... was also in the... pile." I put my hands on my hips and suck in a breath.

*Why is it so hard to breathe?*

"It's the elevation." Ethan reads my mind.

I narrow my eyes at him. "But you're fine." Literally, he's not breathing the tiniest bit hard.

It's a stupid thing to point out because Ethan is *fit*. Like, *oh my gods, look at those muscles* sort of fit. Whereas I like to go on walks.

Regular walks.

Not walks through dense, deserted forests with mountain lions nearby.

And I don't know how long it will take to go *a couple miles*, but I know it's more than the ten minutes we've been walking.

"I've lived at elevation pretty much my whole life," Ethan explains reasonably. "You're still acclimating."

I make a noise of understanding rather than trying to form words.

A few more minutes pass, and I try not to notice the way I can feel my boots rubbing my ankles wrong.

I've had this pair for a while, and even though they look like combat boots, they're more fun than function. So I certainly wouldn't have chosen them for a hike.

And because I was so stressed out this morning about having to see my family, I put on the wrong socks. I'm wearing my super-shorty socks, which are great for my ballet flats because they don't show, not the thick wool socks I usually wear with these boots. Meaning there is no barrier between the boot and most of my skin.

If the walk is too long, I'm sure my toes will be hurting too, but I can already feel that bony part of my ankle rubbing against a seam I hadn't realized was there.

Pursing my lips, I focus on oxygen and not my feet.

At least I remembered to put my stretchy chub-rub shorts on under my dress. If I had to deal with chafing on top of my boot issue... I'd be crying.

After a few more minutes, I decide I can't spend the next few miles listening to my own breathing. "Can you talk about something?" I shove the question out quickly between inhales.

"What would you like me to talk about?"

"Anything." I don't have the lung capacity to talk about any of the things we need to talk about. *Like the fact that we got married today.* So I gesture at a bush before dropping my hand back to my side. "Plants."

"Plants?" I can hear the humor in his tone.

"Yeah, Mr. *I'm Gonna Give You a Ticket.*" I try to mock his deeper tone, but it just puts me more out of breath.

*Honestly, what is with elevation? This is nonsense.*

"I'll remind you that I did *not* give you that ticket."

Without turning my head, I reach out and blindly pat his arm. "Appreciated."

Then I think about how much money I'm about to inherit

because he agreed to this marriage, and I accept that I could afford a few tickets now.

But again, we'll talk more on that when I can actually breathe.

Hand still on his arm, I finally look over. Then I give his bicep a squeeze.

*Good gods.*

I look up and catch the hint of a smirk.

I squeeze him again, then drop my arm.

"What do you want to know about plants?"

"I don't know. Just use your khaki power-ranger skills and fill the silence." I suck in a noisy breath.

"Khaki. Power ranger."

"What's poisonous. What's not." I make a *keep going* gesture with my hand. "Ranger stuff."

"Ranger stuff."

I shoot him a glare. "Just talk and keep the animals away."

Ethan shakes his head. But then he does what I ask.

He talks.

He points to different species of trees and tells me their qualities.

He tells me how to get sap from a maple tree if I'm ever stranded with no food.

He makes me drink water.

He points out a plant that will cause itching and tells me that poison ivy and poison oak don't tend to grow this high in the mountains.

*Score one for elevation.*

He tells me what to do if we spot a bear. Explains why making yourself look big and keeping eye contact with mountain lions is important.

He talks, in his soothing deep voice, for hours.

My feet ache.

My ankles feel like they might be bleeding.

My bladder tells me that I'm going to have to pee soon.

My mind tells me that if I try to pee squatting next to a tree, there is a one-hundred-percent chance I'm going to get pee on my boots.

Ethan makes me drink more water. And we share a protein bar, even though I told him I wasn't hungry.

I'm too stressed to be hungry.

But he told me to eat it anyway. *For fuel.*

And he's the expert, so I listen.

I listen as he points out different animal tracks.

I try not to freak out over how many animal tracks he's identified.

And even though we're walking nonstop, I button up the flannel I'm wearing because the sun is setting and it's getting chilly.

A giant black bird lets out a loud caw as it launches from a branch overhead, and I stumble.

Ethan's large hand grips my upper arm, keeping me upright. "Easy."

I press my lips together, trying to keep the wince off my face.

But I'm not successful.

Ethan stops, looking down at my feet. "Did you twist something?"

I shake my head.

"Matilda."

"No, I'm fine." Even though we've been walking for forever, my breathing has finally evened out. "Let's keep going."

Ethan clenches his jaw. "I saw your look of pain. You're hurt."

I sigh. "My feet hurt, but not from... the bird. Can we just keep going? Please?"

He looks like he wants to argue, but he dips his chin and starts walking again.

The first few steps hurt extra bad. *Stopping was a mistake.*

But I inhale through the discomfort.

*It's nothing I haven't been through before.*

We keep going, but Ethan turns his head in my direction every few steps.

That loud bird made me think of Quackers, and since I think we both need a distraction, I think of a new topic for Ethan. "Will you tell me about the cabin?"

"Fine. But when we get there, you're taking those boots off."

I lift two fingers to my brow in a salute.

*As if pulling these godsforsaken boots off wasn't going to be my very first action.*

"My dad and some of his high school buddies used to come out here every summer. It's government land, so they weren't supposed to, but no one ever noticed, and eventually it became an annual camping trip where they'd come out and just tool around in the woods." Ethan hooks his thumbs in his backpack straps. "One of the guys was an architect, and, as my dad told it, they all got drunk one night and convinced him to draw up a design for a cabin that they could build themselves. He did. And the next summer, they used four-wheelers to haul the material in and spent two weeks building the cabin."

"Wow. That's... ballsy."

Ethan chuckles. "And illegal. But they got away with it. And the next summer, they figured out a way to dig their own well. They could've just built next to the river and saved the hassle. But people occasionally come out this way to fish, so building farther in the woods was the smarter option."

I have no idea what any of that would require, but I'm still thoroughly impressed. "And now it's just yours?"

"Since it was illegally built on government land, there's no paperwork. No deed. No real owner. But all the other guys moved out of state. And I don't think any of their kids know how to find it. They might not even know about it at all. So yeah, I think I'm the only person who's been here in the last ten years, which essentially makes it mine."

"Look at you, breaking rules."

Ethan grunts.

I try to picture this built-by-hand cabin. But I struggle with

the visual, my mind flipping between some Hansel-and-Gretel
cottage and some wonky-looking shack.

"Any chance they built a bathroom?"

"They did."

I almost stumble again. "Seriously?"

"Well, it's an outhouse. No running water. Or electricity. But
there's a toilet seat."

"Luxury," I say with adoration. Because honestly, not having
to pee on the ground is apparently my love language.

*Love.*

*Ugh.*

I don't know if it's safe to fall for this man. But I can already
feel it happening.

Ethan just spent hours talking to me about nothing because I
asked him to.

He *married me* because I asked him to.

He scared off a mountain lion...

I look at his chiseled profile. "Do you have a girlfriend?"

Ethan slowly turns his head to face me. "No. I have a wife."

*Oh.*

*Wow.*

Heat that has nothing to do with muscle strain rolls through
my body.

I look forward.

We walk in silence for a few more minutes. And then I
see it.

The woods don't thin out.

There isn't a clearing.

And I suppose since they were trying to keep their secret cabin
a secret, it makes sense.

Because there, just ahead, surrounded by towering pine trees,
is a cabin.

A perfectly normal-looking cabin with glass windows and
wood siding and a little outhouse a dozen yards away.

My steps slow.

There isn't a porch, and the front door looks to be about a foot off the ground, but it all looks solid. Well cared for.

A couple yards in front of the house is a water spigot with a red-handled pump sticking out of the ground. And next to that is a circle of rocks designating a firepit. Four wide stumps, which have maybe seen better days but still look sturdy, are arranged around the firepit.

Ethan strides ahead of me. "Everything looks fine, but stay here while I check."

I stop.

*Check for what?*

He reaches the front door and turns the handle.

There isn't a lock. He just opens the door and steps inside.

Not liking my back to the woods as I stand by myself, I turn around so my back is to the cabin.

My eyes have adjusted to the dimming light, but I still squint, trying to look for any movement.

Then I lift my gaze to the trees, remembering how Ethan told me that mountain lions like to sit in trees. *A fact that will surely give me nightmares for the rest of my life.*

Footsteps crunch behind me, and I look over my shoulder. Ethan exits the cabin, then crosses over to the outhouse.

He pulls a flashlight out of his pocket and turns it on as he opens the door.

There are no windows in the little structure, so it's completely dark inside. Which is creepy. But still... toilet seat.

Ethan steps out. "All good."

"What were you checking for?"

He opens his mouth, then purses his lips. "Do you really want to know?"

I take half a second to think about it. "No. No, I don't."

I'm assuming it's snakes and spiders. And if he says it's all good, then I'm going to take his word for it.

Ethan holds the flashlight out to me. "You can use this or leave the door open."

I stare at him. "I'm not leaving the door open."

He lifts a shoulder. "I usually hold the flashlight in my mouth if I need my hands, but you can just lay it on the floor if you want."

Giving him side-eye, I take the flashlight into the outhouse with me and lay it on the floor.

A small shelf is built into one wall, on which a large coffee can and a bottle of hand sanitizer sit.

The can is helpfully labeled TP, so I open it. Finding a roll of toilet paper inside a Ziplock bag, I use a few squares to wipe down the seat.

I haven't done much as far as wilderness goes in my life, but I've stopped at a few rest areas along long stretches of highway, so I've encountered the no-flush setup before.

Those are usually gross, but this one is surprisingly clean and stink-free.

*Probably because it gets used once a year.*

Finished, I use the hand sanitizer. Twice. Then I come out to find Ethan standing next to the water spigot.

"Boots off."

# CHAPTER 74

## ETHAN

My teeth grind as I stare down at my Mountain Fairy's perfect little toes.

"Matilda."

Sitting on one stump with her heels up on another, she looks at her feet, then lifts a shoulder.

I clench my fists at my sides at her shrug.

Her *shrug*. When her feet...

I swallow.

Her ankles are bleeding.

Both of them.

And the top of her toes are red, rubbed raw.

"You should've told me." I try to keep my voice calm, but I'm furious.

She wiggles her toes. "It's not that bad. And it's not like I have other shoes to change into."

"It is bad," I argue. "And I have a first aid kit. I could've put Band-Aids over the spots that were rubbing. I could've jogged ahead and gotten the extra socks I have stored in the fucking cabin." I point at the structure behind her.

She looks down. "Oh."

I watch as she bites her lip.

Like she always does when she's distressed.

*I'm making her distressed.*

But I just promised her that I wouldn't let anything happen to her. And here we are. With her feet bloody and in pain.

I drag a hand down my face, then storm past her into the cabin.

Seconds later, I'm back outside, and I set the metal wash basin under the water spigot and work the pump.

Cold water splashes into the wide bucket. "You're going to put your feet in here for a few minutes. The cold should help." I'd put her feet in a bucket of ice if I had it, but cold well water is the best I can do right now.

"I'm really okay," Tilda says quietly. "I've dealt with worse shoes."

I pump more water as I turn my head to look at her.

*The way she said that...*

"What do you mean?" I ask slowly. And the look that comes over her face tells me she didn't mean to give so much away. "Tell me the truth."

"I didn't—"

"Matilda Iris Wright. Do not lie to me right now." I know I'm being intense. Probably more than is warranted. But I don't care.

She lets out a breath, and her shoulders sag. "You met my family."

I stand up straight and face her, immediately hating this.

She shrugs again. "I... I like *girly* things. Sparkles and dresses and that sort of stuff." I think about her yard, dotted with suncatchers. "When I was young, my mom put me in beauty pageants. I was excited at first, ya know? Because it meant I got to dress up."

Dread seeps into my chest. "What did she do?"

"It wasn't..." Tilda doesn't finish her sentence.

I'm sure she was about to say it *wasn't that bad.* But I bet it was.

"Tell me."

She keeps her eyes on her feet. "She bought everything a size too small."

Rage causes my blood to simmer.

Tilda wiggles her toes again. "It sucked. Because I loved the dresses. They were frilly and colorful, and... I loved them. But they were always too tight. And it made it hard to breathe. But the shoes were the worst." Her fingers twist in the material of her skirt. "Like I know she did the wrong-sized dresses to try to... I dunno... encourage me to lose weight. But the shoes... Even if I was skinny, they'd still be too small." She wiggles her toes again. "The shoes were the worst part."

I thought I was furious before.

I thought...

The oxygen in my lungs ignites into flames.

Her mother...

Her fucking mother...

I...

My teeth ache from how hard I'm clenching my jaw.

I've never wanted to end a person's life more than I want to right now.

Turning away from Tilda, I stride into the woods.

# CHAPTER 75

## TILDA

I LIFT MY GAZE AND WATCH ETHAN DISAPPEAR INTO THE trees.

I look back at my feet.

And I grimace when I flex my toes.

I didn't mean to bring any of that up. I was trying to make him understand that this isn't the worst thing I've experienced. But as soon as he told me to *tell him the truth*, I knew it wasn't going to go over well.

Usually, I wouldn't share a story like that.

Usually, I wouldn't admit such a shameful, outlandish thing.

But Ethan's met them.

*Her.*

So I knew he'd believe me.

A branch breaks somewhere out of sight.

*He definitely believed me.*

Sighing, I gingerly get to my feet and carefully take the few steps to the bucket.

# CHAPTER 76

## ETHAN

MY CHEST HEAVES AS I LOOK DOWN AT THE PILE OF branches by my feet.

I don't feel any better.

I don't think anything could make me feel better right now.

I can't...

She said *when I was young*.

When Tilda was *a child*, her mother put her in painful clothing so *her child* would want to lose weight.

My vision is blurry with anger as I think of my own mother.

She would've loved Tilda.

She would've loved every fucking thing about her.

She would never, not ever, have done that to her.

I can still hear my mom's voice, telling me how perfect I was when I'd come home upset after someone teased me about my eye colors.

I can still hear her muffled voice from when I listened outside her door as she chewed out the school's principal.

And that was just over words. If I'd been physically hurt...

She would've burned the world down.

That's what every kid deserves.

That's the bare fucking minimum.

And Tilda...

She deserves that too.

She deserves that now.

Tilda deserves world burning.

Tilda.

My wife.

I turn back toward the cabin.

One way or another, I'll be the man she deserves.

I stride forward. Out of the woods.

And I find her.

Standing in the bucket of cold water.

Standing.

Not sitting on the stump with her feet in the bucket.

Standing. On the very feet that are paining her.

She didn't move the bucket.

Didn't wait for me to come back and help her.

She just got up, walked over, and stood in the fucking bucket.

There's dirt on her pretty yellow skirt.

There's a tiny twig stuck to the sleeve of her flannel.

And she looks... uncertain.

She looks like she's doubting herself.

And I can't take another second of it.

I close the distance between us.

"Ethan—"

I barely slow as I scoop her up.

She feels right in my arms.

She feels fucking perfect as I carry her bridal style through the open front door of the cabin.

And she looks like *mine* when I drop her onto the mattress.

# CHAPTER 77

## TILDA

I BOUNCE ON THE SPRINGY MATTRESS, THE AIR RUSHING from my lungs.

"You're fucking perfect. You know that, right?" Ethan growls as he stares down at me.

I blink up at him.

*Perfect?*

"Every fucking inch." His eyes are feral as he trails his gaze down my body.

I squeeze my knees together.

I can feel my skirt against my thighs, but it's ridden up. And I know I'm showing a lot of skin.

A lot of suddenly hot, feverish skin.

"Fuck." Ethan reaches up and starts undoing the buttons of his flannel.

He... gods... he's acting so... hungry. So... wild.

I work on my own flannel. But I only get halfway through before Ethan is shrugging his shirt off.

And my fingers stop working.

I lift my head off the mattress to get a better look at him.

*Holy...*

The bed is low, just a standard mattress on a basic wood frame, giving me a full-body view of him.

"Keep those eyes on me, Starlight." He reaches for the front of his jeans. "Keep those perfect fucking eyes on me."

He doesn't need to tell me. Not twice. Not even once. Because a mountain lion tapping on the window wouldn't be enough to drag my attention away from his absurdly fine body.

The tattoos cover his chest. And shoulders. And arms.

And...

I've never seen such defined muscles.

Not in real life.

*How is this real life?*

Ethan shoves his jeans down.

I lift my head higher.

My mouth opens.

I've felt it.

I've felt his cock through his jeans.

Felt it rubbing against my core.

I freaking came because of that thing rubbing against me.

But...

I lick my lips.

The outline of it in his black boxer briefs...

*I think I won the husband jackpot.*

He kicks his jeans and boots off. Then he moves like he's going to get on the bed with me.

I make a sound of disagreement and point. "Off."

He pauses.

I shift up onto my elbows. "Be a Good Boy and take the rest of your clothes off. Show me what's mine."

He stares down at me and drags his tongue across his bottom lip, like he might defy me.

But then he hooks his thumbs in the waistband of his boxer briefs and drags them down.

And down.

And...

I sit all the way up.

*Is that a piercing?*

On top of the base of his dick is a barbell.

I was already turned on.

But that...

Wetness floods my core.

The piercing is in just the right spot. So when he's inside me... when he gets that thing all the way inside me, the smooth metal will be right where I need it.

I reach for him.

He takes a step back.

I whimper.

He shoves his last piece of clothing all the way off.

And I whimper again.

Because it's so pretty.

His dick is just so damn pretty.

"You can touch me anytime you want, Wife. But right now." He grips his length. And even in his large hand, it still looks big. "Right now, I need to show you how perfect you are. Let me do that."

*Perfect.*

*He keeps using that word.*

He strokes his length. "Give me permission."

Eye level with his hard cock, I lick my lips.

"Starlight," he growls.

I lift my gaze to his. "You have my permission."

Ethan reaches down, grips the front of my flannel, which is still half buttoned, and rips the sides apart.

*Rips.*

Fabric tears.

A button bounces off the wood floor.

My core throbs.

Ethan places his palms on my shoulders and shoves me back.

I land flat against the mattress.

"Perfect fucking feet." Ethan lets go of his dick and traces a fingertip down the front of each of my legs, from my knees to my ankles, careful to avoid the painful spots.

Goose bumps erupt across my body.

He drags his fingers back up to my knees, then he flattens his palms and slides his hands up my thighs.

Up. And up.

His forearms push the skirt of my dress up. And I can feel when he reaches my shorts.

They're pale blue. Practically see-through. Not sexy. And not doing anything to *control* or *tuck* any part of me. They're just there to keep my thighs from rubbing. And I'm too turned on to feel weird about them.

Ethan slides his hands higher, fingers finding the top of my shorts.

He starts to pull them down, nails lightly scraping over my skin. "Perfect fucking hips."

He drags them all the way off and tosses the shorts aside, then places his hands on my inner thighs and shoves my legs apart.

I'm still wearing my thong, which is becoming more and more soaked with every touch.

Ethan kneels on the bed, between my spread legs, and glides his hands up my thighs, stopping when his fingertips are just an inch from the damp material.

"Fuck..." He drags the word out, then I feel him drag his thumb up my seam.

I arch my back. "Ethan."

He does it again, pressing the material between my lips.

Then he starts to bend forward. And I try to close my legs.

Ethan looks up at me, eyes hooded, as he tugs the material of my thong to the side.

His eyes are on mine, but I can feel the cool cabin air against my bare flesh.

"Why are you trying to stop me?"

I clutch at my skirt, bunched over my stomach. "I'm all sweaty."

The edge of Ethan's mouth pulls up. Just a bit. "I don't care."

"But—"

"You're my wife, Matilda. And you're going to let me treat you like my wife."

Every damn word he says...

"And do husbands like to go down on their wives?" I twist my fingers in my dress.

Slowly, so I can watch him do it, Ethan lowers his gaze down my body.

Over my chest.

Over my stomach.

Lower.

I watch his mouth open.

Watch him pant out a breath.

As he looks at *me*.

As he tugs my thong even farther to the side.

"God dammit." He reaches down with his other hand and drags a finger down the length of my slit.

I can feel the wetness as it coats his finger.

My eyelids flutter.

"Please." He groans as he does it again.

I want to say yes.

I want to feel his tongue on my clit more than anything.

But I don't want to be self-conscious about it. And we just hiked for hours.

"No." I try for commanding, but it comes out as a breath.

Ethan meets my gaze.

And then his finger is there.

Pressing into me.

"Fine." He pushes his finger in an inch.

We both moan.

"This is your warning." He pushes in another inch. "I'm eating this perfect fucking pussy for dinner tomorrow."

I squirm as my inner muscles clench around him.

He pulls his finger free, dragging it up and over my clit.

I moan, and my eyes close on instinct as my back arches.

"We're going to talk later about how you got this so smooth." Ethan sounds torn as he says it. Like he likes the fact that I've had every pubic hair lasered off my body. But that he hates the idea of someone else touching me there.

"It was a woman." I force my eyes open and lift my head again. "Who did that piercing?"

Ethan smirks down at me. "A woman."

I lift my leg and put my foot on his chest. So I can shove him off the bed.

But he presses my leg straight, propping my heel on his shoulder.

Opening me.

Ethan leans forward, and I feel the head of his cock brush against my core. "It was purely professional. And I never saw her again."

I drop my head back down. "Good."

My leg slips off his shoulder as he leans forward even more. And I widen my thighs, inviting him closer.

Ethan braces a hand on the mattress next to my head. "Good what?"

With him this close, I can't resist touching.

I slide my hands up his tattooed pecs to his shoulders. "Good Boy. Now kiss me."

His mouth is on mine the instant I finish my command.

His lips are warm. Demanding.

Ravenous.

And I groan. Because he feels so good.

*His muscles shifting under my hands.*

*His cock rubbing against my entrance.*

*His tongue in my mouth.*

He feels so freaking good.

And I can't wait for tomorrow night. When he *eats my pussy for dinner.*

But right now, I need more.

I hook my feet around the backs of his thighs and try to pull him in.

He nips at my lip. "Bad Girl. I'm not done yet."

There's a tug on the bow holding my wrap dress together, and then Ethan pulls the two halves apart.

Then he groans and drops his forehead to my chest.

My smile is wide as I feel his breath on my skin.

"Bad fucking Girl."

When tied properly, my dress is tight around my boobs, doing all the work of a bra. So I don't have to wear one.

Still on one elbow, Ethan sucks one pierced nipple into his mouth.

A moan rattles around in my chest. The warmth of his lips spears straight through my body.

His fingers tug at my other nipple. My silver barbells are almost a perfect match to the one at the base of his dick.

I bring my hands up to Ethan's hair.

He switches, sucking the other nipple into his mouth, his teeth clinking against the metal as he swirls his tongue around it.

"Oh. Gods."

He flattens his tongue and gives me the slowest, firmest lick.

I tilt my hips up, and he presses down into me so the underside of his cock is nestled in my cleft.

"Ethan." I tighten my grip on his hair as I wiggle beneath him, trying to line up his tip with my entrance.

He gently bites my piercing. And the moan that comes out of me is so loud that I'm glad we're in the middle of nowhere.

Ethan rolls my other nipple between his fingers. "Who did these piercings?"

"A man." I pull on his hair, bringing his mouth back up to mine. "It was purely professional." My lips brush against his. "I never saw him again."

"Good." Ethan seals his mouth to mine.

His fingers tug on my nipple again.

His weight shifts.

He opens my mouth with his.

He rocks his hips. And the head of his dick pushes into me.

Our mouths are still pressed together.

Our lips parted. Inhaling each other's exhales.

And we don't move.

But he keeps pushing his hips forward.

He keeps sinking into me.

And I squeeze my eyes shut tighter.

I dig my fingers into his shoulders.

I struggle to take him.

"Relax," Ethan whispers against my lips. "Breathe."

I focus on relaxing my muscles.

Ethan slides in deeper.

I focus on breathing.

He pushes in deeper.

Ethan softly kisses me. My muscles loosen. And he shoves the rest of the way in.

My spine arches. My chin lifts.

Ethan presses a kiss against my throat, then settles his cheek against mine.

"That's it, Wife." He rolls his hips, our bodies as close as they can get. "You've taken all of me now."

Then he rolls his hips again and I can feel *it*.

I can feel his piercing.

And...

"Oh gods." I wrap my limbs around him.

I hold him as tightly as I can.

"Feel good?" Ethan keeps his weight on me as he pulls his hips back, his length sliding out.

He pushes all the way back in.

"Tell me it feels good." His words rumble against my ear, our cheeks still pressed together.

"You feel good." I cling to his shoulders. "So good. I'm so full."

He moans and rocks his hips faster this time. "Say that again."

I lift my knees higher. "You fill me so good."

"Fucking perfect." He shifts and moves a hand under my shoulders.

And he hugs me closer.

Just like what I'm doing to him. He holds me tightly.

Our exhales become deafening. Until it's all I can hear.

And his heat is all I can feel.

His body against mine.

His breath on my skin.

His cock inside me.

It's all heat.

He grinds into me.

His piercing rubs against my clit.

He pumps and grinds and works his hips into me like we've done this a thousand times before.

Pleasure builds in my core.

The stretch of him.

The motion.

The way he won't stop holding me.

The way he's groaning, like he feels just as good as I do.

"Ethan," I gasp.

He grinds into me.

"Ethan." I lift my head, curling into him.

He rolls his hips.

His chest hair is the perfect friction against my stimulated nipples.

"I... I..."

"Let go, Perfect Girl."

He rocks into me. His rough exhale hits my ear. And the heated metal of his dick piercing rubs against my bundle of nerves just right.

I press my open mouth against his bare shoulder as my composure shatters.

My teeth bite into his skin as my pussy convulses around his length. And my thighs tighten against his sides.

I come around him.

Squeezing and tensing.

Noises trapped in my throat.

"That's it. That's it," he grunts as his movements become choppy.

His breathing becomes heavier.

His hold on me gets tighter.

And as I cry out against him, he comes apart.

Ethan groans loudly as he pushes in as deep as he can go.

His body shakes.

And his exhale is choked as he pulses inside me.

Filling me.

And it's so much.

Too much.

Emotions I can't even identify crash over me.

Tears form and drip from the corners of my eyes.

I've never...

Not like that.

# CHAPTER 78

## ETHAN

I BLINK AWAY THE STARS SPOTTING MY VISION.

My heart is beating almost painfully. And I relish it.

Relish the feeling of being alive.

Because that's what this woman is.

She's life.

I bury my nose in the side of Tilda's neck and roll my hips one last time.

The wetness of our simultaneous releases makes me groan.

*Fucking. Perfect.*

Tilda is still shuddering in my arms, her pussy fluttering around my sensitive flesh.

I know I'm crushing her. Just like last time. But I can't move yet.

Her hold on me loosens, but she doesn't drop her arms away.

Tilda slides her soft hands down my back. Then she drags her fingertips up my bare sides.

A shiver dances up my spine.

"Sorry." Tilda starts to pull her hands away.

I grunt against her neck and shimmy my shoulders.

I feel her huff against my neck. "Again?"

I nod.

She does it again, lightly trailing her fingers over my skin. Tracing muscles. Teasing ribs. It's delicious torture.

I relax. Not realizing I've gone deadweight on her until her next exhale comes out as a wheeze.

"Shit." It takes more effort than I'd like to admit to lift my top half off her. I look down into her pretty brown eyes. "Can you breathe now?"

She smiles as she nods. But in the waning light, I can see a tear track on her cheek.

My brows furrow.

I shift my weight back to one elbow and lift my other hand, using my thumb to wipe the mark away.

Her smile is soft. "I'm okay."

I watch her, needing to believe her. "You're sure."

"I'm sure." Her smile is wider this time. "That was... a little overwhelming."

I think about the way my vision started to fail me. "I know what you mean."

She snickers, making her muscles clench around me.

I grunt.

"Sorry." Tilda widens her eyes, but I hear the humor in her tone.

I smirk. "You're not sorry."

She grins as she shakes her head. "No. But I don't know how you do laundry out here, and I'm trying not to make a mess on this blanket."

I take notice of the blanket spread beneath her. "Ah, right. But just so you know, wool is easy to clean."

She makes a face.

"I didn't mean... I've never brought a woman here before." I know we don't owe each other anything in regard to who we've been with before we met. But I still feel like she should know. Even if it's an awkward thing to say while my dick is still inside her.

Tilda presses her lips together like she's trying not to laugh.

I narrow my eyes. "What?"

"Nothing." She smiles as she says it. "But I sorta figured you hadn't crashed a plane in the woods and hiked to this cabin with another woman before."

"It was a controlled emergency landing. The crashing into a tree happened after."

"Uh-huh." She runs her nails up my sides, and I jolt.

Her laugh is so light and pretty I can't stop my smile.

*I don't even try.*

Leaning down, I press a kiss to the tip of Tilda's nose. Then I lift myself off her, slipping free from her delectable heat and climbing off the bed.

She presses her legs together, keeping her knees up.

I stare down at her.

She's still wearing her dress and my flannel, but they're spread open around her like a robe, leaving her wonderful nakedness on display.

I smirk. "I can't believe you've been hiding pierced nipples from me."

She lifts a brow. "Like you're one to speak."

I shrug.

My piercing was a *drunken night out* decision. I'd convinced myself it would be good for my sex life. So I got it.

Then I found out I had to wait *months* before I could do anything with it.

I had regrets.

But those regrets are gone.

Pretty sure if Tilda asked me to get more, I'd do it.

I almost laugh at myself.

Pretty sure she could just *tell me* to do it, and I would.

Tilda shifts, and my attention snags on the bright red marks on her ankles.

My mouth pulls into a frown. "You better not have hurt your feet more."

Tilda wiggles her toes. "I'm fine, Ethan."

"The bar for your health is higher than fine, Matilda." She looks surprised by my statement, and that, in itself, annoys me. "Just... stay put."

# CHAPTER 79

## TILDA

I STAY SILENT AS ETHAN MOVES AROUND THE CABIN, suddenly aware that the front door was open the whole time.

*Thankfully, we didn't get any oversized feline visitors.*

The bed is parallel to the front door, with the head of the bed pressed against the wall that's to your left when you walk in. It's not all the way against the back cabin wall, but it's close, with just about a foot of space allowing for someone to get into the bed from either side.

The wall across from the foot of the bed, to your right when you walk in, is filled with floor-to-ceiling cabinets. And Ethan opens one of the center doors and pulls out a large plastic tub that's two-thirds full of paper products.

I don't know why I'm surprised by it. There was toilet paper in the outhouse. But it still seems a little funny out here in the middle of the woods.

Ethan takes out a roll of paper towels and rips one off.

I lift my brows when he turns and hands it to me.

He shrugs a shoulder. "Easier to carry in lightweight stuff like this and burn it than it is to carry out garbage."

"Makes sense." I accept the towel. But Ethan continues to stand there, completely nude, watching me. "Please turn around."

His jaw works like he might argue. But thankfully he just huffs. "Stay there." Then he walks out the door.

Completely nude.

I make quick work of cleaning up the best I can. Then I sit up.

Craning my neck, I can see Ethan through the window, back to me, next to the water spigot.

Droplets splash around him, and his shoulders hunch.

*Is he washing his dick in the cold well water?*

I grin. Then I remember Ethan's promise to go down on me tomorrow. My grin pulls into a grimace as I realize I will also need to take an ice-cold standing bath.

*Tomorrow.*

*I can do that tomorrow.*

Ethan bends down, giving me a great view of his toned ass. And I nearly pout when he pulls on a pair of gray pajama pants.

*Where...?*

I look around the cabin again and spot another plastic tub on the floor, open, with clothes folded inside.

Ethan steps back into the cabin and moves straight to the clothing tub.

He takes out a pair of pants, exactly like the ones he just put on, and a waffle-weave long-sleeve shirt. "Put these on."

I take them and set them on the mattress as I scoot toward the edge.

"Stay on the bed."

I give Ethan a look. "Standing will make getting dressed a thousand times easier."

"Your feet."

"The bottoms of my feet are fine. It won't hurt anything for me to stand while I change." I lower my feet to the floor and stand. "Your concern is cute. And truly appreciated." His nostrils flare, but I keep talking as I struggle to get the dress and flannel off my shoulders. "And I promise, I will lie right back down, as soon as—"

Ethan grips my shoulders and turns me around so my back is to him. "Let me help." He pulls the material down one arm, guiding my movements. Then he does the other side. "Take your thong off too. We'll wash clothes in the morning, then they'll be dry for Sunday."

"Industrious."

Ethan steps closer. Until his body is flush against mine. And I arch into him. Pressing my ass against his groin.

He slides his hands over my hips, then grips the top of my thong.

I try to hold still as he lowers behind me. But his breath tickles across my back, and I can't stop my shiver.

"Step out."

I follow his orders and lift one foot, then the other.

A moment later, an oversized shirt is lowered over my eyes.

Ethan tugs it down over my head, and I slip one arm, then the next, through the surprisingly soft material.

"This is nice." I run one hand over a sleeve.

"It's warm." Ethan grips my shoulders again, and this time, turns me to face him.

Then he crouches in front of me, holding the sleep pants out.

He's not looking up, so he doesn't see me shake my head.

Humoring him, I brace my hands on his shoulders as I step into the pants. And I keep my hands on his shoulders as he rises, pulling my pants up as he does.

"On the bed." He nods to the mattress.

"I want to go to the bathroom again before we go to sleep." I know it's not too late. But it's getting dark, and I'm tired enough that I'm sure I'd pass out if I could just close my eyes for two minutes.

He points to the bed. "You can go after I take care of your feet."

"Ethan—"

His hand is gripping my chin before I even notice him moving. "Matilda. Sit your ass on the bed and let me take care of your feet. Then I will walk you to the outhouse. Then we will come back, I'll make the bed, and you'll go to sleep. Then tomorrow, you will select a book from my collection, and you will spend the day lying in bed reading. Or sitting outside. But your feet will be up, and you will not defy me on this."

*Okay. Demanding Ethan is hot.*

I swallow.

"Now sit."

I sit.

"Lie down."

I sigh. But I lie down.

He fetches something else from the wall of cabinets, then stops at the foot of the bed.

"Feet up."

I lift my feet, and he sits. Then he presses a hand to my knees, and I lower my legs so they're resting across his lap.

And... I decide to enjoy this.

I have a half-naked, hot-as-sin *husband* tending to my injured feet. After he thoroughly ravished me in a way I've never been ravished before.

*What. A. Day.*

"This is going to sting, and I'm sorry." Ethan warns me, holding up a small spray bottle.

When he turns his head toward me, I realize he's waiting for me to say something. "Okay."

He looks back down at my feet, but he still hesitates.

And affection fills my chest.

*He doesn't want to hurt me.*

"Ethan." He looks back up at me. "Be a Good Boy and do your job. Make me better."

His face remains stoic, but his thighs tense under my calves.

Then he blows out a breath. "Tell me if it's too much."

I know the antiseptic spray is going to sting, so I don't know what he'd do about it if I said it was too much. But I agree anyway. "I'll tell you."

Ethan slides my pant legs up. Then keeps his hand on my shin, anchoring me, as he mists the spray.

I bite down on my lip and avert my gaze.

Ethan's thumb rubs soft circles against my skin as he makes a sound of discomfort.

*It's too much.*

I blink.

"I'm sorry, Starlight." His tone sounds like heartbreak. And I have to blink more.

The sudden tears aren't from the pain.

But I can't tell him...

If I tell Ethan I'm overrun with emotion because no one—and I mean *no one*—has ever cared for me like this. So sweetly...

If I tell him this is the most genuine love I think I've ever received... He'll either run for the mountains, or he'll find a way to fly us back to Vegas so he can murder my entire family.

*Neither outcome is ideal.*

"I'm going to do the other foot." He slides his hand over to my other shin, his thumb immediately rubbing those perfect circles. "Then the worst is over."

I blow out a breath through pursed lips. "I'm ready."

*I am ready for the pain. But I'm not sure I'll ever be ready for all that is Ethan.*

He sprays my other foot, making a humming sound that sounds suspiciously like a purr. Reminding me of the mountain lion.

I roll my head to the side and look at the door. "You didn't unlock the door when we got here."

Ethan's hand leaves my shin, and I hear a tiny click as he presses the cap back on the spray bottle. "No. If someone finds the place, it's better if they just open the door and come in than break a window. But there's a dead bolt on this side, so I can lock it while I'm here."

I consider that. "Has anyone ever broken in?"

"Not that I know of." He hums as there's a quiet rip.

I glance back down, and he tears open a tiny packet and takes out what I'm guessing is a sanitizing wipe.

He meticulously cleans each of his fingers before setting the little wipe down on the blanket and picking up a tube of ointment.

He meets my eyes. "I'll try to be gentle. But if it hurts, tell me."

I let him see my smile. "How do you make everything sound so sexual?"

His brows furrow. But then I can tell he's replaying his words in a sexual setting because he shakes his head. "You're a dirty girl, Matilda."

My smile turns into a grin. "It's a newly acquired condition."

He huffs, then lowers his attention back to my feet.

"Do animals break in?" It feels like a silly question, but I don't know what else to call it.

"Rodents are the most likely."

I pull a face. "Oh."

"There's no evidence of such a break-in, so fret not." Ethan is practically whispering as he *oh-so-gently* smooths his fingertip over the top of my toes. "Mountain lions mostly leave structures alone. And bears have trouble with the round doorknobs."

"Huh. The more you know." I take in the rest of the interior of the cabin as Ethan continues to meticulously apply ointment to each and every spot he can find.

The mattress below me isn't horrible. There are no pillows, but he said something about making the bed. So I have a feeling one of those cabinets is hiding some.

A large bucket is in the front corner of the cabin, across from the head of the bed, with two axes, a hand saw, a long clipper thing that I think is meant for branches, and a broom sticking out of it. Next to that is a rack with a few pieces of firewood on it. But other than that, there's really not much in here.

The windows are a decent size. There are no curtains. But I guess if there's no one around, then you don't really need them.

I push away the thought of a random person being out here. Because coming across a person in this setting would be way more terrifying than any wild animal.

Then I remember Ethan's gun and decide I'm in good hands. Hands that are still tending to me.

I look down at the man. "I figured there'd be more beds."

"Hmm?" Ethan looks up, then around the mostly bare cabin. "There used to be bunk beds. But I dismantled them when it was clear it would just be me coming out here." He focuses his gaze on mine. "This particular situation is one I didn't plan for."

"Wish you still had those bunks?" I tease him.

He shakes his head, expression staying serious.

My cheeks heat, and he looks back at my feet.

I stay silent as he applies bandages over each spot of ointment. And I continue to stay silent as he lifts my feet and slides off the bed.

I watch as he opens another cabinet, takes out another bin, and pulls out a pair of thick socks.

They're way too big. But they're soft. And I know they'll help keep my Band-Aids in place while I sleep.

I let Ethan help me up. And I let him help me slip my feet into a pair of really old-looking tennis shoes that came out of another bin.

They're gigantic, but Ethan ties the laces so they'll stay on. Then he walks me out the door and across the few yards to the outhouse.

"Here." He hands me the solar-powered lantern he pulled from another cabinet.

He checked it when we were still in the cabin. The glow was dim but still better than the thin band of light from the flashlight.

Ethan mentioned needing to charge it tomorrow, that it should be brighter, but I'm grateful for it as I carry the lantern into the tiny building.

Before I close the door, I eye him, standing feet away. "Ethan?"

"Yeah."

"Please don't stand there."

He looks down, then looks back up at me. "Why?"

I roll my eyes. "I don't mean *that exact location*. I mean, don't stand so close you can... listen."

Ethan drops his chin and looks at me like I'm being absurd.

I lift the hand not holding the lantern and point at him. "I'm serious. Go pee in the woods or something."

Ethan sighs but doesn't argue. And he doesn't go back to the cabin for his flashlight. He just walks off into the dark woods.

*Oh, to be a man with no sense of fear.*

With the lantern on the floor, the outhouse is filled with a cozy glow as I do my business.

I was wondering about the lack of fireplace in the cabin, thinking the winters must be pretty cold out here. But the more I consider it, I figure Ethan just doesn't come out here in the winter.

The trek alone would be nearly impossible with a couple feet of snow on the ground.

And since the toilet seat is chilly right now, I can't even imagine what it would feel like in freezing temperatures.

When I exit, Ethan is standing a few feet farther away than he was before, next to the well.

"Here." He holds out a bar of soap.

I happily take it and use the water as he pumps it out to give my hands a proper wash. Then I soap up my hands again and scrub them over my face.

It's harsher than my usual face wash, but I need the refresh.

Ethan hands me a paper towel, and I smile at him as I use it to dry my face.

Then I gasp, because the next thing he hands me is a toothbrush and a tube of toothpaste. "You're like Mary Poppins with those damn cabinets."

When I'm done, I turn my back to Ethan, ignoring his sigh

over my attempt at modesty as I rinse my mouth and spit onto the ground.

I use the damp paper towel still in my hand to wipe my mouth, then I give him back the toothbrush.

He applies more toothpaste and puts it into his mouth.

And I have to clench my thighs.

*That should be gross.*

*But it's not.*

*It's not gross at all.*

Ethan holds eye contact as he brushes his teeth.

The sun has officially moved below the horizon, and the heavy tree cover means we're in full darkness.

But the lantern is sitting on the stump beside me, and it's just enough light to watch Ethan watch me.

He doesn't turn away when he's done.

He doesn't turn away when he spits into the grass.

And I know I'm screwed.

Because I've never found these things hot before.

*Being a Bad Girl.*

*Having a Good Boy.*

*Sharing a toothbrush.*

*Spitting...*

I swallow.

I've never found these things hot before because I've never tried them before. But Ethan...

Ethan makes it easy.

He makes everything easy.

*Talking. Teasing. Touching...*

And I want more of it.

*So much more of all of it.*

Ethan grabs the lantern, and the light sways, sending shadows across his handsome face. "Come on, Starlight." He holds the lantern in the direction of the cabin.

I take a step.

S.J. TILLY

"Careful." He grips my arm.

And I bite my lip again.

That's another thing Ethan makes easy.

*Caring.*

I swallow again. For a different reason.

He's so good at caring.

The gentleness.

The way he rubs his thumb in circles.

The concern.

Being careful, I step up into the cabin.

It's even darker in here.

"Wait." Ethan steps in behind me.

I wait, staying where I am near the foot of the bed as I hear the door click shut. Then another sound, a muted thud, as Ethan turns the lock on the door.

The light moves around to my side as Ethan crouches next to me.

And I stay where I am as Ethan unlaces my shoes.

"Let me grab bedding." He leaves the light where it is and goes to the cabinets. As expected, he pulls out another bin, opens the lid, and removes two pillows.

*Caring.*

"Now?" I let him hear the smile I force into my voice.

I'll find a way to manage my emotions, my feelings toward Ethan. I don't need him knowing that everything he does makes me fall more than a little in love with him.

*He's probably like this with everyone.*

"Almost." My smile turns real at his response. "Hold these."

I take the pillows from him and hug them to my chest.

Ethan drags the blanket off the bed and drops it in a pile on the empty pillow bin. Under the blanket was a mattress protector, but no sheets in sight. Then I notice a handful of little sachets.

"What are those?"

Ethan grabs the little pouches. And I can smell the answer before he speaks. "Lavender."

"Fancy."

"They're losing their potency, but they're good for keeping bugs and rodents away." He drops them on top of the discarded blanket. "So, at least if something gets in the cabin, they should stay out of the bed."

My mouth pulls into a frown.

Maintaining a cabin in the woods comes with all sorts of logistical issues.

I press my nose against the pillows as Ethan pulls out a full set of bedding from another bin.

Inhaling, I notice the pillows have the same laundry scent as the clothing he gave me.

"Can I help?"

Ethan lifts his head to look at me from across the mattress, the answer written all over his shadowed expression.

I let him see me roll my eyes. "Fine, I'll just watch you do everything."

"Good."

*This man is something else.*

Not helping, I take another sniff of the pillows. "When were you here last?"

"November."

My eyebrows lift. "Seriously?"

Ethan circles the bed, securing each corner of the fitted sheet. "Yeah. Why?"

"Everything is so... fresh."

He does a snapping motion with the flat sheet, and it drapes perfectly into place. "I've had lots of practice learning what works best." He unfolds a heavy wool blanket, similar to the one that was on the bed before, and it falls into place on top of the sheets. "Plus, the elevation keeps things dry. Humidity would make everything moldy."

Coming from Vegas, the literal desert, I don't have much experience with things being humid. So I take his word for it.

Ethan smooths the blanket with his palms, then pulls down

the top edge. When he holds his hand out to me, I hand him the pillows.

He sets them in place. "You're on that side."

I step out of Ethan's big shoes and walk around to the far side of the bed. "I thought you hadn't brought women here before."

"I haven't." The bed creaks as I climb into it. "But I'll always sleep between you and the door."

The lantern turns off.

The room goes dark.

And my breath catches in my throat.

*I'll always sleep between you and the door.*

Putting himself between me and any danger.

Telling me he'll always do it.

Implying there will be more nights together. Not just a weekend stranded in the wilderness.

The bed creaks again as Ethan climbs in, and I lie on my side, facing him, head settled on the pillow, blanket pulled up over my shoulders.

"Ethan?"

"Yeah?" His reply is close, his body turned to mine.

"I just want you to know I'm on birth control. The arm implant."

"Good."

I wish I could see his expression. "Good because...?"

*Because he assumed I was?*

*Because he doesn't want kids?*

"Good because I plan on coming inside you again."

A sleepy snicker sneaks out of my chest at his seriousness.

Followed by a yawn.

"Ethan?" I close my eyes.

"Yeah?"

"Thank you for today." I feel my body getting heavy with sleep. "I'll explain it all tomorrow. But... thank you."

His knees bump into mine. "Are you thanking me for involving you in a plane crash?"

My lips pull into a smile. "It was a controlled emergency landing."

Ethan's exhale ghosts over my lips. "Go to sleep, Wife."

*Wife.*

*What a pleasant word to fall asleep to.*

# CHAPTER 80

## ETHAN

My lungs fill on a sharp inhale, and my eyes open.

My heart is thudding, and I know a dream woke me, but I don't remember what the dream was.

I exhale.

The smallest amount of light is coming in from the windows, letting me know it's morning. But barely.

I blink. And I blink again.

Tilda's face is inches from mine, her head sharing my pillow.

*She came to me.*

We started centered on our halves of the bed. But sometime in the night, Matilda came to me

And our limbs are... entwined.

We're on our sides facing each other.

One of her knees is between mine.

Our arms are tangled.

Her chin is resting on the backs of my fingers.

I focus on my body. On the pressure and warmth of every spot where we're touching.

I don't move my head. Don't move at all. Don't chance disturbing her.

Because I don't have to *see*. I can *feel* her palm against my chest.

Over my heart.

I close my eyes. And I focus on the contact.

I focus on my Starlight.

On the way she makes me feel.

And with a smile tugging on the edge of my mouth, I let myself fall back into sleep.

Something hard slams into my nuts, and pain explodes through my body.

My lungs struggle to suck in oxygen.

*What the fuck?*

"Sorry! Oh my gods, I'm so sorry!" Tilda's voice is scratchy with sleep. And very close.

I pry my eyes open as my balls continue to throb.

Tilda is staring back at me, eyes wide, lips pressed together. Shock and guilt and... *humor* are all over her face.

A small laugh pops out, and she slaps a hand over her mouth.

But our arms are still tangled together, so her sudden movement pulls my arm up. And still stunned and racked with the pain that only comes from smashing your nuts, I'm not able to stop the motion. I watch in horror as the back of my hand connects with the edge of Tilda's jaw.

She lets out a squeak at the contact, and my heart disintegrates.

"Matilda. Fuck." I yank my arm free of hers and roll her onto her back.

The leg she had between mine, the one that kneed me in the balls, gets caught in the blankets at the motion.

And then I remember her injuries.

"Feet! Fuck." I'm up, pulling the blanket off the bed, before she can get caught up in it more. "I'm sorry. Are you—"

Laughter bursts through my bubble of panic, and I lift my gaze to Tilda's face.

Her palms are pressed against her stomach. Her eyes are squeezed shut. And she's not just laughing. She's *laughing*.

Full-body shakes. Legs crossed. The kind of laughing that makes your eyes water and your stomach hurt.

The tension drops from my shoulders, and I heave out a breath. "Dammit, Matilda."

She keeps laughing, but she pries her eyes open. "Sorry." Her voice hiccups. "Sorry."

I place my hands on my hips. "For laughing? Or for making me punch you in the face after you kneed me in the nuts?"

Tilda closes her eyes again as her laughter gets louder.

She waves her hand like she's trying to apologize again but can't form words.

I wait.

"Feet!" She tries to mimic my voice. "Fuck." She tries. But she's hardly able to breathe.

I shake my head. And wait her out.

"Sorry." She snickers around the word, finally sounding like she means it.

"Is your chin okay?" I can't join her humor until I know for sure that I didn't hurt her.

Tilda wipes at her cheeks. "Man, I needed that."

Tilda's eyes are sparkling. Her purple hair is spread across the pillow. And she looks like a sleepy Mountain Fairy, napping in my cabin, wearing my clothes.

*My* Mountain Fairy.

I inhale as the memory of yesterday shimmers between us.

*My wife.*

I exhale. "Matilda. Did I hurt you?"

She shakes her head as she looks up at me. "Swear you didn't."

Barely grazed me." She reaches up and runs her fingers along her jaw.

"Promise?"

Her smile is softer. "Promise. Didn't hurt at all."

I relax the rest of the way. "Good."

Tilda's smile turns into a grimace. "I'd ask if I hurt you, but I'm pretty sure I know the answer. I'm really sorry about that. Whatever I was dreaming about made me jerk myself awake and..." Her eyes drop to the front of my pants. "I would never hurt *that* on purpose. Sorry."

*That* starts to stir at her attention. Previous pain forgotten. "I'm fine. I—"

Tilda's stomach growls.

"Fuck." I drag a hand down my face over the instant sense of failure that hits me. "I didn't feed you last night."

Tilda snickers again. "I'm not a lizard."

I drop my hand. "What?"

"I'm not a pet you have to *feed*. I know where your backpack is with the food." She swings her feet off the bed and sits up. "But it is your fault for distracting me."

She stands, the bed between us.

"I'm not going to apologize for that."

Tilda smirks. "I wouldn't accept it if you did. Now, will you please do your ranger thing and make sure there isn't a scary carnivore between here and the outhouse?"

# CHAPTER 81

## TILDA

"Thank you." I accept the metal coffee cup from Ethan.

He grunts and pours steaming water from the metal teapot into his own mug, dissolving the instant coffee.

Then he pours water into two bowls, each containing a few large spoonfuls of oatmeal, a scoop of sugar, and a dash of cinnamon.

Ethan holds out the bag of sugar to me with a clean spoon.

"Thank you." I repeat myself out of habit.

He lifts a brow at me.

I set the plastic bag on my lap and use the spoon to scoop up a tiny amount.

"Next time I come out here, I'll bring more supplies. Use as much as you want."

I hesitate, then decide to take him on his word and lower the spoon again, filling it with sugar.

Ethan takes the bag when I'm done, and I stir my coffee as I watch his fingers squeeze the zipper bag shut.

"I'm impressed you have sugar." I take a sip of the surprisingly good cup of coffee.

"Long shelf life." Ethan uses his spoon to stir the first bowl of oatmeal, then the second. "And it's a good source of calories for quick energy."

He pours a little more water into each bowl and catches me trying not to smile.

Ethan narrows his eyes. "What?"

"We just have such different lives." I mean it in a lighthearted way, but Ethan frowns. "I'm not a... camper." I lift my cup and gesture to the woods around us, explaining before he loses his marbles over nothing. "And I like casual walks, not thrill-seeking hikes. So I've never had a need for *long shelf-life, quick-energy calories.*"

Ethan's mouth flattens in that way he does when he's trying to look annoyed. But I really think he's trying not to smile.

I lift my cup to my lips. "You're an impressive man, Ranger Grant."

"Please go into the cabin." I keep my eyes on Ethan's, refusing to get distracted by the fact that he's been walking around shirtless for the past hour.

Ethan sighs, but he sets the pair of washcloths and bar of soap on the stump beside me. "Fine. But try to keep your feet dry."

I lift my hand to my forehead.

Ethan gives me a look. "Park rangers don't salute."

I keep my hand up. "That one guy saluted you."

"What one guy?"

"The one... I can't think of his name. He was in the parking lot when you helped me with Quackers's pool."

"Fisher?" Ethan rolls his eyes. "Fisher's an idiot."

"Roger that." I finish the salute anyway, then drop my hand.

Ethan shakes his head as he turns around.

I wait for him to disappear into the cabin. And then I wait

another moment until I hear the creaking sound of him dropping onto the bed, where I've spent most of the day.

Turning so my back is to the cabin, I strip off the shirt and sleep pants I've been wearing since last night and set them on another stump.

It's almost dusk. So the light is dimming, and the air is cooling, reminding me I should hurry.

I use the hair tie I found in my backpack to secure my long braid, then I dunk the washcloth into the bucket of warm water and scrub the soap bar against the wet cloth until it suds.

Today was... good.

Like really good.

Especially considering we're stranded here because of a plane crash.

After breakfast, Ethan made me sit with my feet up while he handwashed my clothes from yesterday, using the well water and powdered detergent. Then he washed his own clothes, minus his jeans.

As I rub the soapy cloth over my body, I look around at our clothing hanging from tree branches.

I re-lather the soap, then wash lower.

After the laundry, Ethan insisted I spend the afternoon reading in bed—with my feet up.

I picked a well-worn thriller and woke up two hours later to find Ethan outside. Chopping wood. With his shirt off.

I stood at the window for a long time, eating a protein bar and enjoying the show.

Then I lay back down, flustered. And by the time I got up again, I caught the top of Ethan's butt cheeks as he pulled on his boxer briefs, having just done his own standing bath.

My nipples pebble at the memory.

I bend down and dunk the washcloth in the water again.

Like this morning, Ethan used the firepit to heat water in the teapot, and he added it to the bucket of cold water so it wouldn't be frigid for me. But it's getting cooler by the moment.

I squeeze out some of the excess water, so it won't drip too much and get my socks wet.

The air out here... It's the same as the air at *my house.*

Fresh. Clean. Crisp.

I switch hands and run the cloth over my other arm.

A month ago, I was surviving, one day at a time, living in a concrete box, walking down busy sidewalks, and breathing in exhaust.

And today...

Today I'm standing naked in the woods, with the sunset and a sexy mountain man as my company.

And I feel free.

I'm stranded. Stuck in the woods with someone I'm just starting to know. Waiting for another person I've never met to rescue us. And yet...

I've never felt more alive.

Never felt more connected to this planet we live on.

I dunk the washcloth again and work my way down my body.

Something creaks in the cabin, and I resist turning around.

If that was Ethan getting off the bed to watch... I don't need to know.

The sun is setting, but it's not so far gone that Ethan wouldn't be able to see every inch of me from there.

A flush creeps up my stomach to my chest.

Ethan is probably the hottest man I've ever seen in real life. His face. His energy. His endless muscles. And yet, I've never felt more confident around a man.

He's seen me in my favorite dresses. In my pajamas. In basically nothing.

He's seen me fall, lose my cool, cry...

He's met my family.

And he still looks at me like he wants me. Like he likes what he sees.

*Perfect fucking hips.*

*I'm eating this perfect fucking pussy for dinner tomorrow.*

I hurry through another round of rinsing off.

Spending all day near each other, but not touching each other...

I drag the cloth down my chest, the fabric feeling rough over my sensitive skin.

I'm ready for the touching.

Bending, I soak the cloth for a final time.

But then I hear a new sound.

And it's not coming from the cabin behind me.

Still bent over, I tip my head up.

My eyes stare into the forest. But I don't see anything.

Letting go of the cloth, I stand slowly, scanning the tree line.

*Nothing.*

I reach for the dry washcloth. But just as my fingers brush the cotton, a chirp comes from the shadows.

I freeze.

*I know that sound.*

My breath catches in my lungs.

I take a step back.

And the mountain lion steps out from behind a tree.

Naked, terrified, shaking all over, I take another tiny step back.

I try to remember Ethan's survival lessons.

"Stay back." My command is a croak. But I keep facing forward. Keep eye contact with the animal. And I slowly lift my arms out to my sides.

*Make yourself bigger.*

*Shout.*

I swallow. "E-Ethan!"

"Right here." Ethan's shoulder brushes mine. There's a metallic click. "Cover your ears." Ethan holds the gun out in front of him.

"Don't kill it."

"Not unless I have to."

I lift my hands and press them to my ears.

"Go on!" Ethan shouts it so loud I feel the vibration in my bones. "This is *my* land. You will *not* come closer."

The cat doesn't move.

Ethan shifts his stance and braces his left hand under the grip of the gun. "Leave."

The cat lifts a paw.

Ethan fires.

Bark explodes out from a tree a few feet in front of the lion.

I shriek at the sheer volume of the gunshot.

"One more." Ethan warns me, then he pulls the trigger again.

A different tree trunk, three feet on the other side of the mountain lion, blasts the cat with a rain of wood chips.

And this time, the mountain lion spins and disappears into the forest.

My hands are still pressed to my ears when Ethan turns toward me, dips down, presses his shoulder into my stomach, wraps his arm around my thighs, and stands.

The motion has me letting out a different noise of surprise as the warm palm on my bare thigh reminds me that I'm completely naked.

I brace my hands against Ethan's back as he does a quick turn so he's facing the spot where the cat disappeared.

"I got you." He presses a kiss to my hip, his beard scratching in the most perfect way. "You're good."

Ethan backs toward the cabin.

He looks over his other shoulder, and I reach a hand out to guide us through the doorframe.

Ethan kicks the door shut, wraps his other arm around my waist, and tips me back, dropping me, once again, onto the mattress.

# CHAPTER 82

## ETHAN

MY LIDS LOWER AS I WATCH TILDA'S TITS JIGGLE.

As I watch *all of her* jiggle.

Keeping my eyes on her, I step back until I can reach the door, and I flip the dead bolt.

My heart has never beat so hard.

I don't think I've ever felt such instant fear before.

The engine failing in the air.

Even the first mountain lion across the river.

*Which I bet is the same mountain lion.*

I step closer to the bed.

Tilda sits up.

I was lying on the bed, right where she is now, listening to her splashing around in that damn bucket.

It was torture.

I knew she was naked. Standing outdoors. Surrounded by the forest.

My literal Mountain Fairy.

And I cracked. Gave into the craving.

With zero shame, I stood from the bed, went to the doorway, and I watched her.

Stared at her as she glistened with water droplets in the

waning sun.

And it took me too long.

I spent too long staring at her ass, focused on the spot of sweetness between her legs as she bent over. And I didn't notice.

Didn't notice the stillness.

Didn't see where her attention was.

Didn't realize she wasn't alone until I heard that chirp.

I take another step closer to the bed.

That fucking chirp.

It's a friendly sound. Not one of aggression. A curious cat checking things out.

But a cat checking out *my girl*.

And that's when the fear hit.

It consumed me as I reached for my gun.

It filled my lungs as I rushed out of the cabin.

It pressed down on my heart.

Because for just a moment.

A second.

I thought of a life without Matilda in it.

My mind tried to imagine an existence where I had her and lost her. And I couldn't.

I couldn't imagine it.

My future was nothing but a void.

I take the gun out from where I tucked it into my waistband and set it on a bin near the foot of the bed.

"Ethan?"

I lift my gaze slowly.

Tilda's sock-covered feet. The way her calves curve. Her bent knees. Her thighs squeezed together.

Her soft stomach.

Her arms crossed over her full breasts. Hiding those piercings.

*Those fucking piercings.*

I lift my eyes to her throat. To the flush of her cheeks. To her parted lips.

I lift my gaze to hers.

"You did a good job calling for me." I step forward, stopping when my legs bump against the foot of the bed. "And I need you to do it again."

"Wha—"

I reach down, grip her knees, and drag her toward me.

She falls onto her back, and I don't stop until her ass is at the very edge of the mattress.

But I don't let go of her legs.

I spread them.

"Ethan," she gasps. But she doesn't struggle.

I keep her legs open as I lower to the ground, kneeling between them.

I lower my face to her bare pussy, stopping with my mouth an inch from her core.

And I breathe her in.

I inhale the scent of my wife.

My fingers flex against her thighs, her flesh molding perfectly to my touch.

She makes a whimpering sound, and I keep my face where it is, but I lift my eyes to hers. "I need you to be loud, Starlight. I need to hear you moan." I lean in, just a little. Until my lips are brushing against her smooth flesh. "Show me how alive you are."

She opens her mouth.

And so do I.

I lean into her, flatten my tongue against her. And I lick.

I lick the length of her slit.

Then I do it again.

And on the third pass, I press in. I part her folds with my tongue, and I taste my wife.

Tilda lets out a strangled sound.

I do it again.

And again.

I push my tongue into her as far as I can.

I feel the heat of her against my mouth.

I consume her.

Tilda groans and presses her heels against my shoulders.

I groan back, sending vibrations through her body. And she squirms.

I palm the backs of her thighs and push her legs up, so her feet lift off my shoulders.

*Her poor, injured feet.*

I lick the length of her again.

"Ethan. Oh my gods." I glance up to see her hands reaching for me, but when I push my tongue into her hole, she gives up and reaches for her tits instead.

She pinches her nipples. The light catches on her piercing. And I growl against her slit.

Tilda's neck arches.

And I press my tongue against her, dragging it all the way up this time. And when I reach her clit, when I feel that warm pearl of sweetness, I suck.

Tilda cries out.

She squeezes her tits.

And I keep my mouth sealed over her bundle of nerves as I continue to create suction.

I suck and I lick and I trace every contour with the tip of my tongue.

"I... I..." Tilda's labored breathing fills the cabin.

I trail my hand down the inside of her thigh, my other hand still holding her legs spread.

Then I lean back. So I can watch.

So I can *see* as I slide my middle finger through the wetness coating her lips.

"Perfect fucking pussy."

I push my finger inside her.

Heat clenches around me.

And a sound of satisfaction leaves my throat.

I pull it out.

Then I push two fingers into my Tilda.

We both groan.

I twist my wrist. I rub my fingers against the inside of her. And I drop my mouth back to her bud.

Her clit is practically pulsing.

I lap at it.

I suck on it.

I rock my hips against nothing.

My cock is so hard.

Leaking.

And I want to fuck her.

I want to shove my dick into Tilda. Want to come deep inside her.

But I want her to come against my tongue more.

"Take it out," Tilda pants. "Ethan, take it out."

I lift my head, my mouth leaving her pussy. And I start to slide my fingers out.

"No." She shakes her head. "Your cock." She tilts her hips, like she's trying to get my fingers deeper. "Take your cock out. I want to watch you stroke it."

I push my fingers in until they're as deep as they can go.

Then I reach down with my other hand and jerkily undo my jeans.

"Is it out?" Tilda arches her neck, trying to see.

I lean back, sitting on my heels, and drag the front of my boxer briefs down.

I pull my dick free. "It's out."

Tilda moans. "Good Boy. Now stroke it."

I slowly drag my fingers out of her heat as I drag my other hand down my length.

I stroke up. I push my fingers in. And my lids lower as I pant at the sight of it all.

Tilda shifts up onto her elbows, trying to see below the foot of the bed.

Trying to see *me*.

I keep my fingers deep inside her pussy.

I rub my thumb against her clit.

And I lift up onto my knees, bringing my cock into her view.

Her eyes bounce from one hand, between her legs, to the other, stroking my length.

"Like what you see, Wife?"

Her pussy clenches around my fingers, giving me her answer even as she nods.

"Tell me what you want." I squeeze my dick tighter. "Tell me what to do."

"Keep... keep stroking." Tilda's words are choppy. "But make me come with your tongue."

I tighten every one of my muscles, trying to control my reaction to her demands.

I increase the pressure of my thumb on her clit as I lean down. "And when can I come?"

"After me." Tilda drops her knees to the side, opening herself to me. "You can come after me. But not before."

Lust pulses through my blood as I lean in and replace my thumb with my tongue.

"That's it." Tilda shifts her weight onto one elbow, reaches down, and grips my hair. "That's my Good Boy." She tilts her hips. "Don't stop." She moans and tightens her hold on my hair. "I'm almost..."

I keep licking.

Keep dragging my tongue over her bundle of nerves as I pull my two fingers out of her heat. And push three back in.

"Oh my... Yes..." She can't stay still.

And I'm ready to fucking blow.

I hum against Tilda's pussy.

"Ethan..." Her hips rock. "I'm... I'm gonna come."

I seal my lips around her clit. Push my fingers deeper. And hum again.

She combusts.

Her body arches and her head tips back as she lets out a whine of pleasure.

Her core throbs around my fingers. Against my tongue. And she soaks my chin.

I don't let up.

Don't stop.

Not until she tells me to.

Not until she pulls roughly on my hair.

I press my tongue flat against her as I look up her luscious body, into her sated eyes.

"Stop." She drops her hand from my hair.

I freeze all motion, my dick hard as an axe handle in my grip.

"Stand up. And let me watch." Tilda drops onto her back and drapes her arms above her head.

I pull my fingers free of her as I stand.

The bed is low.

She's below me, looking up.

I'm in the position of power. But I have none of it.

It all belongs to her.

"Stroke your dick."

I do.

Her eyes rove all over my body.

My cock. My stomach. My face.

"Are you close?"

I nod. "So fucking close."

"Do you want to come?"

"God. Yes." My bicep bulges as I continue to stroke. And, *fuck*, I'm so close. "Please," I beg. "Please tell me I can come."

Tilda makes a throaty humming sound. "Lick your fingers clean, then you can."

Pressure builds in my balls.

That sentence is going to be burned into my memory until the day I die.

"Where?" I look down at her glorious body as I lift my fingers to my mouth. "Where should I come?"

I part my lips. And I lock my gaze with Tilda's as I lick her shine off my fingers.

"On me." She whispers the demand. "Come on me." I suck a finger into my mouth, filling my senses with her taste. "Now, Ethan. Come now."

My body obeys, and the first pulse of release splashes across her stomach.

The second lands on her tits.

"Good Boy."

I keep stroking.

"That's my Good Boy."

I keep painting her with my pleasure.

Tilda lowers one hand and drags a finger through the streak on her tits, and my cock jolts a final time.

A wave of dizziness washes over me, and I sway.

I blink away the spots in my vision.

But then I see Tilda with her finger in her mouth.

The finger she just dragged through my release.

And my balls pulse again.

# CHAPTER 83

## TILDA

With Ethan's taste on my tongue and his heaving body standing at the foot of the bed, I smile.

His body twitches as he releases his cock. His super pretty cock.

"That was... wow." I try to catch my breath, wishing I could take a photo of this moment.

Ethan shirtless, jeans open and shoved down his hips, still-hard cock exposed.

He really is something.

Ethan blinks. Slowly. And I snicker.

"You okay, Ranger?"

He nods and swallows.

I snicker again.

Then a shiver dances across my skin, reminding me I'm even more naked. And no longer clean.

"One second." Ethan turns toward the door, his shoulders shifting as he adjusts himself back into his jeans.

And before I can stop him, he's opening the door and walking outside.

"Ethan!" I squeak and scramble up from the bed. "The mountain lion!"

I catch myself on the doorway, not wanting to go outside.

"Stay there," he calls back as he picks up the second washcloth and pumps clean water onto it.

Clean, freezing water.

Ethan squeezes the cloth, then turns and strides back toward me.

His eyes are locked on my body, not showing any concern for the woods around us.

Then I remember my pajamas are still sitting on a stump.

I hold my hand out for the cloth as he approaches. "Can you grab my clothes too?"

I feel like a giant chicken. I know I'll have to go outside to get to the outhouse. But I'm not ready yet.

And I won't do it alone.

I look around at the trees and bite my lip as I use the cloth to clean up the mess Ethan left all over me.

The trees look like the same ones that are on my property. Same ones in the state park.

Same habitat. Same climate.

"Um." I'm afraid I already know the answer, but I decide to confirm. "Are there mountain lions where we live too?"

Ethan picks up my clothes and shakes them out as he walks back. "Yes. But it's rare to see them."

I step back so Ethan can enter the cabin. "Yes? Like for sure?"

He shuts the door behind him, then drops my pajamas onto the bed. "It's estimated that there are three to five thousand mountain lions in the state of Colorado."

My mouth drops open. "What?"

"But." He turns the lantern on, filling the cabin with a warm glow. "They generally avoid humans. So even though they're around, they're rarely spotted."

With Ethan's back to me, I use a clean spot of the washcloth and quickly drag it between my legs.

Wrappers crinkle as Ethan grabs a pair of granola bars.

"So what's with this one, then?" I pick up my pants and pull them on. "It doesn't seem to be avoiding humans."

Ethan grunts. "Hopefully he will now."

"He?" I tug my shirt on.

Ethan lifts a shoulder. "I think that's the same one from the river. His actions make him seem young, but he's on the bigger side, so I'm guessing male."

"But you think you scared him away?"

Ethan hands me one of the bars. "His behavior wasn't aggressive. I think he just wanted to see what we were up to. But now he knows we're noisy and scary, so I don't think we'll see him again."

I take the bar and bite into it as Ethan changes his jeans for pajama pants.

"Ethan?"

He grabs the lamp and carries it to the bed. "Yeah?"

I lower the wrapper to my side. "Uncle Jack left me two million dollars."

Ethan lifts a brow.

"I, um, I had no idea. I thought the twenty thousand he left me was all of his savings. And even that amount... It felt unreal. But two..." I blow out a breath. "That's why we—I—had to get married. He put it in the will. That I only got the money if I was married by my thirtieth birthday. And if I didn't... He said if I didn't get married, it would all go to *them*. Which is bonkers. Because he hates them. *I* hate them. And the money would just go to, I don't know, a random stranger. Or disappear altogether. I never would've asked. Or pretended like that wasn't the plan already. I just... I know Uncle Jack would roll in his grave if they got his money." I shift on my feet, feeling so uncomfortable and wishing I'd already told him about all of this.

"Tilda."

"I'm not greedy." I rush the words out. "I'll share the money with you. Whatever's fair. And I'm going to get a job. I've started looking. I just... I—"

"Matilda." I stop fidgeting and meet Ethan's gaze. "I get it." I open my mouth, but he lifts his brow again, so I stay quiet. "I get it, okay? I wouldn't give those people a nickel if I found one on the floor."

My shoulder sag. "They're the worst."

Ethan nods. "And I don't need your money."

"But—"

"I won't take any of your money, Tilda."

I lift my hands, then let them drop back to my sides, the empty wrapper crinkling with the motion. I'll find a way to give Ethan some of the money later. "I just don't understand *why*. Like, *why* did Uncle Jack do this?" I take a breath and finally admit what we both must know by now. *The hired pilot and driver. The will. The nearest wedding chapel expecting us...* "Why would he force me to marry *you*?"

# Chapter 84

## Ethan

I swallow.

*Because he wants me to watch over you.*

*Because he asked me to keep an eye on you.*

*Because he sent me a letter telling me to help you.*

But I don't say any of that.

I should.

I should tell her everything. Lay it out so she knows.

But I can't forget her reaction from before. When I casually mentioned I was hired for the job.

And I don't want to see that look on her face.

Not again.

And the rest of it—it doesn't matter. The web that Jack wove, it doesn't fucking matter. Not to me.

So I'll tell her later. When we've built more trust between us. When I'm certain she'll listen to everything I say.

I pull back the blankets. "Get in bed, Matilda."

She does. "Can I wake you up when I have to use the outhouse?"

"If you don't, I'll be upset." I turn off the lantern and climb in on my side.

We shuffle closer, facing each other in the mostly dark until our knees bump together.

I reach under the blankets, lift Tilda's top leg, and slide my knee between hers.

*I will not be kneed in the balls tomorrow morning.*

She lets out a humorous huff but doesn't resist the new position.

My forearms brush against hers. "When's your birthday?"

"Tuesday."

I close my eyes, putting that date into my memory.

"The will..." Tilda lets out a defeated sigh. "It said that the two million would be given to me over four years, on my birthday. I don't know if there are specifics. Like if I have to be married to the same person the whole time. Or just *married* in general."

My stomach sinks, and I open my eyes.

Tilda's outline is barely visible, but I stare at her.

The woman who has made me smile more than anyone else ever has.

The woman who's made me laugh.

Who's given me her body. And her control.

"You aren't marrying anyone else." My tone is low.

"I just mean, like, if you... If you want to be done. Before the four years are up. I know it's a long time."

"Tilda."

I feel her exhale across my lips. "Just promise you'll tell me. If you want to be done."

"Matilda."

"Just promise?" she whispers.

"Promise," I whisper back, knowing I can keep that promise. Because I'll never want to be done.

I can feel her nod against the pillow.

I shift closer, and she slides one of her arms between mine.

"Go to sleep, Starlight."

"Why do you call me that?" Her voice is a whisper.

And I answer just as quietly. "I'll tell you later."

# CHAPTER 85

## TILDA

My nose twitches. And my eyes open.

Sunlight fills the cabin.

The blankets are pulled up to my chin. I'm curled on my side. And I'm alone.

But the door is open, allowing a stream of fresh mountain air to breeze over me. And with it, the scent of coffee.

We're getting rescued today. And I'm excited for running water and electricity. But being here... It's been nice.

Relaxing even.

Minus the encounters with the mountain lion.

I smile against the pillow, remembering Ethan last night.

I have no idea what time it was when I woke up having to pee. But true to his word, he got up and walked me to the outhouse. And he stood outside the door, flashlight in hand, since I had the lantern, and he hummed. The "Happy Birthday" song.

My smile turns into a snicker.

It was so bad. And the most random song choice. But also incredibly sweet of him to oblige when I told him I couldn't go with him listening.

And then after...

I swallow as my humor fades.

After, when we got back into bed...

I blink as I look at his empty side of the mattress.

It was like the other times. Us getting in on our sides. Moving together. Limbs tangling.

But last night, Ethan pulled me even closer. Our arms squished between our bodies. And... I loved it.

Loved the warmth.

Loved the feeling of being intertwined.

Loved sharing a pillow.

Loved falling asleep with his lips against my forehead.

I... I remind myself to enjoy the memory. That there's no need to feel sad.

Just because we're leaving today doesn't mean I'll never sleep in the same bed as Ethan again.

*We are married, after all.*

Married.

Which is just another reminder of how good Ethan is.

Like just... *good*.

When I told him about the money and the will, he didn't judge me. Didn't want anything. Just told me he understood.

Ethan might act like a grump, but he's a good man.

*My Good Boy.*

Heat creeps up my chest as more memories from last night come to mind. And that lightness from before returns.

No, last night was not the last time I'll share a bed with Ethan.

This might be complicated. Absurd even. But the chemistry between us is real. And the scent of coffee reminds me that today is only just beginning.

# CHAPTER 86

## ETHAN

MY EYES TRACK TILDA AS SHE EMERGES FROM MY CABIN, and tightness fills my chest.

*She's mine.*

Her purple braid is frizzy.

Her pajama outfit, which she's been wearing for over twenty-four hours, is wrinkled.

And she's wearing my way-too-big-for-her spare pair of tennis shoes.

I take a sip of my coffee, memorizing the moment.

*She looks perfect.*

Tilda covers her yawn as she sits on the stump across from me. A small fire crackles in the pit between us.

I'm back in my flannel and jeans. And I've folded all the laundry we had hanging from the trees and set it on the stump farthest from the fire so they won't smell like smoke.

"Coffee?"

"Yes, please." Tilda's voice is still sleepy. Adorable.

I use a cloth to grip the handle of the tea kettle and pour hot water into the mug I set out for Tilda, instant coffee and sugar already in the bottom.

After giving it a stir, I hold it out for her.

"Thank you." She takes it from me with an easy smile. "Any visitors this morning?"

I shake my head and add a bit of the hot water to my mug, warming my coffee. "Saw a hawk, but no cats."

I don't like that Tilda is worried about mountain lions. But it's a reasonable worry. They do leave humans alone for the most part, but they aren't an animal you want to fuck with. And they aren't an animal you want to try to befriend. Unlike a duck.

Tilda holds her mug in both hands. "I hope Quackers hasn't left."

That newly constant desire to smile sinks into my chest.

*It's like she read my mind.*

"Pretty sure you had enough food out to last her a week."

Tilda hums as she takes a sip. "I hope so."

I debate telling her about the couple I know who practically adopted a bear. Or the other couple who built a whole damn house for a fox. But I decide she doesn't need encouragement. If I tell her, she'll probably spend all that inheritance money building a damn duck habitat.

"Hungry?" I put my mug down and pick up the two bowls I set on the ground.

Tilda nods. "Yes, please."

I set the bowls on the edge of the firepit and add water to each.

Like the coffee, the ingredients are already inside.

Oatmeal. Sugar. And some wild strawberries that I picked this morning.

While the oats soak, I add more water to the kettle and set it back in the fire.

"How come there isn't a fireplace in the cabin? Too hard to get the materials here?"

"That." I nod. "But we also have to keep fires small out here. We don't want anyone seeing the smoke and reporting a wildfire." I stir the oatmeal.

Tilda is quiet for a long moment, and when I look up, I find her lips pressed together.

I narrow my eyes. "What?"

She loses the battle against her grin. "Will you say it?"

"Say what?"

"You know…" Tilda lifts her brows. "What the bear says."

"What the bear says?" I tilt my head as I look at my mysterious girl.

She glances at the fire.

And I think I get it.

I shake my head.

Tilda sets her mug down and places her palms together. "Please?"

Grabbing one of the bowls, I stand. And I slowly walk around the fire to Tilda.

She lowers her hands to her lap as she watches me. Her eyes wide. Her expression hopeful.

And I know I'll do it. Because I'd do anything for my Starlight.

Stopping before her, I grip Tilda's chin and tip her head back. Then I bend down, stopping when our lips are just inches apart.

Holding her gaze, I lower my voice. "Only *you* can prevent forest fires."

A puff of air leaves her parted lips.

I set the bowl of oatmeal in her hands. "Now eat your breakfast."

# CHAPTER 87

## TILDA

MY FINGERS CLUTCH AT THE BOWL.

*Sorry, Ranger. But there is definitely a fire. In my pants.*

Without looking, I put a spoonful of the oatmeal into my mouth, needing to wet my suddenly dry throat.

Fresh fruity sweetness bursts across my taste buds, and I jerk my attention away from Ethan's jean-clad ass down to my bowl.

"What is this?" My question is garbled as I talk with my mouth still full.

"Wild strawberries." Ethan sits and picks up his bowl.

"From where?" It's a dumb question, but I can't stop myself.

Ethan tips his head to his right. "Found a patch over that way."

I look in that direction, pausing my spoon midway between my face and the bowl. "Oh."

"I kept the cabin in sight. And I left the door closed."

I blow out a breath. Ethan once again says exactly the thing I need to hear. "Sorry. I know I'm being a scaredy-cat. This whole *nature thing* is still new to me."

"You're not a *scaredy-cat*, Firecracker. It's good to have a healthy respect for this *nature thing*."

I give him a half smile. "Thanks." Then I use my spoon to

scoop out a tiny strawberry and eat it. "This is really freaking amazing."

When I look back up, Ethan's looking at me like he wants to ask something.

"Yes, Berry Ranger?"

He smirks. "Is there a reason you don't swear?"

I open my mouth, then shrug. "I swear."

He purses his lips, like he's trying to remember a time.

I poke at a strawberry with my spoon and sigh. "My family swore a lot. *Swears* a lot. And I'm not like *offended* by it. But when I was younger, I just... didn't pick up the habit. And I guess it stuck. I don't even really think about it anymore."

Ethan's expression is so serious that I know he's thinking the worst.

And I'd like to tell him they didn't swear *at* me. That they didn't call me a *fucking waste of space*. Or a *stupid ass* when I didn't do well on a test.

I'd love to tell him that.

But I won't lie to Ethan.

"Do you want me to stop swearing?" he asks with complete sincerity. And that's what does it.

Pressure builds in my eyes.

Ethan swears all the time. It's part of his vocabulary. But he still asks.

I shake my head, biting down on my lip.

"I can try." He insists, melting my heart even more.

But I need him to believe me. So I make sure he hears how much I mean it. "I appreciate the offer. But I don't want to fucking change you, Ethan."

# CHAPTER 88

## ETHAN

*I DON'T WANT TO FUCKING CHANGE YOU.*

This girl.

*This fucking girl.*

Tightness shaped like a word that starts with *L* wraps around my throat.

And I have to work to keep my voice even. "I don't want to change you either, Starlight. Now eat your fucking oatmeal."

# CHAPTER 89

## TILDA

"I'M FINE."

Ethan reaches for my boots, and I swat his hands away.

He grumbles as he stands, "Fine. But you *will* tell me if anything starts to hurt."

I salute him, just to be annoying. "Sir, yes, sir."

Ethan doesn't react. And his nonreaction makes me grin.

Then I hold my hands out to him. "Help me up?"

His big hands engulf mine, and he pulls me to my feet.

Back in my dress, clean panties, and shorts, I feel like me again.

Mostly.

I did another quick washcloth bath, this time with Ethan standing ten feet away, facing the woods on mountain lion duty. My hair is begging to be washed, but that will have to wait until I'm home.

Then I dressed, sniffing everything and thinking I might have to start hanging my clothes from trees to air dry them. And now...

I look around the cabin.

Now, with everything packed back up the way we found it, we're ready to leave.

Ethan insisted on re-treating every tiny mark on my feet and ankles. Covering everything with Band-Aids. Then giving me a new pair of his socks as another barrier between my skin and my boots.

He also tried to convince me to let him give me a piggyback ride to the *extraction site*. And even though I'm sure Ethan—and all his muscles—could do it, there's no way I'm letting him carry me.

I follow Ethan out of the cabin, and while he double-checks that everything is shut tight, I take my phone out of my mini backpack and turn it on.

Ethan wasn't happy about me carrying my own bag, but he's done so much for me already. And I wanted my phone handy so I could take some pictures.

I snap one of the cabin. A few more.

I take a picture of the firepit, now empty of any debris. The ashes buried and mixed with dirt to ensure no flames come back to life.

I take a video of the forest, turning in a slow circle to get the full view.

I take a picture of Ethan walking toward me.

And a second.

And I'm grinning by the third, when he's close enough to fill the whole screen.

He takes the phone from my hand, turns it around, and takes a photo of me.

I'm still smiling, and I don't care how bad I must look. This is a memory I'm happy to keep.

"Let's do one together." I move so I'm standing beside him, the cabin at our backs. "To remember our honeymoon," I say jokingly.

Ethan switches the camera so it's facing us, puts his arm around my shoulders, pulls me into his side, and presses a kiss to the top of my head.

And that's when he takes the picture.

When his lips are on me. And when my expression is full of... joy.

I can only describe it as joy.

Because no matter how things turn out once we're back home, I'll always have this moment.

# Chapter 90

## Ethan

"It's just a little farther," I tell Tilda.

She sighs in response. "My feet are literally fine, Ranger Obnoxious."

I side-eye her, pretending I don't like the names she makes up for me.

It's only about half a mile from the cabin to the landing site—which are the coordinates I gave Stoleman for the pickup. But I hate making Tilda walk that far. Her feet might not be bleeding anymore, but they can't feel great either.

"When we get home, you need to spend a full two days with your feet up."

Her annoyed exhale is adorable.

Then I realize what I said.

*When* we *get home.*

To our own homes.

My jaw works as my steps crunch over downed pine needles.

We're married. Even if we weren't dating before this weekend, it doesn't matter. Because we're married now. I should be able to live in the same house as my wife. *I* want *to live in the same house as my wife.* But... I don't know how to accomplish that.

"I meant to ask you..." Tilda pauses as I grip her upper arm and help her over a log. "Have you ever done that landing thing before?"

"What landing thing?"

"The *no engine* landing thing."

I let my fingers trail down the bare skin of her arm as I lower my hand. Then I tell her the truth. "No."

She jerks her head in my direction. "No?"

I lift a brow as I look at her. "That surprises you?"

"Well, I don't know." Tilda puffs out her cheeks. "You did a good job, so I assumed you'd had practice. I mean, a good job except for that tree."

I narrow my eyes at the dig. "That tree shouldn't've been there."

She nods seriously. "It was awfully inconsiderate."

The backs of our hands brush against each other, leaving my skin tingling. "I have a question too."

"Hmm?" Tilda's fingers reach for mine.

I entwine them. "Did that lawyer have a whistle?"

Her laugh is bright and loud. "You heard that?"

I smirk down at her. "Pretty sure the whole building heard that."

Tilda shakes her head. "Uncle Jack had apparently given it to the lawyer. And even put a line in the will saying... Oh, what was it? Something like, *Don't embarrass me by making Richard use the whistle.* But the lawyer didn't read that part until after he used it the first time." She laughs again. "The whole thing was... I don't even know. But Uncle Jack wrote some pretty direct things to the family that were immensely satisfying to hear. They"—she gestures with her free hand, meaning the whole lot of them— "were not happy about it."

"I'm sorry I missed it."

She smiles up at me. "We'll get a copy, and I'll recreate the scene for you."

I squeeze her fingers.
She squeezes mine back.
And then we step out into the clearing.

# CHAPTER 91

## TILDA

Ethan looks at his watch.

"What time is it?"

"Seven minutes to noon." He tips his head back and looks up at the bright blue sky. "Put your flannel on. It's gonna be cold up there."

*Up there.*

Stress swirls in my stomach as I untie the sleeves of Ethan's flannel from around my waist.

I've been making a point to *not* think about our flight home. I've never loved flying. And now that the last flight I was on ended with a *controlled emergency landing*, I fear I may be developing a phobia. But now that we're here—literally *here*—there's no more avoiding it.

I start to pull one sleeve up my arm before I remember to take my backpack off.

"Let me help." Ethan's voice is steady as he takes the flannel from my grip. "It's going to be okay."

"I know." My voice cracks, giving me away.

Ethan makes a deep sound in his throat as he helps me take my backpack off.

He sets the backpack at my feet. "Arm."

I slide my arm through the sleeve as he holds the flannel up.

Ethan circles behind me to my other side. "Other arm."

I try to start the buttons, but my hands have started trembling.

Warm fingers grip my chin, and I lift my eyes to Ethan's. "I won't let anything happen to you."

"I know," I whisper. "I don't mean to be scared."

"It's okay to be scared, Starlight." Ethan leans in, pressing his lips lightly against mine. "But right now, you don't have to be. I've got you."

*Starlight.*

He seems to only call me that when he's being sweet.

And I love it.

"Tell me you believe me."

I force my shoulders to relax. "I believe you."

Ethan nods, then drops his hands to the front of my flannel. But instead of buttoning it, he ties the bottom corners together, cinching it around my waist.

He steps back, taking in his handywork. And the edge of his mouth turns up. "Cute."

I start to smile back.

But then I hear it.

The *whomp, whomp* of an approaching helicopter.

# CHAPTER 92

## ETHAN

I HAND TILDA HER BACKPACK. "STAY HERE."

She nods, and I jog into the center of the clearing.

It's a natural break in the trees. An easy spot to see from above and close to the cabin, so these are the coordinates I have memorized.

Squinting against the sun, I look up. And a second later, a helicopter flies low into view.

I raise my arms and slowly wave them back and forth, my red flannel visible among the trees.

The chopper does a tight circle, letting me know he sees me, then I drop my arms and jog back to Matilda.

She's hugging her little backpack to her chest, and she's put her sunglasses on.

She looks nervous. And it makes my stomach ache.

I take her hand, and her fingers tremble against mine. But she doesn't pull away.

Taking my own aviators out of my pocket, I put them on, and together we watch the helicopter land.

The skids touch down, the helicopter aimed right at us. But the pilot doesn't get out. He just waves us forward.

Tilda must see the motion too because she takes a step. Even afraid, even with the rotor downwash blowing over us like a storm and the incredible noise, she still takes the step.

Holding my hand the whole way, Tilda follows me around to the passenger side of the chopper, crouching low like I do when we get close.

And I'm so fucking grateful she wears those cute little shorts under her dress. Because her dress is flying all over the place. And if the pilot saw her ass, we'd have problems.

I pull the door open, take Tilda's backpack from her, then grip her by the hips and help her into the fuselage.

She slides to the center of the bench seat, and I hand up both backpacks before I climb inside.

Settling next to Tilda, opposite corner from the pilot, I shut the door, then face forward.

The pilot twists in his seat and hands two headsets back.

I take them both and help Tilda put hers on, then place mine over my ears.

The noise-canceling effects work immediately, dampening the sound of the blades.

The pilot is an older dude. Bushy gray eyebrows sticking out over the top of his sunglasses. And an equally bushy mustache covering the entirety of his top lip.

His mouth moves, and I hear it through the headphones. "Welcome aboard."

I nod. "Appreciate the ride."

"People call me Vulture."

I think of that stupid code name Stoleman gave me and have to force myself not to grimace. "I'm Bunny."

I hear Tilda's snort through the headphones, and Vulture's brows lift into his hairline.

"Thought the name was Ranger, but whatever floats your boat, kid."

Tilda snickers, and I sigh.

"There is no code word, is there?"

Vulture's mustache jumps when he grins. "Nope."

I sit back in the seat. "Stoleman's an asshole."

The man laughs as he turns around to face front but doesn't disagree. "Buckle up, Mr. and Mrs. Bunny. We're taking off in one."

I help Matilda with her seat belt, then do my own.

I lift my elbow away from my side, and Matilda immediately slides her arm through mine.

*Ready?* I mouth.

She nods.

"Ready," I say.

And then we lift off the ground.

# CHAPTER 93

## TILDA

THIS TIME, I CLOSE MY EYES WHEN WE LAND.

But instead of gripping Ethan's thigh, I hold his hand. In both of mine.

The flight was smoother than I expected. And the views were obviously beautiful. But I'm glad to have my feet on the ground.

I exhale and open my eyes.

I know I'll have to fly again at some point in my life, but I really don't want to.

Like, I *really* don't want to.

Ethan shifts beside me, then he reaches over and unbuckles my seat belt.

I watch his capable hands and accept that whenever I do have to fly again, I want it to be with him.

*My husband.*

The noise lessens, and the vibrations around us come to a stop.

Ethan points to his headset, then he takes it off.

I do the same and hand mine to Vulture. Then I follow Ethan out of the helicopter.

After a quick thank-you and goodbye to the pilot, Ethan and I walk to the little restroom building together. And when I'm done, I wash my hands three times in a row, more grateful than I've ever been for running water.

When I step outside, I find Ethan talking to the guy who was with him Friday morning, when I first got to the airport.

He grins at me. "Welcome back."

My answering smile feels tired. "Thanks. Glad to be home."

His attention moves back to Ethan, and he asks about the damage to the wing. So either Ethan or Vulture told him about the *landing*.

Ethan's fingers grip mine, and the three of us start walking toward hangar five, where our trucks are parked.

It's not late in the day, still early afternoon. But I'm ready to go to bed. And I bet I'll sleep for twelve hours straight.

I lift my arm and yawn into my flannel sleeve.

Ethan squeezes my other hand.

I look up at him, our matching sunglasses reflecting each other's distorted image.

"If you feel okay to drive, you should head home. Before you get too tired."

I nod, knowing he's right.

Honestly, I felt fine—scared but fine—all day. But as soon as I got my feet on the ground, exhaustion took hold.

And if these two are going to stick around, talking plane terms, I will definitely fall asleep on the pavement.

Ethan lets go of my hand and hooks a finger in one of my backpack straps. "Get your keys out, Tilda."

*Right.*

I pull one arm free from the shoulder strap and hold my backpack against my front as I dig around for my truck keys.

Warm fingers grip my chin and tip my head up.

"Yes, Ethan?"

"Are you sure you're okay to drive?"

"I'm sure."

He waits a beat, then he releases me. "Go straight home. Get some rest."

I lift my hand to my forehead, saluting while my keys dangle from my fingers.

The other man chuckles.

And the edge of Ethan's lips twitch. Just a little. "Straight home."

I drop my hand. "Straight home."

Then I turn away from my husband and get into my truck.

THE FRONT DOOR CLICKS SHUT, AND I REACH BEHIND me, turning the lock.

Then I stand in my entryway, taking in my home.

It's how I left it.

Mostly clean.

Those last couple boxes still not unpacked.

It's cozy.

And it's mine.

And... it feels empty.

*I miss Ethan.*

I lean down and unlace my boots.

As I tug them off, I debate throwing them straight in the trash, but the memory of lying on the bed as Ethan tended to my feet prevents me from getting rid of them. So I leave them next to my other shoes under the front window.

I checked Quackers's pool and food dish when I walked up. Still looks clean. Still has a little bit of food. So I don't feel bad waiting until tomorrow to refresh them.

The couch is tempting. But a shower is my top priority.

I take my time, lathering up, scrubbing, rinsing. And doing it all over again.

When I step out of the bathroom with my hair in a towel and my softest pajama shirt on, I feel like a whole different person.

I'm still sleepy. But I'm *clean* and sleepy. And that's somehow different.

As I debate the merits of napping on the couch versus just going to bed, I can't help but notice how quiet it is.

And yes, there it is. The *too quiet*.

The great big kind of quiet that makes you feel alone.

Secluded. With nothing but your thoughts.

Sadness cradles my shoulders.

The cabin, in the middle of absolutely nowhere, was the quietest place I've ever been. And I never felt like this.

Never felt the stress of the silence.

Because I had Ethan.

I had someone to share the space with. And even if he wasn't talking, he was there, exuding energy.

That sadness gets heavier.

I know we aren't *done*. We're married. But we didn't really talk about what happens next.

Feeling more than a little depressed and even more tired than I was a minute ago, I walk into the living room and turn on the TV, playing the DVD that's still in there from before.

Then I go into my bedroom, turn my tablet on, and hit Play on a TV show.

As my house fills with noise, I crawl under the covers and close my eyes.

# CHAPTER 94

## ETHAN

My house comes into view before me, and I feel... off.

It's the same single-story structure it's always been.

Attached two-car garage. Green shingled roof. Dark wood siding. Two bedrooms. Two bathrooms. An eat-in kitchen. Living room with a worn couch and two recliners. And the same coffee table Sandra scratched her initials into when she was bored one day.

After that accident... when Sandra was only twelve and suddenly my responsibility, she told me she didn't want to live in the house that reminded her so much of Mom and Dad. And honestly, I didn't either.

So we sold it. We bought this place. And then we split the rest of the inheritance in half. Hers went into savings for when she got older, and mine went into investments and keeping us alive.

It's been a good home. A solid one. Surrounded by pines. On a handful of acres. Far enough from town to be peaceful. Close enough for driving Sandra to school. Not far from the Lonely Peak State Park entrance.

But it's on the opposite side of the park from Tilda.

Twenty-four minutes away from her front door.

Close enough for a visit. Too far for an emergency.

Pressing the button on my visor, I wait for the garage door to open, then I park my personal black pickup next to my official work one.

Climbing out, I hear a rumble of thunder, and I give a thanks to the sky for waiting. My Mountain Fairy was scared enough on that flight home. Bad weather would've traumatized her.

Leaving the garage door open, I step into my house.

It's quiet.

It's how it always is.

But it feels... stale.

Not bothering with my boots, I start to cross the kitchen, when I see it.

The envelope.

The letter.

I left it on the counter. And it's still there. Staring back at me.

Guilt makes my steps heavy as I cross to it.

And anger at myself makes my fingers numb as I lift it.

I know I should've told Tilda about it. Explained that Jack sent it to me. But... there was never a good time.

*There was never a good time.*

I'll repeat that to myself however many times it takes.

And the letter, it doesn't mean anything.

I pull the paper out of the envelope.

It doesn't mean anything because even if I'd never gotten this fucking letter, I still would have done everything the same.

I still would've flown Tilda to Vegas.

I still would've stood beside her against her shitty fucking family.

I still would've married her.

Without anyone's interference, I still would've married Matilda Iris Wright.

I unfold the single sheet of paper.

DEAR ETHAN,

I'M SURE YOU'VE MET MY MATTY BY NOW. SORRY

*(NOT ACTUALLY SORRY) FOR MISLEADING YOU. BUT IT WAS NECESSARY TO GET YOUR ACCEPTANCE.*

*YOU'RE A STUBBORN MAN, ETHAN GRANT. A REAL ASS SOMETIMES. BUT YOUR HEART IS GOOD.*

*AND MATILDA NEEDS SOMEONE WITH A GOOD HEART.*

*YOU GAVE ME YOUR WORD THAT YOU'D KEEP AN EYE ON HER. AND I NEED YOU TO KEEP YOUR WORD. BECAUSE EVEN IF YOU DIDN'T KNOW IT AT THE TIME, IT WAS A PROMISE TO A DYING MAN. AND SINCE I'M DEAD NOW, YOU CAN'T TAKE IT BACK.*

*SO, ETHAN GRANT, PARK RANGER, OVERALL GRUMP, I NEED YOU TO PROMISE ME ONE MORE THING.*

*THAT YOU WILL KEEP AN EYE ON MATILDA.*

*THAT YOU WILL KEEP HER SAFE.*

*AND FOR THE NEXT THREE MONTHS, STARTING TOMORROW, WHEN YOU FLY TO VEGAS, I NEED YOU TO DO WHATEVER SHE ASKS OF YOU. NO MATTER HOW... UNCONVENTIONAL.*

A HEAVY SCOFF LEAVES MY CHEST.

*UNCONVENTIONAL.*

I shake my head.

A Dolly Parton wedding sure counts as un-fucking-conventional.

My jaw works as I lower my eyes back to the page.

Then my phone rings.

I pull it from my pocket and see it's coming from the park's Visitor Center.

"Ethan." I answer as I always do.

"Hey, man." Conners heaves out a breath. "I'm not sure if you're available, but we had some idiot break the handrail on the west overlook trail. And we're trying to get it fixed before tomorrow morning."

"I'm available." I set the letter down. "I'll be there in ten."

After hanging up, I slide my phone back into my pocket and stride toward the side door.

Anything is better than sitting alone in my house right now.

When I yank the door open, a gust of wind blows through the garage, trying to push me back, but I step through and drag the door closed behind me.

FOUR HOURS LATER, I'M BACK IN THE GARAGE.

I did more than I needed to, well aware I was doing it to stay busy and out of my head. But it worked.

Once I kick my boots off, I walk straight to the envelope that's lying on the floor. Probably blown off the counter by the wind earlier.

And I do what I should've done when it was first handed to me.

I walk it to my garbage bin and drop it in.

I'm married to Tilda because I want to be.

And that's all she ever needs to know.

# CHAPTER 95

## TILDA

"WHAT WOULD YOU LIKE?" THE BARISTA SMILES AT ME from her side of the counter.

"Um..." I roll my lips together as I read the list of specialty drink options. "What's in a birthday cake latte?"

The woman grins. "Standard latte, but we whisk a couple spoonfuls of vanilla cake mix into the milk. Then top it with whipped cream and rainbow sprinkles. It's so good." She wiggles her fingers in a *gimme* motion. "And we use gluten-free mix. I personally think it's better hot, but you can have it either way."

I grin back at her excitement. "I'll take a hot one, please."

"Size?"

"Oh, um... large?"

She nods, confirming my choice as a good one. "Love the dress, by the way," she says while typing my order into her system. "It's so pretty."

"Thank you." My cheeks heat as I smooth a hand down my lacy pink skirt.

I dressed for my own personal birthday party, in a dress that's somewhere between hot and neon pink, with yellow hearts sporadically embroidered throughout the bodice and skirt. It's cute but a little skimpy with thin straps, ending above my knees.

"Would you like anything else?"

I eye the little bakery case off to the side but shake my head.

This drink will be enough of a treat. And... eating a birthday dessert alone is a little sad.

A fact I know from experience.

Some of that is my family's fault for sucking. Some of it is mine for never telling my friends when it was my birthday.

The barista tells me my total, and I use my card to pay, selecting the highest tip amount available on the automated system.

"Aw, thanks, hon."

"You're welcome." I tuck the card back in my wallet.

Knowing I'm getting money today stresses me out. But being able to tip with abandon makes me feel a little better about it.

I step aside to wait as she makes my drink, and I think about the friends I had back in Vegas. People I worked with, mostly, who I don't really talk to outside of the random group invite.

A weird feeling settles in my stomach as I accept the fact that I don't plan on telling them I moved.

As I accept the fact that I'm not close with anyone.

Except...

*A tattooed man sleeping in bed with me.*

*A muscled man scaring off a mountain lion for me.*

*A grumpy man humming the "Happy Birthday" song so I could pee.*

"One birthday cake latte."

I blink and grab the paper cup off the end of the counter. "Thank you."

I was planning to sit inside and enjoy my drink while using their internet, but half of the tables are already in use, and I'm starting to feel a bit overwhelmed. So, I take my latte to my truck.

Thankfully, the wind is cooperating today, meaning it's a little warm, but I don't flash the store as I walk to where I parked.

I left my windows cracked, so when I get in, I don't bother starting the engine.

Settling into the seat, I take a sip. And I groan.

*Wowza.*

I take another sip. And another. And wonder how weird it would be if I went back in for a second.

*Weird enough that I know I won't.*

I pop out the questionable drink holder from the dashboard and set my latte in it. Then I do what I've been putting off all morning.

I check my bank account.

It takes me a moment to connect to the coffee shop's Wi-Fi. And another moment to log into my bank app. And then I press a hand to my stomach.

The balance.

I pull in a slow breath.

The balance is the small amount I had before moving to Colorado. Plus the twenty thousand. Minus the bit of money I've spent since then. Plus... five hundred thousand dollars.

I press down harder on my stomach.

"Fuck me."

I blink.

"Holy fucking shit."

I exhale.

"What the fuck, Uncle Jack?"

It's real.

It's so very real and so very much in my bank account.

I blink again, and a tear drips onto my dress.

If ever there was a time for swearing...

"What the fuck?" I whisper it this time.

I lower my phone to my lap and stare out the windshield.

It's not like I thought Uncle Jack did that whole Vegas thing just to mess with me. But... two million just seemed so unlikely.

But now...

I lift my phone again.

Now, a quarter of that amount is sitting in my bank account.

I pick up my latte and take a drink.

Then another, because seriously, this is stupid good.

Staring at all six digits, I wonder what I need to save from that to pay taxes.

I don't know much about the complication that is tax law, but I'm pretty sure you have to pay on inheritance.

*Is this inheritance? Or a gift? Or does that not matter?*

Putting my latte back down, I find my wallet and pull out the card for Richard and Son, glad I took it off his desk before leaving.

I dial the number.

It won't be a hardship to save a certain amount. I don't really have anything to spend all this on anyway.

The phone starts to ring as I mentally amend that thought. I will definitely be splurging on getting internet at my house.

Streaming shows will be a nice perk. But the lack of overall service is my biggest concern. If I spot a mountain lion, I need to be able to call Ethan.

My heartbeat jumps when I remember I don't have Ethan's number.

*Maybe I could find him at the park? Or I—*

"Richard and Son. How may I help you?" A man answers the phone.

"Hi, um, may I please talk to Richard?"

"And who shall I say is calling?"

"This is Matilda Wright."

"Ah, yes." The man's tone turns cheerful. "This is Richard. Nice to hear from you. And I believe a *happy birthday* is in order."

A swell of emotion catches in my throat, and I have to swallow it down. "Thank you. How are you?"

"Good. I'm good." I can hear the smile in his voice. "Now, what can I help you with?"

"Well, I... got the money." A slightly hysterical chuckle escapes me.

"Not a small sum." Richard's responding laugh sounds much more sane.

"Yeah... I..." I take a breath. "I don't know what I'm supposed to do with it."

"Anything you want, dear."

"But, I mean... Like, do I have to pay taxes on it? Or... I don't know." My voice loses some of its volume. "I just don't know."

Richard gives a hum of understanding. "Ah, right. That's my bad. We got a little derailed during the reading with, well, the whole wedding thing. I'm sorry about that." He clears his throat. "Jack has other money set aside for taxes. You just let me know if you end up working or get income from somewhere else, and we'll factor that into the taxes when we file them for you."

"He..." I shake my head.

How in the freaking hell did Uncle Jack have this much money? Not just the two million. *Plus the twenty thousand.* But enough to also cover four years of taxes.

"Jack didn't want to burden you with anything," Richard says gently. "And if you'd like me to, I can arrange to move a portion of these funds into an investment account. Jack already set them up for you. And the money will still be easily accessible if you need it, but even a small amount of interest adds up when we're talking about these sorts of sums."

I feel slightly dizzy. "Um, yes, please."

"I'll email over some documents for you to digitally sign." He reads an email address to me. "That one still correct?"

"It is."

There's a clacking on the other end as Richard types something. "Do you have any other questions?"

I swallow. "Um, the, uh, marriage part of the contract... Does it say anywhere that I have to be married to the same person for all four years? Or do I just need to be married? Not that I, we, plan to get divorced. But... in case..." I don't bother finishing the sentence.

"Good question." There's some clicking on Richard's end. "It doesn't specify... So, as the executor of this contract, I read it as married, to whomever."

"Okay." I nod to myself, not sure how to feel about that but glad to have an answer. "Thank you."

"Of course. I'll send you that email before the end of the day. But if you ever need anything, you can text this number. Day or night."

There's nothing lecherous in his tone. Just compassion.

And it makes me miss Uncle Jack so much that my voice cracks. "Why are you being so nice to me?"

"Because Jack was my friend. And you're his little Matty. And Stephen and I both pinkie swore to look after you." His tone is so genuine... My throat tightens, making it impossible for me to tell him that I don't know who Stephen is. "Now, go enjoy your birthday. And use some of your money for something frivolous. Jack would want you to."

# CHAPTER 96

## ETHAN

I HOLD THE SPARKLY GIFT BAG—THAT GOT GLITTER ALL over my fucking truck—in one hand. And I knock on the door with the other.

Standing on the front step, I can look through the living room windows and see the TV as it plays another animated movie. And since the windows are open, I hear it as well. The volume isn't super loud, but it must be loud enough that Matilda didn't hear me driving up the driveway.

I knock again.

When she still doesn't answer, I lean off the edge of the step and press my face to the glass.

The sun is setting, sending golden rays through the back wall of windows, outlining Matilda where she stands on the deck.

I'm tempted to try the door handle, but even if she left it unlocked, I don't want to freak her out by just walking in. So I head around the side of her house.

# CHAPTER 97

## TILDA

"MATILDA."

I scream, losing my grip on my hot chocolate and dropping the mug over the deck railing.

I know the voice belongs to Ethan, but my heart is still racing from the surprise.

Hand against my chest, I turn toward him just in time to see Quackers fly up from beneath the deck, flapping straight for Ethan's handsome face.

I open my mouth to yell at Quackers. But before I can tell her to stop her attack, Ethan darts his hand out and catches her midair, his large hand gripping her by the chest.

My mouth stays open.

"Knock it off," Ethan snaps. *At the duck.*

He looks past Quackers to me.

I lift a hand. "Hello."

He lifts the duck. "Happy birthday."

I stare at the man. Possibly in shock. Then I grin as Quackers starts to flap her wings.

It's mayhem. And the perfect amount of goofy. Because Ethan is here. For my birthday. And if I don't let the humor win, I may break into tears at the sweetness of it all.

"Enough," Ethan barks, and Quackers instantly settles. "I'm going to put you down. And if you try to bite me, I'm going to be upset."

He's being so stern. And it's making me warm.

Ethan slowly lowers Quackers to the ground.

She flaps her wings once, then waddles back under the deck.

"Could you please grab my mug?" I point to where I threw it.

The edge of Ethan's mouth pulls up. "Sure thing, Starlight."

That warm feeling turns molten.

Then I spot the present in his hand. And all that heat turns into something tender.

Before he even reaches the mug, I'm rushing through the screenless door, into the house.

# CHAPTER 98

## ETHAN

TILDA DISAPPEARS INTO THE HOUSE IN A CLOUD OF pink.

I shake my head as I bend down, reaching for the ceramic mug that Tilda flung over the railing.

It's no wonder my house has felt so lonely. One minute in Matilda's presence is more interesting than anything I've done in the last forty-eight hours.

I hook a finger through the handle of the mug, and the damn duck darts out and tries to bite my hand.

I hiss at her. She quacks at me. But we come to an understanding, and she waddles alongside me as I circle around to the front of the house.

There's a little splash as she hops into her pool, but I keep walking through the door Tilda is holding open for me.

She shuts it, and I feel satisfaction at the sound of the lock turning.

*My wife knows I'm here for the night.*

Tilda moves to stand before me.

I hold out the gift bag. "I got you something."

She takes it with both hands. "I love it."

And *fuck me*. She's perfect.

Dressed up like a damn birthday cake, she looks like a princess. Like a fucking Mountain Fairy.

Tilda crouches down in front of me.

Before I can ask what she's doing, she sets the bag on the floor, then starts to untie my boots.

My heart thuds as she finishes one, then moves on to the other.

When she's done, I reach down, grip her under her arms, and help her up.

But I can't let her go.

*So I don't.*

I keep lifting her.

Tilda wraps her arms around my shoulders and her legs around my waist. And when our mouths meet, I hug her body to mine.

She tastes like chocolate.

Like decadence.

Sweet as fucking sugar.

And I'm a starved man.

I step out of my boots and carry her across the living room. Into the bedroom. To the bed.

She never stops kissing me.

Never stops touching me.

And I never break our contact as I kneel on the mattress, then lower us both to the bed.

I'm so hard. So fucking ready for her.

And she's so warm. So pliant under my touch.

But I don't feel frantic. Just... needy.

I need her.

I need to be inside her.

So when her hands lower from around my neck.

When they move between us.

When they undo my jeans and pull down my zipper.

I exhale.

And when she wraps her fingers around my dick.

When she pulls her panties to the side.

When she angles her hips up.

I push into her wet heat.

And, for the first time in days, I feel like I'm finally breathing again.

# CHAPTER 99

## TILDA

I MOAN AGAINST ETHAN'S MOUTH AS HE PUSHES inside me.

As he stretches me.

As he fills me.

And I take it. All of him.

I rock with his movements.

I trace his tongue with mine.

And when he goes even deeper, I inhale the scent of him.

We're both still dressed.

Fully clothed. With too much between us.

But it's perfect.

And when he grinds against me.

When I feel that metal right where I need him.

When I relax my core and take him even deeper.

We come apart.

Together.

# CHAPTER 100

## ETHAN

T ILDA STEPS OUT OF THE BATHROOM, HAIR SMOOTHED down, dress straightened. "Can I open my present now?"

My pulse still hasn't evened out, but I nod. Unable to deny her anything. "Yeah, Starlight. You can open your present."

She holds her hand out, and I take it, letting her help me up from my seat on the edge of the bed.

Tilda grins as she spins and heads into the living room.

She scoops up the gift bag and the *apparently unbreakable* mug that I don't remember dropping on the floor, and walks into the kitchen.

Tilda puts the mug in the sink, then turns around and sets the gift on the section of countertop that divides the kitchen from the dining area.

Suddenly feeling very unsure of myself, I move to the other side of the counter and sit on one of the wooden barstools.

Sitting like this, I'm still slightly taller than Tilda, but it's a perfect vantage point for watching her as she runs her fingers down the edge of the bag.

The iridescent glitter shimmers with different colors under the overhead lights. And the tissue paper sticking out the top is yellow.

I don't know if she actually likes the color, but it reminded me of her wedding dress when I saw it at the craft store.

It *all* came from the craft store.

Well, all except the two cupcakes boxed up at the bottom of the bag.

When I lift my gaze to Tilda's face, I find her biting her lip, staring at the bag.

"You better open it before it runs out of oxygen."

Her gaze snaps up. "What?" Then she realizes I'm not being serious and rolls her eyes. "I'm savoring it. Don't be a party pooper."

A puff of laughter leaves my chest. "No one says *party pooper*. Now open your present, birthday girl."

"Fine." She carefully pulls out one of the sheets of tissue paper, revealing the card tucked along the side of the bag.

I almost shake my head.

I'd figured her for a *rip it open* gift receiver. But my Tilda likes pretty things, and I guess the wrapping stuff counts as pretty. So I should've known.

She smooths the tissue paper out on the counter, then takes the birthday card out.

Resting my elbows on the counter, I concentrate on keeping my hands still.

Tilda opens the flap of the envelope, made from some sort of textured recycled paper, then pulls out the card, made from the same material.

She sets down the envelope and uses both hands to hold the card up in front of her.

Her eyes flit up to mine, then back down to the card.

She lets go with one hand so she can drag her finger over the surface. And I know she's touching the hair.

As time stretches, I mentally kick myself.

It's stupid.

A child's card.

A simple birthday card with a drawing of a pink tiered

birthday cake and a girly fairy in a matching pink and purple dress, with a wand and a crown.

But the hair was blonde. So I bought a purple marker and colored it in.

Tilda presses her lips together. And I can't tell if she likes it, or if she's upset.

"It..." I clear my throat. "It reminded me of you."

Which doesn't explain anything. Because Tilda doesn't know that I think of her as my Mountain Fairy.

Tilda opens the card.

And, if possible, I feel even dumber.

I'd already bought the marker, so I used that to write inside the blank card. But it's a thick marker, so the letters are too big. Too clumsy for the pretty drawing on the front.

Her eyes trace over the words as she reads.

*Starlight,*

*Happy 30th birthday.*

*From, Husband Ranger*

I like when she teases me with her Ranger names. And I wanted to write *love* instead of *from* because *from* looks so formal. But *love*...

I wanted to make her birthday special, not freak her out. But instead I think I made it weird.

"It's—" I stop as a tear slides down Tilda's cheek. "Fuck."

I stand and round the end of the counter.

She quickly brushes at her cheek. "It's perfect. Thank you."

"It's dumb." I pluck the card from her hands and hold it above my head. "I'll get you a better one."

Tilda... laughs. And she smiles up at me as she wipes more tears from her cheeks. "Stop it. Give it back."

Self-loathing and confusion battle for dominance as I stare at her.

She blinks another tear off her lashes and pokes me in the ribs. "Husband Ranger, give me my birthday card back." She pokes me again. "Right now."

"Matilda—"

"Ethan, it's perfect. Give it back."

I lower my arm. "You don't have to lie to make me feel better."

Tilda huffs. "I'm not." Then she snatches the card out of my hand and carefully slides it back into the blank envelope.

I want to ask why that card made her cry. But she's not crying anymore. And I might be a moron, but I'm not a *complete* moron, so I don't bring it up.

Staying where I am, I stand beside Tilda as she turns back to the gift bag.

She sets the card on the counter, then gently takes out the second piece of extra tissue paper, smoothing it out over the other one.

Slower than I thought possible, Tilda finally unwraps the first item.

The fuzzy tan fabric unfurls to reveal the pair of slipper socks. The toe part is white, with gray stitching to designate the toe lines, and the soles have gray rubber paw prints to prevent slipping.

They're cat feet.

And they're soft. So they'll be comfortable on her abused toes, even if I can't see any marks on her bare feet.

"Closest I could find to a mountain lion."

She looks up at me, her eyes glittering. "I love them," she whispers. And these socks are just as dumb as the card. But I know she means it.

Tilda unties the piece of string holding them together, then bends over and pulls one sock on, then the other.

When she stands straight, she wiggles her toes, then smiles up at me. "Cozy." Her voice is stronger this time.

I let out a breath and nod to the gift bag. "Keep going."

Tilda purses her lips, but it's hard to look stern in a pink princess dress and cat feet socks.

I lift my hand and use my pointer finger to boop her on the nose.

She tries so hard not to smile, but I see her lips curling as she turns back to the bag.

The next item takes just as long to unwrap, but Tilda literally gasps when it's revealed.

"Ethan." She holds the clear bag up to the light, and the glass beads sparkle. They're all different shades of purple, some so light they look white. "They're so pretty."

"There's a spool of fishing line stuff in there too."

Tilda reaches into the gift bag and finds it. "This is so perfect. I'm going to make Deerdra a necklace."

"I'm glad you like it." Then I try to think if I've heard her say that name before. "Who's Dear... Who?"

Tilda smiles up at me. "Deerdra." Then she points across the living room.

I jerk my head over, expecting to see a fucking ghost standing behind me. But there's nothing.

Tilda lets out a laugh. "What is wrong with you?"

"Me? Who are you pointing at?"

She snorts as she aggressively points to the opposite corner of the living room.

And then I see it.

The deer head, with bows—made of familiar purple ribbon— tied around the base of each point on its antlers.

"Deerdra," Tilda says again, like it makes perfect sense.

It is a clever name. I'll give her that much. But I have to state the obvious. "You do know that the antlers mean it's a male deer, right?"

She lifts a brow. "You do know it's dead and doesn't care what I call it, right?"

I dip my chin. "Touché."

She's definitely amused *at* me, rather than *with* me, but I'll take that over her tears any day.

"Finish opening your present."

Tilda reaches into the bag and pulls out the last piece of tissue paper, revealing the final item.

A bakery box.

I reach around her and help by holding the bag in place as she pulls the flimsy paper box out.

She looks up at me.

I lift a brow at her.

She huffs, then sets the box on the counter and opens it.

I lean over her shoulder. "They got a little smooshed."

She swipes her finger through the frosting stuck to the top flap of the box and puts it into her mouth.

When she pulls her finger free and swipes it through the second spot of frosting, bringing it back to her mouth to lick it off again, I grip her wrist and lift her hand up over her shoulder.

I close my lips around her fingertip. And I suck the vanilla sweetness off her skin.

I hum my approval as I release her wrist, then I move to the cupboard and take out two plates.

"Which one do you want?" I ask Tilda as I set the plates next to the box.

One is all vanilla; the other is all chocolate.

We spent the weekend eating oatmeal and protein bars, with very limited flavor options, so I don't actually know what Tilda prefers.

She sets one on each plate, then lifts her shoulders. "They both look good."

"Half and half?" I suggest.

Tilda nods. "Yes, please."

She starts to turn, presumably for a knife, but I stop her.

"Wait." I reach into the chest pocket on my flannel and pull out a single birthday candle, shaped like a pine tree, and a book of matches from Rocky Ridge Inn.

I stick the candle in the top of the chocolate one, because it's closest to Tilda. Then I pluck a match from the book and strike it.

"Where did you find a tree candle?"

"Same store as everything else, except the cupcakes." I lean down and hold the match in place while I light the wick. "I'll take you someday."

Candle lit, I shake out the match, then drop it into the empty dessert box.

We watch the candle burn for a second.

"It's customary at this point to make a wish and blow out the flame."

Tilda huffs. "I know."

The candle continues to burn. "And..."

"And... Will you hum 'Happy Birthday' to me?"

*Will I...*

Then I remember.

That night after the mountain lion encounter.

I don't want to.

I *really* don't want to.

But I can't deny my Mountain Fairy.

Not on a regular day. And sure as shit not on her birthday.

Instead of answering, I step so I'm directly behind Tilda, then I wrap my arms around her upper chest and hold her against me.

And then, with our bodies pressed together, I hum.

# CHAPTER 101

## TILDA

THE TUNE OF "HAPPY BIRTHDAY" VIBRATES THROUGH my body.

I close my eyes, leaning into Ethan, tipping my head back against his shoulder.

He continues to hum. And I reach up, clinging to his forearms.

He hums too many syllables for the name Tilda, and I smile through the urge to cry.

When he's done, he releases his hold of me.

I bend and silently wish for more birthdays like this.

Good ones.

Perfect ones.

Then I blow out the candle.

# CHAPTER 102

## ETHAN

TILDA STEPS OUT OF THE BATHROOM, DRESS OFF, LONG pajama shirt on. "You finally ready?"

I roll my eyes at her teasing. "Get in the bed."

"You're on my side."

I shake my head. "Closest to the door, remember?" I double-checked the dead bolt, but if I'm here, the rule stands.

Tilda makes a face like she's annoyed, but I don't think it's real. I think she likes it.

The bedside lamp is on, casting enough of a glow to see by. And enough for me to watch her bare thighs as she crosses around to the other side of the bed.

I hold both plates up as she lifts the covers and climbs in beside me.

She takes a moment to situate herself, then grabs her tablet off her nightstand and taps the screen.

Tilda is sitting cross-legged, but she's pulled the blankets back up over her lap, so unfortunately, I don't get a glimpse of her panty-covered pussy. But still, just knowing she's not wearing pants or shorts or anything but a fucking thin shirt—that I can see her nipple piercings through—and panties, has my cock stirring to life.

344

I shift, best I can, while holding two plates of cake and sitting with my back against the headboard with my legs straight out.

"What're we watching?" I ask to distract myself.

Tilda leans forward, all the way onto her knees, then stretches forward and sets the tablet on my ankles, propped up against my feet.

I crumble to temptation and lean over so I can look at her ass in those pale pink panties.

"Hold still," she chides, adjusting the tablet.

"Sit on my face."

Tilda snickers, like I'm fucking joking, and sits back how she was before.

Resigned, I sigh and hand her one of the plates as the opening of a show I'm not familiar with starts to play.

I pick up my fork. "Do I need any background going into this?"

Tilda shakes her head, turning the plate in her hold so the two halves of the cupcakes are perpendicular to her body. "It's *Second Bite*. The baking competition..." She glances at me. "Have you not heard of it?"

I shake my head and shove some of the chocolate dessert into my mouth.

She widens her eyes at me. "Seriously?"

I widen mine back. "Seriously."

Tilda huffs, like she's disappointed, making me smile. "Okay, so, it's a baking competition. It's awesome. And we'll watch more of the regular episodes another time." As much as I don't give a single fuck about *baking shows*, I don't disagree. Because her talking about watching more means she's accepting that I'll be over here more. "One of the hosts is this guy." She points at the screen, and I turn to see an attractive older man glaring at someone as they use a mixer. "He's Chef Mike. And his usual cohost is awesome, but this is a special fundraiser episode, so his cohost is his wife."

They pan to a happy-looking blonde woman in a brightly

colored dress. *Okay, so good-looking older man and a girl in party dresses. I see why my Mountain Fairy likes this show.*

"What's the fundraiser for?" I ask around vanilla frosting.

"They have a scholarship program thing they're always promoting." She waves her fork, dismissing my question. "This episode is special because it's Alice's birthday."

"Alice?"

"The wife," Tilda says as though I should've known her name.

"Ah."

Tilda hums around a tiny forkful of chocolate cake. "They make all her favorite dishes... And it's just sweet, ya know?"

I nod. *Sure.*

"Okay, shh. It's starting."

# CHAPTER 103

## TILDA

A PRESSURE BUILDS BETWEEN MY THIGHS.

And builds.

And then my eyes pop open because I'm sliding up the mattress.

Ethan's eyes are just inches away, and I can tell from the crinkles next to them that he's smiling. "Morning."

I tighten my thighs around his leg. "Morning."

Unlike that first morning together when I accidentally kneed him in the nuts, this time Ethan's thigh is between mine. And he's using his leg strength to slide me up the mattress so we're eye level.

"How does it feel to be thirty?"

My grin is sleepy. "Not so bad." I wedge one of my arms up between us to cover my yawn. "How does it feel to be... How old are you?"

"Thirty-nine."

I lift my brows in exaggerated surprise. "Wow. So old."

He narrows his eyes at me. "If you don't like 'em old, you should've asked my age before you asked me to marry you."

I scoff. "How dare you suggest such a thing before coffee."

The thought of coffee has me yawning again.

Ethan presses a kiss to my nose. "Go back to sleep. I just wanted to say bye before I left."

"You're leaving?" The jolt of depression that hits my stomach is so instant that it makes me frown.

His replying smile is soft. "I have to go to work."

*Oh. Right.*

"You can shower here if you want. I'll make us some coffee."

"You don't have to do that."

"I know. But I won't fall back asleep anyway. And we can drink it on the back deck." I probably could fall back asleep, but I'd rather start my day now with Ethan than alone in two hours.

"As long as your damn guard duck stays on the ground."

My grin is less sleepy this time. "I can't believe you caught her."

Ethan rolls his eyes. "That little demon weighs all of two pounds."

"Two pounds of flapping wings with a beak."

THE DOOR TO THE HOUSE OPENS, AND I WATCH FROM my chair as Ethan opens the screen door and steps out onto the deck.

And I keep watching as he holds the doorframe open and sticks his other hand through the big empty spot where a screen should be.

He lifts a brow.

I shrug. "It was like that when I moved in. I usually just step through it."

He lets the door shut and grabs the mug of black coffee sitting on my armrest. "I'll fix it."

Rather than replying, I take a sip, enjoying my sweetened

creamer but thinking about the instant coffee with sugar I had at the cabin in the woods.

Ethan is dressed in jeans and one of his tan short-sleeved ranger shirts—which he fetched from his truck this morning.

I tuck one leg under me and shift in my chair so I can look at Ethan as he sits in the one on the other side of the doorway.

His hair is still damp, combed back from his face. And he looks sexy as always with his tattoos on display.

"Did you always want to be a park ranger?"

Steam trails up from his mug as he lifts it to his mouth.

I'm in my matching blue sweatpants and sweatshirt, good for the cool morning air. But Ethan looks perfectly comfortable in his short sleeves.

He lifts a shoulder. "I always liked the outdoors. But hadn't really thought about it as a career when I was growing up."

"What did you want to do?" Being a ranger seems so right for Ethan that I can hardly imagine him doing anything else.

"Firefighter."

I nod as I consider it. "Still a service to your community. A sexy uniform. I guess I can see that." He shakes his head at my uniform comment. "So what stopped your firefighter dream?"

He hesitates, and I get the feeling that I shouldn't have asked. "I was in the process of applying for a position down in the Springs when my parents passed away."

The sour taste of regret coats my tongue, and I drop my eyes to my lap.

I can't believe I brought this up.

"I'm so sorry. I shouldn't've asked." My voice comes out weak.

"Tilda."

My heart aches for Ethan. "I really didn't mean—"

"Matilda." He uses his serious tone, and I finally meet his gaze. And... he doesn't look upset. Not at all. "I'm okay talking about this. I swear."

"I—"

"I fucking swear." His lips pull up into a small smile. And I think I believe him.

"But if you don't want to—"

"I want to tell you."

I heave out a breath. "Fine. But I can't promise I won't cry."

He shakes his head. "You're too good for your own good." I scrunch up my nose, but he ignores me and keeps talking. "I was nineteen and had just moved into an apartment with some friends. Probably should've saved my money and continued living at home, but I'd lived in this town my whole life and wanted to see something else."

"Lonely?"

Ethan nods. "I'd never known any firefighters, but it sounded like a fun job, and you can do it without extra schooling. My parents always offered to pay for college, but that was never my thing."

"That's a nice offer." I hold my mug in both hands, feeling colder than before.

Ethan sighs. "Yeah, they were good people."

"So... nothing like my family?" I try to joke.

His next sigh is a little heavier. "I wish you could've met them."

"Me too," I whisper, meaning it.

Ethan takes a sip of coffee. "They were heading to the airport to go on vacation... and there was a freak accident on the highway. It was awful, but from what I was told, it was instant, so they didn't suffer. And I think that's the best anyone can ask for."

I swallow, the urge to cry already building in my chest. "When you were nineteen?"

"Yeah." He says it casually. Like you're not still practically a child at that age. "My sister was twelve."

"Sister?" I choke out. "Was she...?" I can't finish the question.

I didn't know he had a sister. And if she died...

Ethan's soft expression gives me the answer before he speaks it. "She's fine. She wasn't with them."

I exhale. "Thank fuck." He smiles at my cursing. But then I realize how bad that sounds and hold up a hand. "Not that the rest isn't awful. Just—"

"You don't have to explain. I know exactly what you mean. She was staying at the neighbor's for the weekend. If I'd lost her too..." Ethan shakes his head. "It was bad. But that would've been worse."

*Nineteen.* "What did you do?"

Ethan lifts his mug and tips it toward me. "I'll tell you, but drink your coffee, Starlight. Don't let it get cold."

I lift my mug to my lips and sip, even though the flavor tastes too sweet now.

"I packed up all my shit that night, after the call." *The call. When he found out his parents died.* "And I moved back home to take care of Sandra."

"I can't imagine."

He blows out a breath. "It was definitely an adjustment for both of us. But we've always gotten along."

"Is that when you became a ranger?"

"Not right away." Ethan takes another drink. "Our parents... We had a modest house. They had normal jobs. My mom was a dental hygienist. My dad worked at a factory as a floor supervisor. But after they passed, we discovered they both had pretty large life insurance policies. And some saved money that, as far as I could tell, came from my mom's dad. It was... a shock." He shakes his head like he can't believe it all over again.

I give him a crooked smile. "Family members are like that sometimes."

He lifts his mug in a toast, catching my meaning.

"It was a surprise and a safety net that meant I didn't need to work right away. So while Sandra went to school, I worked on getting my degree in natural resource management. I hadn't wanted to go to college, but deciding I wanted to be a park ranger motivated me."

"What made you decide?"

"The hours of being a firefighter wouldn't work, not with having to take care of Sandra. And I knew I couldn't pick a career that dangerous. Sandra... well, you get it." I nod, glad he doesn't voice what could've happened. "But I still wanted to do something that left an impact. I wanted to work outdoors. I've always liked nature and wildlife and getting my hands dirty. And I knew being a ranger was something my parents would've been proud of."

That wave of emotions builds in my eyes again. "That's really sweet."

Ethan sighs and points at me. "Keep drinking your coffee."

I sniff. And pretend to take a sip. "So do you still live in the house you grew up in?"

"No. There were too many memories there, and neither of us was willing to move into Mom and Dad's old bedroom, so we sold it and downsized into the house I have now."

"Where is it?" I feel weird asking, even though I know I shouldn't.

"About twenty minutes from here, other side of the park entrance."

"So, close to your work."

He nods.

"And Sandra?"

"She lives near the Springs, just a few minutes from the salon where she has her own booth."

"Salon?"

"She does hair."

I perk up at this detail. "Oh, that's cool."

Ethan's eyes lift from mine to take in my purple locks, which are currently a frizzy mess from sleeping.

And it makes me think of the birthday card. And the way he used a marker to color in the hair. And how he used that marker to write inside it. And how it's now my most prized possession.

I bite my lip. "Can I give you a hug?"

Ethan pushes himself up to standing, sets his mug on the armrest of his chair, and holds his arms open. "Come get your hug, then I gotta go to work."

I'm careful not to spill what's left of my coffee as I do the same thing Ethan did, leaving my mug on the chair.

Not wasting any time, I walk straight into Ethan's body.

He lets out a grunt at the collision but doesn't move, just wraps his arms around me.

I grip the back of his shirt with both my hands, holding him tight.

His exhale ruffles through my hair, and then a weight—that I imagine is his cheek—rests against the top of my head. "Don't feel sad for me." He strokes a hand down my back. "They were great parents, and I miss them, but I'm okay."

"It's still sad." My face is squished against his pecs, so the words come out muffled.

Ethan takes a deep inhale, his chest expanding with the motion.

I want to ask if I can meet Sandra. I'd like to get to know her. But I stop myself from voicing the request.

We might technically be married, but we only met... two weeks ago? *One?*

He can't exactly introduce me as his wife. And I don't want to make a terrible first impression by being the girl who pressured her brother into marriage.

Ethan wraps his arms high around my shoulders, and I feel his body relax. Like he's settling into the position. "What did you do for work before you moved here?" His question rumbles against my ear.

I make a face; my job history is not impressive. "Don't you have to go?"

"I have time."

"What time is it?"

He hums. "Don't know."

I smile against his chest. "You're a dork."

I feel him shake his head. "You can do better than that."

"Huh?" I try to look up at him, but he moves a hand to the back of my head, holding me in place.

"You can come up with a better insult than *dork*."

A laugh bubbles out of me as I remember my previous attempt. "I guess I'm not properly motivated."

"I'll work on that." He slides his hand back to my shoulder. "Now tell me. If it's something you think I won't approve of, I promise I won't judge you."

I'm not sure what sort of job he's imagining, but I believe him. He wouldn't judge.

"It's nothing exciting. Just retail."

His chest does that vibrating thing again. "Tell me more."

"I hated it."

Instead of laughing, Ethan holds me tighter. "I'm sorry."

I relax into his hold. "No, it's okay. I'm just being dramatic."

"It's not dramatic if it's true."

*Wow. Okay. That's validating.*

"Thank you." I can't say it louder than a whisper.

"What sort of retail?"

"A makeup store. A lighting showroom. A wholesale kitchen appliance store." I exhale. "Some other crappy places, all paying minimum wage. I know I could've made more working for tips in a restaurant but..." I shake my head. "Short interactions with customers were enough."

"Now that you're here... Is there anything you want to do?"

I take time to think about the question, but the answer is the same as it was last week. "I don't know." I flatten my hands on Ethan's back. "I moved out on my eighteenth birthday. Graduation was a couple weeks before. I had some money from... Uncle Jack." My throat tightens as I remember that detail. *I'd forgotten.* "He sent me a card and check in the mail that was enough for first and last month's rent. And I'd already been working after-school jobs..."

Ethan's strong fingers curl around my upper arms. "I'm glad you had that."

I nod. Then I nod again. "Ethan?"

"Yeah, Starlight?"

"Can I tell you something?" Emotion threatens to choke me. But I need to tell someone.

"Anything." Ethan presses his mouth to my hair. "Always."

# CHAPTER 104

## ETHAN

"UNCLE JACK..." TILDA'S VOICE CRACKS, AND I HOLD her tighter. "He had a terminal illness. And he... In one of his letters, he told me that he chose to end his life through the death with dignity program."

I stare over Tilda's head at the trees.

I...

I was not expecting that.

"And I get it." Tilda's fingers are back to gripping my shirt. "I do. And I'm glad he was able to leave this world on his terms. But I... I feel like such a jerk even thinking this."

"No." I run a palm up and down her back. "You're anything but that, Matilda Wright."

Her back rises as she inhales, and her voice is steadier when she continues. "I just don't understand why he did all *this* with letters and lawyers and... It was all a surprise to me. I didn't even know he was sick. And instead of... *this*, he could've just told me."

I press a kiss to the top of Tilda's head.

Then I do it again.

"I don't mean to sound ungrateful for—"

"Stop right there." I can't stand to listen to her justify the absolute chaos Jack has caused. "I know you're not ungrateful.

And I know you're glad he didn't have to suffer through whatever pain awaited him. But that doesn't make all of this any less fucked up."

A laugh pops out of Tilda, just as I'd hoped.

"Jack clearly had enough free time to arrange this whole board game of surprises. And he could've just as easily called you on the phone. In fact, it would've been way fucking easier to just call you on the phone." I press my lips to her hair again, hating that she's thought about this all on her own. "But Jack was a man. And we're not always good at confronting our emotions. And maybe this was the only way he knew how to give you *this* without having to hear your voice when he told you he was dying. Or see your face when he said there was no other way. Or listen to you argue—because I'm sure you would—that he should give everything to someone else."

Tilda sniffs, but I feel her nod against my chest.

"Doesn't mean you can't be a little mad at him for it."

She sniffs again.

And I kiss her hair again.

"Doesn't make it right, but Jack always was about the drama. And as out of line as the whole plan might've been, he orchestrated it admirably well. Down to the Dolly Parton wedding."

Tilda's sniff sounds a bit like a laugh this time. "He really did, didn't he?"

"The more I think on it, the more I wonder if he didn't manage to get his ghost ass into my plane. Still can't figure out what happened to my computers before we—"

"Crashed."

"—had to execute a controlled emergency landing."

Tilda hums. "I wouldn't put it past him. Maybe I'll find a stash of airplane books next."

We stand for a moment, absorbing each other's heat.

Then I decide that since Tilda gave me a truth, I can give her one in return.

"I don't know why Jack did things this way. But I do know that I'm grateful to him for bringing you here."

"Thank you." Tilda sniffs. "I'm glad he did too."

I hug her tighter.

An alarm on Tilda's phone goes off, and she jolts in my arms.

"Crap, sorry."

I loosen my hold, and she moves to grab her phone off the deck railing.

"Time to wake up?" I slide my hands into my pockets.

"Yeah, actually. I forgot." She turns off the alarm, then reaches up and brushes at her cheeks. "When I was in town yesterday, I called about getting internet. Someone is coming out today to put up the satellite."

"Who?" I don't like the thought of someone coming over here when Tilda is home alone.

I don't like it at all.

"Um, the guy on the phone said the tech would text me their ETA with a picture of themselves. But my service out here sucks, so I don't know if I'll get it." Tilda sniffs again, then finally looks up and meets my eyes. "Which is why I set my alarm so early. I want to make sure I'm ready and not in the shower when they show up."

My jaw ticks. "I'll take today off."

She blinks at me.

"So you don't have to be alone," I explain at her confused look.

Her smile is kind, but she shakes her head. "Thank you, but you don't have to do that."

"I know I don't have to. I want to."

She shakes her head again. "No. What you *have to do* is go to work. You're probably late already."

"Tilda—"

"Nope." She reaches out and pokes me in the ribs. "I will not be the reason you mess up what I'm sure is a perfect attendance record of rangering. I'll be fine. I've lived alone for twelve years. This is just a new location."

"You know that doesn't make me feel any better, right?"

Her smile lifts into something bright. "Tough shit."

I roll my eyes but can't resist my own smile.

# CHAPTER 105

# ETHAN

"BUT WHERE ARE THE BUFFALO?" A DIRTY FINGERNAIL taps against the paper map.

I lift my gaze from the map to the man. "There are no wild buffalo in the park."

He narrows his eyes. "But they're wild. Can't they go anywhere?"

The amount of self-control I use to *not* leg sweep this man should be commended.

"Sure." I shift my grip on the branch trimmer I have resting against my shoulder. "And a herd of buffalo last moved through this area in 1884."

His expression doesn't change "1884? Really?"

"Overhunting and loss of habitat in the late 1800s caused buffalo to nearly go extinct in this state. There are still some wild herds in the mountains a few hours north of here. So, yes. Really."

The man's jaw works. And I know the only reason he isn't calling me a dick is the fact that his three kids are listening to our every word, looking back and forth between us.

He might also be upset that his wife, who is standing beside him, has been blatantly staring at me since the moment they approached.

*This* is why I don't like working in the Visitor Center.

*People.*

And *this* is precisely why I traded duties with Liza today.

She wanted the air-conditioning. I wanted to wander around on my own, clearing trails and daydreaming about my Mountain Fairy.

But *no.* This cocksucker with an attitude had to flag me down the second I exited the building to ask me where to find the buffalo.

I lift a hand and point in the opposite direction of where I'm going. "If you go about a quarter mile that way, you'll find the Quail Trail. We've had a lot of wildlife sightings on that stretch in the past few weeks."

"Like what?" one of the kids pipes up.

"Like chipmunks. Turkeys. Hawks." I lean down a little. "Snakes."

Their eyes widen. "Ooh."

I nod, then straighten. "We also have bobcats, foxes, bears, deer, elk, mountain lions..."

"Cool!" Another kid inches closer.

"Very cool." My tone is still even. But I agree. It is cool. "Just make sure to stay on the posted paths. And if you're lucky enough to see an animal, don't approach it."

The dad sighs and reaches down to corral his offspring. "Thanks a lot." *He doesn't mean it.*

"You're welcome." *I don't mean it either.*

Not looking at the wife, I turn and head down a trail that needs some maintenance.

I've never been this anxious to get through a day of work.

But I've also never had a wife before.

And my thoughts are consumed by her.

*Since the day I met her.*

And knowing she's close, but out of reach... It makes my skin itch.

I start to slide my hand into my pocket, wanting to text her, but stop when I remember we haven't exchanged numbers yet.

My steps slow.

I'm heading in the wrong direction, but I could find an excuse to go to the border fence on the other side of the park.

And I could stop by. For just a moment.

Check on her internet installation.

Make sure she's okay.

I stop. But then I shake my head.

I'll go after work.

That will have to be soon enough.

# CHAPTER 106

## TILDA

I hold the hose, refilling Quackers's pool with fresh water.

The internet people have already come and gone. And I was tempted to just rot on the couch, catching up on some shows. But it's nice out. And even with the noisy distractions, my mind wouldn't settle.

The sound of the water is soothing, and I wonder how hard it would be to set up some sort of fountain.

Nothing grand, just enough to make it sound like I have a bubbling brook running through my front yard.

Looking out at the trees and my strings of crystals swaying in the breeze, I take in how different my life is now.

And how much I like it.

I'd always thought I was an indoor cat. Never considered an outdoorsy life.

Probably because I always lived in a city, so for me the outdoors were still urban.

But this...

I know this isn't for everyone.

And I'm still adjusting to the quiet.

And I miss food delivery.

But I don't think I could go back.

A butterfly lazily flutters past me and lands on the bush on the other side of the kiddie pool. The one Quackers likes to sleep under.

*I definitely couldn't go back.*

Careful not to splash the butterfly, I pull the hose away and lay it under the closer bush, then I walk around to the side of the house where the hose connects and turn the water off.

With the amount of money Uncle Jack left me, and the fact that the house is paid off—leaving me without a mortgage or a car payment—I'm not worried about finding a job.

But even if I can make the money stretch for years and years, I still need something to do with my time.

Making my way back to the front of the house, I stop beside a tree and watch its suncatcher sparkle in the light.

Maybe I can make stuff?

Sell it?

Not with the beads Ethan bought me for my birthday. Those are mine. But maybe...

A sound cuts through my thoughts.

I stand still.

Is that...?

I take a step farther out into my driveway.

I stop again to listen.

And then my heart rate jumps.

Spinning around, I rush back to my front door as the sound of tires on gravel gets louder.

I'm not expecting anyone.

No one should be coming here.

Adrenaline that I'm becoming all too familiar with fills my body as I wrench my door open.

I swing it shut and lock the dead bolt just as a car comes into view.

I don't recognize it.

But I don't linger.

I dart straight to my bedroom, where I can hide without being seen.

My lungs burn as I stand just inside the threshold to my room.

And my eyes burn.

I want to call Ethan.

I start to reach for my pocket but remember we never exchanged numbers.

That pressure in my eyes intensifies.

*I have a husband, but I don't have his phone number.*

The crunching sound comes to a stop, and then what sounds like *two* engines turn off.

I hear two doors slam.

*Why are two people here?*

I lean a little out of the doorway, wanting to catch a glimpse.

"Matilda!"

I halt. Frozen in place.

*My mom is here.*

More car doors slam shut, and I take a step back.

It's bright outside, and I don't have any lights on inside, but there are no curtains over the living room windows. So if anyone gets close enough—out of the glare of sunlight—they'll be able to see inside.

But that's all they can do.

I locked the front door.

The windows are the crank-out kind, and they're all cracked open, letting in the fresh air and allowing me to hear what's happening. But they're only open a few inches.

And if any of them try to pull open a window to crawl through, I'll be using my new internet connection to call the police.

*Ethan would be better.*

Backing farther into my bedroom and completely out of view, I wonder if there's a way for me to climb off the back deck and circle around into the park without being seen.

I look down at my dress, the one I was wearing the last time I went into the park, when I got all tangled up in the barbed wire fence, and know I won't be able to make it out unnoticed.

The back of my legs bump into my bed, and feeling so incredibly tired of these people, I let my knees give out and sit on the mattress.

# Chapter 107

## Ethan

Gravel kicks up behind me as I make my way down Tilda's driveway.

I wanted to come here straight from work, but I had to run into Lonely to get a screen door kit from the hardware store.

I also got a bag of takeout tacos because I plan to stay.

I make the last turn in the long driveway and take my foot off the gas.

"What the..."

Two cars are parked, blocking the driveway.

Blocking the way between me and my girl.

Two cars. With Nevada plates.

And as I get closer, I see the *group* of people standing in front of Tilda's house.

I press my foot down on the gas.

Being reckless, and not giving a single fuck about it, I steer off the driveway, up into the grass, my truck at an angle as the ground slopes up toward the park.

All heads turn my way. And when I veer back onto the driveway, I slam on my brakes, sending a dust cloud and bits of rock at Tilda's rotten family.

# CHAPTER 108

## TILDA

MY FAMILY HAS BEEN OUTSIDE FOR HOURS.

When they first got here, they shouted things at the house. I heard them jiggling the doorknob, testing if it was locked. I peeked out the bedroom curtains to see my cousin circle the house.

And I wanted to scream.

Wanted to shout at them to *get off my lawn*.

But since my garage door is closed and I haven't made a peep, I'm pretty sure they think I'm not home.

They're still here, though. Waiting.

And if they...

I sit up

Then I scramble off my bed.

At the doorway, I pause, then peek my head out into the living room.

My family is still there, standing outside, but now they're faced away from the house.

And my heart lurches when Ethan's truck roars into view.

# CHAPTER 109

## ETHAN

I PRY MY GRIP OFF MY STEERING WHEEL AND TAKE A calming breath as I turn off the engine.

It doesn't work.

So I give up on calm and let rage fill my chest as I climb out of my truck.

"What the actual fuck is going on here?" I let them hear my anger.

It's all the same people from Vegas. Tilda's mother, the shitty aunt who was at our wedding, more people I don't care to remember. And her cousin Ralph.

*I haven't forgotten about Ralph.*

Tilda's awful mother steps to the front of the gathered crowd. "We're just here to check on Til—Matilda."

My footsteps are heavy as I cross to where she's standing. "Leave."

She plants her hands on her hips. "You can't stop me from seeing my daughter."

I plant *my hands* on *my hips*. Right next to *my gun*. "Oh, I can. And you have quite the fucking nerve calling her your daughter."

"Now, son…" An older man shuffles closer.

"Shut the fuck up," I shout at him. And they all jump.

My dad called me son. No one else gets to do that.

Tilda's mother tries to keep the stoic look on her face, but I can see her darting her eyes back toward their cars. "We just want to—"

"What? You just want to *what*? Terrorize her? Intimidate her? Tell her why all that money should belong to *you*?" I shake my head.

"That's not—"

"How long have you been here?" I ask in a low tone.

Tilda's inside. I *know* she's inside. And these *people* have been standing out here, making her a prisoner in her own home.

"We just—"

"How long?" The question booms out of my chest.

She takes a step back, bumping into the simpering man. "Just a couple hours. We just—"

I take a step forward, and she snaps her mouth shut.

*Hours.*

*They've been here for fucking hours.*

"Here's what's gonna happen." I roll my shoulders out and regulate my volume to an even tone. "You're going to leave. And you're never going to come back."

"She's my daughter." She says it like it's some sort of ownership.

I lean into her space. "She's my wife."

I catch movement in the house through the windows, but I keep my attention on the woman before me.

And I remember the sight of Tilda standing in that bucket with her feet hurting.

I remember her not complaining because she was used to the pain.

Because her mother, this vile human in front of me, used to buy her shoes that were too small. On purpose.

This creature used to force my perfect fucking Starlight to wear dresses that were too small. On fucking purpose.

This biological sack of shit let my wife's cousin threaten her life over *money*.

I inhale the rage.

"You do not get to call her that." My voice comes out so low it's almost a whisper. "You don't get to call her anything. You are so fucking far from deserving the title of mother... You're not even in the same species." I think about my mom. I think about the love she would have *poured* over Tilda. And I think about the way Tilda felt in my arms just this morning. "If my wife decides she wants you in her life, that's her choice. But until she does, you will not set foot on this property ever again. You will not contact her. You will not so much as think her fucking name." I exhale the anger. "I won't ever be violent toward a woman. No matter how much you might deserve it." I slowly turn my head until I'm looking Ralph in the eye. "But I will hurt a man."

I see fury reflected back in his gaze.

But it's a selfish fury.

One of greed and jealousy.

A fury that can never match the heat of my own.

Because mine isn't for me. It's for *her*.

# CHAPTER 110

## TILDA

Tears blur my vision as I yank open the front door.

My aunt lets out a shriek of surprise as the whole group turns to face me.

But I don't look at them.

I look at Ethan.

At his handsome face and the protection shining in his eyes.

Never. Never ever have I felt this much gratitude toward someone.

But I feel it now.

I hold my hand out. "Come here, Husband."

Ethan doesn't hesitate. He strides forward, shouldering through my family.

Looking exactly like my avenging angel.

His hand closes around mine, and the calm I haven't felt since he left this morning returns in a wave.

Behind him, my family reanimates, realizing I've been home this whole time.

"What the fuck—" Ralph's curse turns into a shout as Quackers flies up from beneath her bush.

He tries to swat her down, but he's not Ethan. And Quackers isn't messing around this time.

Loud, angry quacks fill the air, and everyone finally rushes toward the vehicles.

Still holding Ethan's hand, I step onto the top step so I can watch the mayhem.

Quackers dive-bombs Ralph, and I think I see a chunk of hair in her mouth when she flaps back up, out of his reach.

He screams something at me, but it's jumbled.

Feeling light and free and invigorated from watching Ethan face down my family, I grin.

"Hey, Ralph!"

He pauses at his car door, hunched like he's expecting another duck attack. "What?"

I grin wider. "Suck my dick!"

# Chapter 111

## Ethan

PLACING AN ARM BEHIND HER BACK, I SWING TILDA UP into my arms.

She lets out a laugh as I hold her to my chest and step over the threshold into the house.

I kick the door shut behind me, then smile down at my Firecracker. "You can suck my dick, Wife."

She's still grinning. "You deserve the biggest blow job ever for all that."

I start across the house. "How does one make a blow job *big*?"

Tilda hooks her arms around my neck. "Not sure. But when I figure it out, I'll show you."

"Deal." I step into the bedroom. "But you can figure it out another time." And I drop her onto the bed.

# Chapter 112

## Tilda

Me: How was work today?

Grumpy Ranger: Fine.

Grumpy Ranger: People are idiots.

Grumpy Ranger: How was your day?

I grin at his grumpy answer.

Me: It was nice. No idiots over here. Just made some suncatchers on the front step while Quackers played in her pool.

Grumpy Ranger: Show me.

Me: She seemed so happy.

I send him a video of her splashing around in the water.

Me: Pretty sure I spotted some of Ralph's hair tucked under a rock by the food dish.

> Grumpy Ranger: We should've shaved him bald and given her all his hair as a reward.

I snort.

> Me: She really was magnificent.

> Grumpy Ranger: She was. And this is a good video. But I meant for you to show me the suncatchers you made.

The microwave dings, letting me know my popcorn is done, but I don't reach for it.

I just stare at my phone, reading Ethan's text again.

That very first day, when we very first met, he called me ridiculous.

And it hurt my feelings.

A lot.

But even in the moment, I knew he didn't mean it *that way*. The way my family always meant it.

It's just a word people use.

But it still made me cry.

I didn't want to cry. Didn't want to do that in front of a stranger. But so much had happened... it was the final straw.

And Ethan... He looked horrified. I could tell he felt bad for saying it, for making me feel that way.

Since then, he hasn't said that word around me again.

And now, instead of calling me silly for playing with beads, Ethan *bought* me beads.

And instead of ignoring it as some foolish hobby, he's *asking me* to show him.

I know it's too soon.

I know we still have so much to learn about each other, that we need to spend more time together. But I also know that I'm cooked.

A goner.

A girl falling in love.

Me: It's a work in progress.

I hold up the suncatcher in one hand and try to angle it under the kitchen lights just right before I take the photo.

It's roughly the shape of a wind chime. With a ring of beads at the top and single strands of varying lengths hanging down.

But the ring is more of a wonky oval. And the strands keep getting tangled.

Grumpy Ranger: Make me one.

Grumpy Ranger: Please.

I roll my lips together.

Me: Since you asked like a Good Boy…

Grumpy Ranger: You only get to say that in person.

Me: Why?

Grumpy Ranger: You know why.

Grumpy Ranger: Bad Girl.

Good Boy: What are you doing tonight?

I sit up from my lounging position on the couch.

Me: Perfecting dessert popcorn.

I wanted to text Ethan all day.

Actually, I wanted to ask him if he'd come over tonight. Or ask if I could go to him. But I didn't want to come off as needy.

So instead of spending my evening with my hot husband, I'm spending it alone.

Again.

> Good Boy: What's dessert popcorn?

> Me: Regular popcorn but you add melted butter, cinnamon, and sugar.

I look down at the sugar crystals sprinkled all over my pajamas.

> Me: It's a little messy. But worth it.

> Good Boy: I'm putting in my official request to try this.

> Me: What are you doing tonight?

I feel a surge of hope that his answer will be *you*. But he dashes that hope a second later.

> Good Boy: About to teach a class on water conservation.

My brows lift.

> Me: Wow. That's nerdy.

> Me: Kidding.

> Me: Really, that's cool.

> Me: Sorry. I didn't mean to call you nerdy.

Good Boy: Dammit, Starlight. You made me laugh out loud, and now everyone in the room is staring at me.

Me: Sorry.

Good Boy: You're not sorry.

I grin down at my phone.

Me: I'm not sorry.

Good Boy: Such a pest.

Me: What does Starlight mean?

Good Boy: I'll tell you later.

Good Boy: Now wish me luck.

Me: Good luck, Husband.

Sighing, I set my phone down on the couch cushion beside me.

I wish I'd known about this class thing that Ethan is teaching. I would've gone.

Maybe not for the topic, though I'm sure it's very important. But more because I want to spend time with him. And if that time is spent just staring at his handsome face... so be it.

Which leads me to wonder about the people who are attending.

Are they locals interested in the topic?

Is it at the park?

Is the room filled with horny women who, like me, just want to stare at Ethan for an hour?

Is it longer than an hour?

Dropping my head back, I let out a groan.

I really need to find something to occupy my evenings.

# Chapter 113

## Ethan

I grab a bag of beef jerky off the display next to the register and set it on the counter beside the trail cam.

"Anything else?"

I shake my head and pay the total.

Not needing a bag, I shove the receipt in my pocket, then grab the box and my jerky and push through the door into the afternoon sunshine.

It's warmer here down the mountain, but the stores in Lonely don't have what I needed. So I took my lunch break to drive another town over, to a larger outdoor store, to buy the highest-rated trail camera.

But it's not for a game trail. It's for Tilda's driveway.

I open my truck door and toss the goods onto my passenger seat. I'm about to climb in when a flash of color across the street catches my attention.

I step to the side so my door isn't blocking any of my view, and I watch as my pretty little wife steps out of a dispensary with a paper bag clutched to her chest.

My Matilda.

My Firecracker, buying some sort of weed so she can get high.

*Dear lord.*

I pull my phone out of my pocket and dial her number.

She's in that red dress she was wearing the day she bought the pool for Quackers. And since the wind is strong again today, I'm once again grateful for the length.

Tilda stops walking, reaches into her little purse, and pulls her phone out.

And her smile hits me right in the fucking heart.

She sees my name on the screen. And she smiles.

I watch her lift the phone to her ear. "Hello, Husband."

"Hello, Wife."

Her smile grows even wider, and I have to remind myself there's a busy road with traffic between us, because all I want to do is walk straight to her.

"Shouldn't you be working?" Tilda turns so the wind blows her hair out of her eyes. And I know she doesn't see me yet. But she's facing my direction.

"Just on my lunch break. Had to do some shopping."

"Oh yeah? Find anything fun?"

I smirk. "Sure did."

"And... what is it?"

"A Firecracker dressed in red."

Her head tilts, like she's thinking about what I said. Then it clicks. And in an instant, her eyes lock on mine.

# CHAPTER 114

## TILDA

FOR A MOMENT, I'M SPEECHLESS, STARING ACROSS THE road at Ethan, and he stares across the road at me.

Then I remember the store I just walked out of.

"Busted," I laugh as my cheeks heat.

I can see Ethan's smile from here. "And how about you? Did *you* find anything fun while shopping today?"

"You know I did." I try to lift the bag higher, but I'm holding it one-handed against my body, so it doesn't really work.

"Have you ever gotten high before, Matilda Iris Wright?"

I shrug. "Maybe."

"You doing some tonight?"

I grin. "Maybe."

"You doing it alone?"

I snort. "No, I'm having all my friends over."

"Tilda."

"Cool your pants, Sexy Ranger. Of course I'm doing it alone. It's not like I have anyone to invite over." I mean it, and it's true, but I didn't mean for it to sound so self-pitying.

"Starlight—" Ethan says my favorite nickname in that soft voice of his.

"You need a party buddy? I'm free tonight." The deep voice

382

startles me, and I jerk my head to the side to find a man approaching.

"Oh, um..." I blink.

"Fuck off, motherfucker!" Ethan's shout carries across the road, and we both turn to look at him. He's pointing a finger at me. "That's my fucking wife."

I bite down on my lip, trapping the gleeful sound trying to escape.

"Jeez." The man puts his hands up and takes a step back. "Just offerin'."

He says it at a normal volume, but Ethan must be able to hear him through the phone because he keeps shouting. "Offer somewhere else."

When the other man disappears into the building, I grin at Ethan. "Such a Good Boy." Then I hang up and get in my truck.

# CHAPTER 115

## ETHAN

THE SUN IS ALREADY STARTING TO SET BY THE TIME I park in front of Tilda's house.

I wanted to be here sooner, but I had to make a few stops.

First, home, to change into clean jeans and a T-shirt and to fill my backpack with spare clothes. Second, to get ingredients for dinner.

Through the windows, I can see another animated movie playing on the TV. And since the windows are open, I can hear loud music that doesn't match the movie playing from inside the house.

I shift my grip on the grocery bag and knock on Tilda's door.

She screams.

I shake my head. "Let me in."

A moment passes. Then she speaks through the door. "Move to the side so I can see you."

"Tilda."

She doesn't answer.

Rolling my eyes, I shuffle to the side.

She peeks her head around the window frame, then disappears.

Two seconds later, the door unlocks and she swings it open. "Hi."

Her expression is so bright I swear it makes my heart glow. "Hi, Starlight."

"What does that mean?" She asks it with such a big smile that I know she's teasing me again.

"I'll tell you later." My voice comes out thick. "Now let me in, Wife."

Tilda steps back, holding the door.

It's not late, but she's already wearing pajamas.

Her hair is down in wavy lavender curls. Her shirt is solid black but thin. And like the last one—like all of them since she doesn't wear a bra to bed—I can see her nipples.

I lower my eyes, trailing them over her body and stopping on her feet.

On her socks. That go halfway up her calves and look like cat feet.

*Fucking perfect.*

I step into the house, then pull the door shut and lock it.

Tilda watches me take my backpack off and set it on the floor. Her lids are lowered, and her movements are a little slow. And she looks cute as fuck.

Tilda pinches at the sides of her shirt. "Are you staying?"

I can hear the hopefulness in her tone, and I know I made the right call packing.

"Yes." I left my boots untied, so I kick them off and lift the grocery bag. "Are you hungry?"

"Yes." Tilda nods. "Are you cooking?"

"Yes." The corner of my mouth pulls up. "Are you high?"

"Yes." Tilda snickers, and my smile lifts to a full one. "Are you high?"

"Not yet." I step closer to my happy girl. "Do you like peanut sauce?"

"Yes." Tilda says it slowly, with her eyes wide.

"Good. But before you sit down, I have one more question."

"Yes?"

"What color panties are you wearing?"

She presses her teeth into her top lip as she reaches down to the hem of her nightshirt.

I think she's going to show me.

*My cock thinks she's going to show me.*

But she spins away, giving me her back, before she lifts the bottom of her shirt and looks.

*Fuck me. Why was that hotter?*

I use the hand not holding our dinner to adjust my cock as Tilda turns back around to face me.

"Black." She shrugs. "I forgot I wanted to match."

My eyes focus on her waist, and I debate the merits of blowing off dinner and dragging Tilda to bed. Just like I did last time.

"Who did you want to match for, Tilda?"

Her cheeks pinken as she tries not to smile. "Deerdra."

A laugh grates out of me, and I shake my head. "Go sit down."

Tilda turns, and I look across the living room at the damn deer head.

And smile at its new purple beaded necklace.

Tilda turns off the small speaker blaring music, then settles herself on one of the stools.

Taking over the kitchen, I unpack the groceries on the other side of the counter.

I start to tell her about the trail cam, but it quickly becomes apparent that she's more intoxicated than I thought. So instead of talking cameras, I answer her thousand questions about what I'm cooking. When I learned to cook. How often I cook. What's my favorite food.

I tell her noodles with rotisserie chicken and peanut sauce is one of my favorite things.

She says she wants to try that.

I remind her that's what I'm making.

"Want one?" Tilda slides a small plastic container across the counter.

I pick it up, reading the label. "This what you had?"

She nods. "They're good."

I don't know if she's talking about the flavor or the effects. But... fuck it. I want to let go with my girl tonight.

I take off the lid and pull out one of the watermelon-flavored gummies.

Tilda grins when I put it in my mouth.

"What?"

"Nothing." She doesn't stop grinning. "I'm just really excited for this."

"Good."

"Do you want to put your pajamas on?"

I look at her chest, then back up at her. "Do you want me to put pajamas on?"

I don't actually have pajamas, so I don't know what I'll do if she says yes. I just wore sleep pants at the cabin because it was our first time sleeping together. Normally I just wear my boxer briefs.

Tilda shrugs. "You don't have to. I just changed before I took my edible because I didn't want to forget how."

"Forget how to do what?"

"Put pajamas on." She says it so seriously.

I nod back just as seriously. "If I forget, you can help me."

She agrees.

We go back to talking about food, and I plate us each a heaping pile of peanut noodles.

And as we eat and talk and smile, I feel my own lids lower.

I feel my body getting a little heavier.

And I feel so good having Tilda this close.

She tells me how delicious the noodles are. She tells me more about that baking show she likes. And... I feel like I've known her all my life.

I get up and put our dishes in the sink. She gets up to follow.

I face her. "Turn the music on."

Tilda doesn't question me. She just does it.

The speaker crackles to life.

I don't recognize the music, but it doesn't matter. It's upbeat. Feels good.

I grip Tilda's hand and take her with me as I walk around, flipping off light switches.

The sun is nearly down, so the house is dark. But the glow of the TV flickers through the room.

With the lights off and the door locked, I walk us to the couch and sit in the center.

Tilda starts to sit beside me, but I stop her.

"Don't sit there." I grip the hem of my T-shirt and drag it up over my head. Bare from the waist up, I lean against the back cushion and undo my jeans. Then I smooth my hands down my thighs. "Sit on my lap."

Tilda is moving toward me before I finish my command.

I grip her hips, turning her back to me, and help her lower onto my thighs.

I tug her back until she's snug against my front, then I roll my hips.

My cock is already hard. It's been on alert since we walked in and found her looking so sweet and fuckable.

Tilda relaxes into my body, dropping her head back against my shoulder.

She's so warm. So fucking soft.

My hands glide from her hips, up her sides, to her breasts.

*So. Fucking. Soft.*

I press my mouth to the side of her exposed throat and groan.

Tilda squirms, and I pluck at her nipples through her thin shirt, tweaking the little metal bars.

"Shit," Tilda whispers.

I smile against her skin as I tug on her nipples just a little bit harder.

This time she moans and rocks her hips in my lap.

Matilda reaches up and sinks her fingers into my hair. "Ethan?" She practically pants my name.

"Yeah, Starlight?" My lips brush her skin with every movement.

She tightens her hold on my hair. "Are you my Good Boy?"

Heat spears through my body, and my balls squeeze.

I grit my teeth. "Fuck yes, I am."

She rolls her head to the side and looks up into my eyes.

Her knees spread, and she hooks her feet around the outside of my legs.

Opening herself to me.

"Then touch me."

My cock pulses, and I clench my stomach muscles.

I'm not coming in my pants tonight. But I'm getting my wife off at least once before I shove inside her.

# Chapter 116

## Tilda

With his left hand, Ethan slowly pulls the hem of my shirt up while sliding his right hand up my thigh, higher, closer to my center.

I drag my nails over his scalp as I lower my hands.

Then I grip his forearms, wanting to feel his muscles flex and move while he touches me.

Ethan's mouth presses against my throat, and I let my eyes close as he drags his tongue across my skin.

"So good." I grind my ass against his erection.

The palm on my thigh shifts, and Ethan groans as he cups my pussy.

I widen my legs.

He keeps his hand flat and starts to rub.

Slow movements, but with enough pressure that my panties start to soak through.

"You wet, Bad Girl?"

A sound catches in my throat as he plucks at one of my nipples with his other hand.

I squeeze his forearms tighter. The sensation of feeling his fingers on me and feeling his muscles and tendons moving under my hands...

I feel him everywhere.

In my core.

In my throbbing nipples.

Under my ass.

Against my back as he rumbles with pleasure.

And I lose myself in it.

Music fills the room, and my heartbeat fills my ears as I lie draped over Ethan.

He slides his hand under my shirt, and the feeling of his hand on my bare breast pushes me that much closer to the tipping point.

I start to shift. Rocking my hips. Seeking more.

Wanting more.

The pressure builds.

My lungs feel hot.

And... his hand leaves my core.

I whimper. "No—"

My panties are shoved aside, and fingers replace them.

"Oh gods."

Ethan presses his lips to my temple as he pushes two fingers inside me.

I clench, my muscles squeezing, trying to keep him there, trying to take him deeper.

"So fucking hot for it." His other hand kneads my breast. "So fucking hot for me."

I nod. "Always."

"Always." He grinds his palm against my clit. "I like that."

His breath is warm, and his touch is relentless.

He plays me perfectly.

Strumming and plucking.

Over and over.

My body tenses.

My lungs hitch.

"Come for me, Firecracker." Ethan flexes his thighs, bouncing me on his lap, shoving his fingers deeper.

He pinches my nipple and drags his palm across my clit. And that's it.

I'm tossed over.

He doesn't stop the pressure.

And I can't catch my breath.

Ethan shifts me.

A hand leaves me.

Fingers still play between my legs.

A hand lifts me.

And then I'm sinking onto Ethan's thick cock.

# CHAPTER 117

## ETHAN

TILDA CRIES OUT AS I FILL HER WITH EVERY INCH I have.

I rock my hips. Dragging my cock in and out of her heat.

I keep my right hand between her legs and wrap my other arm around her waist, holding her to me.

Keeping her *impaled* on me.

Her sounds make my dick impossibly harder as she moans and whimpers.

I reach farther, keeping my palm against her clit and spreading my fingers around my dick, feeling where I disappear inside her.

It feels amazing.

It feels so fucking amazing.

"Have I been good, Tilda?" I ask brokenly as I continue to pump into her.

"Yes." Her voice cracks on a moan. "You've been such a Good fucking Boy."

My balls tighten.

Hearing Tilda say fuck while she calls me a Good Boy...

"Say that again. Reach down and touch my dick while you say that again."

Tilda slides her hand down my arm, leaning forward until her fingers are covering mine.

I pull my hand back, just a few inches, but she keeps hers there.

Her fingertips press against the base of my cock as mine start to rub circles around her clit.

Tilda clenches, and I grip her hip with my other hand.

To hold her. And to rock her.

Tilda rolls her hips with a gasp. She settles her free hand on my knee as she leans forward even more. But her other hand is still between us.

Still trying to grip me. Fingers slipping against my slick cock.

I keep rocking her. Getting closer and closer.

I managed to shove my jeans down a few inches, and now I can feel her wetness all over me.

"I'm so fucking close," I warn Tilda.

"Me too." Her pussy flutters around my length.

I focus on her clit.

On the way it feels.

How slippery it is.

"Come for me, Starlight." I can tell how close she is. "Hurry up and come for me."

I watch her shake her head. "Be a Good Boy, and you go first."

She leans forward even more and slides her hand down to cup my balls.

Her fingers flex.

Her core tightens.

She squeezes and oh-so-gently pulls.

"Holy fuck."

I explode.

My abs contract.

I wrap my left arm around her waist as I sit up, curling into her.

And I hold her tightly as my dick pulses, filling her so full I can feel it dripping out of her.

Tilda tenses, and with one final rub of my fingers, she comes. Again.

# CHAPTER 118

## TILDA

PANTING, I'M DEADWEIGHT, SPRAWLED OVER ETHAN like a life-sized rag doll.

We both collapsed back after the shockwave subsided. He still has an arm banded around me, his other hand on my thigh, and I can feel the wetness of our combined releases on his fingers.

A perfect mess.

"Firecracker." Ethan wheezes the nickname. I try to sit up, but he just holds me in place. "Where're you going?"

My struggle is weak. "I'm crushing you."

Ethan chuckles. "You couldn't crush me if you tried."

The movement causes his dick to finally slip free.

I squeak and try to press my thighs together.

"Quit wiggling." Ethan nuzzles his nose against my cheek.

This time, I start to chuckle. Which only worsens the state between my legs. "Ethan, I'm making a mess."

He lifts his hand from my thigh, and I think he's going to help me up, but he just reaches down and pulls my panties back into place. "There." He pats my pussy.

I jolt. "Ethan."

"What?" He drags his nose up to my temple and inhales.

"You're like a cat." A shiver works its way down my spine at the feel of his scratchy beard against my cheekbone.

"A happy cat." His fingers knead into my stomach.

"I always wanted a cat," I sigh. Then I give up the fight and go back to my deadweight state.

A rumble vibrates through Ethan's chest. Like a purr.

"Good Kitty."

Ethan's hand goes back to cupping me between my legs. "Pretty kitty."

Letting my eyes drift closed, I grin. "I remember thinking you had a pretty penis."

Ethan chokes, then lightly smacks my pussy.

"Ethan!" My eyes snap open.

He leaves his hand there. "That's for calling it a penis."

I snort. "That's what it's called."

"Cock. Dick. Shaft." He hums. "I'm sure there are others. But never penis."

I shake my head, my hair ruffling against his shoulder.

Ethan smacks my pussy again, and it makes a wet slapping sound. My panties are completely soaked by this point.

"Ethan!"

"And *that* is for knowing how to tug on a man's balls like that."

I huff as I shake my head again.

He keeps his palm pressed firmly against me. "Where did you learn that?" His fingers flex against my panties. "Better yet, don't tell me."

His jealousy warms me all the way to my toes.

So I tell him. "Porn."

I can feel him slowly lift his head to look at me.

I keep my eyes up, watching the colors from the TV dance across the ceiling.

"Matilda Iris Wright." He says it so sternly that I snicker.

He rocks his palm against my core.

S.J. TILLY

"Are you telling me that you watch filthy, ball-fondling pornography while you touch this perfect little slit of yours?"

I start to squirm.

*His words.*

*His body beneath mine.*

*His fingers putting pressure on my entrance.*

I lift my heavy arm and reach down to grip his forearm. "Ethan."

He slides his hand up until his fingers reach the band of my underwear, then he slides them back down. With nothing between us. "Tell me, Starlight. Tell me what you do."

He starts to work his fingers, our combined releases coating his hand.

And it's so slippery.

Gods, it's so freaking slippery.

Ethan groans.

Then we're sitting up, my body moving with his.

He's eager now.

Hands moving quickly to pull my pajama shirt off.

"On the floor." He uses his foot to shove the coffee table forward, making room for us. Then he slides us off the couch.

I kneel on the floor, collapsing forward, elbows on the coffee table.

"Tell me, Bad Girl." He kneels behind me, dragging my panties down. "Tell me what you do when you're alone."

I open my mouth.

But then he shoves inside me.

And all that comes out is a cry as he roughly thrusts into me.

I squeeze around him.

It feels so good.

He digs his fingers into my hips.

So damn good.

"Touch yourself, Tilda." He doesn't slow. And I can tell it's not going to take him long. "Show me how you make yourself come." He keeps going, keeps *fucking me.* "Use those fingers on

398

that perfect pussy." Blindly, frantically, I reach one hand down and start rubbing at my clit. "That's it. That's my Bad Girl." His words send me higher, send me closer. "Keep going. Don't fucking stop. Don't you dare stop until you're coming on my cock."

"Ethan. Oh gods. Ethan."

He grips my hips even tighter.

His movements get even rougher as he pounds into me.

"Fuck. Starlight. Fuck."

My fingers can barely stay where I need them because I'm so freaking slippery.

"Tell me, Wife. Tell me when you're coming."

That's it.

*Wife.*

That's all I needed.

"I'm coming," I choke out as my body spasms. "Husband, I'm coming."

"Fuck," Ethan bellows as he slams his hips forward, burying himself as deep as he can go.

Flames bloom in my chest.

Sparkles dance in my vision.

Muscles pulse and clench, and pleasure consumes me.

Ethan groans and moans and twitches inside me.

It's bliss.

*Heaven.*

Then my head starts to swim, and my hand drops from my core.

I slump forward, and when my forehead bumps against the coffee table, I gasp in a breath.

Ethan makes a garbled sound of alarm as he wraps his arms around me and lifts my top half off the table.

"I'm okay." I put my palms on the table and start to snicker. "I forgot to breathe."

"Don't do that." Ethan sounds so distraught. And I feel bad. But...

My snicker turns into a full-body laugh.

Ethan grumbles as he, once again, slips free from my body.

I can't stop laughing.

That was all so... intense. I don't even know what to do with myself.

Ethan's heat leaves my back. Followed by a thud.

Turning my head, I find him flat on his back. On the floor. Chest still heaving. Pants and boxer briefs around his knees. Dick shining in the glow of the TV.

What a perfect night.

# CHAPTER 119

## ETHAN

A SMALL GROAN LEAVES ME AS I OPEN MY EYES.

Tilda makes a matching noise as knuckles press into the base of my throat, her hand somehow wedged between her forehead and my neck.

A sleepy smile starts to pull at my lips, but it gets demolished by a yawn.

I feel like I lay down and didn't move a single muscle after falling asleep.

I blink, trying to wake myself up.

And that smile returns when I remember last night.

My Firecracker is a goddamn sex goddess.

*Rounds, plural, of sex.*

*A shared shower.*

*Another shared edible before we climbed into bed.*

Said Firecracker shifts. Her knee jams into the center of my thigh, and the hand not threatening to choke me somehow pulls my chest hair.

My smile widens.

*She's pure chaos. And I love it.*

I press my lips to the top of her messy hair.

I want to stay in bed, fall back asleep. But I also want to get that trail cam set up on her driveway before I have to leave for work. And being able to keep an eye on Tilda takes precedence over sleep.

Resigned, I start to roll away from Tilda, but the mattress sinks more than it should as I move.

Pausing, I shift my top leg back, feeling with my foot. And yep, this little menace has me trapped on the very edge of the bed.

If I try to roll onto my back, I'll land on the floor.

Tilda murmurs and snuggles into my chest.

But I was already starting to lean, and the added pressure on my body pushes me past the tipping point.

"Fuck."

I reach for the headboard and hook my fingers over the top of the plain wood as my top half slides off the mattress.

My fingers strain, but my grip holds.

Then my ass slides off the bed, and rather than dislodging my shoulder, I let go.

I grunt when I hit the floor, my boxer briefs doing little to soften the landing.

A purple-haired fairy peeks over the edge of the mattress, looking down at me. "Ethan?"

I sit up. "Morning."

She squints at me. "Did you sleep down there?"

"No." I get to my feet. "You pushed me off the bed."

She starts to deny it, then looks down. She's mostly on her stomach now, with me out of the way. And her shoulder is right at the edge of the mattress. Where I was.

Tilda rolls onto her back and slaps a hand over her mouth.

"Laugh it up." I roll my neck out. "Next time I'm taking you with me."

"Sorry," she says from behind her hand.

I look down at her. And even though I know she's hiding a smile, I know she really is sorry. "Go back to sleep."

She shakes her head and drops her hand as she starts to sit up. "The least I can do is make you coffee before you go to work."

I place my hand on her chest and push her back down. "Go back to sleep."

"But—"

"Get up in an hour and make me coffee."

She glances at the clock, seeing it's early. "Sleep with me. I promise I won't push you off the bed again."

I bend lower. "I don't believe you." I press a kiss to her mouth, then stand up straight. "And I got a camera for your driveway. I want to set it up before I go."

Her brows lift. "A camera?"

"Yeah." I cross the room and pick my jeans up off the floor. "I'll hook it up to your Wi-Fi and show you the app. Then you'll be able to watch it on your phone and see who's coming."

"Oh, wow, that would be really cool." She sits back up.

"Matilda."

She waves me off and scoots to the edge of the bed. "I'm awake now. And I'm pretty sure a spy camera deserves French toast."

# CHAPTER 120

## TILDA

ETHAN'S BEEN AT WORK A COUPLE HOURS.

I've put the extra clothes he brought into a dresser drawer. Hung up his extra ranger shirt in the closet. Cleaned every dish from breakfast. Had a second coffee.

I pace across the living room for the fifth time and finally force myself to stop.

"Just text him."

I sit on the couch.

Then I remember what we did here last night, and I stand.

If I sit there and think about *that*, I'm going to end up back in bed with my hand up my dress.

I move to the kitchen counter and pull out the stool.

This is where I watched Ethan cook last night. Still a sexy experience. But a safe one to think about.

> Me: Do you have plans for tonight?

As soon as I send it, I worry that I'm acting needy.

Then I tell myself to stop overthinking it. Ethan and I clearly have a good time together. If he didn't like hanging out, he wouldn't have brought extra clothes to leave here.

Only a few seconds pass before he replies, and that mollifies the rest of my anxiety.

> Duck Whisperer: I have to go to the gym after work.

Me: To work out?

I roll my eyes at myself. *Obviously.* What other reason would he go to the gym?

Me: Ignore that question.

> Duck Whisperer: What question?

I grin, glad I married a clever man.

> Duck Whisperer: I do plan to lift some weights while I'm there. But I really just need to go check on things. Make sure it's good.

I make a face at the phone.
*Huh?*

Me: I have no idea what you mean.

> Duck Whisperer: I have a cleaning team, but I need to make sure the cameras and stuff are running correctly.

Me: Hi, whoever you are. Can you put Ethan on the phone?

> Duck Whisperer: I hope you're happy. I just laughed, and now Liza is looking at me like I ate the fly off the windowsill.

I almost gag.

Me: What. The. Fuck.

Me: Did you eat a fly?

Me: Ethan. Answer me.

I press a hand to the base of my throat, feeling literally sick at the idea.

My phone lights up with a call.

I answer. And laughter greets me.

The hand on my throat drops, and my disgusted frown disappears.

*Ethan's laugh is one of my most favorite sounds.*

"Starlight." He's still chuckling. "You're killing me."

"You're the one who said you ate a fly."

His exhale scratches over the line. "I said she was looking at me *like* I ate the fly."

"It was a very specific thing to say."

"Dammit, woman." I can picture him shaking his head. And I can hear the smile in his voice. "I needed that."

My brows furrow. "What? Why? Did something happen?"

Ethan sighs. "Quit being perfect. Nothing happened."

My cheeks warm, but I decide to ignore the compliment. "If nothing happened, then why did you need that?"

"Matilda. I swear. Everything is fine."

"But—"

"I was thinking about you. Then you texted. And started cursing at me. Acting all outraged… It was adorable. Are you done staring?"

I blink. "Me?"

"No, not you, Tilda. Liza, I can see you. You know that, right?"

I bite my lip.

I shouldn't ask.

*I shouldn't.*

"Who's Liza?" Jealousy stains my tone green.

"*Liza.*" Ethan enunciates her name, and I assume she's still listening. "Is supposed to be stocking the maps. But she's too busy gawking over our conversation."

"I'm *gawking* over the fact that you're *laughing*," an unfamiliar voice says. "I didn't know you could do that."

"Yeah, well, surprise," Ethan deadpans.

I snort. "You're a turd."

"You're the turd," he whispers back.

I snort again.

"Who are you talking to?" the woman asks, clearly still stunned by this playful side of Ethan. And it makes me proud to be the one who brings it out.

Ethan keeps whispering. "Should I tell her? Shock her some more?"

I have no idea what he's about to say. But I enjoy being in on the joke. "Tell her."

Ethan clears his throat, then raises his voice. "I'm talking to my wife."

*Wife.*

I hear paper rip.

Then the woman screams the type of scream that's accompanied by jazz hands and running in place.

And I decide I like Liza.

"Let me talk to her." The voice is louder. Closer.

My eyes widen.

*Talk to a stranger?*

*No, thank you.*

"Ethan," I hiss into the phone. "Ethan."

"I'm putting you on speaker."

"Wait—"

"Tilda, meet Liza. Liza, meet my wife, Tilda."

"Oh heavens. Is this real? Did our boy Ethan run off and get married?"

"I'm almost forty," Ethan replies.

The woman huffs. "You're the same age as my son. Now zip it."

I snicker, and their dynamic gives my jealousy a swift death.

"Was that her?" Liza's voice is quieter, like she's asking Ethan.

407

"Tilda, put me out of my misery and say something."

"Um, hi."

Someone—Liza—claps their hands. "Oh, my Jesus. You're real."

"As real as the fly Ethan just ate." I'm grinning so hard my cheeks ache.

"I didn't eat the fly." He sounds so put out that I dissolve into laughter.

"Oh, I like her." Liza sounds like she's beaming.

"I like her too." Ethan says it easily. "When she's not being a pest."

"You like when I'm a pest."

Ethan hums. "Maybe. Now, Liza, if you don't mind, I'm going to take my call outside."

"Oh, but—"

"We have visitors."

"Well, crap," Liza huffs. "It was nice to hear your voice, Tilda. I hope to meet you soon."

"Same to you," I tell her honestly.

"Okay," Ethan says a moment later. "I don't even remember what we were talking about before."

"Um... I don't—Oh, you were talking about the gym. About cleaners?"

"That's right. My part-timers would let me know if something was up, but I still like to check for myself."

"Part-timers? Do you... work there?"

"I own it."

Silence.

Crickets.

"You own... what?"

*Are we back to talking about the cleaning crew? Does Ethan have a cleaning company?*

"I own the gym."

I blink. "You own the gym. The one where we...?"

"Where I first got my mouth on you? Yes."

My pulse thuds at the memory of our first kiss.

That was so hot.

I shake my head. *Not the time, Tilda.*

"Since when?"

He makes a thinking sound. "Sixteen years ago."

"Sixteen?"

"Remodeled it about five back."

"How?"

"New flooring. Machines. Updated—"

"Ethan."

He chuckles, clearly proud of his own joke. "I told you, my parents had a lot of life insurance. Sandra and I split it. I bought a gym."

"Well..." I can't believe Ethan owns a gym, and I had no idea. I try to think back, if he gave any hints. But my time there is overshadowed by the kiss we shared.

"Well?"

"Well, I want a free membership."

Ethan barks out a laugh. "Done. Any other demands, Wife?"

I tap my fingers on the counter. "I want to come with you tonight."

"Done." Ethan's using that warm tone now. And it makes me want to hug him.

"Glad we could come to an agreement." I blow out a breath and stand from the stool. "Okay, slacker, go back to work. I have a duck to feed."

"Bye, Starlight."

# CHAPTER 121

## ETHAN

Wife: Do you have a moment?

Me: Yep.

Wife: To call?

I SHAKE MY HEAD.

Me: Yes.

Sitting at one of the picnic tables behind the Visitor Center, I open my container of leftover peanut noodles and set the lid aside.

It's a little later than I normally eat lunch, but Tilda's French toast, which happened to be store bought and frozen, was damn good. And apparently I ate enough to keep me working through the noon hour without realizing it.

I'm picking up my fork when my phone rings. But not with a voice call, a video one.

I swap my fork for my phone and answer.

Tilda's pretty face greets me. "Hi."

"Fuck, you're pretty."

She presses her lips together, embarrassed. "Thank you. You're very handsome."

I smirk. "Thank you."

Tilda is sitting on her front step, in the shade of the house.

"You hangin' out with Quackers?"

"Um, Quackers is nearby." Tilda's voice is pitched too high.

I narrow my eyes. "What's going on?"

"I, uh, found a kitten."

My shoulders relax. "Okay. Well, you said you always wanted a cat. We can make sure it doesn't belong to anyone."

"Right, so, the thing is..."

My tension returns tenfold. "What's the thing, Tilda?"

"I don't think it's a normal kitten." Tilda bites her lip, then switches the view to the front-facing camera.

The day is warm, but a chill coats my skin. "Matilda." I swing my leg over the bench, abandoning my lunch, and stand. "You need to go inside."

"What? Why? She's really nice."

I watch as Tilda reaches out and scratches the belly of a tiny fucking mountain lion.

A mountain lion that is laid out in her lap, on her long purple skirt, furry little paws sticking up in the air as Tilda plays with it.

"Matilda Grant." The camera view jerks at my use of her *real* full name. "A baby mountain lion means there could be a mama mountain lion nearby. Looking for it."

The inhale tells me she understands. "Oh."

*Yeah, oh.* But I can't even verbalize the danger that represents. Because... losing Tilda in any way would destroy me. Losing her in a violent way... That would fucking end me.

I swallow down my rising fear as I step through the back door into the Visitor Center. "Now, please."

Tilda palms her phone, blocking the camera, and I listen to fabric rustle as she gets up.

She grunts. And her muffled voice says something I can't understand.

I clench my jaw to stop myself from yelling at her to hurry.

Phone still held before me, I stride down the hall and cut over to the counter area that separates the office from the public.

Liza looks up at my approach.

I speak before she can. "Call Shelia. Now. Please."

Her eyes widen, but she doesn't ask questions.

Liza takes her phone out of her pocket and dials, then puts it on speaker as she sets it on the counter between us.

It starts to ring at the same time I hear Tilda's door shut.

Shelia answers. "Hey, Liza."

"Shelia, it's Ethan."

"Oh, hey, is Liza okay?"

"I'm fine," Liza answers so I can ignore the question.

"I need an animal pick up. No injuries, just rescue."

"Where?"

I give her Tilda's address.

I hear Shelia pick up a set of keys. "What's the animal?"

"Mountain lion cub. Maybe two months old." As I answer, Tilda's camera comes back into focus. "Dammit, Firecracker." I hang up the call with Shelia.

"Aww..." Liza is leaning against the counter to see my phone.

And the baby mountain lion that is back on Tilda's lap.

"I gotta run," I tell Liza, already turning away from the counter.

"What?" Tilda asks like she honestly doesn't know what the problem is.

"I told *you* to go inside."

"I did."

"And you brought the cat?"

"Well, I wasn't gonna leave it."

I shove out the front doors and stride toward my truck. "Just... don't bring any other wild animals inside. Okay? I'm on my way."

# CHAPTER 122

## TILDA

In less time than it probably should've taken Ethan to drive here, I get an alert on my phone that someone just passed the driveway camera.

"He's almost here." I run my hand down the baby's back.

She's the prettiest thing I've ever seen. And I already love her. But I can't bring myself to give her a name.

Because I heard the other conversation Ethan was having, and I bet that person is on their way too. Which means I'll probably never see this sweet baby again.

I press my finger against her sleeping nose.

*There's also the tiny detail that this sweet baby will grow up to be a lethal weapon.*

"Yeah." I boop her nose again. "You're gonna grow up to be a killing machine, aren't you?"

She yawns. And my heart melts even more.

I hear Ethan park his truck just as my phone notifies me of another car passing the driveway cam.

The front door opens, and Ethan walks in. But I keep my eyes on the baby. Wanting to soak her in as much as I can.

Ethan sighs as he crouches next to where I'm sitting on the floor.

I didn't want her falling off the couch. And I figured, in case she pees on me, then at least this way it's just my dress and not any furniture.

Ethan's warm palm settles on my bare shoulder. "She's cute."

I nod. "Super cute."

We both hear the other car pull up, and Ethan stands to go wait by the door.

The baby cat blinks her eyes open.

"Such a pretty girl," I whisper as Ethan and the stranger step into the house.

I keep my gaze on the cat.

The furball stretches, her front legs reaching out, her claws catching on my dress.

I help her untangle, then finally lift my eyes to Ethan. "Sorry."

He lowers back to a crouch beside me. "You don't have to be sorry."

"After I called you, I did an internet search about what you should do with abandoned mountain lion cubs." I wince as I say it, and we both know why.

Every search turned up with the same thing. *Do not touch them.* For a plethora of reasons.

Ethan runs his tongue along his teeth. A move I suspect is meant to hide a smirk.

"Turd," I whisper.

He runs a hand over my hair, petting me like I'm petting the baby. "Yeah, but I'm your turd."

The other person, a woman in her thirties, sets a pet carrier on the floor a few feet away from me. "Hi. I'm Shelia."

"Hi, Shelia. I'm Tilda." I look back down at the feline in my lap. "You gotta go with Shelia now. But I promise you'll like her."

I sniff against the urge to cry.

I want to ask where the baby's mother is.

How they'll find her.

But I don't ask because I'm afraid the answer will end up being something sad.

Shelia pulls leather gloves on, and I stroke the baby's back one more time before she picks her up.

Shelia expertly gets the cat secured, tells us goodbye, then carries the mountain lion out of the house.

Ethan, still next to me, leans in and presses a kiss to my temple. "I'm sorry, Starlight." He kisses me again. "We can get you a regular cat if you want."

I exhale the sadness. "I'm allergic."

An engine starts, and a vehicle drives away.

Then a quack sounds through the stillness, and we both watch through the windows as Quackers flies down from the roof.

"Good thing you're not allergic to ducks."

"It is a good thing." I sniff but can't stop my smile. "I don't think Quackers liked her much."

Ethan hums, then kisses my temple again. "Come on, Starlight." He stands, then steps over so he's straddling my extended legs. "Let's go wash your hands, then have some lunch."

He reaches down, hooks his hands under my arms, and lifts me to my feet.

I look up into his eyes, soaking in the colors. "I like how strong you are."

Ethan smirks as he slides his hands down my sides. "I like that you like it."

I start to reach for him but stop with my hands in the air between us when I remember what he said about washing my hands.

I wrinkle my nose. "She was a little stinky."

Ethan lifts his brows. "Wild animals."

I sigh as I drop my hands back to my sides. "Guess I should probably wash my dress too."

"Not a bad idea." He flexes his fingers against my hips, then steps back. "You do that, I'll start lunch."

Gratitude fills my stomach. "Thank you for coming. I'm sorry if I scared you."

Ethan steps forward, closer than he had been. "You never have to thank me, Starlight." He leans in, slowly, and presses his lips to mine. "Now hurry up. If we eat fast, I might still have enough time on my lunch break to eat *you* for dessert."

I inhale, then sprint to my bedroom for a new dress.

# CHAPTER 123

## ETHAN

I GROAN AS I BEND DOWN TO PICK UP A STICK. AND groan again when I toss it off the trail.

After work last night, after I stayed late to make up for my long lunch break, I took Tilda with me to the gym.

She walked, looking cute as fuck and distracting as hell, in another pair of painted-on shorts. And I lifted weights.

A normal amount.

To start with.

But then she came over and sat on the bench next to mine, telling me she wanted *to watch*.

And since I'm not one to disappoint my wife, I kept going. With heavier weights. And more reps. And goddamn, I am feeling it today.

I roll out my shoulders and swing my arms back and forth.

If I get my blood pumping, then maybe my aching muscles will shut the fuck up.

I glance at the woods to my right, then down at my watch.

Not even ten thirty. Too early for lunch.

This part of the park is less traveled. The trails are less manicured. Mostly used by staff, like me, to check on the property lines and to make sure no one is camping where they shouldn't.

I glance off to the right again.

Toward Tilda's property.

It's strange how it feels like hers now.

For so long, it was Jack's. Now...

Now it's *hers*.

I inhale the scent of pine.

Jack really did a fucking number with his little death plan. I don't know if it's psychotic or brilliant. *Probably both*. Definitely unethical.

But even without his interference, I feel certain.

*I feel it in my fucking bones.*

Tilda would still be mine.

I went over there *that day*, looking for Jack. Checking in. And I found *her*.

I found her, on the very same day she moved in, and I haven't stopped thinking about her since.

Without Jack, we wouldn't be married. Yet. But I would've kept finding her.

She's impossible not to find.

*She's my way home.*

I turn to the right.

It's early.

Too early for my plan to surprise Tilda by showing up at her door for lunch.

But...

I take a step.

I can't help myself.

I specifically came to this side of the park so I could see her.

My phone alerts me with a notification, and I pause.

I'm almost out of range for service. But I have enough to see the image of a car passing the trail cam on Tilda's driveway.

I don't recognize the vehicle. But when I zoom in on the image, I recognize the man in the passenger seat.

Fury and fear fill my lungs.

I exhale the fear.
I send a text.
Then I start sprinting through the woods.

# CHAPTER 124

## TILDA

I ACCIDENTALLY CLICKED THE WRONG THING WHEN MY phone alerted me to someone on the driveway, so I'm still standing in the garage, trying to find the notification, when a text comes through.

> Gym Owner: Stay in the house. I'm on my way.

"Stay in the house?"

I start to type a reply. Then I hear the sound of a car approaching.

*Stay in the house. I'm on my way.*

Goose bumps erupt down my arms.

Ethan must have the camera connected to his phone too.

And he must know who's coming.

Leaving the pile of gardening tools scattered on the ground, I rush across my front yard straight to my front door.

The car is close. And I know they're within sight when I reach the door. But I don't look back.

My hands are shaking as I shove the door open.

And brakes screech as I step inside.

My pulse is pounding in my ears when I slam it shut.

And anxiety has tears prickling my eyes when I twist the dead bolt.

I step back from the door just in time to hear someone shout my name.

But it's not Ethan's voice.

It's Ralph's.

"Get back out here, you bitch."

I scramble for the handle on the closest window and quickly crank it shut.

From a few yards away, he sees what I'm doing and darts for the other open window.

I do too.

But I'm closer.

The window is still open an inch when he tramples through Quackers's bush. And I'm so grateful I saw her flap away half an hour ago.

I get the window shut all the way just as Ralph tries to wedge his fingers in the opening.

He presses his hands against the glass and sneers at me. "You think a little glass is going to save you?"

I take a step back.

"Uh, Ralph." The other voice is muffled.

I look past my cousin to see a second guy, about the same age, standing next to the driver's door of an older sedan.

So, he came with a friend. Not more of our family.

"Ralph!" the guy shouts again.

"What?" Ralph shouts back.

The guy points.

Away from the house.

Toward the park.

"Company."

Ralph and I both turn our attention in that direction.

Toward the state park property line.

Toward the angry park ranger.

# CHAPTER 125

## ETHAN

My CHEST IS HEAVING.

But not from the run through the forest.

From the sight of a man. *This fucking man.* Standing with his filthy hands against my wife's window.

"You." My voice is low. Gritty.

Ralph steps away from the house into the driveway.

His eyes are wide. Wild. But he's more angry than scared.

And this motherfucker needs to be more scared.

My boots crunch on gravel, the width of the driveway the only thing between us.

"This doesn't concern you," the weasel whines.

"You just threatened my wife." My stride is steady. Measured. "And that should fucking concern *you.*"

His chin wobbles, but he holds his ground. "What're you gonna do? Arrest me?" His eyes dart to the gun at my hip as I continue to cut the distance between us.

"No. And I'm not going to shoot you." I roll my head side to side. "I'm going to punch you."

Blood sizzles through my veins as I take the last two steps quicker.

Then, in a blink, I do exactly what I said I would do.

I shift my stance.

I pull my right arm back.

And I throw my weight forward and out.

He tries to step back. Tries to lift his arms in defense. But Ralph is slow. And my fist connects with his jaw.

The sound is *loud*.

His head snaps to the side, and his arms flail as he trips over his own feet and falls to the ground.

I bend down and grip the front of his shirt with my left hand.

And I lift him.

His eyes are unfocused as he tries to shove my hand away.

"If you ever show up here again..." I keep my hold of him as I dart my right fist out, slamming it into his stomach.

He chokes on his own breath.

I shove him away from me.

He stumbles back.

"If I ever see your bitch-ass face again..."

I kick my leg, sweeping his out from under him.

Ralph lets out a pitiful cry as he lands back on the gravel.

"If you ever put your dirty fucking hands on anything that belongs to Matilda again..."

The vision of him with his hands against her window grates over my senses.

Ralph rolls onto his stomach and starts to crawl.

I kick his wrist.

Hard.

He screams and lands face-first in the dust.

I use my boot to roll him onto his back. So he's looking up at me.

So he can't miss what I say next.

"If you *ever* threaten my wife again, I *will* kill you. And no one will ever find you." I step over him. "You want to know why, *Ralph*?"

He shakes his head.

But I bend down anyway, putting my face closer to his.

"Because I know where the animals live. And I will feed you to them, piece by fucking piece, until all that's left of you is a pair of empty fucking shoes."

Ralph whimpers, and I straighten.

My eyes settle on something up ahead. On the ground. And I step over Ralph's head.

I hear him scramble behind me, getting to his feet.

I don't hurry.

Don't run.

I just walk toward Tilda's garage, and from the pile of tools on the ground, I bend and pick up the axe.

I let the rusted head drag across the rocks as I turn around.

Ralph is cradling his wrist to his chest as his other hand fumbles with the handle for the passenger door.

I hoist the axe up, and through the back window, I make eye contact with the driver.

His engine turns over, and he screams at Ralph to get in.

This is *his* car.

The car he drove to my wife's house.

To help Ralph torment her.

Ralph scrambles into the car.

He slams his door shut.

And I swing the axe.

# CHAPTER 126

## TILDA

THE PASSENGER WINDOW SHATTERS, AND PIECES OF glass shower over Ralph as Ethan's axe cuts into the doorframe.

I pull open the front door and step outside.

The driver steps on the gas, but Ethan's grip on the axe doesn't falter. He pulls it free as the car jumps forward.

But the car is facing the wrong way, and he has to turn around.

I can see movement through the windshield, the driver frantically trying to turn the wheel. And I can hear Ralph screaming through his now windowless door. But I can't pull my attention away from Ethan.

He's...

*Gods, he's so hot.*

My Ranger swings the axe again.

Metal hits metal, and Ethan tears a hole in the rear passenger door.

The engine revs as the car lurches and goes up into the grass. But there's not enough room with the hill. And the driver has to back up to fully turn around.

Ethan sidesteps the rear bumper, the driver focused on leaving, not running him over.

But Ethan's not done.

When the car shifts back into drive, Ethan steps forward. And with a final swing, he smashes one of the rear taillights.

The tires spin, kicking up dust, then catch, and the car disappears.

*Holy. Shit.*

My heart is racing.

My body feels hot.

And when Ethan turns to face me, that heat travels straight to my core.

His expression is wild.

Feral.

I take a step backward.

Not trying to get away.

Trying to get him to follow.

He steps forward, lowering the axe to his side.

I part my lips so I can pull in deeper breaths.

He takes another step.

I step back.

And we keep eye contact.

Keep staring at each other as I back into the house.

As he drops the axe on the ground.

As I back toward my bedroom.

As he kicks the door shut behind him.

We're both breathing heavy.

Both feeling the effects of the adrenaline rush.

And when my legs bump into the bed.

When Ethan enters the bedroom.

We still hold eye contact.

We hold it while we tear our clothes off.

Hold it while we fall onto the mattress.

We hold it, and each other, as Ethan enters me.

As we rock.

As we moan.

And we hold it the whole time. Until we come apart.
Then our eyes close. And we exhale.

# Chapter 127

## Tilda

Quackers takes the pea from my palm.

"You like that?" I smile and take another one from the bowl, holding my hand out.

She takes it, then waddles over to her pool, and I set the bowl of partially thawed peas next to me on the front step.

The day is beautiful.

The sun is out, but it's not too hot.

The sky is a bright, vivid blue.

And I... have no idea what to do with myself.

Quackers hops into the water.

"What do you think?" I ask the duck. "Should I get a pet?"

She lets out a mild quack.

"Yeah, but you aren't a pet. You're a... neighbor."

She paddles away, giving me her back.

I tap my shoes against the ground.

I really am allergic to cats. And dogs seem fun, but I've never had one.

Quackers turns back around, and I toss a pea into the water.

She dives after it.

I toss some more as I think about my options.

But that's the problem. There are too many options.

I have money now. And not just like *enough savings to cover me for a few months*. Like *I have every option available to me* money.

I could work part-time and earn just enough to help with expenses while giving myself something to do.

I could work full-time and make enough that I don't use any of the money from Uncle Jack.

I could use the money to pay for a college degree. No loans needed.

But... I don't have the first idea of what I'd go to school for. And, if I'm being honest with myself, I don't want to go to school. I didn't really like it the first time around, and doing it by choice seems like the worst choice of them all.

I toss another pea into the water.

"You don't know how good you have it."

Quackers chomps the pea.

"Okay..." I toss another pea. "What do I like to do?"

In general, I'm easy to entertain. But the things I enjoy...

*Ethan.*

My mind just keeps going back to Ethan.

I enjoy life when we're together.

All of it.

The conversations and the expressions he makes. The sex.

I snort.

Sex with Ethan is not a viable profession.

But...

I bite down on my lip, glad no one but Quackers can see me as my cheeks flush. Because a profession I'd never really considered before might also be an option.

The duck paddles in place, looking at me.

"What do you think? Would I be an okay mom?"

Quackers flaps her wings.

I toss her a pea.

I've never given kids too much thought. I've never been in a serious enough relationship to have the conversation with anyone before. But I've thought about it enough to know that I didn't want to be single and pregnant, so I've always been on birth control.

But...

I tap my toes on the ground a little faster.

Ethan and I are new, even if we're technically married. But it still feels serious.

Like it's getting serious.

I think about Ethan beating up my cousin yesterday.

Feels like maybe we're already serious.

And it's probably too soon to talk to him about kids. But maybe... I could be a stay-at-home mom.

Maybe.

One day.

I blow out a breath, and Quackers snaps her beak.

"I know, I know." I toss her two peas. "I'm getting ahead of myself."

But thinking about Ethan makes me think about yesterday.

*Freaking yesterday.*

Ethan was... perfect.

His timing.

His words.

The way he looked while punching my stupid cousin in the face.

My mouth pulls into a smile.

Ethan was so perfect, handled it so perfectly, that I can sit out here today, feet away from where Ralph put his hands on my window, and smile.

Ethan did it all so perfectly that I'm not at all worried about Ralph coming back.

First, he probably spent yesterday in the hospital because I'm pretty sure his wrist is broken. It's also probable that his face is broken.

Second, Ethan looked intimidating as hell swinging that axe around.

Hot. But intimidating.

And third, I think Ethan was telling the truth.

I think he was telling the truth about his cousin that one time too.

I think, if pushed to it, Ethan could feed a man to the mountain lions and feel completely at peace with the idea.

And that, combined with the time he ran my whole family off, reminds me that I owe him the biggest blow job ever.

# CHAPTER 128

## ETHAN

I CHECK MY WATCH AGAIN.

Tilda messaged me earlier asking if she could bring me lunch.

Of course, I said yes. And she said she was on her way.

And now I need to find a way to track her location, because the fact that she should've parked four minutes ago has me spiraling over all the things that could've happened to her between her house and here.

"Fuck it."

I pull my phone out of my pocket and call her.

It rings twice, then I see her.

I'm behind the ticket counter in the Visitor Center, standing at the opening that separates the office from the public space. And I have a view straight across the center to the front doors.

She's on the other side of the glass door, walking toward me in a white sundress. And she looks like a goddamn wet dream with her legs and tits on display.

The phone rings again, reminding me that I'm calling her.

Tilda stops, reaches into the floral tote bag she's carrying, and pulls her phone out.

She smiles as she answers. "Hey, Ranger."

"Hey, Starlight."

She glances back toward the parking lot. "Did you move?"

"Nope."

She looks at the door. "Are you in the building?"

"Yep."

"So... Why are you calling me?" She takes a step forward.

"You were late."

She pushes the door open. "I'm right on time."

I hear her in stereo through the phone and through the space between us.

We lower our phones, and Tilda doesn't break stride as she crosses the room to me, grinning.

I lean forward, resting my elbows on the tall countertop as I wait.

Tilda's eyes bounce around the space, taking in the displays of merchandise, looking at the walled-off office area, all while she smiles at me.

Seconds later, which feel like an eternity, she stops on the other side of the counter. "That's a fancy hat."

I keep my expression even. "It's called a campaign hat."

"Right. Of course." Tilda says it seriously as she slowly lifts her hand to her forehead. In a salute.

I clench my jaw, resisting a laugh, and start to slowly lift my hand.

Tilda's eyes widen. "Oh my gods, are you gonna do it back?"

I drop my hand. "No. Now get back here."

Tilda drops her hand and mock glares at me. "Party pooper."

"Uh-huh." I step back from the desk. "Door's back around the side."

Dressed in my tan flat-brimmed hat, button-down shirt, and green pants, I walk the fifteen feet to the back of the office, past the low counter with the computers and rolling chairs, to the door.

A functional office with plenty of space for Tilda to have lunch with me. And if she wants to hang out for a while afterward, she can do that too.

*I hope she wants to stay.*

I open the door that leads into the back hallway, and a second later, Tilda steps through.

She sets her floral bag, which must contain food, on the counter, then does a turn. "This is nice."

"I'll give you the tour." I gesture to our surroundings. "This is the back half of the office." I place my hand on Tilda's back and walk her to the spot with the pass-through, where were talking a moment ago. "And this is the front half of the office."

Tilda looks up at the overhead rolling door that can be pulled down to meet the counter, closing off the opening. "I feel like we're in a concession stand."

I nod. "Basically the same thing. Except we don't have nachos."

"A shame." Her gaze focuses on my hat. "I really like the hat."

"I'm glad."

"How come I haven't seen it before?"

"We have to wear it when we're working in official buildings. But not when we're out in the field."

"I want to wear it." Tilda reaches up and pinches the brim of my hat. "While I'm riding you."

She gives the brim the smallest tug, and I feel it in my balls.

"I like that idea." I grip Tilda by the waist and pull her closer.

She lets go of my hat. "Good." Her fingertips touch my shoulder, then drag down my chest. "Where is everyone?"

I flex my fingers against her sides. "We're short-staffed today. And the morning rush of visitors has died down."

"So... no one else is coming back here?" She drags her touch down to my stomach.

I shake my head. "Very unlikely."

"Good."

"Why is that good, Firecracker?"

Her fingers reach my belt. "Because I figured out what a big blow job is."

My cock pulses to life. "And what is it?"

434

"Doing it someplace special. Or dangerous." Tilda stares up at me, bites her lip, then lowers to her knees.

"Fuck. Tilda."

She sits on her heels, back to the wall below the counter.

The counter comes up to the bottom of my rib cage, and the flat surface is wide. Plenty of space for people to set down the items they want to purchase. Plenty wide to hide the fact that a woman is hiding below. And with the walls surrounding the cutout, it means Tilda is invisible to anyone outside the office.

There are no cameras in here.

No reason for any of the few other employees to show up.

Tilda presses her hands to my legs, just above my knees. Then slides them up. Slowly. Firmly.

I stare down at her, my dick already straining against my zipper.

"Tilda."

"Hands on the counter."

On her knees, with lust in her eyes, Tilda is completely in charge of me.

*Tilda is always in charge of me.*

I place my palms on the counter.

"Good Boy." Tilda sits up and presses a kiss against my fly, over my cock.

"Fuck," I groan, as she places her palm against my bulge. "I don't think I'm gonna last long."

She grips the tab of my zipper. "That's part of the big blow job."

"Coming fast?"

Tilda nods and starts to pull my zipper down.

The sound of it in the silent room makes me even harder.

And fucking hell, I'm glad she's expecting this to be fast. Because it's going to be.

This is the first time I'll be in Tilda's mouth.

She's offered before.

And I've wanted to before.

But my impatience over wanting to fuck her always wins.

And now that it's happening, it doesn't matter that we're in public. I can't stop her.

I don't want to stop her.

And whether it's here or at home, there's no way I'll be able to withstand the pleasure for long.

Tilda drags my zipper all the way down.

And the front door opens.

My head snaps up, and I take a small step forward.

My stomach presses against the counter, and I hear Tilda's quick inhale of surprise as I crowd into her. But I can't let anyone see her. Not like this. Not on her knees with sex in her eyes.

And I *really* can't let this guy see her.

The man in question lifts his hand as he and his wife walk into the Visitor Center. "Howdy, Ranger Dickhead."

A snort comes from under the counter, and I clear my throat to cover the sound. "Rocky. *Mature* as ever."

His wife grins, getting the joke.

"And that's why I call you a dickhead."

I grunt in reply.

Tilda places her hands back against my thighs.

I grit my teeth to keep from groaning as she slides her hands up higher.

She goes up. Then down.

"Joe sends his regards with the latte," Rocky says while spinning the postcard rack.

"What latte?" I focus on the couple with nothing in their hands, not on the hands rubbing up and down my thighs.

"The one he told me to bring." Rocky shrugs and turns his attention to the stickers. "But I don't take orders from that old man, so you can get your own latte if you're thirsty."

I grunt again. Because Tilda's hands are moving higher. And higher.

Rocky stops beside Kendra in front of the T-shirt display.

One of Tilda's hands grips the side of my pants, holding the material to keep her balance. And then her other hand...

I grit my teeth as her fingers slip through my open fly.

My button is still done, and my belt is still on, so she can't get my dick out. But she can reach in.

Her fingers are warm through the cotton of my boxer briefs.

And I feel my dick pulse with the contact.

I clear my throat. "Can I help you find something? Like the door? No offense, Kendra."

Rocky points a finger at me. "Dick. Head."

*Yeah, Rocky. I'm fucking trying.*

Rocky drapes an arm over his wife's shoulders. "We were out running errands. Needed to use the bathroom." He shrugs. "Figured I'd come use mine."

His.

I shake my head.

Tilda's touch disappears. And I open my mouth to ask how Buddy is doing. But then Tilda's hands reappear. On my belt.

I hold still as she tugs at the leather.

And I hold my breath as she moves to my button.

With my pants open, Tilda palms my dick through my boxer briefs.

Then her other hand grips the elastic band, and she starts to tug down the only barrier between my cock and her lips.

And my pulse climbs.

Tilda's fingers trace over my barbell before they wrap around the base of my cock. Skin on skin. And she holds it tight as she pulls my dick free.

My knuckles turn white as I grip the edge of the counter. And if Rocky walks any closer, I'm going to have to reach up and pull down the overhead door.

Warm breath ghosts over my sensitive skin, and then a tongue licks my tip.

"F—" I clear my throat. Again.

"Yeah, yeah, we're leaving." Rocky holds up his middle finger as he heads toward the front door.

"Bye, Ethan." Kendra waves at me.

I lift a hand, holding it up as they leave.

Tilda's lips close around the head of my cock.

The door closes.

And I drop my hand, my fist thudding against the counter. "Fuck."

Tilda's tongue swirls around me. And she hums.

I black out for a heartbeat.

Then I step back.

I *have to* step back.

*I need to see.*

The movement pulls me free of Tilda's mouth, but she chases me.

Her hand is still around my base, holding me steady. And her other hand clutches my thigh.

She shifts forward on her knees, and my jaw goes slack as she sucks my dick into her mouth.

She's so pretty.

So perfect.

So fucking hungry for it.

Her cheeks hollow as she sucks.

The pressure in my balls builds.

I let go of the counter with one hand and reach down, gripping a handful of her hair.

Her tongue swirls again.

I tighten my hold, the backs of my fingers against her scalp. "Matilda." Her eyes flutter, and she looks up at me. "A big blow job means I'm putting my dick all the way down your throat."

# CHAPTER 129

## TILDA

MY CLIT THROBS AS ETHAN USES HIS HOLD ON MY HAIR to pull my face closer.

To shove his dick deeper.

I let go of the base of his dick and brace both my hands on his thighs.

"Breathe through your nose, Firecracker."

He bumps into the back of my throat.

He drags my head back.

Then he pulls me forward again.

"Fuck." He repeats the motion. "Relax, Matilda." Back, then forward. "Relax your throat."

His words are quiet. And his groans are restrained.

But his body is tense. And his cock is so hard.

It's hot and throbbing, and it feels so good in my mouth.

Ethan keeps going. And I keep trying to fit him.

Keep trying to take him.

Every time he hits resistance, I feel it in my core.

Every time my throat constricts, I feel it in my clit.

And when he groans again, I can't take it anymore.

I inhale through my nose, and I drop my hand from his thigh.

I let him use me, use my hair to control me, as I slip my hand under my skirt.

Planning for a sexy scenario, I'm only wearing a thong under my dress.

Panties that are easy to push aside.

I moan around Ethan's cock as my fingers glide through my already soaked slit.

My eyes roll back when I drag my finger up over my clit.

*Gods.*

The more I touch myself, the more my throat relaxes.

I keep going.

Keep rubbing.

I feel myself start to tremble.

*Everything is so sensitive.*

"Firecracker, I'm close," Ethan grunts.

I tilt my head, keeping him in my mouth, as I look up and meet his gaze.

I lean forward, pulling against his grip to go just a little deeper.

"You like this, Wife? Do you like…" His attention lowers. And his cock pulses against my tongue. "Are you touching yourself, Matilda?"

I nod.

"Fuck." He holds me still and pulls his hips back. "Such a Bad Girl." He thrusts his hips forward. "Such a filthy little Wife." He pulls back out.

I rub my clit faster.

His grunts get louder. And his hips thrust quicker.

Ethan fucks my mouth as I touch myself. In the middle of the day. In a public building.

And I'm so close.

So damn close.

"Fuck." Ethan's breathing is choppy. "Have you ever swallowed before?"

I hum my no as I give my head the smallest shake.

Ethan's eyes close as he wedges his cock deeper. Then he opens them on a groan as he slides back out.

"Just once. I just need you to swallow one time." He stares down at me, commanding it. "You can spit out the rest."

My body starts to tense.

My orgasm a moment away.

I want to swallow.

Want to try it for Ethan.

Want to do anything for him.

"You want that?"

He fucks my mouth.

"You want to swallow me down?"

My pussy clenches.

"Get ready, Wife. Keep rubbing your little clit and get ready."

He holds my head in place.

My heart beats once.

Then Ethan starts to come, pulsing and throbbing and spilling his release across my tongue.

I swallow.

I do it again.

And it's all so overwhelming.

My throat works. And my senses implode as an orgasm rocks through me.

I sway at the intensity, and Ethan grips my head with both hands.

Waves of pleasure crash through my body.

I swallow once more as I pull my hand away from my core.

Ethan's hold on me loosens, and I slump down onto my heels, exhaustion taking over as I fight to catch my breath.

Ethan wavers and braces a hand back against the counter. "That was... a big blow job."

A snicker starts in my chest. "I'm glad we agree."

# CHAPTER 130

## ETHAN

When I know I can manage, I let go of the counter, tuck myself away, then haul Tilda to her feet.

She wobbles, smiling like she's drunk.

And... Fuck it.

I press my mouth to hers.

She kisses me back. Chastely.

But what she just did... she deserves more.

I push my tongue into her mouth, and she groans.

My hands roam her body.

Gripping her sides. Clutching at her hips.

Tilda tilts her head, letting me deepen the kiss.

I do.

And I taste myself on her tongue.

Moaning, I hold her closer.

The brim of my hat rubs against the top of her hair.

And then the door opens.

We jerk away from each other, but when I look up, I see we've already been spotted.

"Is this her!" Liza practically shrieks from the doorway.

I look down at Tilda.

Her hair is mussed.

Her lips are swollen.

And her cheeks are a deep shade of pink.

She's a mess.

Her eyes widen as she discreetly taps at my belt, reminding me that my dick might be put away, but my pants are still hanging open.

*Okay, so we're both a mess.*

I press my lips together to stop myself from cracking up.

But if I start, I won't be able to compose myself before getting caught.

Liza wouldn't rat me out. But she'd never let me live it down either.

I run a palm down the back of Tilda's head, smoothing her hair, then look back up at Liza. "Come back here and I'll introduce you." I tip my head, gesturing to the office.

Tilda gives me a look that says I'm an idiot, but as soon as Liza steps out of view, heading down the back hall, I quickly zip up my pants and work on my belt.

Having caught on to the fact that we have approximately three seconds to put ourselves in order, Tilda bends at the waist, flipping her head upside down. Her hair hangs almost to the floor, and she shakes her head, then flips her hair back as she stands up straight again.

My brows lift. "Impressive."

The door handle starts to turn, and Tilda darts past me, reaching for the bottle of hand sanitizer on the counter.

She gets one pump of the clear gel into her palm when the door starts to open. Then she quickly rubs her hands together.

And when I get it, I grin.

"Clever girl," I whisper, before turning to face Liza.

# CHAPTER 131

## TILDA

THE WOMAN WITH SHORT GRAY HAIR AND STRIKING cheekbones hustles across the little office toward us.

"Oh, Mother Mary, you..." Her voice catches. "You're so pretty." She stops before me and holds her hand out. "I'm Liza."

I'm sure I look... flustered. But I'm really hoping she attributes it to our little make-out session and doesn't assume Ethan just came down my throat.

Hoping the gel did its job, I lift my hand toward hers. "I'm Tilda."

Our palms are an inch away when Liza shakes her head, then pulls me in for a hug.

Taken off guard but also slightly relieved, I hug her back.

When she finally releases me, I step back and lower the hand that was just up my skirt to my side. "Nice to meet you. I've heard lots of good things." *I haven't. But it feels like the right thing to say.*

"Oh. Well. That's so sweet to hear." Liza presses her hands to her chest. "And can I just say how happy I am that Ethan has someone special in his life? He's..." She sniffs, and her chin quivers. "He's just such a nice guy. I've been praying for love to find him. I just knew there was someone out there. Boy or girl."

444

I bite down on my lip so I smile the normal amount, not the open-mouthed grin that's trying to take hold.

"And then you." Liza gestures with both hands toward me. "You look like an angel."

Ethan snorts.

I backhand his stomach.

And Liza bursts into happy tears.

"She's sweet." I plop myself onto one of the office chairs.

Ethan shakes his head and lowers himself into the other chair. "She's something, alright."

I snicker as I spin to face the counter and reach for my bag.

"Did you really bring lunch too?" Ethan rolls his chair closer to mine.

"Too? Like I brought the blow job."

He smirks at me. "Oh, you brought the blow job, alright. And you're welcome to bring me that for lunch anytime you feel like it."

I roll my eyes and pull out a plastic container. "Those are for special occasions, remember?"

"Beat up Ralph, get a big blow job. Got it."

"Exactly," I laugh. "Come to think of it, you probably earned one for scaring off that mountain lion."

Ethan grips the brim of his fancy hat and tips his chin in a *much obliged* gesture.

I take out a bag of grapes and two camo-printed paper napkins from my bag, then open the container and place one of the sandwiches on a napkin for Ethan.

He picks up his turkey and cheese and lifts a brow. "Nice napkins."

I pick up my own sandwich and roll my eyes. "I found a box in the garage that I thought was all wrapping paper and gift bags and stuff. But half of it's just napkins. For like... any holiday you can think of."

"And what holiday is this for?"

I look at the tan-and-green camo print. "Not sure. But they're the *big blow job* napkins now."

Ethan huffs a laugh, and we lazily eat our sandwiches.

Once we're finished, I start putting the items back in my bag. "Do you want to come over tonight?"

I'm pretty sure he will, but I still feel a little shy asking.

Ethan nods. "Yeah. I have to run to the hangar to sign some paperwork, then I'll bring dinner over."

I almost ask if I can go with him to the airport, just for something to do. But I'm still a little traumatized from those flights, so I don't.

He lets his gaze travel from my eyes... down.

"And keep that dress on."

I was already excited to see him again. But with that look in his eye... "Deal."

# CHAPTER 132

## ETHAN

I GRAB MY BACKPACK OFF THE PASSENGER SEAT AND climb out of my truck.

Tilda already has the front door open and is standing there, smiling at me.

"Put shoes on," I tell her. "Walking ones."

Her smile freezes, then, without asking for more information, she darts through the house to her bedroom.

She comes back a moment later with socks on her feet. And after she puts her tennis shoes on, she steps outside and pulls the door closed behind her.

Her hair is still down, and her pretty white dress is still on. And my heart squeezes as I hold my hand out for my Mountain Fairy.

Tilda puts her palm in mine. "Where are we going?"

I lead her away from the house. Toward the Lonely Peak State Park fence line.

"I was reminded today about the time I caught a couple trying to have sex in the park."

"What?" Tilda laughs her question.

"Uh-huh." We step off the driveway and keep walking.

"What happened?"

I lift a shoulder. "I found them as they were about to start stripping in the back of his truck."

"And then...?"

I shrug. "Then I stood there until they left."

"Seriously?"

I nod. "Then I blackmailed him for thirty thousand dollars to upgrade the public toilets."

"Ethan!"

I grin. *Good memories.*

# CHAPTER 133

## TILDA

ETHAN HELPS ME THROUGH THE FENCE, AND ONCE I'M on the other side, I click my tongue at him. "Not very Good Boy of you. *Illegally entering* park property."

He swats my ass.

I squeak but keep smiling.

Playful Ethan is maybe my favorite Ethan.

I purse my lips.

Or maybe it's sexy Ethan.

Or Good Boy Ethan.

Or... *swinging an axe at my cousin* Ethan.

A quack has us both turning back to the fence.

Quackers is waddling toward us from the other side.

Ethan whistles and points to the house.

Quackers snaps her beak, then turns around and waddles back.

Or... maybe it's duck whisperer Ethan.

"Oh. Wow." My steps slow as we come out of the woods into a large grassy patch.

I have to turn my head side to side to take in the view.

It's breathtaking.

Before us, the land slopes down.

And down.

All the way to the bottom of a valley. And across the valley is a mountain shooting up from the earth.

It's so tall. And perfectly formed.

It feels like I'm standing in a postcard.

I take it in.

Amazed.

"Ethan, this is—" I turn my head toward him and find a blanket laid out in the grass.

He unclips his fancy hat from where he had it hanging off his backpack. And he holds it up to me.

I slowly reach out and take it. "What am I supposed to do with this?"

"Wear it." Ethan lowers himself to the blanket. "While you sit on my face."

# CHAPTER 134

## ETHAN

MATILDA LIFTS MY *FANCY HAT* AND PLACES IT ON HER head.

I lie on my back but keep my gaze on her.

The hat is a little big on her, so she tips it back, causing the brim to frame her head like a halo against the setting sun.

Purple curls. Ranger hat. Skimpy white dress.

I reach down and adjust my dick.

Tilda sucked the life out of me just this afternoon, but knowing what I'm about to do is making me hard all over again.

Holding eye contact, Tilda reaches up under her skirt, and torturously slowly, she pulls her panties down her legs.

I want to watch her hands, but I can't tear my eyes away from hers.

The heat in them.

The excitement.

I hold my hands up, then gesture for her to *come here*.

My Starlight bites her lip. Then she walks closer.

I drag my tongue across my lower lip.

She pauses. Then steps over me. One foot on either side of my head.

Shadows dance under her skirt. But I can see.

*I can fucking see.*

I slide my hands up the backs of her calves. And she lowers.

One knee presses into the blanket.

Her dress settles over my head.

I slide my hands up her thighs until I'm gripping her bare hips, helping her balance.

Her second knee presses into the blanket on the other side of my head.

My fingers flex against the softness of her ass.

I stick my tongue out.

And I pull her down.

# CHAPTER 135

## TILDA

I CRY OUT AS I TREMBLE. ETHAN'S TONGUE IS LAPPING at me, dragging my orgasm out until I can't take it anymore.

"Ethan." I'm bent forward, one hand on the ground.

I reach down with my other hand and grip Ethan's hair through my skirt.

After one final slow lick over my clit, he grips my hips, lifting me and moving me backward.

I use my hands to help as I crawl down his body.

And then I feel him.

There.

Ethan's hands left for a moment when his tongue was buried in my pussy. And now I know what he was doing.

He was taking his dick out.

His tip presses into me.

And he uses his hold on my hips to push my body down.

"Oh gods." I brace my hands on his chest. "Ethan."

He pulls me onto him deeper, groaning, until he bottoms out, until I'm sitting on his pelvis.

My strength is nearly gone.

I can barely hold myself up.

But Ethan doesn't let go.

He holds me steady as he lifts his knees behind me, plants his feet, and thrusts up into me.

# Chapter 136

## Ethan

"Come here." I lean back against the inflatable pillow and hold my arm out.

The sun has set.

Our dinner of cold gyros has been consumed.

And it's time to look at the stars.

Tilda zips the hoodie I brought for her, then crawls up the blanket and snuggles into my side.

I wrap my arm around her shoulder, holding her to me.

"Didn't you bring a sweatshirt for yourself?" Her cheek is pressed against my chest, so I can feel her mouth move as she speaks.

"No. I'm good."

She hums. "I still can't believe how cool it is up here. It gets cold in the desert at night, but not like this."

"Elevation makes all the difference."

Tilda is quiet for a moment before I feel her speak again. "How long until the first big snowfall?"

"A couple months. We'll get snow in October, but if you're talking about a lot of inches, that might not happen until November. Then it will keep happening until May."

"May?" Tilda blows out a breath. "Plenty of time to learn how to shovel, I guess."

"I know a guy who plows. We'll get him hired for you." Then a thought occurs to me. "Have you never seen snow?"

She shakes her head against me. "Not really. There were a few dustings that I can remember. Which were exciting." I know she's being serious, but I still smile. "But the times there was a rare Nevada snowstorm with measurable amounts, it was never where I lived."

"I promise, where you live now, you'll see snow."

Tilda taps her fingers against my chest. "I'm excited for it. A little nervous."

My smile softens. "There's nothing to be nervous about. Just stay home and don't drive in it until I can teach you how."

"I can agree to that. It's probably from being forced to watch too many scary movies growing up, but *lost in a snowstorm* is one of my biggest and, until now, most unlikely fears."

I hug her tighter to my side, then lift my other hand and point to the sky. "You see the Big Dipper there? The seven stars that make the ladle shape?"

Tilda shifts her head. "Yeah. I remember the name from school."

"Well, if you're ever lost at night, look for the Big Dipper."

"Is it always there? Visible, I mean?"

"Yes. In this part of the world."

Tilda makes a humming sound and lifts her hand to trace the pattern in the sky. "How will it help me?"

"The Big Dipper is a part of a larger constellation, Ursa Major. The Great Bear." I rub my thumb in a circle on Tilda's shoulder. "The handle part of the Big Dipper is also the tail of the bear. But if you see the cup part." I shift my arm as I point. "The two stars on the end, opposite the handle. If you start at the bottom one, draw an invisible line up to the top one, then keep going..." I draw a line in the sky with my finger. "You'll find the North Star."

Tilda matches my movements, her hand tracing the lines between stars.

"And when you're facing the North Star, you're facing north." I lower my hand. "The Rocky Mountains run north and south, and we live on the eastern edge. So, if you find your starlight, you'll always know which way is home."

# CHAPTER 137

## TILDA

ETHAN'S VOICE IS THICK.

And I think about the stars.

The comfort they've brought humans for centuries.

With my eyes, I trace the path again.

Memorizing it.

Refusing to forget it.

I flatten my hand on Ethan's chest and feel the thud of his heart under my palm.

The stars are filled with stories. Dreams. Hidden truths. Famous myths.

But this man right here.

The one beside me.

He's solid.

Real.

*Mine.*

And as we walk back to the house.

As he guides me in the dark.

I think about the time he called me Matilda Grant.

And I think about the way his hand feels in mine.

And I think about how I want him to stay mine.

Forever.
Until all that's left of this world... are the stars.

# Chapter 138

# Ethan

Me: When we go to sleep tonight, we're starting on your side of the bed.

Wife: Don't blame me for you falling out of bed.

Me: You literally pushed me.

Wife: Don't blame me for what happens when I'm asleep.

Me: Your. Side.

Wife: Do you want to go to the gym today?

Me: Sure.

Me: Do you want to go on a walk? I could take you to a trail.

Wife: I want to watch you lift weights.

Me: Thanks for bringing me lunch today, Starlight.

Wife: Anything to see you in your fancy hat.

Wife: Can you pick up some duck food when you're in town tomorrow?

Me: Yes. But I'm coming over tonight, remember?

Wife: I remember, but I don't want to forget about the duck food.

Me: Do you want to go out for burgers tomorrow night?

Wife: Duh.

Me: There's also a bake sale this weekend.

Wife: If you don't take me, I'll be upset.

Me: You didn't even know about it until now.

Wife: And?

Me: Solid point.

Wife: Did you order this?

Wife: This is the longest floor mat I've ever seen in my life.

Me: That's for the bedroom.

Wife: It's a kitchen floor mat.

Me: It's for my side of the bed. In the bedroom.

Wife: Are you serious?

Me: I'm seriously sick of busting my ass on the wood floor.

Me: Can you tell me if there's an outlet on the front of your house?

Wife: It's a little early for holiday decorations.

Me: But not too early to put that fountain you
wanted in the duck pool.

Wife: Don't joke about this.

Me: Hand to Quackers.

Wife: I just looked. There's one by the door.

# CHAPTER 139

## TILDA

Hot Husband: If you come to the Visitor Center before three today, you can see a hawk.

Me: What kind of hawk?

Me: Don't answer that.

Me: I'm leaving now.

Me: Do you think Quackers will be able to tell I cheated on her?

Me: I'm still sorting through all the stuff I got at Which Craft.

Me: Thank you for taking me.

Me: We should've done that weeks ago.

Craft King: It's your fault for always distracting me with sex.

Me: You're the one who carries me over their shoulder into the bedroom every Tuesday.

Craft King: You're right. You should carry me next time.

Craft King: Is it actually always Tuesdays? Or are you making that up?

Me: You really are too handsome.

Me: I made cupcakes today.

Just Tell Him You Love Him: Your favorite.

Just Tell Him You Love Him: What's the occasion?

Me: I accidentally bought a box of cake mix and frosting.

Just Tell Him You Love Him: What a nice accident.

# CHAPTER 140

## ETHAN

TILDA PULLS THE BATHROOM DOOR SHUT WITH A CLICK, about to start her shower, and I top off my coffee.

Pushing open the screen door, I step out onto the back deck and cradle my mug while I stand and admire the view.

Most mornings I wake up here.

In the past... two and a half months, since we got married, I've spent more nights here than at my house.

I've spent hardly any time at my house.

It's a good house.

Nothing wrong with it.

But I don't want to be there.

I've lived there for almost twenty years, yet Tilda's house feels more like home to me.

I fill my lungs with the crisp morning air.

*Tilda feels like home.*

And I want to... move in.

My house is bigger. More rooms, more bathrooms. More space for a future. *Children.* But even when I imagine it, I imagine that future here.

I want to fill half her closet, empty my fridge, and figure out what to do with my house later.

I want that so much, but Tilda hasn't even been to my house. Not once.

We've talked about it. But I haven't put any effort into it. For no reason other than I like it here better.

*Maybe I can bring Tilda over there this weekend. And while we're there, I can casually make a comment about clothes. And we can casually pack a suitcase of my stuff. And I can casually move the rest of my existence into her house.*

My phone rings.

I'm off today, so I almost don't take it out of my pocket.

But I do. And I see something else I've been avoiding.

"Hey, Sandra."

"Finally." My sister sighs. "I feel like we've been playing phone tag forever."

I grunt. Because we have. But also because I've been calling at times I knew she'd be busy. Because I haven't told her I'm married.

An idea forms. Two birds, one stone. "What are you doing tomorrow?"

"Umm." Sandra's tone is suspicious. "I don't think I have anything planned. Why?"

"Why are you lying to me?"

"I don't have anything planned. I'm not lying."

"You're lying about something." I sip my coffee. Loudly.

I do it again.

On the third time, Sandra caves. "Oh my god, fine. Just knock it off."

I smile.

She sighs. "*We* don't have any plans for tomorrow."

My smile drops. "Who is *we*?"

"Me and my, um, boyfriend."

I exhale. Loudly.

*Fine. I'll invite everybody.*

*Three birds, one fucking stone.*

"Bring him with."

"Uh." Sandra hesitates. "Bring him where?"

"The house."

"And what are we going to do at *the house*?"

I roll my eyes up to the sky. "We're going to murder and dismember your boyfriend."

"Hilarious."

"I'm gonna grill veggie burgers. You can bring the dessert." I think about it, then specify. "Cupcakes."

"Cupcakes... Inviting the boyfriend over without asking a single question... What's going on?"

I take another loud sip of my coffee, then audibly exhale. "I have someone for you to meet too."

"Oh?"

"Yep." I'm being evasive on purpose. But she deserves it with this *boyfriend* bullshit.

"And who am I meeting?"

"Tilda." I can't even say her name without smiling anymore.

"And who is Tilda?"

I turn and look through the windows into the house, and I spot Tilda walking out of the bedroom in nothing but a towel.

"She's my wife."

The line is quiet. Then my sister shouts incoherent nonsense into the phone.

"Show up at four."

She shouts something else, but I end the call.

Because my wife is dropping her towel.

# CHAPTER 141

## TILDA

My palms are clammy against the steering wheel.

Keeping an eye on my phone GPS, I run one hand, then the other, down the skirt of my dress.

I chose my yellow dress, the one I got married in, for today.

Sure, last time I wore it I was in a plane crash. But that day also felt like the start of something new. And not just because of the crash. Or the fact that night was the first time Ethan and I had sex.

It... it feels like since then, I've unlocked a part of myself.

The adventure part.

The outdoor part.

The confident part.

The desirable part.

I'm still unsure what to do with myself. What job to get. What hobbies to pursue.

But I also feel more like *me* than I ever have before.

And because of that, I really want Ethan's sister to like me.

My phone alerts me of my final turn in half a mile.

I wipe my hands off again.

Ethan wanted to come get me, but he had to run to the park for something this morning, and it didn't make sense for him to backtrack to my house after that. Though now I'm regretting my decision to drive alone. Because my nerves are *frazzled*.

I press the brake and get ready to turn into Ethan's driveway.

We didn't talk about what happens after dinner, but I have a bag on the passenger seat with some overnight things.

It's weird that this will be my first time over here. But it's also been nice having Ethan at my house so much.

Moving from my apartment to a house in the mountains was a huge adjustment. And I think if we'd spent half the time at Ethan's over the last couple months, I wouldn't feel nearly as comfortable as I do now at my house.

Plus, there's Quackers.

I know she'll be fine.

She has fresh water in her kiddie pool. I did turn her little fountain off, though, just in case something knocks it over when I'm not there to fix it. But her food dish is full. And even though fall is upon us, her bush is still leafy, and it's still her favorite place to sleep.

And... she's a wild duck that knows how to take care of herself.

Still, I'll be happy to go home to her tomorrow.

I read the numbers on the mailbox, confirming Ethan's address, then I turn.

# CHAPTER 142

## ETHAN

I PULL TILDA'S DRIVER'S DOOR OPEN THE SECOND SHE shuts off the engine.

"Hi, Starlight."

She smiles at me. "Hi, Ranger."

Tilda turns in her seat to climb out of the truck, and my eyes travel down her body.

That sense of *home* she always brings me intensifies in my chest.

I reach out and trace my fingertip along the low neckline of her dress.

*The* yellow dress.

Her wedding dress.

"You look nice." My voice comes out quieter than I intend.

"So do you." Tilda places a palm against my chest.

I'm in a black T-shirt and jeans. Hardly a match to Tilda's beauty.

"Did I beat them?" Tilda asks, referring to my sister and her boyfriend.

I nod, then grip her by the waist and drag her out of the truck. "They'll be here soon." When her feet touch the ground—in sandals, not the boots I still want to burn—I lower my mouth to hers. "We should have enough time to make out for a little while."

She smiles against my lips. And she lets me kiss her. But then she pokes me in the ribs.

"What?" I pull back just enough to speak.

"Show me your house quick. I don't want your sister to know I've never been here."

I sigh. "Fine."

I place my hand on her back and lead her toward the house.

But before we can reach it, we're stopped by the sound of another vehicle on the driveway.

We turn back around, and Tilda tenses as I keep my hand on her spine.

"Don't be nervous." I press a kiss to her hair.

I feel like maybe *I* should be nervous—meeting Sandra's mystery boyfriend, having her meet my wife. But Tilda and I discussed it last night and agreed we were going to be truthful. About all of it.

Sandra is pretty much my only family, and therefore, pretty much Tilda's only family. And we don't want to censor our history around her.

So no, I'm not nervous. I'm excited. Ready for the two most important people in my life to meet.

I kiss Tilda's hair again. "My bedroom is at the end of the hall, and you can use the bathroom in there. The first room you pass in the hall used to be Sandra's, but she took her furniture a long time ago and now it's an office that never gets used. There's another bathroom next to that room. The living room and kitchen are all connected. And I already set the table on the back deck, so the only thing we still need are water glasses, and they're to the right of the sink."

Tilda beams up at me. "You're the actual best. You know that?"

I lift a finger and tap it to the tip of her nose.

She bites her lip.

Then the vehicle comes into view.

A vehicle that is not my sister's car.

But... it's still familiar.

"What the..."

Tilda glances at me, then back at the truck. "What is it?"

The afternoon sun reflects off the windshield, preventing me from seeing inside. But I know I know that pickup.

I slide my hand down Tilda's back, silently comforting her, even though I feel like I'm going to want to throw a punch in about ten seconds.

The truck comes to a stop behind Tilda's.

The passenger door opens first, and my sister hops out.

Her smile is huge as she waves. "Hi!" She slams her door shut and hurries around the front of the truck toward us. "Now, before you lose your shit, I want you to remember that you just told me *yesterday* that you're *married*." Sandra puts her hands on her hips. "So keep that in mind."

My jaw works.

And then the driver's door opens.

A tall man with wavy hair and a dopey grin climbs out.

"Afternoon, Ranger Grant." He lifts a clear package of cupcakes in greeting. "Congratulations on the nuptials."

I heave out a breath and turn to Sandra. "Fisher? Really?"

She lifts a brow. "Married? Really?"

# CHAPTER 143

## TILDA

I CAN'T HELP IT. I SNORT.

Both of the Grant siblings turn their attention to me, and my eyes widen. "Sorry."

Ethan shakes his head, amusement pushing past his obvious annoyance. "You're not sorry."

I bite my lip, then shrug. "She has you."

Sandra laughs, then steps forward and pulls me into a hug. "I like you already."

Tension drains from my body as I hug her back. "Sorry you just learned about me. But I've heard lots about you, and I'm so excited to finally meet you."

It's true. The nerves are also true. But I can already tell she'll be just as easy to be around as Ethan.

We pull apart just as the boyfriend, Fisher, steps up.

Together, they look a little opposite.

She's edgy. Short black hair. Piercings. A tight floral top. A studded belt. And black denim cutoffs.

He's dressed... a lot like Ethan. Jeans. Gray T-shirt with the logo for a lodge on the chest.

Opposite, but they fit.

A lot like me and Ethan.

And it takes me a moment, but then I recognize him too.

He grins. "Saw you guys buying that kiddie pool."

It comes back to me. Ethan's hat on my head. Standing so close. And I feel myself blush. "Hello, again."

"Wait, what?" Sandra turns to Fisher. "You knew?"

He shakes his head, his smile still in place. "No idea they were married. Just saw your brother here helping her get one of those little plastic pools into her truck."

"We, um, weren't married yet," I add, just in case that helps.

I almost tell them the pool was for my duck, but that detail feels unnecessary.

"How long?" Ethan crosses his arms as he stares at Fisher.

The other man cocks his head. "Two, maybe three months ago?"

Ethan's jaw ticks. "How long have you two been dating?"

"So..." Sandra starts, and I have to hold in another laugh.

Ethan drops his arms as he lets out an exasperated sigh. "Just tell me."

"Ten months." Sandra grabs the cupcakes from Fisher and holds them out to Ethan like a peace offering.

"But that's only because it took me a few months to get the courage to ask her out." Fisher drapes his arm around Sandra's shoulders.

"How'd you meet?" I smile as I ask, because they really do look cute together.

"She cut my hair." Fisher looks down at Sandra, and I can feel the affection between them.

"Yeah, and he came back two weeks later for a trim." Sandra rolls her eyes. "And every two weeks after that until his hair was almost as short as mine before he asked me to dinner."

Ethan wrenches the dessert container open and pulls a pink cupcake out. Then he puts it, top first, into his mouth and bites off all the frosting.

Sandra and I share a look.

And it's confirmed. I like her a lot.

475

"And how did you guys meet?" Her gaze travels over my hair, and I'm glad I took extra time styling my loose curls today. "I love your color." And I'm extra glad I touched up the dye last week. But before I can reply, Sandra tilts her head. "Wait. Purple..." She slowly shifts her attention to Ethan. "That ribbon? It was for her, wasn't it?"

Ethan peels the paper wrapper off the base of the cupcake, and I find myself grinning again when he shoves the rest of it into his mouth.

# CHAPTER 144

## ETHAN

"You crashed your plane?" Sandra drops her spoonful of pasta salad.

"It was a controlled emergency landing."

Tilda snickers, and I bump my knee into hers under the table.

Sandra scoffs. "You're an idiot. How did you get home?"

I lean back in my chair. "Had a chopper pick us up. Two days later."

My sister holds her hands up. "You were stranded in the woods for *two days*, and you never told me? I don't want to hear you say another word, ever, about me and Fisher."

I glare at the man across the table from me.

I don't actually mean it. He's a decent guy, and Sandra's smart; she wouldn't be with him if he didn't treat her well. But I'm not going to smile at him. That's not what I do.

Not that it matters, because Fisher is apparently immune to intimidation, looking as content as he always does, sitting on my deck like he's been here a dozen times before.

Probably has something to do with the fact that he's worked for the asshole who runs Black Mountain Lodge for years.

Tilda makes a contemplative sound. "The mountain lion was

probably scarier than the crash landing." We all turn our heads and look at her. "What? It was."

Sandra rests her elbows on the table. "What mountain lion?"

I drape my arm over the back of Tilda's chair and let her tell the story.

We didn't tell them the dollar amount of the inheritance. And Sandra and I don't really have firsthand experience with shitty family members. But Sandra still gets it. Nodded her head the whole time we told her about Jack demanding that Tilda get married to keep everything.

And I don't know Fisher's family history, but he was nodding too. Understanding and not questioning, no looks of judgment. Which put another point in his favor.

Sandra presses her hand to her chest when she realizes we stayed in the cabin Dad built with his friends. And when Fisher puts his hand over the one she has on the table, I begrudgingly give him another point.

I knew Tilda and Sandra would get along. But to see it confirmed... I feel complete.

I twirl my finger in a lock of Tilda's hair.

Tonight, my wife will be staying under my roof. And tomorrow, I'll convince her to let me move in full-time.

# CHAPTER 145

## TILDA

THE URGE TO CRY HAS BEEN PRESSING AGAINST MY EYES since the first time Sandra hugged me.

And now that she's gone, hugging me twice more before she left, I'm finding it harder to resist.

Today was... everything I've ever wanted in a family.

Funny, snarky, peaceful.

No fighting.

No name-calling.

No shaming.

Just an enjoyable time.

Ethan even clapped Fisher on the back by the end of it. But I think we all could tell his earlier mean mugging was just show, something he did because he's the older brother. Because he cares. Because he's a protector.

A sparkly string wraps itself around my heart.

A string that feels like family. That wants to tie all my broken pieces together.

And I want to let it.

I want to stay here, in this family, with these people.

I want to stay with Ethan.

Here or at my house.

I just want to *stay.*

I want to keep feeling safe and loved. And...

And I need to tell him.

I need to tell Ethan how much he means to me.

Tell him that we may have started because of Uncle Jack's scheme. But it's not a scheme anymore.

Without the money.

Without an inheritance.

I'd still pick *him.*

I'd stay *with him.*

My inhale feels choppy.

*You can do the hard things, Matty.*

*I believe in you.*

I reread Uncle Jack's letters last week, wanting to feel closer to him.

Wanting to thank him for pushing Ethan and me together.

We'd already met. And I like to think that even without the whole ruse, we'd still have found our way together. But I still feel like I owe Uncle Jack for speeding up that timeline.

These last couple months would've been lonely without Ethan.

"I'm gonna take a quick shower." Ethan steps into the kitchen through the deck door. "I smell like the grill."

"Okay. I'll bring my bag in."

Ethan takes a step toward the front door. "I can get it."

"No, no. It'll give me something to do." I wave him off.

"Fine." Ethan turns toward the hall. "I won't be long."

"Take your time." I mean it. I need a moment to gather my composure. And a moment to decide how to tell Ethan I love him.

I slip my sandals on and step outside.

I could sit him down, tell him I have something to say. And then just say it. *I love you.*

Or I could wait until later. When we're having sex, because I'm sure we will. And I could say it then.

I could cling to his shoulders and whisper it in his ear.

Opening my passenger door, I make a face at that idea.

I don't think he'll have a bad reaction to it. I have a pretty good feeling he might even say it back. But... what if I say it and it turns him off? Having him clam up would be bad enough. But if I told Ethan I loved him during sex and he lost his erection... I don't know how to recover from that.

My eyes snag on the beaded suncatcher I made for Ethan, and I grab it off the seat before slinging my backpack over my other shoulder.

After sex.

Or in the morning.

One of those options.

Casually.

*Good morning, Ethan. I love you.*

I step back into the house, confident that's the right choice.

Distracted, I set the suncatcher on Ethan's dining table, then swing my backpack down.

A clatter startles me, and I spin to see a plastic water cup that I must've knocked onto the floor.

"Crap." I leave my backpack on the dining table and rush toward the kitchen sink.

I grab the pair of hand towels next to the sink and hurry back.

Thankfully the cup didn't break, but there is a puddle of water spreading across the hardwood floor now beneath the couch.

Down on my knees, I set the cup upright, away from the puddle, and start to soak up the water.

As I push the towel, I accidentally send more of the water under the couch.

Sighing, I grab the second towel and, holding one corner, flick my wrist so it spreads out on the floor below the couch, hopefully catching everything.

But it makes a... papery sound.

I drag the towel toward me, and it comes out wet. But it catches more than just water.

A folded piece of paper is stuck under the other end of the towel.

Not wanting to ruin whatever it is by dragging it through what's left of the puddle, I let go of the towel and reach for the paper.

It's a single sheet of paper. Folded in thirds.

Like a letter.

Unease crawls up my arms as I hold the paper in front of me.

*It's just paper.*

*It's a lost piece of mail.*

*It's... making my hands shake.*

"It's none of my business," I say out loud, trying to convince myself not to open it.

But the corner of the paper is wet.

And if I flatten it out, it'll dry faster.

Sitting on my heels, I lift the top edge of the paper, opening the page.

And revealing Uncle Jack's handwriting.

That unease inside me turns hot.

"What..."

The paper trembles as I unfold the rest of it.

I shouldn't read it.

I know I shouldn't.

It's not mine.

But it is *my* uncle's handwriting.

And why wouldn't Ethan tell me he got a letter too?

I shouldn't read it.

But my eyes find the first line.

And even though I shouldn't read it.

I do.

Dear Ethan,

I'm sure you've met my Matty by now. Sorry

*(NOT ACTUALLY SORRY) FOR MISLEADING YOU. BUT IT WAS NECESSARY TO GET YOUR ACCEPTANCE.*

*YOU'RE A STUBBORN MAN, ETHAN GRANT. A REAL ASS SOMETIMES. BUT YOUR HEART IS GOOD.*

*AND MATILDA NEEDS SOMEONE WITH A GOOD HEART.*

My heart races as I read each line. I remember now, Ethan making a comment about Uncle Jack asking him to keep an eye on me. But I didn't think more of it.

It's just a thing people say.

But as I start to read the next line... I feel sick.

*YOU GAVE ME YOUR WORD THAT YOU'D KEEP AN EYE ON HER. AND I NEED YOU TO KEEP YOUR WORD. BECAUSE EVEN IF YOU DIDN'T KNOW IT AT THE TIME, IT WAS A PROMISE TO A DYING MAN. AND SINCE I'M DEAD NOW, YOU CAN'T TAKE IT BACK.*

My throat feels tight as I swallow.

It *wasn't* just a thing people say. It was more than that.

And Uncle Jack wrote Ethan to remind him.

*SO, ETHAN GRANT, PARK RANGER, OVERALL GRUMP, I NEED YOU TO PROMISE ME ONE MORE THING.*

*THAT YOU WILL KEEP AN EYE ON MATILDA.*

*THAT YOU WILL KEEP HER SAFE.*

*AND FOR THE NEXT THREE MONTHS, STARTING TOMORROW, WHEN YOU FLY TO VEGAS, I NEED YOU TO DO WHATEVER SHE ASKS OF YOU. NO MATTER HOW... UNCONVENTIONAL.*

The sparkly string around my heart starts to loosen.

Ethan received this letter the day before we got married. The same day I got mine.

Ethan knew something was going to happen.

He... he agreed so easily. He...

My eyes trace over the next sentence.

*AND IF YOU DO THIS, IF YOU PLAY ALONG WITH MY PLAN FOR THREE MONTHS, THEN $250,000 WILL BE*

DEPOSITED INTO YOUR BANK ACCOUNT. MY LAWYERS ALREADY HAVE THE INSTRUCTIONS. SO, AS LONG AS THERE'S NO BAD NEWS, THREE MONTHS FROM NOW, YOU'LL BE A LITTLE BIT RICHER.

IF THERE IS BAD NEWS, YOU'LL GET NOTHING.

AND I'LL HAUNT YOU FOR THE REST OF YOUR GRUMPY LIFE.

ALL MY LOVE, JACK

The string dulls as it unravels, releasing all the broken parts of me back into my chest.

A drip lands on the page.

Then a second.

And when I blink,

more tears fall.

*Money.*

*It's all been about money.*

Cold seeps through the floor into my knees.

Ethan got this letter from Uncle Jack, offering him a quarter of a million dollars to... *play along.*

The cold spreads down to my toes and up my thighs.

Ethan got this letter before I ever set foot on his plane.

He got this before I met with the lawyer. Before the wedding ceremony.

He went along with all of it because he was getting paid.

He got this letter before...

The cold spreads to my stomach

Ethan got this letter before we slept together.

My broken inhale feels like ice as the cold reaches my lungs.

*This whole time.*

*This entire time.*

*Ethan's had a motive.*

He wasn't just being an amazing guy. He didn't just marry a woman he barely knew to spite my family.

Ethan did it for money.

It's all been for money.

My fingers go numb as the cold travels down my arms.

*Like my family.*

*Like everyone I know.*

*Like every other person I should've been able to count on, but who let me down over and over again.*

*Ethan needed me for money.*

Despair, like I didn't know was possible, drapes over me, making it hard to breathe.

I was going to tell him I loved him.

I was going to tell him and...

*Three months.*

The despair gets even heavier.

*Three fucking months.*

This letter says Ethan will get paid three months after that day.

It's been two and a half.

We're two weeks short of the deadline.

*In two weeks, Ethan will get his money.*

*In two weeks, Ethan will be free to act however he wants.*

*And if I told him that I loved him tomorrow...*

A sob crawls up my frozen throat.

If I told him tomorrow, would he have said it back even if he didn't mean it?

Would he have smiled but not denied it?

*In two weeks...*

The paper shakes as I hold it in one hand while I press the other to my mouth.

If I found this letter in two weeks, after the deadline, and I told him then...

If I found this letter in six months and nothing between us had changed...

If the deadline had come and gone, and Ethan still... if he still acted like he loved me... Maybe I could believe him.

But I didn't find it later.

I found it now.

And I can't pretend that I didn't.

I can't pretend to be okay for two weeks, just to see if he changes.

I *won't* pretend for two weeks, waiting for him to break my heart.

So I have to go.

With numb limbs, I climb to my feet.

The paper crinkles in my grip as I pick up my backpack.

And I focus on breathing as I walk out the door.

# CHAPTER 146

## ETHAN

I SCRUB THE TOWEL OVER MY HAIR ONE LAST TIME, then pull a clean pair of boxer briefs on.

I'm clean. My stomach is full. And I'm ready to get Tilda naked.

"Wife." I step out into the hall.

I was hoping Tilda would be waiting for me on my bed, but I don't mind throwing her over my shoulder.

She doesn't call back.

It's quiet.

I stop when I reach the front of the house.

And I can see that it's empty.

I turn back around, but I can see the door to the second bathroom from here. And it's open.

"Tilda?" I walk through the kitchen and look out the glass door onto the back deck.

Empty.

"Starlight, where are you?"

Nerves start to dance over my skin.

*Where could she be?*

I start striding back toward the hall, wondering if I somehow missed her, but then I see the towels on the floor.

My pulse thuds in my ears as my first thought is that maybe she hurt herself. Slipped in the water and fell.

But she would be here.

Lying on the floor.

And she's not.

*What if she really hurt herself? Broke a bone.*

I shake my head.

She would've yelled for me. Or waited for me. She wouldn't just drive herself to the hospital without a word, when I'd be out in ten minutes.

I'd drive with shampoo dripping into my eyes if I needed to.

She wouldn't drive herself.

Gritting my teeth, I stride to the front door and rip it open.

Tilda wouldn't drive herself to the hospital but...

Her truck is gone.

I step outside in just my underwear.

The driveway is empty.

I fight against panic as I stare at the empty spot where her truck was parked.

My mind reels with possibilities, each as unlikely as the next, as I step back inside and cut to the door that leads into the garage.

I pull it open. But it's just my trucks. There's no room for a third vehicle.

My panic increases.

She wouldn't drive herself to the hospital.

She doesn't have anyone in her life who would call her with an emergency.

Something twists inside my chest.

*Tilda doesn't have anyone in her life who would call her with an emergency.*

*Tilda only has me.*

A bad feeling mixes with my panic.

It's that same feeling I had when I answered the phone twenty years ago. Before the stranger told me what happened to my parents, I already knew it was going to be bad.

I could sense that my life was going to change.
And this...
I slowly turn, looking in every corner.
This empty house feels a lot like that phone call.
A lot like my life is about to change.

# Chapter 147

## Tilda

My phone rings.

I wanted to turn it off. Because I knew he'd call. I knew Ethan would find me missing, and he'd call.

I wipe at my cheeks, then reach over and send him to voice-mail as my GPS tells me to take the next left.

As soon as I'm on the main road, I'll turn my phone off.

It rings again.

*Just Tell Him You Love Him* flashes across the screen.

I take the turn, recognizing where I am, then I reach over and power off my phone.

# CHAPTER 148

## ETHAN

I KNOCK MY ELBOW INTO MY DRESSER AS I YANK JEANS up my legs.

Tilda rejected my call, and now it just goes to voicemail.

I want to text her, but she's driving. Wherever the fuck she's going, she's driving. And that truck she drives is too fucking old to read her texts to her.

Gritting my teeth, I drag a flannel off its hanger and shove my arms through the sleeves.

I don't know what's going on, and I fucking hate it.

I dial her again as I stride down the hall.

It doesn't go through.

Tilda seemed good during dinner. Great, even.

I can't think of any reason for her to leave.

The hospital option slams back into my mind.

Grabbing my keys, I step into the garage and open the over-head door.

I climb into my truck and turn it on.

I need to do something. Have to go after her. Help her. Whatever is happening. But I need to know where to go.

I open my GPS and type *hospital* into the map search.

Tilda wouldn't know where to go, so this is what she would do.

*But she wouldn't turn her phone off.*

I don't know...

A notification shows up on my screen.

Motion detected on Tilda's trail cam.

That doomed feeling makes my hands unsteady as I open the app to see the image.

It's blurry.

She's going too fast.

But it's Tilda.

She went home.

# CHAPTER 149

## TILDA

MY HANDS SHAKE.

But I embrace the cold.

I remind myself that I'm strong.

That I can do the hard things.

Ethan's truck comes to a stop in front of my house, and I grip the door handle.

As my husband approaches, I open the door.

And I remind myself that I'm worth more than money.

# CHAPTER 150

## ETHAN

MY WIFE STEPS OUTSIDE.

Still in her yellow dress.

Still looking beautiful.

Looking unharmed.

My racing pulse calms. Just a little. And I exhale. "You're not hurt?"

Tilda presses her lips together, but she doesn't answer.

"I thought maybe..." My steps slow, and I stop an arm's length away at the bottom of the two steps.

The energy is off. *Her* energy is off.

Different.

"Tilda?"

The sunset is vibrant.

Burning orange glows around us.

And it masked it.

Made it so I didn't notice.

*Her eyes...*

*She's been crying.*

"What happened?" The words taste like that phone call.

They taste like doom.

And when Tilda swallows.

When she works to keep her composure.

I know...

I know this is going to hurt.

"I found the letter," she whispers. And I hear every word. But I don't understand.

"What letter?" I whisper back.

And the look she gives me... is disappointment.

I swallow, knowing I'm failing. But...

"What letter, Tilda?"

She lifts her hands that were hidden by her skirt, holding out two things.

I take the first item.

A glasses case.

The aviators.

The ones she's had since she first sat in my copilot seat.

And my heart feels suddenly too heavy. Like it's turned to stone.

It feels like it can't beat anymore.

"Why are you...?"

Then I see the second item.

It trembles in her grip. So I take it.

The piece of paper.

*No.*

*It can't be.*

*I threw this away.*

"I need you to promise me one more thing." Tilda's voice cracks as she repeats the words Jack wrote to me. "You'll let me find someone else to marry before we tell the lawyer it's over."

"No." I shake my head. "No, Tilda. Don't do this."

"I'm not doing anything, Ethan. Nothing will change for you."

My breath claws at my throat. "Nothing? You're not marrying anyone else. This isn't—"

I start to take a step closer, but Tilda holds her hands up. Stopping me.

A crack forms through the stone of my heart.

*She stopped me.*

"It's all I'm going to ask of you." She tries to smile.

Matilda tries to fucking smile as tears spill down her cheeks.

And it's just like that first time.

Just like that first fucking time.

"Please..."

*Please don't cry.*

*Please let me explain.*

*Please don't treat me like I'm the stranger you met. Right here. Months ago.*

"I don't care about the money. I know I should've told you." I try to keep my voice even. Try to fight down the panic. Try to prevent the doom. "I threw that letter away. I don't know how..."

"It was under the couch." Tilda lowers her hands and twists her fingers in her dress. "Throwing it away wouldn't stop the deposit."

I crumple the letter in my fist. "I don't care about the money. I... I haven't thought about it in weeks. I was going to call the lawyer. Cancel it. I never wanted it."

"Did you?" I can see the hope flicker in her eyes. "Did you cancel the payment?"

And fuck. I want to lie.

I want to lie so fucking bad.

But I can't.

Not to her.

I slowly shake my head, watching in real time as I break the rest of her heart. "Starlight..."

"Did the letter arrive on time? Did you get it before Vegas?" More tears roll down her cheeks. "Before our wedding? Before... th-that night?"

She's so still.

So quiet.

But her eyes give her away.

They're filled with so much fucking pain.

"I..."

"Yes or no, Ethan."

Doom defeats panic. And sadness coats my skin.

She's asking me if I knew about the money before we had sex.

And I don't think I've ever hated myself more than I do right now.

*It wasn't like that.*

*I didn't think of the money once.*

*It had nothing to do with us.*

But that's not the question she's asking.

And that's not the answer she wants.

So I give her the truth. "Yes."

She blinks, releasing more tears.

And they're my fault.

Each and every one.

Her fragile, fake smile finally breaks. "Okay." She nods. "Okay."

"It's not okay." The words drag across my tongue. "I haven't been *staying* for the money. I don't *need* the fucking money, Matilda. I've told you before. I have my own."

She lifts a shoulder. "You need to fix your plane."

I shake my head. "I already have a new one. It's done. Without *this* money." I lift the crumpled paper.

She stares at me. And I know she doesn't believe me.

Because I didn't tell her.

I knew the idea of flying still scared her, so I didn't tell her.

"That day I had to go sign paperwork at the hangar. It was paperwork for my new plane. It was delivered that day." I plead for her to understand. "Please believe me."

"I want to."

"But you don't." Pain streaks through my chest. And that crack in my heart expands. Bits of stone chipping away.

It fucking hurts that she doesn't believe me.

That she thinks I'd use her. Sleep with her. Spend so much time with her. For money.

It hurts that she doesn't give me the benefit of the doubt.

But why would she?

*That fucking letter.*

The fucking letter that makes me like everyone else she knows.

All the people in that lawyer's office.

Her reaction the first time we met. When she asked if her cousin sent me.

To shoot her.

Because he threatened to kill her over money.

It's always been about money.

The betrayals.

The verbal abuse.

The fear.

For Tilda, her abuse has always been about money.

And now... I'm just another person in that line.

Another person who hurt her for dollars.

"I know I'm being a hypocrite. Money is the reason we got married in the first place." Her words are quiet as she shakes her head.

"That's not... I don't want the money. I'm sorry I didn't tell you." My voice breaks.

"You could've told me. There were so many times you could've told me the truth." Her composure finally cracks, and more tears pour from her eyes. "But you didn't. You never said anything." She takes a step back. Into the doorway. "Two weeks, Ethan."

"Tilda."

She takes another step back. Into the house. "Tomorrow morning... I was going to tell you I love you."

My shoulders sag as my heart breaks in half. "Matilda."

"But I found the letter instead." She takes another step back.

"Starlight."

"And now I'm not your problem anymore."

She shuts the door.
And turns the lock.
And it's exactly like that phone call.
Something inside me dies.
And it's exactly like that fucking phone call.

# CHAPTER 151

## TILDA

I PUT MY BACK AGAINST THE DOOR AND MY FACE IN MY hands. And I sob.

I slide to the floor. And I close my eyes. And I let my heart fall to pieces.

# CHAPTER 152

## ETHAN

I STAND ON THE OTHER SIDE OF THE DOOR.

On the outside.

And I listen to her cry.

I listen to what I've done.

And when the weight inside my chest makes it too hard to stand, I sit.

I sit on Tilda's step. And I close my eyes. And I force myself to listen as everything between us breaks.

# CHAPTER 153

## TILDA

WHEN I CAN'T TAKE IT ANYMORE, I GET TO MY FEET.

And I walk through the dark house.

I don't look out the windows.

I don't look for Ethan.

I go to my room.

And I crawl into bed.

Knowing this will be the last time I wear this dress.

Knowing that when I take it off, it's really over.

That when I take off the dress I married Ethan in, I'll never put it on again.

I curl up on top of my blankets.

My lashes are still wet when I close my eyes.

My mind is still stuck on a loop of sadness and betrayal.

But eventually, exhaustion reaches out from the shadows and pulls me into unconsciousness.

And I sleep with Ethan near me.

One last time.

# CHAPTER 154

## ETHAN

SOMETHING SOFT BRUSHES AGAINST MY HAND, AND I
open my eyes.

My heart lurches, thinking it's Tilda.

That she's waking me up to let me in.

But it's not her.

It's her duck.

And I can't sleep on Tilda's front step.

I don't deserve even that.

Not yet.

"I'll be back." I lift my hand and stroke it down Quackers's
back. "I'm going to fix this."

Then I stand.

And in a body that feels too heavy, I stagger to my truck.

# CHAPTER 155

## TILDA

LIGHT PRESSES AGAINST MY EYELIDS.
But I'm not ready.
Not for being awake.
Not for the day.
Not for facing my emotions.
I'm not ready for reality.
It's already too hard.
I woke up earlier, in the middle of the night.
I took my dress off.
I cried in the bathroom.
And I can't do that again.
Not yet.
So I roll over.
And I pull the blankets up over my head.

# CHAPTER 156

## ETHAN

MY PHONE BLARES FROM SOMEWHERE NEARBY, AND I SIT up with a gasp.

My eyes feel gritty.

My throat hurts.

And it takes a second.

Only one second.

Then I remember.

I remember every awful moment of yesterday.

Of last night.

My phone keeps blaring, and I finally shove my hand into my pocket.

I fell asleep fully dressed. On top of my blankets. In a bed that Tilda has never slept in.

Silencing my alarm, I stare at my phone.

I've never called in sick to work for emotional reasons. But as I work to swallow down my despair, I'm tempted.

It would be warranted.

But... I can't sit here all day.

Can't stand to sit with myself all fucking day.

I drag myself out of bed and strip on my way to the bathroom. A trail of laundry behind me.

I know my own motives.

I *know* I wasn't with Matilda for the fucking money.

But what I know doesn't mean shit.

I need her to know.

I *need* Tilda to understand.

And I'm not sure how to accomplish that.

I squint against the light as I turn it on.

And I avoid my reflection in the mirror as I start the shower.

But I don't avoid my thoughts.

I've earned every bad feeling I have.

I've earned them. But I'll find a way to make up for them.

I'll find a way to prove to Tilda that I love her.

That I...

I brace my hands on the edge of the sink as I gasp for breath.

I love her. So much.

*I was going to tell you I love you.*

*But I found the letter instead.*

The pain threatens to take me to my knees.

Because she *loved* me too.

She was going to tell me today.

I was going to spend this morning hearing the words I've wanted to hear for so long.

But instead, I'm alone.

And so is she.

# CHAPTER 157

## TILDA

I STEP OVER MY DISCARDED DRESS AND INTO THE shower.

I can't sleep anymore.

Every time I nod off, I wake up a moment later with Ethan's name on my lips.

So I'm up.

And I'm going to wash the rest of him away.

# CHAPTER 158

## ETHAN

I PAUSE.

The towels and water cup are still on the floor.

Still mocking me.

I don't know how...

I close my eyes and think.

We'd just gotten home. We'd spent the weekend at the cabin. I came home, and I read that fucking letter. I... got a call and went to work. And when I came home, I threw it away.

I *know* I threw it away.

But I didn't. She found it under the couch. I...

I picked it up off the floor when I got back from work.

The wind blew it off the counter, and I... threw away an empty envelope.

All this time.

All this fucking time, the letter was here.

Waiting.

Just when I think I can't be any madder at myself...

Swallowing, I bend and scoop up the damp towels and empty glass.

I walk them straight to the trash and drop them in.

I'm not keeping them.

I won't.

I...

Morning sunlight cuts through the window, and tiny rainbows dance around the room.

My breath catches.

What...

Then I see it.

And that pressure in my eyes becomes unbearable.

My boots are quiet on the floor as I cross to the dining table.

My fingers tremble as I pick up the suncatcher.

The purple beads make a quiet clinking sound as they bump into each other.

It's like the one I saw her working on before. But even better.

There's a loop of fishing line to hang it from. And the top of the suncatcher is a horizontal circle of beads. But it's stiff. Like she found wire to use. Then, hanging from the circle are half a dozen strands of beads of different lengths.

It's delicate.

Beautiful.

Made from Tilda's birthday beads.

I hold it carefully as I walk outside.

I didn't park in the garage last night. Couldn't find the energy.

So I cross the driveway to my truck, holding my gift up to the sunlight, watching it sparkle.

And I know she must've set this down before she found the letter.

But it's still mine.

And I'm going to keep it.

Just like Matilda Iris Grant is still mine.

And I'm going to keep her.

# Chapter 159

## Tilda

The screen door slams shut behind me as I carry my coffee to my chair.

I want to ignore it. *The screen door.*

The way it reminds me of Ethan.

I want to rip the screen out.

Want to turn it back to the way it was before.

But I don't.

If he can use me, I can use him.

I can keep the things he did for me.

I...

A tear slips free.

"I hate this," I whisper to the trees.

There's a rustle, then Quackers flaps up from below the deck and perches herself on the railing.

The edge of my mouth pulls up into a sad smile. "Morning."

She does her little shoulder shimmy.

"You know what I hate most of all?" I ask my best friend. "I hate feeling stupid. It's... it's such a bad feeling. The worst."

Quackers hops down from the railing onto the deck.

"You get it. Don't you?"

She waddles over to me, stopping at my feet.

I hold my mug out of the way and pat my lap. "If you want—"

There's a flapping of wings, and I close my eyes on instinct. Then I feel a gentle weight resting on my thigh.

I slide my eyes open.

And I find Quackers sitting on my lap.

I sniff.

Then I sniff again as more tears fall.

"You're such a good duck." I move my hand so very slowly before stroking it down her back.

Quackers makes a soft sound and stretches her head out.

"Does that mean you like this?" I do it again.

This time she scrunches her neck up so her chin... beak... is resting on her chest.

I keep petting her, keep soaking in the comfort she's giving me.

And then I tell her the truth of it all.

"I don't want to love him."

# CHAPTER 160

## ETHAN

I WANT TO CALL HER.

I want to message her.

I want to explain it all to her.

But I know I can't do any of that until the next two weeks are up.

And I know denying the payment now wouldn't prove anything.

It would be seen as guilt. Nothing else.

But I've talked to my own lawyer.

And it's going to take time.

Resources.

Coordination.

But I have a plan.

And it's going to work.

# CHAPTER 161

## TILDA

"Just the one box?"

I nod at the woman. "Making some room in the closet." I try to say it like a joke, but it sounds as sad as I feel.

Today is the three-month mark.

My three-month wedding anniversary.

The day Ethan gets his money.

Standing at my open passenger door, I take the box off my seat and hand it to the woman.

"Do you need a donation receipt?"

I shake my head.

"Then you're all set."

"Thank you." I force out a smile. Then I circle around the back of my truck, and I drive away.

# CHAPTER 162

## ETHAN

I'M NOT STALKING HER.

I didn't follow her into town.

I was already here.

I just happened to see her leave on the driveway camera.

Guilt tries to push into the forefront of my mind. But I've been swimming in enough guilt to sink a fucking yacht, so this is nothing.

Easy to ignore.

And I didn't come here to find her.

I was just already here. At the post office. Seeing a notary.

And the Lonely post office happens to be in sight of the town's donation center. The sort of place where you can donate clothes and home goods that they sell to fund charitable causes.

It's a good place.

But Tilda doesn't have a lot of extra stuff. So I'm curious. And I watch.

I stay in my truck, and I watch as Tilda gives a box to the woman working the drop-off lane.

Tilda is in a blue dress today. And her hair is in a braid. And...

I press a hand to my chest.

She's so fucking pretty.

I miss her so fucking much.

My wife gets into her truck and drives away, her back to me so I can't see her expression.

"What are you giving away?"

The woman carries the box to one of the giant rolling bins filled with other recent donations. And just before she lowers it out of sight, a gust of wind blows the top of the box open.

Yellow fabric catches on the breeze and flaps in the wind.

My hand drops from my chest to my lap.

*Did she...*

Nausea swirls in my stomach.

"Aw, Starlight. Don't... Don't do that."

I put my truck in drive and pull out of my parking spot.

My suncatcher bounces as I clip the curb, turning onto the frontage road. And I reach up, gently grabbing it to stop its swinging.

Hanging from my rearview mirror, the suncatcher is big enough to be illegal in the state of Colorado. But I refuse to put my gift anywhere else.

I need to have Tilda with me. Always.

After rolling through a stop sign, I pull into the donation drop-off lane.

It's never that busy, and no one else snuck in before me, so as I stop under the overhang, I can see the box that Tilda handed over.

During my one-minute drive over, the woman disappeared inside the building. And I wonder if I can just snag the dress and go without getting caught.

My door is open and my feet are on the ground when the side door of the center opens and the woman steps back out.

"Hey, there. Dropping off?" She's all smiles, and I accept this is about to get really awkward, really fast.

"Um, no."

She lifts a brow and crosses her arms over her chest, reminding me of my stern third grade teacher. "Then what can I help you with..." She moves her eyes over my outfit, then to the side of my truck. "Ranger?"

I debate lying. But I can't think of anything good enough to justify what I'm about to ask. So I go with honesty.

"The woman who just came through is my wife. And she, uh, donated some stuff in anger."

The woman makes an impressed face. "I see."

"Yes, well, I'd like to... purchase the dress back. Please."

The woman tilts her head. "How do I know you're telling the truth and not some creep?"

*Valid question.*

"I... have a photo." Her skepticism goes nowhere, but when I ask if I can show her, she nods.

I go to my photo albums on my phone and open the one titled *Wedding*.

My throat tightens as the array of photos shows up as tiny thumbnails on my screen. But I keep my emotions in check as I select one of Tilda and me standing side by side.

"This is us." My words aren't exactly steady, but I hand my phone over to the woman.

She looks at it, then goes over to the box and flips the top back open.

The yellow fabric matches the dress in the photo.

She hands the phone back to me but doesn't pull the dress out. "What did you do? Must've been bad for her to come here, donating her wedding dress."

"I..." I swallow, and I can feel myself losing my battle for composure. "I kept something from her."

"Another woman?"

"No." That nausea returns as I shake my head. "Never. It... it's a long story. But I'm going to fix it. And when I do, she'll want that dress back."

The woman watches me for a moment. "Here's what we'll do. You're going to go over there." She points across the street. "And get me a caramel latte and something for yourself. Then you're going to come back, and you're going to tell me this story. When you're done, if I think you'll be able to *fix it*, I'll give you the dress. In exchange for a two-hundred-dollar donation."

Ninety minutes later, I drive home, slightly more confident than I was before, with Tilda's wedding dress on my passenger seat.

# CHAPTER 163

## TILDA

QUACKERS WADDLES BESIDE ME AS I WALK DOWN THE driveway.

Yesterday, on my way home from the donation center, I didn't have it in me to stop at the mailbox.

I didn't have it in me to do anything.

Didn't even turn the TV on. I just lay on the couch. In the silence. Wishing life didn't have to be like this.

Wishing I didn't want to call Ethan.

Wishing it didn't hurt so much that he hadn't called.

I kick at a rock and watch it bounce down the driveway.

Quackers flaps her wings, flying ahead a few feet, chasing it.

"You show that rock who's boss."

She lets out one of her loud quacks, and something that sounds like a laugh cracks out of my chest.

She quacks again, and I toss her a pea from the baggie in my pocket.

"You're happy, right? Living life on your own. Doing whatever you want?"

Quackers snaps her beak, and I toss her another pea.

We walk the rest of the way in companionable female silence, listening to the breeze.

I don't really get mail other than junk mail. But I get enough junk that I need to empty my box before too many days go by.

I toss three peas onto the ground for Quackers, then put the baggie back in my pocket so I can use both hands to remove the small stack of mail.

Tucking it in the crook of my left arm, I close the mailbox.

"Show me that one-eighty."

Quackers picks up the last pea, then flaps her wings as she turns around and starts waddling back up the driveway.

A smile that only an animal can cause tugs on my lips. "Such a smart girl."

Quackers flaps her wings again.

I try to keep the happiness she brings me. But happiness doesn't seem to stick to me anymore.

"Stop," I whisper to myself.

Except I can't stop feeling awful.

Over the last few months, Ethan went from Stranger, to the person I wanted to be with most of all, back to Stranger.

And I think it's worse. Having the good memories.

Because it's not the first time someone has used me. But the other times... Those were from my family. And they've never been kind to me. Not the way Ethan... was.

All I've known from them was disappointment and pain.

But Ethan...

Ethan made me feel like I mattered.

He made me feel wanted.

Valued.

Ethan made me feel loved.

I hug the mail to my chest, trying to ease the ache in my heart.

I'd never felt like that before. And the sadness that coats me makes me fear I'll never feel that way again.

I pause my steps. Close my eyes. And breathe.

*I will be okay.*

The sun is warm on my face. And I tip my head back to soak it in.

*I'm going to be okay.*

I exhale, then open my eyes.

"I'll be okay."

Quackers looks up at me as I look down at her. Then we start walking again.

As we round the turn in the driveway, I start to flip through the stack of mail.

Flyer for a roof estimate. Offer for a credit card. Letter from Uncle Jack.

I stop.

Frozen in place.

*Letter from Uncle Jack.*

I grip the corner of the envelope and pull it free.

It's a plain white envelope. Like the others he sent me. But this one went through the mail.

The writing is all done in his neat handwriting.

My name and this address are there.

The name on the return address label is his.

But it's not for this house. The return address is from another city in Colorado.

"What..."

I shift my thumb and look at the date stamped onto the envelope.

This was put in the mail just a few days ago.

*Someone* put this in the mail just a few days ago.

Part of me doesn't want to read it. Because I'm afraid of what it might say. What demand he might make next.

But I can't *not* open it.

I glance up the driveway to the house.

Not wanting to wait, I tuck the other mail under my arm, and I rip the envelope open.

Then, slowly, I unfold the paper from inside.

*MY LOVELY MATTY,*

*THIS IS MY LAST LETTER TO YOU.*

*I hope everything has worked out exactly as I planned.*

*You and Ethan really are perfect for each other. And it might take you both a moment to see that, but three months is enough time.*

*After three months, you'll know.*

*Sometimes it's the little things.*

*The laughs. The meals together. The hand holding.*

*Sometimes it's the big things.*

*The moments that feel like they might've saved your life.*

*Usually, it's everything.*

*The big and the little. The explosive and the slow.*

*Love can be all of that. And so much more.*

*So, my sweet Matty, if you love him, stay married to him.*

*You can thank me in the afterlife.*

*Uncle Jack*

My vision blurs as tears swim across my lashes.

I don't want to love Ethan.

I *don't.*

But I can't make myself stop. No matter how hard I try.

*The moments that feel like they might've saved your life.*

My tears spill over as I think about those moments.

Landing the plane. Scaring off the mountain lion. Swinging an axe at my cousin.

Hugging me on the deck. Kissing my hair. Bandaging my feet.

Ethan saved my life so many times.

My lungs hitch as I inhale.

It's so hard to look back at it all and believe his motivation was money.

And maybe it wasn't *only* money.

Ethan was upset when I handed him the letter. I don't think he was faking the pain in his eyes.

And knowing that he might be hurting too somehow makes it worse.

Because if we're both sad... That just feels so pointless.

Just like this letter is pointless.

It's not *me* who has to love Ethan. It's *Ethan* who has to love me.

I refold the paper and put it back in the stack with the rest of the mail.

When we reach the house, the duck goes straight to her pond, cooling herself off in the water. And I go inside.

I set the mail on the counter and reach for my phone, wanting music for my shower.

But then I pause.

Because I have a message.

I lift my phone and open my texts.

> Ethan: It was never about the money. And if you give me time, I'll prove it to you.

The tears that just won't stop drip down my cheeks.
*He's waited two weeks to message me.*
*Waited until the day after he got his money.*

> Ethan: Please give me time.

My fingers tremble.

He's sending these texts now.

Ethan's on the other end of this phone right now.

But I don't know what to say to him.

So I don't reply.

# Chapter 164

## Ethan

I'm putting my lunch in the refrigerator when Conners walks into the office.

"Hey, man."

I nod as I close the fridge door.

He sets something on the counter. "My wife got these for our daughter's class, but she wasn't feeling well, so she didn't go to school today. And the wife said I had to get them out of the house."

I stare at him blankly.

He points at the counter. "Cupcakes."

I couldn't give a fuck about his kid not going to school but... cupcakes.

"Thanks," I grumble as we switch places.

He puts his lunch away, and I take an eight-a.m. cupcake.

"Are you really doing that whole duck thing over on the eastern edge?"

"Yeah." I hold the cupcake in one hand and grip the door handle in the other. "It's all on schedule."

Conners huffs out a laugh. "Surprised us all with this one, Grant."

I grunt in reply as I leave.

Surprising my coworkers doesn't matter to me.

Convincing Tilda that I love her does.

Outside, I put the cupcake on my palm, and I take a picture of it.

Then I text it to Tilda.

It shows up in the thread after the message I sent yesterday. The last in a line of daily texts from my first, a week ago.

They're simple. No questions. I'm not asking her for anything, not yet. Just letting her know I'm thinking of her.

I put my phone in my pocket, then peel the paper off the dessert.

# CHAPTER 165

## TILDA

I cross the driveway, my shoes crunching over the gravel.

I feel like I'm losing my mind.

Every text Ethan sends me puts me that much closer to replying.

But I don't know if I should.

I don't know what to believe.

My feet carry me forward, up the little hill, toward the tree line.

I don't want to make the wrong choice and get hurt all over again.

I can't—

My steps slow.

He...

I look to the left. And to the right.

And for as far as I can see...

Purple ribbon.

For as far as I can see, Ethan has wrapped purple ribbon around the barbed wire fence that separates my property from the park.

I step closer until I can touch it.

It's the same ribbon he gave me.

The same ribbon he bought me.

It's... vandalism.

It's beautiful.

I pull my phone out of my pocket.

I don't know what to say.

No idea where to start.

But I need to let him know I've found this.

I need—

My phone rings.

I stare at the screen. I don't know the number. But... I feel like I should answer it.

I lift the phone to my ear. "Hello?"

"Hello. Is this Matty?" The older man's voice is frail.

The oxygen disappears from my lungs, and I can't reply.

*Is this...*

"My name is Stephen."

*Stephen.*

A manic laugh tries to break free.

It's a man named Stephen. *Not* Uncle Jack calling from beyond the grave.

"Hi, Stephen. I'm Matty."

There's a raspy cough on the other end of the line. "I'm so glad I got you." The man's voice sounds weak. "I know this is an imposing request. But I'd like to meet you."

"Me?"

"Yes." He clears his throat. "I was a... particular friend of your uncle. And I promised him I'd check in on you. After..."

The name comes to me then.

The lawyer had said it when I called him on my birthday.

*Stephen and I both pinkie swore to look after you.*

"I'd like that." I agree before I can overthink it.

"That's good of you. If you could do it... soon. This week."

My poor, bruised heart squeezes.

This man just lost Uncle Jack a few months ago, and now it sounds like he's...

I swallow. "If you're close, I could come... day after tomorrow. If that works."

"That would be wonderful." I hear the raspy cough again. "I'm not too far. Just outside Denver. But Jack never drove that old truck of his this that distance."

"Oh." I bite down on my lip, wondering how I should get there.

"When we hang up, I'll text you the name of the little airport near me. From the one near you, it's less than an hour flight."

*A flight.*

My palms start to sweat. "Oh, I—"

"Thank you, Matty. This means a lot." Stephen's voice hitches. Then he hangs up.

I lower my phone. Then stare as two texts pop up immediately.

And I don't know why it surprises me that a man who might be on his deathbed knows how to text... but it does.

I look at the first one. And it's the name of a regional airport.

I look at the second address. The one he's titled *Home.* And it looks familiar.

Turning away from the ribbon-wrapped fence, I read the address over and over as I walk back to the house.

I swear...

Inside, I cross to the dining table, to my growing pile of mail, and pick up the envelope I got from Uncle Jack.

The return address label has Jack's name. And Stephen's home address.

# CHAPTER 166

## ETHAN

I REST THE HANDLE OF THE SHOVEL AGAINST MY shoulder and pull my phone from my pocket.

If this contractor is about to tell me he's delayed again...

I stare at the screen.

> Wife: Do you know someone who can fly me to Laurel Bell Airport in two days?

My pulse thunders in my ears.

> Me: I'll fly you.

> Me: Just tell me what time.

I don't know why she has to fly there. And it doesn't matter. Tilda is reaching out to me.

Asking me.

> Wife: You don't have to. I can pay someone to do it.

I'm shaking my head as I read.

Me: I'm flying you.

Me: Just tell me what time.


An eternity passes.
I barely breathe.
I worry she'll disappear.
Then she replies.

Wife: I'll be at your hangar at ten.

# CHAPTER 167

## TILDA

I PARK BESIDE THE BLACK TRUCK THAT I NOW KNOW IS Ethan's.

And my heart won't stop racing.

I don't have to do this.

I know I don't have to.

I could chance my truck making it.

I could drive to the next town over and rent a car.

I could hire someone else.

Anyone else.

But...

I don't want it to be anyone else.

The next time I fly, I'm going to be scared

And I don't want to do it alone on a giant commercial plane.

And I can't do it on a little plane with someone else.

So... it has to be him.

The man who broke my heart.

The man I can't stop thinking about.

The man I want to see again, even if it hurts.

I turn off my engine and exhale.

*It has to be him.*

The soles of my tennis shoes hit the blacktop.

Just in case something... *goes wrong*, I wore my most comfortable pair of walking shoes.

And because I want to look cheerful for a man who's possibly dying, I wore my floor-length rainbow-striped dress.

It has a high neckline, leaving just my arms exposed. But in my bag, my largest purse, I have a light blue sweater. And some protein bars. And a bottle of water. And an extra battery charger for my phone. And a bag of nuts. And a Swiss Army knife that I found in the garage.

Just in case.

I hoist the bag onto my shoulder and slam my door shut.

I'd hoped that the stress of flying and the stress of seeing Ethan would maybe cancel each other out. Dull my senses.

But as my heart continues to gallop, I accept that's not true.

It honestly feels like the stress might kill me.

*Hopefully before a plane crash does.*

I fill my lungs.

*Stop it, Matilda.*

I brace myself, then I step through the side door into the hangar.

It's the same.

Looks just the same.

Except the plane is different.

It's similar. Same size. Possibly the same type.

But the paint is different.

It's... purple.

I press my lips together.

Ethan's plane is purple.

I bite my lip.

He did buy a new one.

I blink against the heat.

Ethan bought a purple plane.

I force in a breath.

He bought a new purple plane.

And maybe he lied. Maybe he bought it in the past week. With the money he got. But...

The man who haunts my every thought steps out from behind the plane. And he's as devastatingly handsome as I remember.

His muscled body is wrapped in red flannel. And I have to fight to keep my eyes on his because... I think that's his wedding shirt.

I think it's the one he was wearing when he married me.

When he promised me forever in front of a fake Dolly Parton.

He stops before me. "Hi—"

His mouth starts to form a word. But he stops himself.

And my heart aches. Because I think he just stopped himself from calling me Starlight.

*What does that mean?*

*I'll tell you later.*

I swallow. "Hi, Ethan."

His eyes dip. Just for a second. And I catch his hand moving at his side. His fingers flexing around nothing.

"Are you ready? Or would you like—"

"I'm ready." I stopped at a gas station two minutes away to use their bathroom. Knowing that if I don't immediately get on the plane, I'll turn around and leave.

Ethan nods. "I've checked everything three times." He holds out his hand. "Do you need anything from your bag?"

I shake my head and hand it to him.

He takes it, and I wait while he secures it in the back.

Then I focus on everything *but* where his hands touch me as he helps me into the plane.

# CHAPTER 168

## ETHAN

IT'S A SPECIAL SORT OF TORTURE, SITTING THIS CLOSE. Being this close. And hurting this bad.

I can see it in her too.

The pain.

And I want to pull her into my arms. I want to hold her tight.

I want to make her understand.

Make her believe me.

But I secure my seat belt instead. There's a process to this.

And *this*—flying her—that's step one.

I hold out a headset, and Tilda takes it from me and puts it on.

When she puts her hands in her lap, I release the brake, and the plane rolls out of the hangar.

She twists her fingers in her skirt, and I can see them shaking.

I want to grab her hand and put it on my thigh.

I want to do it like we did last time.

But I reach into a side pocket instead. And I hold out the pair of sunglasses.

The ones she gave back to me. With that awful letter.

Her gaze darts to mine.

And I can see the shimmer.

And fuck. I hate this.

Her lips tremble as she takes them from me.

I put on mine as she puts on hers.

And when her hands are back in her lap, back to clutching her skirt, I turn us toward the runway.

Tilda's inhales are rough through the speakers.

"Relax, Matilda."

She tries.

"Breathe."

She lifts a shaking hand and wipes at her cheek. But she doesn't lower her hand back to her lap. She stops at her chest and grips the seat belt.

Clings to it.

That all-too-familiar tightness wraps around my neck, but I need to push my voice through it. Because I need to distract her.

And I need to tell her.

"I didn't tell you about the letter because I didn't want you to think I was like them." I keep my voice steady, needing her to *hear* me. "Except now you think I'm worse."

I finish the turn, lining us up for takeoff.

"But it's only ever been about you, Matilda."

We start rolling forward.

"I need a few more weeks." The plane picks up speed. "Then I'll show you."

The plane vibrates.

"Show me what?" Tilda whispers.

"How much I love you too," I whisper back.

Then the nose of the airplane lifts, and the wheels leave the ground.

# CHAPTER 169

## TILDA

I'VE STAYED SILENT.

The whole flight. The landing. While Ethan got the rental car. I've stayed silent.

Since we left the ground. Since Ethan said he loved me. Since *I'll show you how much I love you too.*

I know he saw me wiping at my cheeks.

And even though I have a thousand questions, I'm grateful he didn't say more.

Didn't spend the flight trying to convince me of anything.

He just flew.

Only breaking the silence at the end. When he reminded me to relax. To breathe. As we landed smoothly.

The sunglasses are still covering my eyes, and I turn my head just a little to see him in the driver's seat.

I wanted to tell him to stay at the airport, that I could drive myself. But I couldn't bring myself to speak.

I want his love to be true.

I want it to be true so badly.

But I don't trust myself to be smart right now.

So I let him drive.

The car slows to a stop.

We're here.

Ethan turns off the engine, and we both climb out.

He hasn't asked me anything about who I'm seeing. But now that we've arrived, a new stress starts brewing inside me.

I've never visited anyone at the end of their life. I don't know how to do this.

Ethan waits for me on the sidewalk in front of the car, in the small visitor's parking lot.

Signs point in different directions, labeled with numbers.

When we got in the rental, I copied the address Stephen had given me, building number included, and texted it to Ethan so he could use his phone to navigate.

Without touching me, he holds out his hand, gesturing to the path that leads to building nineteen.

Anxiety is freely flowing through my veins when we reach Stephen's building. And I stand still before the door.

This place is a community of small homes. Almost tiny. But not quite.

There are flourishing gardens around the houses, with paved walking paths, weaving every which way, dotted with benches and shade.

It's pretty.

Peaceful.

"Do you want me to come in with you?" Ethan's voice is close beside me.

I stay facing forward, looking at the brightly painted cottage.

I want to say yes. I want to say it so badly.

But I shake my head.

And Ethan doesn't press me.

Focusing on breathing, I climb the single step to the front door. And I knock.

A moment later, it swings in. And a man stands before me.

He's tall. Thin. In tan shorts and a teal polo shirt. With bright white hair and a matching goatee that stands out against his dark complexion.

"What a beautiful rainbow princess." His smile is wide as he takes me in. "You must be Matty."

His voice... is not frail. There's no sign of a cough. And when he holds his arms out for a hug and I accept, his hold is tight. Strong.

A real smile forms on my face for the first time all day. "And you must be Stephen. It's a pleasure to meet you."

He shakes his head. "The pleasure is all mine." He steps back, holding the door open. "Please, come in."

# CHAPTER 170

## ETHAN

TILDA DISAPPEARS INTO THE MAN'S HOUSE. AND HE stands in the doorway for a moment, looking at me.

He doesn't say anything, but the edge of his mouth quirks before he shuts the door.

Then the small square window next to the front door opens.

And when he tells Tilda to have a seat on the couch, I hear the words clearly.

I lift a brow.

*Okay, old man.*

Taking it as permission, I sit on the front step and listen.

# CHAPTER 171

## TILDA

THE INTERIOR OF THE HOUSE IS SMALL BUT NOT cramped.

The kitchen is off to the side, open, with a peninsula island, much like my house. And the living room is bright, with a sliding glass door that looks out over a little pond, letting in a lot of sunlight.

I take a seat on the emerald-green couch as Stephen lowers himself into one of the two peach-colored armchairs opposite me.

Between us is an antique lacquered coffee table with gold inlay tracing the edge.

And on the table is a plate with four types of cookies.

"Sadly, they aren't homemade." Stephen gestures at the plate. "Jack was the baker."

He sounds... happy. But there's a hint of that sadness I feel in my chest.

I lift my gaze to the wall behind Stephen.

And it's all right there.

The framed photos.

The two of them.

Arms around shoulders. Smiles and soft expressions.

"I always told him we should tell you." Stephen's voice holds no admonishment. "But he was a stubborn man."

"I..." I press my palms against my thighs. "I would've been happy for him. I am. I wish..."

"He knows. He was never afraid you wouldn't." The *then why* must be written all over my face because Stephen answers my unspoken question. "He didn't want to burden you with secrets."

"That's stupid."

Stephen huffs a laugh. "Stubborn, remember? But I told him I was going to do this." He gestures across to me. "And he didn't even try to tell me not to. Honestly, I think he wanted me to. And I think the whole elaborate inheritance plan was his way of apologizing. He was always bad at that."

"Apologizing?" I try to smile as I reach up and brush away a tear.

My body is so tired of these mixed emotions.

Joy for Uncle Jack, knowing he wasn't alone. That he had someone.

And sadness that he never told me. That I had to find out now.

*Sometimes it's the little things.*

*The laughs. The meals together. The hand holding.*

*Sometimes it's the big things.*

*The moments that feel like they might've saved your life.*

*Usually, it's everything.*

*The big and the little. The explosive and the slow.*

*Love can be all of that. And so much more.*

Stephen nods as he leans forward and nudges the plate of desserts toward me.

I take one of the cookies shaped like an elf.

Stephen takes a square one that looks like lemon.

And as we take bites, a tiny dog walks out from behind the second chair, startling me.

The dog yawns, his gray fur sticking out in all directions, looking like he just took a winter-long nap.

Then the dog coughs. A raspy cough.

And my mouth opens.

Stephen scoops up the tiny dog and sets him on his lap. "Cena always has allergies this time of year."

I gape at the man and his little dog too. "I thought you were dying."

He grins. "Did you?"

I try to scowl at him, but I can't find it in me. I'm more impressed by the trickery than upset over it. "You two really were made for each other."

Stephen winks at me as he scratches Cena behind the ears. "The wrestling DVDs were mine."

I slump back against the plush couch. "Did Uncle Jack really not drive his truck back and forth? Or was that a ploy to get me to fly with Ethan?"

"Jack did not drive that old-ass pickup back and forth. The truck stayed at the mountain house year-round." Stephen takes a bite of his cookie. "He drove his Corvette."

"Corvette," I deadpan.

Stephen grins. "He left that to me. Your man can buy you one if you want to match."

I press my lips together, but I think Stephen might be my only family now, so I decide to tell him the truth. "I found the letter Uncle Jack sent Ethan. About the money."

Stephen lets out a heavy sigh. "I told Jack not to do that. Told him it was a bad idea that would backfire. And that Ethan wouldn't need the nudge. But Jack wasn't willing to risk it. Said he needed to make sure the wedding would happen. It was the idea of an old, foolish man. And the fault of that lands on him, not Ethan."

I let his words settle against me as I absorb them. "Have you met him? Ethan?"

"That handsome man waiting outside?" Stephen shakes his head. "No. Our paths never crossed. Jack mostly went to the mountains by himself, when he wanted to disconnect and be one with the trees. But Jack told me all about him. And I believe him to be a good man."

I shove the rest of the cookie into my mouth.

# CHAPTER 172

## ETHAN

Tilda spoke with Stephen for almost two hours.

I heard all about how he and Jack met.

Heard that damn dog coughing.

Heard Tilda's laugh for the first time in weeks. And I let myself smile over the sound as my ass went numb from sitting on the concrete.

Tilda was silent on the drive back to the airport. And silent the whole flight. But something felt... lighter.

*Feels* lighter.

The engine slows to a stop, and I climb out of the plane first. Then I help Tilda down.

We stand before each other, inches apart. But there's still so much between us. An invisible barrier that keeps us from moving closer.

Tilda is still wearing the aviators, and I wish I could see her pretty eyes instead of my reflection.

I watch her press her lips together. Watch her prepare herself to speak.

"Why did we never go to your house?"

Her question isn't what I expect. But I answer honestly. "Because I like yours better."

"The view?"

I shake my head. "I liked being surrounded by you."

She bites down on her lip.

And after a moment, she lifts one of her hands toward her face, like she's going to take the sunglasses off.

But then she lowers it, leaving them on as she steps back.

And hope floods my chest.

"Ethan?"

"Yeah?" My voice comes out choked.

She takes another step back. "Tying ribbons to state park property is vandalism."

Each word sinks into my heart, softening the stone into something... more.

Tilda watches me for another moment, then she turns and disappears.

# CHAPTER 173

## TILDA

I BLINK DOWN AT THE BAG OF DUCK FOOD ON MY FRONT step.

Quackers flaps her wings and bites at the bag.

"Calm your feathers. You have food in your dish." I point, proving myself to the duck.

She quacks. Loudly.

"Fine." I lower myself to sit beside the bag, then I rip open the top and scoop out a handful of the food.

Quackers waddles closer and eats from my palm, making little grunting noises as she does.

I didn't get a text from Ethan yesterday, but that was the day after he flew me to see Stephen.

And he didn't send me a message today but...

I stare down at the disappearing feed in my hand.

He left this here.

He had to have left this here.

With my free hand, I pull my phone out of my pocket, checking to see if I missed any notifications from the trail camera on my driveway.

Nothing.

And this bag wasn't here when I was sitting with Quackers last night.

My eyes lift to the other side of the driveway. To the tree line.

"You're supposed to be my guard duck, ya know? If you're just letting men walk out of the woods onto my property..."

Quackers holds my gaze, then jabs her beak into the center of my palm.

I snort. "You're a greedy bird."

I scoop out another small handful of the duck feed, then I squeeze the resealable bag closed and stand.

Quackers is focused on her food, so I walk alone.

Across the driveway.

Into the grass.

Up the little hill.

Toward the trees.

And everything inside me that's been wondering if I made the right choice...

Everything inside me that wants to believe Ethan.

Everything inside me that's still in love with him... squeezes.

My lips tremble even as they lift into a smile.

I don't find the man.

He's not here.

But he was.

I take a step closer.

The ribbon is still there. As far as I can see, in both directions.

But now there's more.

There are beads.

Every few feet, strings of glass beads hang down from the top wire of the fence.

Beads of varying shapes and shades of purple.

Beads hanging from fishing line.

I turn my head to the right and to the left.

Hundreds of suncatchers.

And everything inside me that doubted him...

Everything inside me that thought he was like everyone else...

Everything inside me that worried my feelings were one sided... starts to crumble.

# CHAPTER 174

## ETHAN

DROPPING ONTO ONE OF THE NEWLY INSTALLED benches, I take my container of cold noodles with peanut sauce out of my cooler bag.

It's all coming together.

Almost done.

I open the lid, lift my phone, and snap a photo of the noodles, careful not to get too much background. Then I text it to Tilda.

It's been almost two weeks since she was on my plane.

And every day since I dropped off that duck food, I've either left something for her—socks, DVDs, mealworms for Quackers. Or I've texted her—photos of food, flowers, things that make me think of her.

She hasn't replied to any of it. But it still feels different.

Ever since the airplane hangar.

Ever since she kept the sunglasses on.

It's felt different.

And I'm hopeful.

"Pretty impressive." A voice interrupts my thoughts.

I look up from my lunch and spot Shelia. "Thanks." I take in the activity around us. "Appreciate your input on the habitats."

She hums and puts her hands on her hips, looking at the pond. "It's nice to be involved in something fun."

"Rescuing mountain lion cubs getting old?"

"Hardly." She laughs, but it morphs into a sigh. "But... ya know."

"Yeah." I do know.

Wildlife management isn't always fun, cute babies. It involves a lot more death and sadness than anyone wants to think about.

Which is why education is so important.

I think about Matilda picking up that mountain lion like it was a fucking house cat. "How's the cub doin'?"

"Real good." Shelia smiles. "You can tell Tilda we were able to put it in a rehab with an injured adult who we suspected lost her own cubs recently. They're bonding well."

"She'll like that."

I want to text Tilda the update right now.

But we'll talk soon enough.

Shelia blows out a breath. "Well, I gotta get back to the clinic."

"See you at the opening?"

"Wouldn't miss it. Tell Tilda hi."

I nod, and she walks down the gravel path toward the parking lot that's just out of view.

My colleagues know this is a surprise for my wife, but they don't know that we haven't been talking.

No one knows. Except Sandra.

My sister loved my wife so much she called me just a few days after that disastrous night, asking when we'd have dinner again.

When I replied with a choking sound, she started freaking out, asking me if Tilda had died.

And... I started crying.

*Big, fat tears* kind of crying.

Then Sandra started sobbing.

Then I had to fight through my tears to tell her Tilda was fine.

Then Sandra screamed at me, saying it was just like the time I showed up at her sleepover to tell her our parents had died.

Which just made us both cry even more.

Of course, that's when Fisher showed up at her apartment, and then I got to listen to him freaking out because he didn't know why Sandra was crying.

And that's how I ended up on speaker phone with Sandra and fucking Fisher, telling them everything.

I told them my plan.

Asked for advice.

Ended up including Fisher in the project. Putting him in charge of stocking the pond and sourcing the fountain.

I shake my head as I dig my fork into my noodles.

*Friends with Fisher. Who'd have fucking thought?*

My phone signals a message, and I chew my food as I set down my fork.

One of the stonework guys lifts his hand as he walks past.

I nod, then look down at my phone.

It's a text.

A photo.

*From Tilda.*

I swallow.

It's a picture of a container, exactly like the one on my lap. Open. With a fork sticking out of it.

And it's on a lap.

A lap covered in a rainbow skirt

And in the corner of the image, I can see an armrest.

The pink armrest from the camping chair I left for her yesterday.

That hope swells inside my rib cage.

She's eating the food I left for her this morning.

And she's sitting in the chair I got just for her.

I hesitate. Then I send her another message.

Me: I miss you.

The hope twists around itself.

It's true. The most true thing I've ever felt. I miss her so fucking much.

But I don't know if telling her—

Wife: I miss you too.

The relief that hits me is so thick I shift back.

I want to go to her.

Right now.

I want to fall to my knees in front of her and beg her forgiveness.

But that's not what she needs.

She needs to believe me.

Wife: I want to believe you.

I press a fist over my heart.

She always said it was like I could read her mind. Like I knew what she was thinking.

But she did it just as much to me. And even now... even apart, it's like we're together.

Me: You will.

Me: Friday. Noon.

I send her the address.

But just the address.

It's two days away. And I don't want to wait that long. But I can. Because a lifetime is on the line.

# CHAPTER 175

## TILDA

I LOOKED UP THE LOCATION ON THE MAP AS SOON AS Ethan sent it to me. But it didn't show anything. All I could tell was that it was next to the state park. Not far from my house, but I have to take a roundabout way to get there.

So I don't know where I'm going, but there are three vehicles ahead of me, and they're all slowing to take the turn I'm headed for.

I follow the row of cars as we all head down the gravel road.

It's narrow and winds between tall trees.

Eventually, the line of cars slows, and I can see we've reached a parking lot.

Someone in a uniform is directing the drivers.

As I get closer, I roll my window down. And not knowing if he's told his coworkers about us, I force a smile onto my face.

Liza grins at me as I stop beside her. "Welcome to Opening Day."

My nervousness mixes with curiosity. "Of what?"

"You'll see." She holds an arm out. "Follow the car ahead of you and park on the right."

She's still grinning as I pull away, and in my side mirror, I watch her lift a walkie-talkie to her mouth.

*Opening day of what?*

The lot is gravel, like the road, and it doesn't have any lines painted on it, but I park as directed, then get out of my truck.

The October air is cool, but the sun is out, so I decide to leave my jean jacket on the seat.

I didn't know what to wear today. I still don't even know what this place is.

But I know I'll see Ethan. So I took my time getting ready.

And I decided today was a fresh start.

A big deal.

Possibly a celebration.

So I wore my white dress.

The one I wore the first time I visited the park. The first time I got to wear his fancy hat.

Keeping my aviators on, I shut my truck door.

I follow the other people as they walk to the front of the lot. And I keep following them down another path that leads away from the parking lot, toward the forest.

The gravel walkway is wide, and the edges are manicured. The wood chips circling the flower beds look like they were just laid out.

It's Opening Day, and whatever this place is, they clearly just finished building it.

My steps slow and my heartbeat jumps.

I turn my head, looking at the flowers on the other side of the path too.

There are different types.

Different sizes.

But all shades of purple.

*It can't be for me.*

*It's a coincidence.*

I bite my lip as I keep walking.

As I keep passing more purple blooms.

*It can't...*

I lift my gaze.

To the sign that arches over the path.

*Uncle Jack's Wilderness Camp.*

I read it twice.

*It can't be.*

I push the sunglasses up into my hair. And I read it again.

*But it is.*

And that string, the one that I thought was gone, it reforms.

It's brighter than before.

Stronger than before.

And as I look up at the sign, as I think about the flowers, it doesn't just wrap itself around the broken pieces of my heart. It sews them together.

Someone moves before me.

And I hold my breath as my eyes meet his.

One green iris. One brown.

Looking back at me.

Standing beneath the sign for Uncle Jack's Wilderness Camp.

"How?" I whisper.

Ethan steps closer. "Because it was never about the money."

I blink, and a tear slips down my cheek.

Because I believe him.

I believe him about everything.

Ethan holds his hand out between us. "Let me show you."

I don't hesitate. I put my palm in his.

Ethan wraps his fingers around mine.

He squeezes them.

I squeeze his back.

Then I walk at Ethan's side.

Down the path. Staying straight when it branches off in both directions.

We keep walking, side by side, through more flowers. Under an archway of trees. Past benches and structures with plaques on the walls.

We walk down a little hill. And when I gasp, his fingers tighten around mine.

A portion of the path cuts down to the left, leading to a wooden boardwalk that goes out over a large pond.

A fountain shoots water a few feet into the air in the center of the pond. And it's like Quackers's pool.

Only bigger.

A whole flock of ducks flap their wings and take off from the pond's surface, flying up into the sky.

I brush a tear off my cheek.

And we keep walking.

Past a mini amphitheater.

Past a giant swing set.

The path splits ahead of us.

The section going off to the right has two cones marking it as closed. The path to the left circles down into a thick section of forest, and I assume it circles back toward the pond.

I start that way, but Ethan tugs on my arm.

Trusting him, I follow Ethan around the cones and up the path.

There's no one else out here.

It's just us.

Us and the quiet noise of a forest filled with life.

We crest the rise and step into a natural opening in the trees. And in the center of the opening is a large gazebo.

We follow the path to it.

Curved benches line the inside of the gazebo, and the sloped roof will protect anyone sitting from rain. But the center of the roof is open.

We step up into the gazebo, and Ethan walks me to the middle.

Stopping, I tip my head back and look up at the clouds.

Then I imagine doing this at night, looking at the stars.

Ethan releases my hand and moves so he's facing me. "By next summer, I want a conservatory. With a telescope for kids to use."

I lower my eyes from the heavens to the man before me. "I... I don't know what to say."

"Say you like it."

I shake my head. "Ethan. I love it."

He exhales, like he's been holding his breath for weeks.

I start to reach for him. Because I want to touch him.

But I stop, not sure...

Ethan grips my wrist, and he finishes my movement, pressing my hand to his chest.

"You make me smile." His tone is serious. And I feel the vibration of it under my palm. "Since meeting you... I've never smiled so much in all my life. You make me happy, Matilda. Being near you makes me happy." He pauses, swallowing. And I have to do the same. "I know I broke your trust, and I'll spend the rest of my days and the rest of my nights proving to you that it was always you. It's only ever been you. Because if you're not in my life... I don't know that I'll ever smile again."

He slides his hand from my wrist to the back of my hand, holding my palm over his heart.

"You're my joy." He places his other hand on top of the first. "You're my Starlight."

My lips tremble. "What does that mean?"

Ethan's lips pull into a soft smile. And this time he tells me. "You're my North Star. My way home. My destination." Letting his hands slip from mine, Ethan lowers. To one knee. "You're the light that guides me. And I don't ever want to lose you." He reaches into his pocket and pulls out a small velvet box. "Tell me you believe me, Starlight. Tell me you still love me."

He opens the box, and I stare down at the glittering star.

Ethan pulls the ring free and holds up the gold band.

In the center is an opal that shines purple. And jutting out around it, covered in dozens of tiny diamonds, are the points of the star.

I blink, and tears drip off my lashes.

Ethan sets the box on the floor and holds the ring between us. "Tell me I haven't broken everything." His voice is quiet. A plea.

I lift my gaze from the ring and meet his. And I tell him the truth. "You haven't broken everything." I hold my left hand out. "I still love you."

Ethan's hand trembles as he slides the ring onto my finger.

I don't look at the diamonds. Don't look at the sparkling ring he must have designed for me. I just look at him.

At the man on his knee before me.

And I use my right hand to grip his chin, making sure he's watching me.

Making sure he hears.

"I believe you, Husband."

# CHAPTER 176

## ETHAN

THE LAST PIECE OF THE STONE FALLS AWAY FROM MY heart as it beats almost painfully in my chest.

*I still love you.*

*I believe you.*

"Say it again." My demand is raw.

Tilda smiles through her tears.

And it's nothing like the day we met.

Her smile is real.

Her hope. Her happiness. Her love.

It's all fucking real.

"Husband."

I reach out and wrap my arms around her, dragging her body into mine.

My cheek is against her stomach. And I hold her tight.

I hold *my wife* tight.

She lets out a laugh. And I can feel it travel through her body.

And that's it.

I shift my hold on her, and I stand, Tilda slung over my shoulder.

She lets out a shriek of surprise and presses her hands into my lower back. "Ethan."

I run my palm up the back of her thigh, loving the feel of her, needing the weight of her.

"Ethan Grant." She tries to sound stern, but I nuzzle my cheek against her hip and hear her sigh.

I slide my hand farther up her thigh and find the tiny shorts she has on under her dress.

I grunt in approval as I carry her out of the gazebo.

No one else should be back here, but if someone catches a glimpse of us, they won't see her bare ass.

I circle around to the backside of the structure, then follow an old footpath farther into the woods.

"Mr. Park Ranger, we cannot fuck in the park."

I wedge my hand between her legs, pressing up against her core.

Her heat spears through me, and I lengthen my stride.

"Language, Mrs. Park Ranger." I follow the path as it turns. "And we're not fucking in the park. I'm taking you home."

# CHAPTER 177

## TILDA

ETHAN SLIDES ME DOWN HIS BODY AS HE LOWERS MY feet to the ground.

I feel all of him.

Every inch of him.

We stand next to his truck that's parked in the middle of the forest, staring at each other.

I want to drag his mouth to mine. And I know he wants to kiss me too.

But we don't.

Because we both know once we start, we won't stop. And we can't get naked in the park. In broad daylight. In moaning distance of *Opening Day*.

Opening Day for Uncle Jack's Wilderness Camp.

The warmth of Ethan's love fills every inch of my body.

And looking up at him, I smile.

Ethan's mouth matches my own, his lips tipping up at the edges.

"Take me home," I whisper.

Ethan opens the passenger door. And I feel his hands on my hips as I climb into his truck.

He shuts the door when I'm settled, and while he circles

around the hood, I reach out and drag my finger down the suncatcher hanging from his rearview mirror.

But I stay quiet as he drives us down some sort of service road.

I stay quiet as I hold my hand out between us. And he stays quiet as he places his palm in mine.

And I recognize the landscape when we come to a stop.

We never went onto a real road, just traveled through the woods. And we're stopped in the clearing where Ethan showed me how to find the North Star.

Where he showed me how to follow his Starlight.

I follow him out of the truck and take his hand again as soon as I can.

And I squeeze his fingers as we walk to the fence line.

I let go of his hand as I step through the fence. As he holds the wires open for me. As the suncatchers dance with the movement.

And once we're both through, our hands find each other again.

Then together, side by side, we walk to my front door.

# Chapter 178

## Ethan

I can feel how real this is.

I can feel it where our hands touch.

I can feel it in the air between us.

And I can see it. Because in front of her house, next to the pink chair I bought her, is a green one that wasn't there before.

She bought it for me.

So we can sit outside together.

Because she means it.

Because she loves me.

Because she believes me.

And I can feel how true it is as she leads me through her house.

I can feel how true it is when we stop at the foot of the bed.

And I can feel the truth *of us* when I lower my mouth to hers.

# Chapter 179

## Tilda

His lips are warm against mine.
And my hands shake when they reach for his sides.
His exhale tangles with mine.
And my fingers curl into the fabric of his shirt.
His tongue is demanding against mine.
And my grip on the past releases.
I let it all go.
I pull Ethan closer. I wrap my arms around him.
And I let it all fucking go.

# CHAPTER 180

## ETHAN

SOMETHING BETWEEN US SNAPS. AND THE NEED TO touch, to feel, becomes frantic.

Tilda rips at the buttons on my shirt, and I fumble with the zipper on her dress.

We shift and we shove and we never break our kiss as we shed our clothes.

We never break our kiss until we're both naked.

When Tilda drops her panties on the floor, I turn us, and I tip her back onto the bed.

She reaches for me.

But I take a moment.

Just a moment

To look down at her.

All of her.

And I think about our first time together.

Our first kiss. Our first touches. Our first night as a married couple.

I think about how perfect she is every time.

And when I think about how I get to do this for the rest of my life, I smile.

"Ethan." Tilda grabs at her tits since she can't reach me.

"I'm right here." I kneel on the foot of the bed. "Now open for me." I hook my hands around her thighs and spread her legs. "Remind me what my wife tastes like."

My tongue flattens against her, and Tilda lifts her head off the mattress as I consume her.

She moans and wiggles and cries my name.

And I lap up every bit of it.

I savor it.

Her.

Until I can't wait any longer.

Tilda tugs on my hair, and I let her pull my face away from her core.

My lips are slick with her flavor as I crawl up her body. And her taste is still on my tongue as I line my hips up with hers.

She reaches for me.

Still pulls me down.

Her eyes flutter as she seals her mouth to mine.

And when I rock my hips, my hardness finds her entrance.

We both still.

And we open our eyes.

And with my gaze locked on hers, I push into my wife.

Inch by inch, I fill her.

I stretch her.

I fight for breath as she gasps at the feeling.

I fight to stay in control as her heat pulses around me.

And when I go as deep as I can.

When we're fully connected.

Tilda wraps her arms around my neck.

And she tells me she loves me.

# Chapter 181

## Tilda

I whisper it to him. Over and over.

Needing him to know.

Needing him to believe me.

And when he wraps his arms under me.

When he holds me as close as he can.

When his words hitch as he repeats the words back to me.

When Ethan tells me he loves me.

I know he believes me.

And when we come apart together. At the same time.

I believe, with all my heart, that this is forever.

# CHAPTER 182

## ETHAN

"Tilda."

She lets out a sleepy grumble, and I smile against her forehead. My wife is still tired from last night.

After the first time, we held each other as I apologized, in every way I could. But Tilda just kept telling me she understood, that I didn't need to apologize anymore.

And then we had each other again. Slower.

Then we ate bowls of soup sitting in our chairs outside, feeding peas to Quackers, as I told her how Uncle Jack's Wilderness Camp came to be.

I told her about the land I donated to the park, land I'd inherited from my parents. And how I knew they'd approve. How in exchange for the land donation—which I got notarized at the post office the day after I received the money—the park agreed to make it official state park property, meaning it would be maintained by the staff.

I told her how I used every dollar I got from Jack to build it.

Then I made her look at my bank accounts, proving once and for all that I still have plenty of money all on my own.

Then I followed her to the shower. And we ended up back in bed.

S.J. TILLY

So I'm still tired too. But I know she's going to want to see this.

"Starlight, wake up."

She mumbles something about buttholes, and my responding laugh is loud enough that she opens her eyes.

I wait for her to blink a few times. Then I tell her. "It snowed." I smile. "A lot."

Her eyes widen, and I recognize my mistake too late.

Tilda scrambles to sit up, pushing against my chest as she does.

And because I didn't check to see how close I was to the edge of the mattress. And because my brain is too sex fogged to react quickly.

I fall off the bed.

"Oh my gods." Tilda looks over the edge of the mattress down at me. "I'm sorry."

I try not to smile. "You're not sorry."

She lifts her hand and holds her thumb and forefinger an inch apart. "I'm a little sorry."

I push up onto my elbow. "I appreciate you leaving the floor mat here."

Tilda climbs off the bed and holds out a hand to help me up. "I couldn't get rid of it."

I keep a hold of her hand when I'm standing. Because being here, Tilda in her pajamas, me in my boxer briefs, it all feels right.

Waking up together always feels so fucking right.

Tilda squeezes my fingers. "I couldn't get rid of the book either."

"What book?"

Tilda slips her hand from mine and opens the nightstand drawer.

I watch her move aside a birthday card. The one with the fairy on the front.

My throat fills with emotion, knowing she kept it.

Then she pulls out a small hardcover book.

The cover is plain, but when I open it, that emotion acts like gravity. And I pull Tilda to me.

I hold her against my side as I turn the pages.

As I look at our wedding photos.

Tilda had it custom printed. With the photos from our ceremony. With photos from the cabin.

The one of us before we left, when my lips are pressed to the top of her head.

"It's perfect." I kiss her hair.

She leans into me. "I got rid of the dress."

Her words are quiet.

An admission.

A regret.

I press another kiss to her hair. "I got the dress back."

Tilda tips her head back to look up at me. "What?"

I press a kiss to the tip of her nose. "It's in my closet."

Her mouth drops open. "How?"

"I'll tell you later." Then I turn us, walk her to the window, and yank the curtains open.

Tilda steps away from me and puts her hand on the glass. "Holy..."

Beyond the glass... is a winter wonderland.

Snow clings to every branch, coats every inch of ground, covers everything in a blanket of white.

And it all sparkles under the morning light.

"What about the flowers?" Her question is quiet.

I place my hand on her back, holding the book against my chest with the other, thinking that I need to put that first scrap of ribbon, and the ticket I never gave her, between the pages.

Tilda looks up at me. "The flowers at the Wilderness Camp."

I lift a shoulder. "They'll bloom again next year."

"Oh. But..." Her eyes widen. "Quackers!"

She rushes away from me, and I shake my head as I follow.

Tilda is already against the window facing the front of the house, and I stop beside her, looking down at Quackers as she paddles a circle in her pool. The fountain prevents the water from freezing.

I smile at the bird as I put an arm around Tilda's shoulders. "You convinced she's fine?"

My wife nods.

"Good."

I scoop her up and carry her back into the bedroom.

"Ethan!"

I back up to the bed, then sit so she's on my lap.

Then I hand her the book. "I want you to show me every page."

"Sitting on your lap?"

I shake my head and drop onto my back. "Riding me."

# EPILOGUE 1

## TILDA GRANT, STAR PRINCESS

"THIS IS FOR YOU, MY DEAR." LIZA HOLDS A PAPER CUP out to me.

I take it and cradle it in my hands, absorbing the warmth. "What is it?"

"Mulled cider. Or wine." She tips her head to the side. "Is there a difference?"

I grin. "Pretty sure the difference is alcohol."

Her brows rise, then she snickers. "Well, good thing my mister is driving today."

She pats me on the shoulder, then spots someone else she knows and bustles away, her skirt kicking up plumes of the fresh-fallen snow.

Ethan appears beside me, and I grin at him. Like I always do when he's wearing his fancy hat.

"What?" He narrows his eyes as he grabs the cup from my hands and takes a sip.

"I didn't say anything." I take the cup back.

It's not just the fancy hat that makes Ethan look extra sexy right now. It's the all-black suit. With his black leather boots. The perfect mix of Grumpy Ranger and Good Boy.

"It's just... so weird," my husband says seriously.

"What is?" I lean against his side.

"Seeing Liza in a dress."

I snort. "You're acting like a kid seeing his teacher in public for the first time. Liza obviously wears more than just her ranger uniform."

Ethan shakes his head. "Nope. It's permanent. She bathes in it."

"You're a turd. And her dress is pretty."

Ethan slowly turns to me. "Your dress is pretty."

"Thank you." I twist side to side, making the skirt dance around my legs, showing it off to Ethan, as though he wasn't there when I bought it.

Not long after the opening day of this place, when we found our way back to each other, Ethan surprised me by bringing me to a custom dressmaker.

He told me he wanted to do it right. To get married all over again. And do it however I'd dreamed of doing it growing up.

Ethan said that he knew I would have wanted to pick out a special dress for the occasion. That if I had known it was going to be my wedding day, I would've worn something different. He promised that I looked perfect in my yellow dress, but said that he wanted to see me in the bridal gown of my choosing.

I, of course, cried on the sidewalk in front of the store.

He panicked.

I told him I loved him.

He calmed down.

And then I told him I didn't want to do the wedding over. That it was perfect and part of our story, and we have the photos to prove it. But... I did want a reception.

So, here we are.

It took a few months to get everything arranged. To get my dress made. An ombre number that's a goldish yellow at the hem of the poofy tulle skirt and transitions up to a bright white at the sweetheart neckline. And the whole thing is covered with glittering embroidered stars.

The short sleeves would be far too cold for this March afternoon, but I have my shoulders and arms covered in a white velvet cape, complete with faux-fur trim and a hood.

The whole thing is frilly and fancy, and I feel like the luckiest princess in the universe.

Ethan slides a hand under my cape and grips my side. "I can't wait to suffocate myself under your skirts tonight."

"Ethan," I hiss.

"You're a pig," Sandra groans as she steps up on his other side.

Ethan laughs, loud and carefree.

My sister-in-law, who insists I just call her my sister, turns to me. "He is a pig, but the dress is stunning."

I roll my eyes even as I grin.

Sandra showed up for two of the fittings, so she's just as familiar with the dress as Ethan is. But it's the most beautiful thing I own, so I appreciate their comments.

"What are you drinking?" Ethan reaches for Sandra's cup.

She pulls it back out of reach. "It's hot chocolate. Go get your own."

Watching these two as siblings has been one of my greatest joys. They're so lighthearted together and always teasing one another, but you can tell how much they love each other. And I love that they have that.

And with Ethan basically living at my house, Sandra has been visiting a lot, spending the weekends, sleeping at Ethan's house.

"Babe!" Fisher jogs up to our group. And as Ethan always does when Fisher calls Sandra that, he tries to hit him. Fisher dodges the backhand. I'm pretty sure Fisher uses the pet name simply to annoy Ethan. And it's another thing I love. "Come watch me destroy these punks in hockey."

Sandra takes his hand, and they rush off toward the small ice rink that was frozen overnight, just for today.

For our wedding reception.

*Kind of.*

We're hosting. And we're dressed for a wedding. But we

decided to make it an event for the whole town, celebrating the success of Uncle Jack's Wilderness Camp since its opening.

We hired food trucks, an on-site candle maker, a face painter, a DJ. And we have people running educational booths, teaching outdoor survival skills, and experts, like Shelia—who has an eagle with her today—showcasing animals.

It's the perfect way for us to enjoy a party while sharing the joy with others.

And since I've been volunteering at the camp, teaching kids about ducks and showing them how to map the stars, I've gotten to know a lot of the locals.

One of the locals, Fisher's boss, walks by with a child dangling upside down from his shoulders. The little girl is cackling, swinging her arms around.

Sterling glares at Ethan. "Thanks for all the free sugar. *Definitely* no side effects."

His wife, Courtney, is a few steps behind. She's beaming at us. "Ignore him. He's just mad he dropped his apple turnover."

I wave at Ursa. The Blacks are here quite a bit, and Fisher usually brings Ursa with him when he comes to check on the fish in the pond. The kid waves back at me. Then she bites Sterling's shirt.

I snicker. She's definitely a handful. But if my suspicions are correct, I think she'll be a sweet and protective big sister.

I take another sip of my drink, sighing over the steam. Everyone here has been so welcoming that I feel like I've been here for years.

I smile against my cup.

This really is my happy place.

The camp. Lonely. Colorado.

*Anywhere with Ethan.*

"And then there's this idiot," Ethan grumbles, then crouches down beside me.

"What're you..."

Ethan stands. And hurls a snowball.

"Ethan!"

Twenty feet away, the sphere thuds against the center of a man's back, causing him to shift forward a step.

Rocky slowly turns around, with something that looks like a brownie raised halfway to his mouth.

He glares at Ethan.

Ethan points at some random guy eating a pretzel.

*A welcoming group of people, where all the men pretend like they hate each other.*

Rocky's wife, Kendra, is in a periwinkle pompom hat that matches Rocky's fleece-lined flannel. And every time I see them, I blush. Because it still reminds me of the first time I gave Ethan a big blow job.

Rocky hands his brownie to Kendra, then reaches for a snow-covered bush.

Ethan starts to back away from me. "I'll... be right back. Gonna get us some more food."

"Chicken."

"That's an insult to Quackers."

I shake my head as he slips behind the doughnut truck, out of snowball range.

A different man appears on my other side. And I bump my shoulder against his. "Enjoying yourself?"

Stephen smiles down at me, emotion bright in his eyes. "This... He would've loved this."

# Epilogue 2

## Ethan Grant, Good Boy

Tilda hums something as she steps into the cabin, her yellow dress disappearing into the shadows.

I smile as I rinse my hands under the cool well water.

Today is our one-year wedding anniversary. And we decided to come back to the cabin.

We opted to avoid aircrafts, driving in as close as we could with my truck, then switching to four-wheelers.

Tilda took some convincing to drive her own ATV, but after a few quick lessons, she handled it like a pro. And with the two vehicles, we were able to haul a fair number of supplies with us. Like extra bedding, dried food, and camping chairs.

My wife was worried about leaving Quackers and her flock of ducklings unattended, but Sandra and Fisher are staying at our house, duck sitting.

"Ethan."

"Yeah?"

"Come here, Husband."

Smiling, I dry my hands on my jeans and stride toward the open cabin door.

*I love when my wife bosses me around.*

"What do you..." My words falter at the determined look on Tilda's face.

She's standing at the end of the bed. "I'm the lion tamer tonight."

She lifts a foot and puts it on the mattress, flashing the fact that she's not wearing anything under her dress.

I swallow.

"And you're the lion."

"Fuck yes." I nod, my dick already throbbing.

Slowly, Tilda lifts her hand from behind her back.

She's holding something leather.

"I'll be whatever you want, Wife," I promise.

"Good." Tilda releases one end of what she's holding, and it unfurls.

Into a collar.

For me.

"Fuck," I groan. Then I drop to my knees before her as my cock strains against denim.

Tilda bends at the waist, and I have to grip my thighs to stop myself from reaching up her skirt.

I keep my eyes on my wife as she clasps the collar around my neck, my pulse pounding beneath her touch.

She hooks a finger under the leather. "One more thing."

I stare up into her beautiful eyes. "Anything."

Her mouth pulls up into a smirk. "I stopped my birth control."

My mouth falls open.

She leans in closer. "So be a Good Boy and put a baby in me."

# Help Protect Quackers
## and our Beautiful Parks

One of the best ways we can support wildlife is by protecting their habitats. Through preserving their lands, we can keep greedy landowners from bulldozing forests. There are all sorts of ways we can do this, but one of the easiest (and prettiest) ways is by visiting our state parks. Paying for your day pass, or your annual pass, helps keep these parks alive.

There is all sorts of information out there on how the destruction of habitats leads to declining populations in animals—and even extinction. And for birds like Quackers, who tend to migrate, the changing landscape can make it hard for them to rest and feed on their routes.

Our planet, and her creatures, are precious. And we need to do everything we can to keep her and them alive for generations to come.

For a list of state parks near you, https://listofparks.com/pages/us-state-parks

And for more information on how protecting lands protects the animals we love, https://www.nwf.org/Educational-Resources/Wildlife-Guide/Threats-to-Wildlife/Habitat-Loss

We can make a difference. Never stop trying.

# Acknowledgments

Thank you to all of my people. My friends and family, who support my chaotic schedule. My early readers. My ARC readers. My dogs for the cuddles. My ergonomic office setup for not completely destroying my body as I hunch over my keyboard.

But for this series, I need to thank Mother Nature herself.

Moving to the Colorado mountains was the inspiration for this series. The mountain peaks. The blue skies. The fresh air. The struggling to breathe at elevation... The driveway camera catching the family of bears that live in our woods, the fox that visits on the daily, the chipmunks and turkeys and deer. The coyotes and squirrels. The skunk who occasionally strolls down the driveway. And the birds. My chunky hummingbird friend. His girlfriend. The songbirds. Tweety Tomforde, who lives outside my bedroom window. The little gray bird, who found his way into our guest bedroom. And the ravens. I love you so much. Please be friends with me.

So, if you're able, go touch some grass today. Or snow. Or sand. Or take a walk down a gravel driveway. And then, when the sky is clear and you're awake after dark, go outside and find your starlight.

# ABOUT THE AUTHOR

S. J. Tilly was born and raised in the glorious state of Minnesota but now resides in the mountains of Colorado. To avoid the snowy winters, S. J. enjoys burying her head in books, whether to read them or write them or listen to them.

When she's not busy writing her contemporary smut, she can be found lounging with Mr. Tilly and their circus of rescue boxers.

To stay up to date on all things Tilly, make sure to follow her on her socials, join her newsletter, and interact whenever you feel like it! Links to everything on her website www.sjtilly.com

# Also By S. J. Tilly

The Alliance Series

(Dark Mafia Romance)

NERO

KING

DOM

HANS

The Sin Series

(Romantic Suspense)

MR. SIN

SIN TOO

MISS SIN

The Darling Series

(Small Town Age Gap)

SMOKY DARLING

LATTE DARLING

The Sleet Series

(Hockey Rom-Com)

SLEET KITTEN

SLEET SUGAR

SLEET BANSHEE

SLEET PRINCESS

The Bite Series

(Holiday Novellas - Baking Competition)

SECOND BITE

SNOWED IN BITE

NEW YEAR'S BITE

The Love Letters Series

(Lost connections)

LOVE, UTLEY

DEAR ROSIE,

The Mountain Men Series

(Hot guys in flannel)

MOUNTAIN BOSS

MOUNTAIN DADDY

MOUNTAIN GRUMP

The Bonded Souls Series – 2026